The Girls Club
Sally Bellerose

Ann Arbor
2011

Bywater Books First Edition: September 2011

Printed in the United States of America
on acid-free paper.

Cover designer: Bonnie Liss (Phoenix Graphics)

Author photo by Mary Vazquez

Bywater Books
PO Box 3671
Ann Arbor MI 48106-3671
www.bywaterbooks.com

ISBN: 978-1-932859-78-2

To my parents
Alice Irene Bellerose and George Merrill Bellerose
with gratitude for their practice of unconditional love
in an era before the phrase was coined.

Acknowledgments

What follows is an attempt to acknowledge a fraction of the many people who have helped this manuscript become a book.

Thanks especially to Susan Stinson, friend and writing collaborator of twenty-odd years and Cynthia Suopis, beloved partner during sublime, mundane and insane times.

Thanks also to steadfast friends and readers: Janet Aalfs, Carol Abbot, Jane Bellerose, Mary Beth Caschetta, Jane Christensen, Meryl Cohn, Sarah Halper, Chaia Heller, Marilyn Huffman, Susan Kan, Diane Lederman, Lesléa Newman, Lynn Paju, Brian Pelletier, Michelle Pelletier, Hilary Sloin, Gail Thomas, Terry Vecchio, and Carol Williford.

Gratitude to members of The Valley Lesbian Writers Group, The Friday Morning Writers Group, The Clam Belly Poets, and The Forbes Library Fiction Group.

Thanks to my agent Amy Hughes.

And thanks to Bywater Books, Kelly Smith, Marianne K. Martin, Caroline Curtis, and Val McDermid.

The author would like to thank The National Endowment for the Arts, The Barbara Deming Fund, and The Millay Colony for granting her money, time, and space to work on *The Girls Club*.

The Girls Club

Part 1

Chapter 1

I sit in ninth-grade English, a freshman in the class of 1970. Twelve minutes, forty-one seconds until the bell rings. I'd be bored to death if my gut wasn't killing me. The mystery loaf they served for lunch went down like a crown of thorns. A burning pain shoots across my belly. My arm jerks, up goes my hand.

Mrs. Raymond, of the straw hair and skinny arms, sits behind her big wooden desk in front of the class. "Yes, Cora Rose?"

I freeze. It's almost the end of fourth period, a bad time to go to the girls' room. Other girls might already be in there. I get another cramp, low in my gut. I hold my face stiff, concentrate on the wetness that wells up in my right eye. Not really a tear, just run-off from the pain. I focus on holding the drop in the corner of my eye, don't blink until the cramp passes. I pretend I'm pushing the hair out of my face and wipe my eye with my baby finger.

"Yes, Cora Rose?" Mrs. Raymond taps her desk impatiently. I stand at attention and squeeze my butt muscles together. All twenty-nine of my fellow freshmen stare at me. "Mrs. Raymond, *may* I please have a bathroom pass?" (I don't say, "*Can* I please have a bathroom pass?" Mrs. Raymond considers poor grammar "an insult to the speaker and listener alike." I don't want to piss her off. I need that pass.) I shouldn't have stood up. Standing makes the pressure worse. I should have waited it out seated.

She takes off her reading glasses and peers at the big round clock behind her desk. Twelve minutes until the end of English, two hours and forty-five minutes until the final bell rings. She turns her naked eyes on me. She's into moral development. Hurry up and decide Mrs.

3

Raymond: Are you going to destroy my character by letting me use the toilet? You think I'm showing off? You think I like being a loser who has to use the bathroom ten times a day? The tops of my legs start to shake.

She sighs and points her glasses at the hook on the wall at the front of the room.

I feel all fifty-eight of my classmates' eyeballs on my back. Fifty-seven eyeballs, if you believe that Larry Shimpsky's right eye got poked out when he was a baby and the cloudy-looking thing in his right socket is glass. My classmates are supposed to be diagramming the sentence structure in "Ode to a Grecian Urn." Mrs. Raymond doesn't seem to care that it's a poem and half the lines aren't even proper sentences. As far as my classmates are concerned, any distraction, even if it's just watching me pluck the laminated bathroom pass off the hook, is better than dissecting truth and beauty.

I make it to the girls' room without an "accident," slip into the last stall, and lean my head against the metal door. I recite a Hail Mary—fast, like a 33 LP being played on 78 speed—to thank Mary for keeping the girls' room empty.

As soon as my butt hits the toilet, I get a bad cramp. I stifle a moan and let the teardrops roll down my face. It's hard holding on. It hurts. Letting go hurts too, but it doesn't take as much effort. The worst part is the smell—gunmetal mixed with rotten egg. It's proof that I'm abnormal, diseased.

My sister Renee named my freaky illness the Dreaded Bowel Disease. She thought it up in Dr. Bello's waiting room while she was reading *Ladies' Home Journal* and I was being tortured in the exam room. Ulcerative colitis is Dr. Bello's name for what's wrong with me. "Relax," he said, then asked me embarrassing questions while he put me in position and looked up my butt through a long, hard, metal thing, some kind of scope.

I examine the paper towels that line my underwear. Renee's the only one who knows about the paper towel diapers. She says they don't make my butt look bigger. Maybe she's just saying that because she's my sister and feels sorry for me. She won't blab to anyone about my homemade

4

diapers. She vowed she wouldn't tell. She's a true believer. Breaking a vow is a mortal sin.

The door to the girls' room opens. Short steps. Water running. I hold my breath and pick up my feet. I don't want whoever it is to look under my stall door and recognize my penny loafers. Maybe she'll just fluff up her hair and get out. A door swings open a couple stalls down, somebody peeing, snapping toilet paper off the roll. Flush. The stall door swings open again. More running water. Silence.

Then a squeaky voice. "Jesus. Something die in here?" Bobbi Lee Paterson. Big loser. Sticks for legs. Wears cotton tights that bag at the knees and ankles year-round, because her father hits her and she doesn't want anyone to see the marks.

"You alive in there?" Bobbi Lee bangs on my door.

I hold my breath. I see the top of her rat's nest of hair peeking over the stall door. Bobbi Lee is a greaser. If you don't count her hair, she's about my height, five foot six. But leave her alone with a can of Aqua Net, she grows six inches and has to duck to get through the doorway.

She jumps on the toilet seat in the stall next to mine and stares at me. "Hi, Cora Rose." She wrinkles her nose like a demented TV housewife looking down into a bucket of dirty water before Mr. Clean rescues her from the filth.

I glare up at her.

Bobbi Lee laughs her stupid laugh. "You *sick* or what?"

I should jump up and wipe the grin off her face. But first I have to wipe myself, and Bobbi Lee's not getting that show, so I sit with my panties around my ankles. "You *queer* or what?" I'm shaking so hard I almost can't speak. I touch my cheeks, no tears.

"Just trying to find out if you're all right." Bobbi Lee stands on the toilet, cocks her head and fakes a pout.

"Normal people don't watch other people . . ." I tug my skirt over my knees and try to sound dangerous. "Pervert. The bell's gonna ring." Help me, Mary, I'm trapped in a toilet stall by Bobbi Lee Paterson.

"So?" She blinks down on me. Her rat's nest of hair is starting to give in to gravity. It falls forward like a great big sticky bun.

5

The first bell rings. The door to the girls' room bangs open. I know it's my sister Renee before the door bangs shut. I don't know how I know. I can't smell her Jean Nate over the Dreaded Bowel Disease smell and the smell of Bobbi Lee's hair spray. Renee takes a few steps, so maybe I know her by her walk, but it's her, I know it's her. Maybe when you're being tormented by the biggest loser in the class of '70 a sixth sense kicks in and you know things you don't know when it's just a regular crummy day at school.

"Hey, Bobbi Lee." Renee's usual chatty voice. "What's up?"

Big silence.

"You're standing on a toilet seat," Renee says, cool, like it's exactly the kind of twirpy thing she'd expect from Bobbi Lee.

"Your sister's having a little trouble," Bobbi Lee answers, snotty.

"Marie?" Renee should know it's me because Bobbi Lee wouldn't have the guts to stand on a toilet and look down on Marie. Maybe she thinks they're passing a cigarette?

"Psst. Psst. Psst." Renee's hair spray.

"Your *baby* sister." Bobbi Lee points down into my stall with a chipped orange nail. "Sick."

Clink. The hair spray can hitting the sink? The door to Bobbi Lee's stall swings open. "Get down, or I swear I'll kill you." Renee, still calm, like she's used to killing assholes who hang over me while I'm sitting on the toilet. Renee is not built to fight. She's built to make boys fight over her. She goes after Bobbi Lee anyway. She doesn't have a lot of muscle, just a lot of nerve.

"Get off me." Bobbi Lee braces herself against the wall. "I was just checking to see if she was all right."

Kicking, then a thud. Renee hitting the floor? Bobbi Lee hitting the side of the stall? I'm frozen to the toilet seat and I can't really tell who's doing what. "Renee, you okay?" I croak.

"Hang on." Renee's puffing like the little engine that could. "You're gonna be sorry when Marie gets her hands on you, Bobbi Lee."

Footsteps running out of the girls' room. The door slams. I'm crying. Bobbi Lee's head pops up over the side of the stall. "You better take off," I say. "Before Marie crams your head down that toilet." Even the teachers are afraid of Marie. Bobbi Lee's eyes dart sideways. There's a sick smile on her face like her mouth doesn't quite know which way to go. Her hair looks like cotton candy that exploded. My chest hurts where my heart is pounding.

"You're just dumb." It comes out kind of soft like I might be talking to myself. "You're the most pathetic girl in school," I say much louder.

Her face clouds up, like a little kid, like when the guys throw spitballs at her and yell, "Bobbi Lee, have my baby."

She gets a real mean look in her eye. "Target practice," she says and spits.

I shudder and try to wipe her slobber off my hair with toilet paper. She grins, satisfied. I'll strangle her as soon as I get up enough nerve to pull up my panties.

The bathroom door bangs open. Then bangs again louder. Bobbi Lee's eyes get big. Her stall door swings open. Crash. One second I'm looking up her nostrils, the next second her head jerks sideways and flies out of view. No crying. No screaming. Fast, but it feels like slow motion. Pulling up my underwear, I try to make a story out of the noise. She fell off the toilet seat? She's lying out there with her head cracked open? They'll think it was me that killed her. I hold my breath and pull down my skirt. Listen. A little scuffle, still no one speaking. Another thud. Smash. Another crash. Heavy breathing. I close my eyes. It's my sister Marie. It shouldn't have taken me the last twenty seconds to figure that out.

Bobbi Lee's crying. "I was checking to see if she was all right."

"Come out of that stall." Marie's voice, hard. Thank you, Mary.

I push open the stall door. Marie, like a tank, way shorter than Bobbi Lee, is bent over, pulling her by the hair. Bobbi Lee is kneeling in front of Marie with her head slammed up against the mirror.

Marie's head whips around to address me. "Don't be such a pussy." Her voice snaps like a rubber band. "What'd she do to you?"

"She spit on me." My voice sounds tough.

Marie twists Bobbi Lee's head like a corkscrew, pulls her hair, and looks right in her face. "You like to spit?"

There's not a scratch on Bobbi Lee. She must have a real hard head.

7

"I was kidding around." Bobbi Lee's voice is cracking. She's still trying to be tough, but it's not working. Tears roll down her face. She's leaking like a sieve.

"I'm kidding around, too." Marie twists Bobbi Lee's head toward me. "Cora Rose, you want to kid around?"

"Sure," I say, like I'm dying to kid around.

Bobbi Lee's eyes catch mine, pleading, desperate. I look away, don't tell Marie to let her go, don't explain that Bobbi Lee has saved me from being the biggest loser in school.

"This is a private matter. You girls are going to have to leave." Renee, always the well-mannered sister, speaks to the crowd gathering outside the open door of the girls' room, guards the entrance like a hostess at the senior prom. The girls right outside the door can see over her shoulders. A couple of them stand on tiptoes and whisper to the girls behind them. Renee stands with her hands on her hips and her feet wide. Nobody tries to push past her.

I'm supposed to do something. Punch Bobbi Lee? Spit on her? Wad up some toilet paper for spit balls? Stupid ideas. Shove it in her mouth? Doesn't seem right. I've got two sisters. There's only one of her. She lunges and bites Marie on the arm. Her teeth leave a red mark, but the skin's not broken. Marie yanks Bobbi Lee's head further back. I do it. I shove toilet paper in Bobbi Lee's mouth, stuff it in her cheeks. I don't look at Bobbi Lee's eyes. We're shaking, me and Bobbi Lee.

"Oh dear Lord. Oh my God." My cousin Lorraine. I can't see her, just hear that voice. I'm making Lorraine squawk, so I must be doing something right.

Marie has a confidential talk with Bobbi Lee, right in her ear, so low that I can't hear. I keep tearing toilet paper from the roll. I'll have to shove it down her throat if she decides to bite Marie again. See, Bobbi Lee, you can't let people spit on you.

"Enough." Marie lets go of Bobbi Lee with a shove.

Bobbi Lee falls on her face, pulls toilet paper out of her mouth, spits toilet paper on the floor. A little blood, a lot of spit, on the cracked gray tiles. The final bell rings, all students are supposed to be in their seats.

Everybody runs. I run to Mr. Cain's fifth-period geometry class, slide into a seat in the last row, my hands folded on my lap, a wad of toilet paper bunched up in my fist.

ೞ   ೞ   ೞ

Four hours later, home in my bed, I pretend to be asleep. It's the only way I can figure out how to be alone. The worst thing about sharing a room with your sisters is that it's always filled with your sisters. I roll over and watch Marie. She's in her slip with her hands spread flat on top of the dresser, blowing on her fingernails, getting ready for the big game tonight: basketball, Chicopee Comp versus Chicopee High. Gigi, our French poodle, cocoa brown hair, soft and clean from her monthly bath, is lying next to me on the bed. I play with the transistor radio. The Dave Clark Five comes in with hardly any static. Renee comes in from the bathroom, naked except for her pink panties.

"You mind?" Renee scowls and stands in front of Marie. Her cable-knit sweater and herringbone slacks are draped neatly on her bed. My sisters glare at each other. The grace period—when they tiptoed around so that their poor, diseased, baby sister could get some rest—is over.

"You can get your stuff when I'm done." Marie blows on her nails.

"Right." Renee rams a dresser drawer against Marie's squatty legs, pulls out the pink lace bra that matches her panties, and slams the drawer shut. "That's for shoving your Pillsbury doughboy body into my blouse yesterday."

Marie, fingers spread out in the air in front of her, knows how to look mean and bored at the same time. "As soon as my nails dry, I'm going to wring your neck."

Renee snaps the bra around her waist backwards, the cups resting on the shelf of her butt. "You and what army?"

Before Renee can rotate the cups to the front and hoist them over her tits, Marie's on her. Marie shoves Renee. Both sisters fall on top of me. Gigi yelps and jumps off the bed.

I yell, "Get the hell off me."

"Girls!" Our mother pads up the stairs. My sisters scramble, sitting

9

on the edge of their own beds, looking innocent by the time Mom makes it up to the second floor.

Mom stands in our bedroom door, wearing Dad's beat-up bathrobe and her own fuzzy pink slippers. She's in the middle of getting dressed for the Buffalo Banquet, her big night out, the only night Dad gets drunk. They go every year with my best friend Stella's parents and our Aunt Josette and Uncle Louie. "Cora Rose, if I hear any more swearing out of you, there will be no basketball game tonight."

I stare at her. I wasn't planning on going to the basketball game. Anyway, swearing should be allowed when something hideous happens, like your half-naked sisters falling on you. "All I said was hell." Only a venial sin.

"All right, no basketball game tonight." Mom trots back down the stairs. Renee stands by the door on her tiptoes, clutches an imaginary robe, her breasts still naked. She looks like a *Mad Magazine* cover: *June Cleaver Does Porno.*

"Cora Rose," Renee giggles and imitates Mom. "Any more swearing out of you; no basketball game tonight."

"You're a bad influence, Cora Rose." Marie clicks her tongue in my ear. "You're lucky we don't wash out your fucking mouth."

I don't care how stupid any of them act. In fifteen minutes, it'll be just Gigi and me. And Stella. We're going to practice sounding tough. I don't want to sound like a girl who has to line her panties with paper towels in case I have an accident. Stella doesn't want to sound like a girl who gives a shit that the boys call her "Sir."

Right now, Stella's watching from her back porch. When our parents drive off, she'll jump the fence into our yard. The whole house will be ours. I would have murdered somebody, probably myself by now, if it wasn't for Stella. I used to think Stella was beautiful. Then I grew up. Stella's too skinny, too stretched out. And she wears her brother's old shirts. All the kids in her creep-infested parochial school think she's weird. It would be the same in my creep-infested public school. She fights, too. Stella says girls like us have to stand up for ourselves or spend our lives taking other people's shit.

I stare out the bedroom window, watch my sisters peel out of the driveway with Rory and what's-his-name in Rory's old man's Buick. Rory, that's a queer name for a boy. I look at myself in the bureau mirror. The only reason I feel bad about not going to the basketball game with them tonight is my hair. I washed Bobbi Lee's spit out of my hair with Mom's good shampoo. Renee brushed it for five minutes. It looks real good. I must have laid on it just right. It happens like that sometimes. I have the best hair in the house, Mom's hair: long, dark, shiny. If I don't sleep on it funny, it hangs stick-straight all the way down my back. Renee's the pretty one and she's not chubby, like Marie, Mom, or me. "My Renee should be a model," Dad says, bragging.

Renee's fifteen, the prettiest girl in school. Marie's sixteen, the toughest. I'm fourteen, the diseased weak link in the LaBarre sister trinity. But both Renee and Marie have shit for hair. Wavy and coarse like Dad's, it looks cheap, always teased up and plastered with hair spray.

I try to see the back of my head in the mirror. Even the back is straight. Sitting through a basketball game and worrying about the bathroom is not worth showing off my hair. Stella will see it.

I'm trying not to use the bathroom until my parents, Stella's parents, Aunt Josette, and Uncle Louie leave. We have two bathrooms in the house now. The new bathroom, right next to our bedroom, used to be a linen closet. It's not legal. Dad put it in, so I wouldn't have to run down to the first floor all the time. The plumbing's shaky and there's no window.

Gigi jumps on the bed with me. Gigi's cool. They call her the *family* dog, but really, she's my dog. I feed her, walk her. She sleeps in my bed. She was an anniversary present from Dad to Mom. Dad thinks a classy poodle named Gigi will make up for living in a dumpy neighborhood. "More work. Somebody else to buy food for." Mom says it almost every day, but never in front of Dad. He knows how she feels anyway. It's easy to tell.

I rub Gigi's head, concentrate on scratching her silky ears. She loves it. With her head on the pillow next to mine, her big brown eyes watch everything I do. Mom would have a fit if she saw the dog with her head on my pillow. Dad just gave Aunt Josette another rum and coke. He's offering Stella's father another Seven and Seven. I keep scratching

Gigi's ears. There's a stabbing pain in my belly and a gurgly noise. Gigi tilts her head. I can see my whole face, twice, once in each of the dog's eyes. Gigi will sit staring up at me all night if I want her to. I use her eyes to arrange my hair so it fans over my shoulders.

They're taking so long down there. Christ. I'm trying not to use the bathroom until they leave. I make the sign of the cross, penance for thinking Christ's name in vain. In case the nuns are right and He is omnipresent, tuned in to every fourteen-year-old lying on a bed with her dog. Aunt Josette and Mrs. Kallowitz are still yakking away down there. Leave. So I can use the illegal bathroom. So I can lie on my bed with Gigi, read Renee's *Seventeen* magazines, and listen to Aretha Franklin. So Stella can jump the fence, and we can sneak into Marie's drawer, take the microphone Marie stole from the music room at school, dance around in the cellar, and sing R-E-S-P-E-C-T, loud, like the tough black girls at school. I'm glad Stella goes to parochial school and I go to public school. She gets picked on. I don't want to see that. I want to tell her my own version of what happened today. I don't want Stella to know she's the only one who thinks I'm cute.

The sheets smell good from the lemon fabric softener Mom uses. In a couple of days, the bed will smell like dog again. I poke around under the mattress. *Lady Chatterley's Lover* is safe. Stella and I have been reading it aloud. I pick *Seventeen* off the nightstand. Mom buys us magazines with "Before" and "After" makeovers so Marie and I will know what to shoot for and Renee will keep up the good work.

I can't wait any longer. Gigi follows me into the bathroom. Dogs have good noses but nothing grosses them out. After ten minutes the adults still haven't left for the Buffalo Banquet. Gigi follows me out of the bathroom.

Our bedroom is at the top of the stairs. I leave the door open so I can hear every word the adults say. It's boring. I listen because you never know when it might come in handy. They finish talking about how many phone calls Renee gets.

"Boys," Mom brags. "I have to put a five-minute limit on her calls."

Next up for discussion is Marie, in trouble at school, as usual. Not because she beat up Bobbi Lee. Bobbi Lee didn't tell. No one told. No one cares if Bobbi Lee got beat up. Marie's suspended for skipping the last two periods of school with some new guy, Fletcher. He's from the South. He has an accent. He came to Massachusetts to find work. Imagine traveling all that way and ending up working at a gas station in Chicopee. Aren't there any boring towns in Georgia where he could pump gas? He's old, twenty, maybe.

"Shouldn't Marie be grounded?" Aunt Josette asks.

My father answers, cheerful. "We'd be happy to ground her at your house, Josette." He must be getting drunk. He doesn't usually make jokes about Marie.

Everybody laughs, except Aunt Josette. She clears her throat and says, "Lorraine's lost twenty pounds." Our cousin Lorraine is Josette's beloved daughter.

"Big deal." My words are muffled in Gigi's soft fur. "That makes over two thousand pounds Lorraine's lost since she was ten. And she's still chubby." The best thing about Lorraine is that, compared to her, the rest of us seem well-adjusted. You almost feel sorry for Aunt Josette. Lorraine's her only child. Pitiful to have only Lorraine to feel proud of.

"Cora Rose and Marie still haven't lost any weight." Mom's voice trails off. She must be walking into the kitchen.

"Baby fat. They'll outgrow it," Dad says. "Renee's never had that problem."

"How *is* Cora Rose?" Aunt Josette's phony voice wafts up the stairs. She sounds concerned, but it's bogus. I don't have to see her to know she's wearing the same ugly green party dress she wears every year. No one says anything. I sit frozen, listening. A glass clinks on the coffee table. Gigi picks up her head, perks up her ears.

"Cora Rose is in the accelerated English class," Mom says, real dignified. Her daughter is diseased, but at least I've read a little Shakespeare.

"Sick again?" Aunt Josette knows I'm *always* sick.

No answer. They're drinking in dead silence down there.

Finally, Mom says, "Cora Rose is a strong girl," like it's the end of the discussion and Josette better drop it. Mom's embarrassed.

If I die, I'm going to leave a note that says Aunt Josette is not allowed at the funeral. I heard of a girl who died of the same Dreaded Bowel

Disease that I have. Ulcerative colitis—getting stuck with a disease with such a hideous name might kill me.

Christ, I'm crying. Gigi's licking my cheek. I hate it when the dog does that. It's disgusting. I slap her snout. She yelps, jumps off the bed, runs to the corner of the room.

They all start talking at once. Going on and on about whose car should they drive to the Buffalo Banquet. I jerk into a sitting position. Like it matters if they take a nine-year-old Chevy or a Ford with a smashed taillight for a three-mile ride?

"Fuck them," I say loud. "Fuck Aunt Josette and my mother and my father." I leave Uncle Louie and Stella's parents out of it. Gigi, watching, cowers in the corner. I fling open *Seventeen*. "Before" and "After" of the same girl face each other. She's beautiful either way. "Before" girls are always beautiful, just not perfectly beautiful. Girls who are really ugly aren't allowed in magazines unless they're somebody important's daughter and then they have to have saved a drowning victim or be dying of leukemia. *Seventeen* thinks "Before's" number one problem is her "Boring, mousy hair." I run my fingertip over "Before's" hair. It looks like Marie's and Renee's hair, brown, teased up. "Before" looks stubborn, nervous. "After" has straightened auburn hair, a green jumper with vertical stripes to make her hips look thinner, and somehow her nose got smaller, her eyes got bigger. She looks perky and spit-shined like the rest of the girls in the magazine.

"Come 'ere, girl." I try to coax Gigi back up on the bed, adjust my attitude, fake it, smile. I hate being mean to Gigi. She cocks her head, doesn't move. She's a good dog, not an idiot. "I won't hurt you." I pat the mattress. "Bobbi Lee, have my baby," I coo like one of those jerk-off boys. Saying that out loud makes me sad. I can't stand it that you can hate somebody and still feel sorry for them. Gigi looks at me with her sad dog eyes and jumps up. I hug her neck, arrange the pillow so she can put her head on it. I brace myself on my elbow, put the "Before" girl between us, rub Gigi's head, and read where the "Before" girl goes to high school, what clubs she's in.

Mom clicks up the stairs in her two-inch heels. Now she's almost five foot two. I shoo Gigi off the pillow. She curls up at my feet. Mom clicks into the room in a cloud of Chanel No. 5. She smiles. "Who were you talking to? The *dog*?" I stare. She could have been a "Before" girl when she was my age if she was taller and thinner. "You can go to the ballgame next time. We love you. Call us at the Buffalo Club if you need anything. Remember, no one in the house when we're gone." She kisses my forehead and whispers, "Close the door when you're done in the bathroom, sweetie."

Chapter 2

Every time I go to confession there's some weird girl who forgets her scarf and has to put a hanky on her head before she's allowed in the church. Today it's me. I keep checking to make sure the stupid lace handkerchief I borrowed from Renee hasn't slid off my head.

An old lady comes out of the confessional. I take her place. I thought she'd take longer. I haven't even asked Saint Anne to ask Mary to ask Jesus to be merciful. I close the heavy door and kneel inside the confessional. I give the inside handle an extra tug so the light that streams through the stained glass windows in the main part of the church can't get in. I make the sign of the cross, bow my head, fold my hands, and try to wipe all doubt and insincerity from my heart. "Dear Saint Anne, please intervene for me, as I am not worthy. Please ask The Blessed Mother to request her Son's mercy on my soul that I may make a complete and sincere confession. Through Christ, our Lord, Amen." I whisper, not just because it's what you do in confession but because it helps to scare me into a confessional state of mind.

The priest mumbles to the person in the confessional box on the opposite side of him. Listerine and Brylcreem. Father Anton is hearing confession. He's nosy, a details man. He's the one who wanted to know if I asked Mary for help or kept thinking about Mrs. Gillmartin's boob after I saw it flop out of her halter top. The old priest was easier. Too bad he died just when my impure thoughts started getting details.

My eyes adjust, focus in the tiny dark room. I sweat and cramp up, not Dreaded Bowel Disease cramps, normal confession cramps. I touch the little accordion pleats on the shutter lightly with my fingertip just to touch something I know is real. Through the closed shutter I can

16

hear the priest but not the penitent. "How does your impatience manifest itself?" There's a faint murmuring that I can't make out, then the priest again. "Are you truly sorry?"

It's sinful to listen to someone else's confession and it's usually not worth the bother. I make an effort not to hear and pray quietly. "Hail Mary, full of grace, the Lord is with thee. Blessed art thou amongst women . . ." Mary is the easiest one to pray to. She never strikes people down in wrath, throws anyone out of temples, or starts floods. Just has babies and looks sad.

Click. The little blind on the opposite side of me shuts. Creaking. The penitent on the other side is leaving. More creaking, someone kneeling in the vacant spot. Total silence, no mumbling, no rustling, not even my own breathing.

Whoosh. The little wooden door slides open. The shadowy outline of the priest's face, a side view, like Alfred Hitchcock, only skinny. My First Holy Communion was seven years ago, but I still get palpitations every time.

"Bless me father, for I have sinned. It's been one week since my last confession. My sins are: I disrespected my mother seventeen times; I disrespected my father four times; I took the name of the Lord in vain, by mistake, one time; I had impure thoughts every day; I smeared the good name of others almost every day; I lied." It's easier to blurt it all in one breath, but I have to stop for a second to suck in some air. "I'm not sure how many times I lied."

"Grievous lies, my child?" His head rocks forward.

"No, Father, I don't think so." Catching my breath was a mistake. It gave him time to think about my offenses.

"The nature of your impure thoughts?" His voice is deep and low.

"I listened to my best friend's impure thoughts and I thought about the thoughts I was listening to . . ."

He cuts me off. "You smeared the good name of others. How?" He sounds like the Wizard of Oz before Toto rips away the curtain, only closer, and not as loud.

"My sister, Renee . . ."

"No names. You gossiped?"

"Yes, Father. I wasted food twice. I disrespected my sister. I adored my best friend, Stella. I spoke impurely." I mumble. Maybe he won't catch some of it.

"No names. You *disrespected* your sister?"

"Yes, Father." I should have said annoyed. Disrespect is too serious for Marie. She's not an elder, a deity, or clergy. But this is good, much better than him going after the "adored my best friend" part.

"How?" He stretches out the word.

"I kind of annoyed her, Father."

"What was the nature of the *annoying disrespect*?" He's irritated and he wants details. He's got me. Now I have to spit out the whole pathetic story. "Me and my other sister wait until the sister we're annoying is asleep, then we scratch her headboard to make her think there's an animal, or something, in the room. I do the scratching because I sleep in the middle. I'm the youngest." Best to seem as young and dumb as possible. "My other sister growls."

The priest squirms around. I wait him out with my hands folded and my elbows resting on the ledge, sticking out below the shutter. My arms tremble.

Finally, Father Anton, in a low, dramatic voice says, "Calling up the devil can have grave consequences." He thinks we're calling up the devil? He must have met Marie. "Remember you are not talking to me." Now he sounds like Perry Mason appealing to the good sense of the jury. "You are talking through me, to your merciful Lord. You have taken part in this activity how often?"

"Once, that worked."

"How do you know it worked?"

Why didn't I just leave it at once? I exaggerate the shake in my voice. "Because she sat up in bed and said 'What the F,' then she whispered The Act of Contrition . . ."

He cuts me off again. "Are you truly sorry for your sins against your sister?" It's hard to tell if he's angry or just disappointed that no exorcism will be necessary.

"Yes, Father." I'm always truly sorry in the confessional.

"You say you *adore* your best friend?" He sounds skeptical. Does this guy ever forget anything? "You *adore* only the Lord and his Blessed Son."

"Yes, Father." Adoring somebody who's not a member of the Holy Family is a mortal sin.

"How does this adoration for your friend manifest itself, child?" Soft, reasonable, like Mom before she blows.

But I've got an answer all ready for him. I've had it for months, ever since Sister Mary Theresa described the "tingly, radiant, feeling" she has for the Blessed Lady. "An emotion," she said in her soap opera voice, "One must reserve for Christ, His Holy Father, and The Virgin Mother." Nuns include Mary as part of the deity you're allowed to adore.

"I feel happy, abundantly happy, when I'm with her." A direct quote from Sister Mary Theresa.

"I see. Is that all?" He asks in the drone he uses when he wants to wrap up.

"Yes, Father." Wow, that's all? You can never be sure what a priest's going to react to and what he's going to let slide.

"For your penance," he announces in a severe tone that makes the hair on the back of my head stand up, "*fifty* Our Fathers, *fifty* Hail Marys, *fifty* Acts of Contrition." He hammers down each *fifty* like a gavel. "You will pray daily to our Blessed Virgin to help you." He clears his throat. "Whenever you encounter or depart from your *friend,* you will declare your adoration for your Lord God above all else. You will try your utmost to remain pure of thought and deed." He leans toward me on the word deed. Peppermint gum. "You will confess your sin against your aggrieved sister and ask her forgiveness. With the power entrusted in me by our Father in heaven, the Lord Jesus Christ, and his Holy Church, I forgive your sins." He makes the sign of the cross. Snap. The little shutter closes.

Shit. One hundred and fifty prayers *and* confess to my aggrieved sister. I've never been more than a ten Hail Mary sinner before.

I wait in line for my turn to kneel at the altar. It's Saturday morning and the church seems bigger than it does on Sunday because the pews are mostly empty. People are lined up in the side aisle, before the confessional box, waiting to kneel and confess. People are lined up in the middle aisle, before the altar, waiting to kneel and repent. I rock on my heels, lightheaded with after-confession calm, humming through my Hail Marys at breakneck speed and clicking them off on my fingers.

Renee, looking contrite, takes her place in line behind me. She nudges my calf with her foot, and whispers, "Quit screwing around."

I turn around and mock her hands-folded-head-down posture. Mom's white lace mantilla drapes her head and shoulders, falls halfway down her arms. I finger the lace. "You look like a bride in the Puerto Rican church."

"So?" She says sharply through her teeth without looking up. Her bangs are curled just right around the mantilla. She's calculated to a quarter-inch how tight a skirt she can get away with wearing to church.

A bald guy gives me the evil eye, so I turn back to the altar. The air in the church seems like it's been breathed and re-breathed since Jesus was born and no one's ever had the nerve to crack the stained-glass window. Angels and saints fly around on the high ceilings. The Stations of the Cross are painted on the walls, Jesus being born, Jesus throwing thieves from the temple, Jesus carrying the cross, Jesus dying, Jesus resurrecting. Two walls, sixty feet long, covered with Jesus. I bow my head and click off ten Our Fathers.

After I make it to the altar and finish begging Mary and her mother to help me, I walk back down the aisle, hands clasped, head bowed. I stick my fingers in the basin of holy water, genuflect, and push through the heavy wooden doors.

Fresh air.

Renee's already on the marble steps, sitting up, dignified, stomach in, chest out. "What the hell took you so long?" The white mantilla covers her shoulders like a shawl.

I pull the handkerchief off my head and sit down next to her. "I told Father Anton about trying to scare Marie."

"What!" She snatches the hanky out of my hand. "Marie's a jerk. She told the bus driver we're illegitimate children that Mom is raising for The House of the Good Shepherd."

"You liked that. You've been smiling at the bus driver like the Little

Match Girl ever since. I keep waiting for him to give you a quarter and ask for a light."

"You vowed not to tell." Her eyes flash, dramatic. "She calls us faggots."

"She calls everybody faggots." I'm not going to tell Renee that the reason I confessed to hassling Marie is because Marie stood up for me in the girls' room at school last week. In public. I figure the least I can do is whisper in the privacy of a little cubicle that I'm sorry for scaring her. Renee won't understand. She'll figure Marie has no choice. That Marie has to stand up for us because we're sisters. "Girls can't even *be* faggots. Anton says I have to ask her forgiveness."

"Ever hear of lesbians?" Renee smoothes her skirt. "Keep your big fat mouth shut. You vowed."

I stand up and tug at my dress. "Normal people call them dykes." Sooner or later the waist of whatever I wear ends up under my tits. "And they don't have *sex* . . . they just don't like men . . . they're like . . . neuter."

"The proper word is lesbian." Leave it to Renee to know the proper word. "And they have sex." She wiggles her fingers in my face. "With their fingers."

I stop in mid-tug. Renee is only a year older than me, but she has a zillion girlfriends, and she talks on the phone by the hour, so she gets a lot of dirt. Sometimes her information is correct. "Kind of skimpy." I look at my index finger and consider the mechanics. I still haven't figured out how a guy fits his thing in, but fingers? "Doesn't seem like it would make much of an impression." I walk down the smooth marble steps, lose my balance, slip, and land on my butt.

"You are the dumbest fourteen-year-old in history. You have more than one finger." She helps me up. "And they have special equipment."

"Equipment?"

She dusts off the back of my dress. "Dildos," she mouths the word, looking around to make sure no one is listening.

"Dildos," I repeat, trying to decide if she's putting me on. But it couldn't be a coincidence that Stella used the same word. I thought Stella made up the word. I almost fell off her bed laughing. I thought it was an extinct bird. "Where do they get them? Excuse me? Can I see your dildo selection?"

21

I can usually count on Renee to laugh at stuff like this, but she's still mad and walks in front of me, fast, then whips around. I almost smack into her. "Did you tell him you made a vow?"

"You've got to let me out of the vow."

"No way. A vow counts more than an order from a priest." Her hands are on her hips. She got the hands on her hips idea from Chicopee High School's production of *Oklahoma*. Girls like Renee are corny enough, they shouldn't be allowed to see musicals. "God will put you in the part of hell He saves for people who break vows." A vow counts more than an order from a priest? May be true. May be a rule Renee made up. She cocks her head. "The hottest part of hell. Boil in your own sweat for eternity."

I wish I either totally believed or didn't believe all this Catholic business. I don't think this boil in your own sweat stuff comes from the Church, that's Renee bullshit. I look around Renee and see Marie in the street, right in front of All Saints Church, scrunched down next to a beat-up station wagon, squinting in the rearview mirror, her big butt blocking half the sidewalk.

Renee walks up behind her. "You better get in there." She jerks her thumb at the church.

Marie ignores Renee. Marie usually ignores Renee.

"Marie." I jump on the hood of the car and blurt, "I scratched your headboard and made growling noises to wake you up."

Renee's standing behind Marie. When Renee realizes what I said, her eyes almost bug out of her head, then narrow to little slits.

Marie slops eyeliner over green shadow. "Big fucking deal. Get off the car. You're making the mirror move around." That's it? Confession to aggrieved sister over? I jump down. No death threats. No hair pulling. Only one swear. Thank you, Saint Anne. Thank you, Mary. Marie licks the tip of her eyeliner, making another smudge across her lid, admires her raccoon eyes in the rearview mirror. Then smirks at Renee. "Did you confess that you have the hots for Father Anton?"

"Gross. You're going to have to confess that." Renee relaxes her mouth, which was all tight and white around the edges, and feels to make sure the straps of her bra aren't showing.

"I'm not confessing shit. I'm not going in." Marie smears her lips with pink lipstick. She has red nail polish on. Chipped. Even a fourteen-year-old knows not to wear pink lipstick with red nail polish. All Marie reads is *Seventeen* and *Cosmopolitan*, but nothing sinks in. She crosses the street. Renee and I follow, stand in front of the rectory, and watch Marie tease up her hair with a black comb she swiped from Dad. "I'm going to find something to do that's worth confessing," she says.

℞ ℞ ℞

"Hi, Memere." I walk over my grandmother's creaky kitchen floor, past the cupboards with no doors on them.

"Fermez la porte, Cora Rose." Memere, bent over her stove, stirring pigs' hocks in a chipped enamel pot, doesn't look up. I close her kitchen door and run into her bathroom. "You got troubles?" She yells so I'll hear her through the closed bathroom door. I don't answer. She doesn't ask again.

When I come out I ask, "Memere, you ever have impure thoughts?"

She gives me one of her looks. She crushes a few bay leaves into the bubbling water, then, without looking up, she says, "Everyone has impure thoughts. The trick is not to dwell, just let them float through your head." She waves the soupspoon across my face. "In one ear, out the other."

I pull up the stool. "Just wondered if old people still have them." She gives me another look that shuts me up. If I make her mad, she'll swat me with the rag hanging from the waist of her apron. I lean on the counter with my chin in my hands, stare at the white hair piled up in a hairnet on top of her head, at her stained apron and laced-up shoes. She plucks the bones out of the broth with metal tongs, puts them on a cutting board to cool, scrapes the meat and marrow, and spoons it back into the pot.

"You ever have a best friend, Memere?" Safe subject. She likes to talk about people from her past.

"Certainly." She stops stirring for a second. A little smile crosses her face. "Marguerite Beaurbeau." She moves the wooden spoon around in the pot again. "Then I married your Pepere and he became my best friend."

"Did you adore them?"

"Adore them?" She smashes dried bay leaves under the flat of the knife blade. It smells like a Christmas candle. "What's on your mind?"

"Nothing." I pick at my cuticles.

She picks up my chin, gives me a once-over. "I suppose I adored your Pepere. And my mother. And the Blessed Virgin."

"What about Jesus?"

She lets go of my chin. "And Jesus." She slides the smashed bay leaves off the knife into the bubbling water with the side of her hand. "I guess Jesus and God Almighty are the only ones we're really supposed to adore, eh?" She winks.

"What if you die without confessing your bad thoughts?" I already know her answer. I just want to hear it again.

She's busy browning flour and butter in the cast-iron frying pan. She pours a few drops of water in the pan. It pops and hisses. She stirs the sauce with a metal whisk until it's thick, picks up the big pan with doubled-over potholders, and pours the hot mixture into the enamel pot. When she's done, she takes a step back and says, "No one ever went to hell for thinking." She wipes her hands on her apron. "It's what we do that counts. Each of us gets so many foolish words when we're born. When they're all used up, we die. We wait in Purgatory. God takes a look at how many foolish things we've done, how many good things we've done, before He decides where we end up. But God doesn't tell you how much foolishness you get, so you better watch what you say." She raises her eyebrows before she pinches a little more salt into the pot. "Once you're dead, it's what you did in life, how you handled the trials and tribulations, not what you thought about doing that counts."

"How much time do you get to live if you're deaf and dumb?"

I've got her with that one. She ignores the question and whacks a head of cabbage into wedges. We both look out the window above the sink. She adds the cabbage to the pot, puts on the lid, and lowers the flame.

"How about singing? Singing count as foolishness?"

"Ah." Memere lowers the flame under the ragout and lowers herself onto a chair. "You remind me of him, all your chatter." She's talking about my Pepere. He's dead. "Tired, Memere?"

Memere never moves too fast, but she doesn't usually sit down while she's working in the kitchen. An old wooden comb is on the windowsill. I pick it up. The wood is shiny and darker between the teeth. It reminds me of Pepere. Sometimes, when I was little, I'd sit and watch as he unpinned her hair and brushed it with the wooden comb.

"Want me to comb your hair, Memere?"

She looks at me funny. "Yes, I do," she says like she's surprised to hear herself say so. Her fleshy arms wobble as she takes the pins out. Her thin white hair falls half way down her back. Her scalp is even whiter than her hair.

I hold her hair, delicate like Mom's lace mantilla, in my hand and drag the comb slowly through it, trying not to break the brittle strands. Three white hairs stick in the comb and fall to the floor. Memere leans back, closes her eyes, and says, "Sing. A nice French song." Some of Pepere's old songs are dirty.

I comb and sing, "Frère Jacques."

Memere sings, "Dormez-vous? Dormez-vous?" She stops singing, shakes her head, pats my hand. "You did a nice thing for your old Memere, Cora Rose. God sees. He'll take care of your troubles by and by." She puts her hands on her knees, stands up slowly, picks hairpins off the table, and walks to the window, pinning up her hair. "Stella." She nods at Stella, who's shooting hoops against the barn. "Go."

Stella and I walk to Memere's barn. We're not supposed to hang around with the cows, unless it's to feed or milk them. Mom thinks it's unsanitary to hang around in a barn. I push up the latch, the doors swing open, light pours into the barn. Stella bolts the doors shut from inside. There are only two cows left. They stare at us and tilt their heads like there's something funny going on. It's not feeding time and it's not milking time. Light streams in from two triangular windows on each end of the high roof and between the missing boards of the dilapidated side walls.

The cow Pepere named Bill moos. He named the cow Bill because he said there were "too goddamned many girls in this family."

Stella climbs over the stall and straddles Bill's back, which is as big as our coffee table. She spits on the floor, holds on to Bill's neck with one hand, and waves her other hand in the air like she's riding a bucking bronco. Stella's skinny, but strong. She's the only girl who ever knocked Marie down and kept her down. "Ride 'em, cowboy." She grins and waves her arm, scabbed up from scratching the rash she gets sometimes.

I grin back at her and scratch the other cow behind her ears. The other cow's name is Molly. There used to be a lot more cows before Pepere sold off the pasture in back of the barn. Men with bulldozers came a few years ago. They were supposed to build apartment houses where the cows chewed grass. The only thing they've built so far is a big pile of dirt.

"Pretty cow." I kiss Molly between her big crossed eyes. She almost never moos.

"Get on Molly's back," Stella says, bossy.

I shake my head. I want to, but I can't screw up before I get communion tomorrow. It's not about disobeying my parents. That's only a venial sin and we already disobeyed by coming in the barn. Stella lays her head on Bill's neck and talks in her dreamy voice, a story about school, her brothers, Lady Chatterley. It doesn't matter what story, something happens to me. She talks and watches me with her dark eyes and I get this feeling. If I sit on the cow, rock, and lay my head on Molly's neck while Stella tells the story, the feeling goes up my legs, making me abundantly happy and very nervous.

I pretend I don't know she's giving me a look, waiting for me to jump on the cow's back. My face gets hot. I can't look at Stella. I pet Molly. Bill and Molly are side by side in the same oversized stall. Stella swings her leg, she'll let it swish back and forth against mine if I get on the cow. Swishing legs—alone in the barn—not the day before communion.

"My Pepere used to let me ride her around the pasture."

"I remember Pepere. He swore a lot. Get on her back."

"I'm too fat," I answer. Sometimes Stella answers, "You are not fat," or "Who cares." She just looks at me, irritated.

"I just went to confession."

"Thou shall not ride a cow." Stella lays her head on Bill's neck. Her long black hair hangs down from the cow like a mane. She scratches Bill's head and studies me. "Your big boobs balance you off."

"*Stella.*" It's the hundredth time she's told me that my big boobs balance me off, the hundredth time I say, "*Stella.*"

"I'll be nineteen before I get tits." She grabs the neck of her t-shirt and looks down.

Because she's still lying on Bill I can see right down her shirt. "*Stella.*" I'm really surprised this time. She's flat as a boy except her nipples are a bit swollen. I knew she was flat, but I haven't had this clear a view since we were ten. "You confess your impure thoughts?" I'm worried for Stella. She's Catholic but hardly ever goes to confession and she says whatever pops into her head. What if it's true, all the stuff Renee and the nuns believe?

"Just to you." She sits up on Bill and tries to wave the flies away from the cows' ears with a fistful of her own hair.

ೞ ೞ ೞ

I lie in bed with my head in my hands, looking up at the ceiling. My sisters are in their own beds on either side of me. Marie's sitting up against her headboard, leafing through *Cosmo.* Renee's sitting on the edge of her bed, head bent forward, setting her hair in huge pink rollers.

"Know the stuff Memere says about getting so many foolish words before you die? Where'd she come up with that?" I ask.

Marie flips onto her stomach and throws the magazine on the floor. "She's tired of people talking shit, so she wants to scare the crap out of them by making them believe they'll die sooner if they don't shut up."

"Hmmm." Renee fluffs her pillow, lays down her big rollered head, and flicks off the light switch. "That's a smart observation."

There's dead silence. I wait for Marie's answer, something snotty like, "You think you're the only one who ever says anything smart," or something about Renee using the word "observation." But there's only breathing on either side of me. Nice. *There shall be ten minutes right before the lights go out when everyone must be nice.* That should be the eleventh commandment. I hear Marie turn and face the wall.

I say three Hail Mary's for Pepere. I can't stop thinking about how sad Memere will be when she dies and goes to heaven if Pepere's not there waiting for her. It will be better for Memere if there's no heaven at all if she can't be with Pepere.

Stella and Marie will probably commit as many sins as Pepere did before they die. If they die before me, will I pray for them? If I make it to old age, if the Dreaded Bowel Disease doesn't get me first, will I still pray? Renee better die last so she can pray for us all. Maybe being sick is penance. I can't remember which came first, adoring Stella or being sick all the time.

My legs move back and forth like scissors on my clean sheets. Not like in the barn. I'm not nervous. My heart isn't racing. The sheets are cool on my legs. We always have clean sheets on Saturday. Fresh sheets remind me of sitting in church with the cool smooth wood of the pew on the back of my thighs. I wish I was still eight years old, sitting next to Memere's big body, safe in the whoosh of all the people as they stand and kneel, the hem of Memere's skirt passing over me like a warm washcloth every time she stands up or sits down, totally taken up in the magic of the altar boy in his white skirt, swinging incense from a gold ball on a long chain. My head in the crook of Memere's arm, breathing lily of the valley until the altar boy and the incense disappears into the vestibule.

I snuggle my blanket up to my face. The priest really believes wine turns to blood because he made the sign of the cross over it? Marie is curled up in a ball, breathing loud. Renee's on the other side, a lump in the dark too.

I lie on my side. Gigi is at my feet. I put my fist between my legs, close my eyes, and rub my face in the clean pillowcase. Stella's black hair hanging down, a piece of straw poking out of it, Molly's soft cow neck. My hips rock, just to help me fall asleep, not enough to disturb my sisters or ruin my confession.

Chapter 3

Stella and I sit sideways on the hammock in my backyard, swinging our feet, comparing our legs for the four thousandth time. Stella's are long and muscular. Mine are short and chubby. Everything about Stella is long and muscular and everything about me is short and chubby. Except our hair. Stella's hair is shorter than mine, messy, and usually covered by a baseball cap. I stroke my hair. It's halfway down my back; doesn't make up for the rest of me, but it's better than nothing.

"Shit." I nod toward the gate where cousin Lorraine, almost sixteen and still wearing butterfly barrettes, jumps off her rickety bike. She opens the gate, walks the bike into the yard, and leans it against the fence. Her hair is matted down with sweat. She just stands there, ten feet away, staring at Stella and me.

"The party's not till this afternoon." My sister Marie sits near us on a lounge chair and slathers suntan lotion under the straps of her sleeveless shirt. She doesn't look up to address Lorraine.

"Guess what I saw, Cora Rose?" Lorraine loves to say my name, because my name is weird and she knows I hate it. "Stella's new house," she blurts without waiting for an answer.

"Congratulations." Marie cradles her hands behind her head, closes her eyes, and lays back in the chaise lounge.

"You're going to live right next door to doctors." Lorraine beams at Stella.

Stella, her foot tapping the air, is more interested than her expression lets on. It's Stella's fifteenth birthday today. Her family is in the middle of packing. Four of her five brothers are helping her father carry furniture and boxes to the new place. The oldest brother moved out after he came home from Vietnam with a fake foot. Stella's mother is taking a break from moving, sort of. She's in our kitchen with my mother doing party stuff. Our families have been next-door neighbors since before either of us was born. Hers is moving out of Chicopee to a nice neighborhood in Agawam, a few towns away. Most of their stuff is already gone. Stella's birthday party, combined with a goodbye party for the Kallowitz family, is going to be in our backyard in a few hours.

Lorraine holds out her wrist so we'll notice the Bulova, a reward from Aunt Josette for not flunking out sophomore year. "It took all morning to get there. You should see the street. Sidewalks on both sides." She walks over to the hose that's lying by a patch of marigolds near the house and picks it up.

"You rode all the way up there on your bike?" Marie, who has been in a bad mood since she started her period four years ago, asks, impressed and disgusted. "Why didn't you ask the doctor couple to drive you back in their Lincoln Continental?"

"Grande Prix," Lorraine corrects her. "Doctor Harold and Doctor Barbara Cohen. A Jewish doctor couple. With a teenage son."

"Mrs. Stella Cohen." Marie pulls her sunglasses over the bridge of her nose to peer at Stella.

Stella gives Marie a who-gives-a-shit look. I love when Stella does that. Then she squints at Lorraine and holds her body stiff so she can lean forward in the hammock. "You talked to my new neighbors?" She collapses back into the hammock, humiliated by the thought. Our shoulders collide. I hang on to her arm to steady myself. "You're gonna *need* two doctors if you don't mind your own business."

"You're thinking of Cora Rose. *I* don't need any doctors." Lorraine flounces her head. Her slicked-down hair doesn't move an inch. "*I'm* potty-trained."

I cringe, speechless. No one in either family, not even Marie, ever talks mean about the Dreaded Bowel Disease.

Stella glares and grips the side of the hammock. Lorraine steps back. "I can ride my bike anywhere I want." Stella keeps glaring and Lorraine keeps stepping backwards until she reaches the spigot attached to the house. She turns the faucet to get a drink from the hose, but nothing comes out.

Marie, scary-looking in her white nail polish and lipstick, opens her eyes and says, "Try turning the nozzle of the hose on." She's been roasting herself in the sun like a hot dog grilling. She's talking to Lorraine, but staring at me and Stella.

"Keep your eye on the hose," Stella whispers as Lorraine turns the nozzle and a whoosh of water hits Marie's chest.

Marie jumps off the chaise lounge and grabs Lorraine by the collar.

"Marie, do you always have to get physical?" Renee, on cue, walks out of the house in pink seersucker shorts and halter top, licking a cherry Popsicle. "You look like Brutus beating up Olive Oyl."

Relieved by the turn the conversation is taking, I lie back in the hammock and giggle.

"Swat the top of Marie's head and send her flying," Stella suggests to Lorraine.

The advice comes too late. Marie has already pulled Lorraine, who is much taller, by the hair. Lorraine is bent forward, down on her knees. This is how Marie wins; she just drags you down to her level.

"I didn't do it on purpose," Lorraine whines. "Unhand me."

"See. She even talks like Olive Oyl." Renee shakes the Popsicle stick at Marie. "Why are you picking on Olive Oyl? Short people have complexes."

"Unhand me? That is so lame. Go home." Marie unhands Lorraine and scowls at Renee. "And why don't you shove your stupid psychology up your ass?"

Lorraine grabs her neck and makes a face like she's been mortally wounded.

"Oh, you're all right. Marie just wrinkled your collar a bit." Renee turns Lorraine's neckband back down. "Which doesn't matter because the rest of the shirt wasn't ironed anyway." Renee's lips are stained cherry red from her Popsicle.

Me and Stella giggle out of control. "Unhand me, you brute." I grab Stella's collar. We laugh so hard I choke and fall out of the hammock. She falls on top of me.

"What are you two lezzies laughing at?" Marie screws up her face.

Stella lets go of my collar, my head hits the grass with a soft thud. The laugh drains completely out of her face. I say, "Shut up, Marie. You're the pervert."

"I'm not the one making out with my girlfriend in the hammock." Marie's wet t-shirt is stuck to her, outlining her bra.

Stella gives *me* a dirty look. Like it's my fault Marie's an asshole and Lorraine's harassing her new neighbors. "We were just talking." She piles her hair back into her baseball cap. A little knot of muscle pops out of her arm.

Marie leans toward us, whispers like a spy passing a secret, "Try lying down in the back seat of a car when you're *talking*. You won't fall out."

Stella's right foot shakes like crazy. Marie and Stella stare each other down. My fingers tense around Stella's arm.

"Sex is all you think of, Marie." Renee steps right between them. "Just because you don't have any girlfriends doesn't mean the rest of us can't." Good old Renee, you can always count on her to butt in.

In a hoarse voice to demonstrate her injured vocal cords, Lorraine says, "You're all a bunch of queers." She fumbles with her bike's kickstand and takes off. Marie sticks the transistor radio's earplug in her ear, pulls down her shades, roasting herself, flat on her back again. Renee saunters back into the house. I hoist myself into the hammock. Stella, already in the hammock, tries to keep space between us, but it's not too easy in a hammock.

Stella's mother, Big Stella, comes out of the kitchen carrying a big metal pan with three naked chickens in it. Their wrinkly legs stick straight up in the air.

"Oh Mae, what am I going to do without you?" Big Stella asks over her shoulder.

Mom is right behind her, carrying a platter of corn-on-the-cob. "Cut up chicken all by your lonesome."

They sit at the picnic table and dissect dead birds.

Stella scrunches up her nose. "Why do they have to cut up the chickens out here?"

Marie walks past the mothers, toward the house. "I'm going to the library for an hour, Mae."

"It's Mom to you. The library? In the summer? On a weekend? You can do better than that, Marie."

"You meet interesting guys at the library. The reference room is air-conditioned. Ask Cora Rose and Stella." Marie pauses, holding the screen door open. "About the air conditioning, I mean."

Mom whacks the wing off a chicken. "Close the door, change your t-shirt, and try reading something while you're there."

I wonder if Mom really thinks Marie is going to the library to meet "guys"? Marie's going to the rat projects to smoke pot with Fletcher. I'd bet my life on it.

When Marie's out of view, Stella relaxes. "Too bad the party can't be just us." She pushes on the ground with her feet. The hammock rocks. We slide closer and watch Stella's grandmother, Babcia, an empty wicker basket in her arms, walk toward the clothesline in the Kallowitzes' yard.

"Fifteen years old," I say with a Polish accent, trying to sound like Babcia. "Eh yup, fifteen years old." I answer myself, bobbing my head, like my Memere answers Stella's Babcia, like it's a miracle that we made it to fifteen. Stella grins. She likes it when I imitate the families.

"They were friends before we were born," Stella says softly. I don't know if she means our mothers or our grandmothers, but it doesn't matter. They were all friends before we were born. She raises her voice to be sure Big Stella can hear. "Old people and teenagers aren't even asked if they want to move."

"Stella, unfold the lawn chairs and put them in the shade, under the tree." Big Stella, a warning in her voice, points to the spot with a severed chicken leg.

"We're taking off," Stella announces as soon as the last chair is unfolded. Our mothers exchange a long-suffering look. Big Stella says, "Stay within hollering distance in case we need you."

I push open the gate, but Stella stops to tie her sneaker, so I let it clink shut and wait for her. Mom stops painting her chicken with sauce and says to Big Stella, "I'm happy for you, but I wish you weren't going.

I sympathize with Stella. Swept away from the only life she's known." Something in her voice makes me realize she thinks we're out of hearing distance. Stella realizes we're invisible too. She puts a finger to her lips. We back up slowly and sit in the shadow of the butternut tree.

Big Stella doesn't answer Mom. She frowns and pushes back a wisp of gray hair with her forearm. Our fathers, Andre and Chester, walk over from Stella's house, sit down at the picnic table next to our mothers. They each have a beer. Either they don't notice me and Stella or they just don't have anything to say to us. A car backfires in the parking lot where the cow pasture used to be. All four of our parents turn around. Dad shakes his head, disgusted; watches a Datsun drive off in a cloud of black smoke.

Mom says, "Before the projects, there wasn't really a neighborhood to move out of—just three houses at the end of a street with a big pasture out back." Now there are these big ugly green things, four of them in a row, like motels on a Monopoly board.

Stella's father stares at the buildings and says, "Went up too fast. First good wind, they'll blow away."

Dad looks over his shoulder. "Imagine trying to live in one of those things. People on top of you. People on both sides of you. People across from you. Ain't healthy."

"No. It's not." Stella's father nods agreeably. "Kids grow up mean like that, like rats in a barn."

"Project rats," Stella whispers.

"Poor Ma. I wish she didn't have to see this." Dad sips his beer. "She'll never leave, though. Why should she? We were here first. My father got screwed when he sold that land. They're not going to screw us too."

"It was a nice little piece of property," Stella's father says. "Good pasture." He doesn't argue about getting screwed. He's moving out.

The men take off. Stella's father nods as he walks past. The mothers sit at the picnic table, making sure all the hair is off the corn, smearing butter, wrapping each ear in a separate piece of tin foil. Me and Stella let a ladybug pass back and forth between our fingers. I'm about to suggest we take off too when Big Stella sighs, "I'm so proud of Chester. He's spent his whole life working for this new house."

34

"Too bad he's going to miss his own party and his daughter's birthday because he has to work this afternoon." Mom's voice has an edge, sounds more like she's talking to Marie than Big Stella.

Big Stella is startled. "He works hard for his family, Mae."

Mom stops picking hair off the corn. "Andre works hard too. We all work hard."

"Some of us just don't get paid much," I whisper to Stella, too loud.

Mom whips around. "What did you say? What are you girls doing here?"

"Nothing." I look down at my feet so she won't read my face. Dad works hard, in a paper mill, by the canals, for lousy pay he always complains about.

Big Stella makes her face blank just like mine and takes an interest in making sure the corn is totally de-haired. Mom, who thinks she's the only one allowed to comment about Dad's lousy job, glares at me. "Eavesdropping. Get out of my sight. Go," she says.

Stella grabs my hand. "Come on." We make it through the gate this time but stare at each other and agree silently to hang back a few seconds longer.

"Mae, forgive me. I didn't mean anything about Andre." Big Stella says the right words, but her voice and her words don't go together. She's angry too.

Mom's eyes are on me and Stella. She knows we're still here, but she turns away, putting all her attention back on Big Stella. Sometimes Mom gets real mad real quick, but it's usually not Big Stella she gets mad at.

"Please, Mae," Big Stella says, irritated herself now.

"Please what? The girls won't even be going to the same school."

Stella and I give each other a look. We never went to the same school.

"It's only twenty miles, twenty-five minutes away," Big Stella says reasonably.

"Christmas, maybe." Mom's voice is flat. "And funerals."

"We'll make a standing date. Friday nights," Big Stella says enthusiastically.

"After working all week?" Mom says, bitchy. "You don't even drive."

"Saturday, then. The buses run on Saturday."

"It would take a miracle." Mom throws an ear of corn on the pile. "The girls will just have to make new friends."

"A miracle. Like nine children between us, every one alive and healthy, nobody in trouble, husbands who come home every night?" Big Stella says, excited, arms in the air, like the TV evangelist preacher that the nuns warn you not to listen to.

"That's your idea of a miracle, Stella? You *have* been living here too long." Mom waves an ear of corn at Big Stella. "It's good you're moving. You need bigger miracles." She turns her back and slaps paper plates on the picnic table.

"Here's your miracle." Big Stella stands, waves her hands in a big circle surveying the neighborhood, her big arms churning the air.

Mom turns around to see Big Stella's miracle. "You see a miracle that you're moving away from here, Stella?"

Big Stella talks fast, on a roll, "You work all your life. You raise three girls. Marie's a little wild. Cora Rose has a medical problem. They'll be all right, work hard, give you cute little grandchildren. Renee, she'll maybe go to nursing school. There's your miracle. You waiting for a big miracle? The Blessed Virgin's gonna visit while we're hanging out laundry? I'm forty-eight years old. I take what comes along. Would you say no to moving your family to a bigger house in a nicer neighborhood? Why not Saturdays? Why not, Mae?"

"What?" Mom says, slow and mean. "You and Stella will spend Saturday mornings on a bus? Or will you finally sneak Cora Rose to the mansion?"

"*Mansion?* Yes, me and Stella, we could take a bus. Sometimes you and Cora Rose could drive to us. What *mansion?* What are you saying, Mae? Who has to sneak?"

"I'm saying . . ." Mom stares at her hard. "That none of the LaBarres has ever seen your new place. We help pack Babcia's crystal from this end, but we don't help you unpack at the other end." Mom's smile is nasty. Big Stella stares with her mouth open. "Why is that, Stella?"

"I don't know. I was waiting . . . until the place was set up, so we could sit and enjoy." Big Stella sits down at the picnic table. "Mae, I'm sorry. What do you think? You think I'm ashamed? You think it's easy for me to leave? You think it's you I'm leaving? Tomorrow, please, you and Cora Rose will come to the new place with us tomorrow?"

Mom shakes her head and sits down next to Big Stella. "I think the old neighbors won't fit the new life. But it's nice you said it, about Saturday. It might happen once or twice." Mom smiles, a sad tired smile. Big Stella takes a tissue out of her apron, blows her nose, and pats Mom's hand. Stella and I look away from each other. A breeze comes up. Our mothers turn to watch the paper plates blow off the table and flatten against the fence.

Finally Mom looks in our direction like she just woke up. "I said go on. Get ready for the party." They're back where they were before Big Stella thought there was a miracle, before Mom yelled at us. She sighs, "Take a little time to say goodbye. This is your last day as neighbors. In a few weeks you start school."

The look on the mothers' faces makes them look younger and older at the same time. I wish Mom hadn't mentioned school. I don't want to think of more than one bad thing at a time.

"Let's go to my house." Stella means her real house, the one next door to mine.

ࠆ   ࠆ   ࠆ

Stripped down, Stella's house feels deserted, like an aftermath of some disaster that the inhabitants have fled. "Everybody at the new house?" I bet Stella's never been alone in her house before.

"The new house." She sounds hollow, like the Ghost of Christmas Past. She sits on her bed with her back against the headboard. It's the only piece of furniture in the room. I squeeze in next to her. Good thing Stella's skinny, or the two of us wouldn't fit. Curtains, shades, Joplin posters; all gone. Nothing but the twin bed is left.

"It's going to be so weird when you're gone," I say.

We listen to the empty house. Someone starts up a lawnmower. A car pulls into the gravel drive at my house. Stella's aunts, carrying big aluminum pans full of golumpkis and pierogi, arriving early for the party?

Our shoulders and hips touch. Stella pulls a silver flask her brother left behind after boot camp from under her mattress, tilts her head back and swallows. It's just water, but her whole body shivers. She plays with the metal cap on the silver chain. She offers me the flask. I shake my head. She wipes her mouth on her bare arm. Her bottom lip quivers. Our legs touch all the way from our hips to my ankle and Stella's calf. I wonder if my legs will always be half as long and twice as wide as Stella's. I try to stay still so I won't cry. Stella almost never cries; even when she was a little kid, she never made a big deal of things. We're both going to hate it if she cries. I stare at her big, bony hand that's resting on her knee, so I don't have to look at her eyes. Her fingernails are cracked but clean, scrubbed for the party. Her fingers are tapered, almost delicate. It makes me feel better to concentrate on just one part of her. Even throwing a basketball or weeding Babcia's garden, Stella's hands are the girliest things about her.

"You're staring." She rubs her hands together.

"You could be a piano player. Or a violinist." I want to give her a compliment, something nice that she'll remember. She stares at her hands. I pick one of them up, turn it over, stare at her palm.

"What are you doing?"

"Think you'll go to the prom in a Grand Prix with the doctors' kid?" It comes out of the blue. I don't even know I'm going to say it until it's out of my mouth.

"Christ." She pushes her shoulders into the headboard and closes her eyes.

I get the crazy urge to kiss her hand. I stroke her palm instead.

She squirms a little, pulls her hand away, and opens her eyes. "*You'll* get asked to the Prom next year. Not me."

"What?" I don't want to talk about next year or the stupid prom. I lean back against the headboard, irritated, even though I brought it up. "Boys don't want to go to the prom with a girl who asks for a bathroom pass ten times a day." I shouldn't have said that, I'm crying now.

She kneels on the mattress and faces me in one quick motion. Her baseball cap falls off, her hair falls down, dark and messy around her shoulders. She stares into my eyes like there's something inside my head that she lost. "You're beautiful," she says like it's an insult. Her face is hard and fierce like those masks in the Social Studies room.

"What are you mad at?" The urge I have to fling my arms around her scares me. "It's not my fault you're moving."

She cringes like she's got pain somewhere. Her face gets soft. She brushes a tear from my eye with her finger. "You're too pretty to be sick. I wish you were never sick again."

"Nobody ever thought I was beautiful except you." She's too close. I have to squeeze the words out. "And Memere. Grandmothers don't count—something in nature makes them think all their grandchildren are beautiful."

She leans closer, her breath on my cheek. "At least I won't have to watch you take off in cars with your boyfriends," she says.

"You're scaring me." My voice squeaks. "You'll have boyfriends, too."

"No, I won't." She pushes my hair back. It's so hot in her bedroom. Air hits the sweat on my neck and gives me a chill. Stella's hand flutters, barely touching my hair. My forehead drops to her shoulder. Her fingers land on my neck.

"I love you." I mouth the words on her shoulder. My body gets stiff with fear. Maybe she didn't hear me. Her breath is warm on my neck.

She pulls me closer. Her cheek is on top of my head. She's leans back, pulling me with her her. My arms dangle, useless at my sides. I put one hand on her back at the base of her neck, to help steady us, fan out my fingers. She pushes her head back into my hand. I feel her pulse in my palm.

I still want to say something nice, tell her she's the only girl I know that never says mean things to people unless they deserve it. Tell her it never mattered how lousy I am in gym because it feels like a part of me is shooting those baskets and making the shot when I watch her out in back of the barn. Tell her that they're wrong, the mean kids; she's beautiful, especially in motion, she's beautiful.

"We'll talk on the phone. They'll let us even though it costs money.

They'll feel bad they made you move." My hand is in Stella's hair. My fingertips are moving.

"My brothers listen." Her voice catches in her throat. "I hate the phone."

My other hand dangles at my side. I rub it against the mattress, naked and slippery with no blanket or even sheets on it. What would we talk about on the phone? One of the things I like about Stella is that she makes me feel like I don't have to talk if I don't have anything to say. I touch her neck with the fingertips of the hand that was just on the cool sheets. Stella's neck isn't cool. It's warm. Stella is skinny with muscles like a boy, but her neck and cheeks are soft and warm. She whimpers; the noise you make when you're not supposed to cry.

I pull her head to mine. I don't let myself think about it. I just kiss her, right on the mouth. She kisses me back. We kiss with our mouths wide open. It feels like forever. Stella leans way into me, her hands are on the mattress, one on each side of my hips. First it's me kissing her. Then we're kissing each other. She's pressing into me, her tongue slow, her breathing heavier and heavier. She doesn't take her lips off mine, not for a second. Her body is moving slowly. I make little noises, shiver. She pulls me under her, lies on top of me, never takes her lips away from mine. Her hips move in the same rhythm as her breath. She pushes her tiny breasts into mine. I follow the beat of her, my sneakered foot rubbing against her calf. Her body starts to quiver.

"Stella! Cora Rose!" Her mother's voice zaps us like a cow prod. We listen to the door slam and Big Stella's heavy footsteps coming up the stairs.

Stella looks at me horrified, like she woke up next to me, wedged in the back seat after some gruesome car crash. She jumps off the bed. I push on the mattress with my heels, scoot up against the headboard into a sitting position, and wrap my arms around my knees. Her eyes dart to the open door. She says, angrily, "We weren't doing anything wrong." Her right thigh twitches and her right foot taps the floor wildly.

Big Stella steps into the room. "Stella, what's the matter?"

Tears stream down Stella's eyes. "You should be ashamed of the new place. It's all snobs there," she says to Big Stella. She whips her head around to me. Her voice shakes, "Go home. Nobody lives here anymore."

Big Stella and I stare at each other.

"Honey." Big Stella tries to put her arms around Stella, but Stella pulls away and sets her jaw against us both.

I get off the bed. The mattress squeaks.

"We'll see you at the party." Big Stella puts her arm around me and guides me out of the room. "I'll take care of her." She walks me to the top of the stairs and goes back to Stella.

I walk out of Stella's house for the last time.

Chapter 4

"Because sex is more fun than school," Marie screams at Mom and storms out the front door. A pair of black panties falls from the big leather purse slung over her shoulder and lands on the threshold. Mom tries to slam the door, but the door catches on Marie's panties and swings back open.

Crouched by the tiny porthole window at the landing of the stairs, wearing only a bra and underwear, I watch Marie throw her feed bag of a purse on a pile of clothes lying on the back seat of Fletcher's '57 Chevy. Marie is a Senior. School is almost over and they haven't thrown her out yet. All she'd have do is show up for the next few weeks and they'd probably let her graduate just to get her out of their hair. The stairway is cold. I should have grabbed my robe when the yelling started.

Marie jumps in the passenger side of the Chevy. I strain to get a view of her belly. Me and Renee think Marie might be pregnant. Fletcher, standing outside the car on the driver's side, waves sheepishly. "Sorry, Ma'am. She'll be all right." He folds his lean, tall body into the car. For a guy with a ponytail, he's really polite and pretty brave. He could get in trouble, maybe, for dating a high-school girl. The car revs up, and they're off.

"I'm calling the authorities." Mom picks up the panties and waves the underwear from the front steps like a start-up flag at Riverside Speedway.

She means the cops. She won't call anyone. She'll stomp around the house, bitch to Dad when he comes home from work, and scream at Marie next time she shows up for a meal. Mom should give up on rehabilitating Marie, like Dad did. Marie will be eighteen in a few months. Then the cops won't care if she goes to school or if she's pregnant with some older guy's kid. If she is pregnant.

Mom turns to me. "The show's over. For God's sake, put some clothes on. You better not be late for school."

Typical. Renee's lying in bed with the oatmeal flu. She threw her oatmeal in the toilet and yelled, "Ma, I'm sick." Mom fell for it, always does. Who would believe that a girl who washes off the bottom of her sneakers after gym class, goes to confession every Saturday morning, and spends Saturday afternoons with Future Nurses of America would do something as gross as making fake puke? If Renee really had an illness as gross as the Dreaded Bowel Disease, she'd never fake it. She'd never call Mom to the bathroom to show off the disgusting proof.

And Marie—comes and goes as she pleases, doesn't even bother to lie.

Being the youngest doesn't count for shit in this family. I'm the one with ulcerative colitis, a diagnosed illness with a real name. Even if I try to pretend it doesn't exist, Mom knows about it. I should be the one getting off easy, but no. I'm the only one doing what I'm supposed to and I get yelled at.

Screw them.

I get dressed, do my hair, and eat a Pop Tart without saying a word to my mother. She doesn't notice. She's too busy being pissed at Marie. It snowed last week. Then it got warm. The far end of our yard, the part that connects with the land behind the projects, is a mud flat. I tug on my stupid laminated looks-like-leather boots with corny looks-like-fur above the ankles. The other girls have high boots, tight on their calves, which come way up, just below their knees. Even Marie found decent boots for her squatty legs. At least I've got my hair. Some girls don't have one cute thing about them.

I walk through the mud in the backyard, thinking about Marie screaming, "Sex is more fun than school." She's been saying that since she was a freshman. I believe her. Sex better be more fun than school. I just wish she wouldn't scream it from the front door. I bet Memere was watching from her kitchen window.

I step over a pile of slush and stand with the project rats at the edge of the parking lot. Carlos, a cute Puerto Rican kid, says, "Where is your most voluptuous sister?" He means Renee. I wish Renee was here too. It's easier when she's here, she knows how to bullshit, how to flirt.

I shrug my shoulders. "Sick."

The rat bus drives up, stinking up the parking lot with farty black smoke. Carlos climbs in. "Tell your sister that Carlos will make it better." The toes of his sneakers, black high tops, are wet. There's gritty black stuff on the bus's metal steps. Two girls with high boots get in behind Carlos and add more muck to the steps. Three guys hunched together, passing around a butt, take a last drag, and climb in. I don't move. I just hang there for a second, then step back.

The driver yells, "Let's go."

I shake my head no. The driver doesn't comment. He looks straight ahead and lets the bus doors hang open for ten seconds before he pulls a lever and the doors screech closed. I suck in the smelly fumes and watch the bus's big square rear end waddle out of the parking lot before I walk toward Fletcher's place. He lives at the end of the last building, apartment 24A. I don't see his car in the lot. I knock on his door. There could be someone else inside or his Chevy could be parked around back. Nobody answers. Fletcher and the guy he lives with both work at the wire company, but some days Fletcher doesn't go to work. I thought Marie would be here. Maybe she went to school. She does that once in a while. Fletcher drops her off on his way to work.

He told me, "Come over any time. Just come on in," even if he's not home. It would feel weird to just go in. Marie and Fletcher could be doing it. I sit on the steps. Someone could be asleep on the couch. People hang out at Fletcher's: hippie guys with long hair and glassy eyes, who laugh a lot, smoke dope, listen to Cream or Jefferson Airplane, and watch a black-and-white TV that gets only Channel 8. They're okay, they pass me the joint if they're smoking. I don't inhale. I'm afraid of marijuana. I'm afraid of hippie guys, but not quite as afraid of them as I am of most people. The best part of the apartment is that the bathroom is down a long narrow hall on the second floor. If no one is in either one of the upstairs bedrooms, it's really private.

I shouldn't be skipping school. I miss enough school when I'm sick. It starts to sleet. Fletcher and Marie can't be doing it if she's pregnant, can they? I knock again and turn the handle. It's not locked, it never is. I open the door slowly, "Anyone home?" I walk around the first floor, which is a big kitchen, and a tiny living room with a huge couch and a long bookcase made of warped two-by-fours and cinder blocks. The shelves of the bookcase were built right across a window. The shelves are empty in front of the pane, so light gets into the small room.

"Anyone home?" I call a third time. Still no answer. I can't believe my good luck.

I kneel on the couch and run my fingers along the spines of the books. Fletcher has great books. Stuff they don't have in the school library. I didn't know how much I like to read until I started borrowing from Fletcher. He lets me take his books home as long as I hide them from Mom. I show them to Renee and Stella.

No, not Stella.

Stella is gone. She's been gone a long time. I called her twice. The first time she said eleven words, "Hi." "No." "It sucks." "The kids are mean." "I gotta go." It didn't even sound like Stella. It sounded like Stella underwater. The second time I called, her mother answered, tripping over some bogus excuse why Stella couldn't talk to me.

I pick out my favorite books. *The Joy of Love, Stranger in a Strange Land, Legal Highs.*

I sit on the couch with the pile of books next to me and place *The Joy of Love* in my lap. I like the pictures, mostly sketches of the same hippie-looking man and woman, naked, having sex in different positions. Renee and I leafed through this book. Renee likes pictures of people having sex and she likes talking about who's doing it with who at school. But she thinks going all the way would be a disgusting mess. Renee's better to look at than most people. She's my sister and even I know this. She looks better than normal, but she's as weird as everyone else is.

I want to get used to seeing guys naked, so if I get a boyfriend, *when* I get a boyfriend, it won't freak me out. Plenty of girls worse off than I am have boyfriends. Aunt Josette has Uncle Louie. Bobbi Lee Paterson has a greasy creep of a boyfriend.

I open the book. The pages are all dog-eared. Lots of the people who come to Fletcher's must be looking at pictures of other people having sex. I turn to a picture of a woman with her feet hooked behind the back of her head, her knees pointed in opposite directions, so her stuff is just hanging out there, dead center, on the page. She's smiling, happy with herself, like cousin Lorraine when she got honorable mention in the school newspaper for her "What Liberty Means to Me" essay. Someone could bend their legs like that without breaking them? Yoga? The caption reads, "The oyster position." "Ouch" is handwritten under the picture in purple ink in Marie's writing. "Ouch" wasn't on this page a couple of weeks ago when Renee and I sat on my bed staring at it.

I turn the pages, stop at almost every one. Try to imagine myself doing this stuff with some guy. Close my eyes. Concentrate. I'm turned on. Good. I've never even kissed a guy. It must be like kissing Stella, only not as crazy-feeling. You probably don't feel like you're riding a wild horse and hanging on for dear life and you never want to stop when it's a normal kiss. You'd probably be embarrassed, but it probably wouldn't feel like the horse got shot out from under you if you almost got caught. If it was a normal kiss.

Dirty books, stuff I hear from Renee, sometimes from other girls talking at school—that's what I know about sex and boys. Renee kissed a guy and she got felt up once. She said getting felt up was gross. Renee likes what she's got too much to share it. Marie knows a lot, but she doesn't give me or Renee much information.

I flip to the table of contents. The chapter on foreplay starts on page 178: "Let's Get Excited." Foreplay isn't until page 178? The next chapter is masturbation, a skipper. I could have written it. Marie's writing in purple ink again: "The sin of wasting seed." Then below it, crammed in small letters, "Or eggs." Marie's a dope. She thinks cuming and ovulating is the same thing. I got over worrying about whether masturbation is a sin or not when the boys got pulled out of Catechism class to be warned about the evils of self-abuse while the girls sat stuffing collection envelopes into boxes. If the Church isn't worried enough about me masturbating to even mention it in Catechism class, I'm not going to worry about it either. I make myself think about boys when I do it. I know how to do it with my pillow, with my sheets, with Stuffy Bear's head. Mom thinks it's cute that I still want to keep Stuffy Bear.

Marie's purple pen crossed out "Celibacy," the title of the next chapter, and renamed it "Renee's Song." Another skipper.

I turn to a chapter titled "Entrées" and a sketch of the hippie couple in the "x" position, lying on their sides, crotches together, heads at opposite ends of the page. Their legs are spread so one foot is on their partner's chest and one foot is on their partner's back, like scissors trying to cut each other in half. He must be inside her. I hope this is specialty stuff. I wonder if it's considered worse than two girls kissing. I bet it's not. Oral sex. I bet most people consider a blowjob worse than two girls kissing. I can't imagine doing any of the specialty stuff with a boy. Straight sex in the missionary position, that's it for me.

I page backwards and land on "Homoerotic." I haven't let myself look at this chapter. It'll give me cramps. Marie's purple pen re-titled this one "Abominable Sin," Sister Angelica's words. Sister Angelica's high clipped voice, "Boys with boys. Girls with girls," angry like it's a sin against her personally, then shivering and dropping the subject, the details of abominable sin making her too upset to comment any further. Funny how you can make something seem really bad by not talking about it.

On the next page two women, young, in their early twenties maybe, are sitting cross-legged. More hippies, a black woman with a big Afro, and a white woman with long straight hair. They're facing each other, knees touching, bare boobs, smiling. Wearing hip huggers, their thin stomachs aren't even flat, they're caved in. The white one is leaning forward, touching the black one's nipple with the tip of her finger. Both of them have hard, really dark nipples that are really sticking out. The white woman's head is sort of cocked, like a puppy not quite sure what's going on. The black woman is laughing with her head thrown back. Their breasts are round and big on their skinny bodies. It's a photograph, not a drawing like most of them. These two actually sat on the grass somewhere and did this? In front of a photographer? A black girl and a white girl. I feel nervous for them. Don't they know anyone could pick up this book and see them? Parents. Grandparents. Gross perverts masturbating in public bathrooms. It gives me the willies. Do they have boyfriends? What if their boyfriends see the picture? Where are these girls now?

I turn the page, sketches again. Two more naked women, lying sideways, their legs wrapped around each other, kissing. Marie smudged this page with her purple pen too. An arrow with "Stella" points to one girl. Another arrow with "C. R." points to the second girl. I can't stop staring at Stella's name and my initials. Why is Marie writing this in a book that anyone can pick up and read? Nobody at Fletcher's knows Stella. Marie is crazy. I pull a pen out of my purse and scratch until there are two holes torn in the page where our names were.

I kneel on the couch and search through the bookcase until I find Fletcher's fat, blue Webster's dictionary. I can't find homoerotic. But I find abominable.

Abominable, 1. very hateful; detestable; loathsome; odious to the mind; offensive to the senses.

Me and Stella on her bed; the Dreaded Bowel Disease.

I get a bad cramp, slam the dictionary shut, and take deep breaths. A noise comes from upstairs, creaking, followed by footsteps. Oh Mary, oh Jesus, somebody's getting up out of bed. Fletcher's roommate? One of his hippie friends? I rip out the page I scratched up. I snap *The Joy of Love* and *Webster's* shut.

Fletcher bounds down the stairs.

"Sorry." My voice is shaky. "I yelled, 'Anybody home?' but no one answered." I shove the page in my pocket, kneel on the couch, and stick the books back on the shelf.

Fletcher flops down next to me. "It's okay, partner. You're welcome here." He strokes his beard. He lights a joint, offers it to me. There's a red crease down the side of his face. I shake my head no. I like Fletcher. I don't feel like I have to take the joint from him if I don't want it. He yawns and stretches. "We fell asleep for a minute." He scratches his beard with his bony hands. He has long nails for a guy. He yells up the stairs, "It's Cora Rose."

Marie walks down the stairs in Fletcher's bathrobe. There are cowboys riding bucking broncos on the robe, like a little kid's, but man-sized. Marie is real short. Fletcher is real tall. The bathrobe is way big on Marie. I'm so pissed about the crap she wrote in that book that I can barely stand to look at her. To make things worse, she sits on his lap, even though there's room for six on the couch, and plays with his fingers. They look at each other with shit-eating grins. Marie slides over, snuggles in the crook of his arm, and sighs. It's embarrassing. They must have just done it. This must be after-play. Did Marie learn this in *The Joy of Love*? Does this stuff just come naturally to some people? If she's pregnant, does he know?

"Want something to eat Cora Rose?" Marie says sweetly.

"No thanks." I'm nervous about Marie's sugary voice and I want to stay pissed about her writing my name in that book. I don't want anything she offers.

"There's orange juice and root beer, I think." She sighs again. "What'd ya do, skip school?"

I don't answer. It's not really a question, just Marie listening to herself coo. I don't stare at them. I feel like a jerk being here. I watch them, only when it's the right time to be looking, like if one of them says something. Both of them are way different than usual, especially Marie. She's calm, just lying there on Fletcher's shoulder, minding her own business. Fletcher is calmer than usual too, but he's always pretty calm, so it doesn't show so much on him. Marie's a mush ball. Drugs? Her eyes are dreamy like drugs. She's in a good mood; that's what it is. She looks like she's going to roll over on her back and purr. From being with a guy? The way they cuddle makes me want to run out of the room, but only because it's my own sister and her boyfriend.

I feel so sad. Maybe if I had a boyfriend, a nice calm guy, he'd help me calm down.

Chapter 5

Memere rocks in her rocking chair, knitting. Her old hands move fast, weaving strings of colored yarn, pink and blue. Marie rocks in a straight-backed kitchen chair, precariously perched on its back legs, her arms wrapped around herself. This is how I find them, their eyes locked, when I walk in.

Mom and Marie had another fight. Mom was too pissed to come after Marie herself, so she sent me. Marie didn't bother to grab her purse when she stormed out, so Mom figured she couldn't have gone much farther than Memere's.

"Hello, Cora Rose." Memere's needles keep clicking. She doesn't move her gaze from Marie's. Her hands are so used to the yarn and her ears are so used to my feet on her floor that she has no need to look at me or the baby blanket. "Marie and Cora Rose, both granddaughters visiting their old Memere on the same Saturday morning?" The clicking stops. "This is an event."

"Hi, Memere." I kiss her on the cheek.

She stands with a grimace. Her knees are getting bad. She pats Marie's shoulder and exhales one of her long patient sighs. She smiles at me calmly. "Your sister wants to cut one foolish mistake in half and make two. Take her to see the priest."

ଔ   ଔ   ଔ

I'm not sure Mom believes me when I tell her we're going to church, but she's ready for a couple hours of peace and quiet and Dad hands over the car keys. Marie drives, staring straight ahead, not saying a word to me until we're ready to go inside. Then, as we're walking into All Saints vestibule, she says, "Slip into the confessional box opposite me so some holy roller doesn't hear my confession."

"Better some holy roller, than me. I'm not even going to confession." Ever again.

"So, don't confess, just fill up the other side until I'm done." Marie's face is even rounder since her belly popped. She looks younger and pudgier, like a big baby. A pregnant almost eighteen-year-old baby, wearing too much mascara, sneering at me.

"Great. Wonderful." Here we go again. Marie threatens abortion and I end up in confession. "How do you expect me to manage getting in opposite you?" There are two lines, one on each side, leading to the confessionals that sandwich the priest. We'd have to wait in opposite lines and hit it just right. "I'll just cut in front of whoever's in line on my side when you go in," I say sarcastically.

"Good," she snaps. "I'd do it for you, too."

She would. She wouldn't think anything of it. She'd think it was funny.

So, when the time comes, I say, "Excuse me, I'm so sorry, my mother is very sick. I have to get back to her. May I please . . ." and a wide eyed twelve-year-old nods and lets me take cuts.

I kneel in the dark and listen to the priest and Marie as they take turns mumbling. This goes on and on. I can't understand what either of them is saying. I should have let the twelve-year-old have his spot. Marie wouldn't have known the difference.

I haven't been to confession since the Kallowitzes moved. I'm out of here as soon as Marie's done mumbling. Some deranged monk, alone in a cave in the fifth century, must have come up with the idea of confession. What would I say, "Bless me, father, for I have sinned. My favorite fantasy is my old neighbor Stella climbing on top of me on her stripped bed?" "Oh, yes, Father, I pray." "I'm sorry to confess, prayer isn't working out all that well for me. Stella's warm neck seeps right through the 'blessed fruit of Thy womb, Jesus.' I try to replace her with the hairy guy in *The Joy of Love*." The hairy guy is a step up from lezzy stuff, but still not what the priest means by "Pure of thought." Anyway, at the

51

crucial moment, Stella's hands and sad smirk bleed right through any dream that tries to replace them. It's because I've never been with a guy. Mom was right. Me and Stella had no business sneaking off to be alone with cows. The cows and Stella moved to greener pastures, so now I can concentrate on good influences. Maybe that's how I'll explain myself to the priest.

Cows corrupted me. That's funny. When I hold my breath and try not to snicker, I hear Marie's voice quivering, then her muted sobs. The priest mumbles again. He mumbles on and on. I roll my eyes. It's not sisterly, but I'm sick of Marie. I'm pretty sure God doesn't need a priest to intercede for Him, but I'd like to try and figure out what I think about that someplace else. Denouncing confession while you're in a confessional has to be a new level of sin even Renee hasn't considered. And I wouldn't be committing it if Marie's wasn't squeezing every last drop of drama out of the bad situation she made all by herself. Well, her and Fletcher. He's probably getting stoned right now. If Marie was really considering abortion, she never would have gone to talk to Memere. This way, she can blame Memere and the priest and the Church when she has the kid. Anybody but herself. Bet she doesn't tell the priest, "What I do with my pussy is nobody's fucking business," like she does me and Renee any time we try to talk to her about being pregnant. What a bitch.

Marie and the priest are awfully quite all of a sudden. Marie inhales a sob that takes my breath away. I know that kind of sob, when you're drowning on your own snot and tears. The kind of sob you don't want anyone else to hear, especially a priest or your sister. I feel like a trapped animal, but my sister sounds like one. She does it again. It's horrible. You should wail like that only if you have someplace to crouch and hide in, like Memere's back pantry room, and even then you should stuff your mouth with a kitchen towel. Her wailing gets me in the chest. I'm afraid she's not getting enough oxygen. The third time she makes that noise, I suck in air, hard, for her. What the hell is she going to do? A baby?

Marie and the priest are quiet again. I listen but don't hear a thing. Whoosh, the little shutter slides open and I gasp. I'm taken off guard by the smell of English Leather and the priest in profile through the screen, sitting in the dark, making the sign of the cross. I'm up. How did this happen? I meant to leave when Marie left. She must have bolted from the confessional in mid-sob. I take a deliberate deep breath.

"Bless me, father, for I have sinned. It has been many months since my last confession." Get up a head of steam and just go. "I ah, disobeyed my parents." Believable, all-purpose sin. "Seven times."

"Yes, go on." His voice is soft, but confession dread trips through me, switched on like the hall light. I know this voice. It's Father Anton. I'm used to his mix of Listerine and Brylcreem. English Leather and black coffee instead of Listerine, but it's Anton all right. I know his white collar is unsnapped in back and stained with hair grease. And, if he doesn't know me by my voice or smell, he's surely figured out who Marie is. Our voices are enough alike that people mistake us for each other, on the phone, all the time. You heard one LaBarre sister, you've heard them all. Anonymous lying to a priest is one thing. Lying to a priest who knows Memere and my parents, who knows I have long brown hair, and an unmarried pregnant sister, is something else.

"My sins are . . ." I have sins, acceptable sins, to report. They dry up in my throat. I know what he wants, sitting there in the dark, patient as the statue of Mary on the left side of the altar, breathing his coffee breath. He may not know what he wants, but I know. He wants me to admit I dream of Stella in shorts, her skinny legs and little round calf muscles, squatting to talk to me as she rubs the top of her thighs with her long fingers, rocking on the balls of her feet. He's not getting my Stella fantasies. He can have lying and gossiping and eating meat on Friday.

"Yes," the Priest prompts me, softly, kindly. Does he know I'm crying? Does he know I have the urge to hit him? "Take a deep breath," he says, so kind, so patient. Somewhere in his big, clean soul, he knows everything. "Tell it simply." His voice is soothing. He can afford to be calm. "We have all sinned." All his sins are safe sins.

"I kissed a girl, Father." Of course, I throw myself at his feet.

"You must never do this again," he says gravely, kindly, like he's really rooting for me to go in peace.

53

"We shall say The Lord's Prayer together, that he may guide us. Pray with me, child." A deep inhale. A deep exhale. "Our Father who art in heaven."

I slip out of the confessional. Oh God, why did I tell him that? An involuntary whimper escapes as I pass by the twelve-year-old who looks at me with the fear of God in his eyes. I leave the poor kid to take my spot. I leave the priest to finish The Lord's Prayer by himself, before he gives me penance, before he forgives my sin and gives his blessing, half expecting him to come after me. He doesn't. He may not even know I'm gone. I look over my shoulder. The twelve-year-old slips into the confessional.

Exposed and unforgiven, I kneel next to Marie at the altar. What kind of ass confesses the sin, then walks out on the absolution? I glance sideways at Marie. Her hands are folded. Her head is down. She's praying like crazy. Not only is her head bent, her eyes are closed, and she's reciting The Act of Contrition out loud, bobbing, droning on, like the old lady who sits in the back of the church. "I am heartily sorry for having offended Thee." She breathes out the prayer in whispers, getting louder and more desperate, until anyone in the front of the church can hear. I smile lamely at the cute guy kneeling next to me. He gives Marie a look. My mouth moves to make a smile again. There is heat coming off Marie. Her sins have made her hot.

I shiver. The cute guy looks back down at his folded hands.

Marie moans. More animal noises, this time a mewling sound, like a cow giving birth, not as loud as that, but still way too loud and raw for church. She is an animal, alive and warm. She is my sister. I have to take care of her.

She better not flip out, right here, up at the altar. "Marie." I nudge her. "Shh." She looks at me, angry, but pleading. Marie needs help. Me trying to help Marie? It's going to really piss her off if she has to let her little sister help her.

"Shh. What's wrong with you?" I hiss. Now I know how it must be for Mom trying to take care of Marie.

She throws her head back, hangs onto the altar with both hands, and lets her body lean back, away from the altar. I'm afraid she's going to really wail. She's in the perfect wailing position. The cute guy stands up. "Should I get help?" he asks. He looks embarrassed to be intruding. I know this guy from Sunday Mass.

"No, no thank you. We'll be okay." I put my arms around her and pull Marie back toward the altar. "Stand up. We're leaving. Now." She lets me escort her down the aisle, her head collapsed on my shoulder.

As soon as we hit the marble steps and the outside air, I ask, "What the hell happened in there?"

She plunks herself down on the steps of the main entrance. Right there with people trying to get in and out for confession. "A kid," she says, in a close to level voice. "A fucking baby."

"No shit," I whisper.

She sobs, upping the volume, "He doesn't want me to have the kid."

I push down the air with the flat of my hand, trying to signal her to lower her voice. It's so strange that Marie is letting me see her sob. I've seen her make a scene many times out of anger, but this is fear. For a second I just watch, like this is a TV show or a movie. Her face is all tortured-looking: nose red, cheeks puffed up and wet. She looks pretty much like everybody else does when they're crying hard.

It hits me, what she just said. "The *priest* doesn't want you to have the kid?" I keep whispering, hoping she'll get the idea to whisper back.

"No," she wails. "Fletcher." She picks up her head and broadcasts, "Fletcher, the father of my child," and collapses on my shoulder again.

"Oh." I try not to knock her off my shoulder as I shrug at the three middle-aged women who step around us. Marie and I haven't hugged since we were toddlers and now she's stuck to me like a barnacle. "What did the priest say?"

"He gave me money," she manages through the sobbing.

I put both arms around her, afraid if I don't keep her wrapped tight she'll lie down and clog up the whole width of the steps. The priest gave her money to keep the baby? "Not the priest," I say, catching on.

She picks up her head and glares at me. "Fletcher," she repeats louder, "Fletcher." Then really wails, "He offered abortion money, *then* offered to marry me."

Two teenage girls, who, thank God, I don't know, stop, stare at us, and raise their eyebrows at each other before trotting up the marble steps of All Saints to take care of their own sins.

"Abortion money." I whisper more to myself than Marie. "Are you going to?"

A guy in a Sunday suit comes out, stands on the top step behind us, and clears his throat. He expects us to move so that he doesn't have to take a step to the right like everyone else to get by. "Excuse me," he says in a tone that means "Get out of my way."

I give him a dirty look. "We're having a spiritual crisis here, Sir." I wrap my arms tighter around Marie, who ignores him, maybe doesn't even know he's there.

"It's too late for an abortion. Fuck him. Fuck anyone else who thinks I'm having an abortion," Marie says fiercely into my neck. The front of my good pink cotton blouse is wet with her tears.

The guy behind us grunts and his eyes get big. He must have heard "abortion" or a muffled "Fuck." He says, "You are on the steps of the house of the Lord," indignantly sidesteps us, and huffs away.

"Marry Fletcher," I say. "You're crazy about him, aren't you?"

"I'm not marrying anybody who's only marrying me because I'm pregnant." She sits up, her back straight, her hands grasping the hard marble steps. Black lines of mascara run down both cheeks. There are little puddles of black on my pink blouse. She hisses, "The prick." She's not talking about the priest.

The reality of Marie's pregnancy, like the fact that she still knows how to cry, hits me. This is real. It's not Vietnam on TV. It's one of Stella's brother's getting shipped home without his foot. Until I saw him on the La-Z-Boy, all depressed looking, I didn't believe it. How could that happen to a boy who once apologized for calling me Fatty? I shake my head. No. No. This is not as bad as that. But Marie, who won't feed the dog, having a baby? Everything is too real. I don't want Marie to have an abortion. I don't want Marie to have a baby. Where will she live? Where will she get money, food, diapers? The kid will be swearing like a trooper before it's potty-trained.

"How will you take care of a baby?"

"Shut up." She hugs herself and nods toward the church doors. "He says the baby's bigger than my fist now. Says it has a heartbeat. Eyes. Ten formed fingers and ten formed toes."

"Marie." I wish she was still in my arms.

"What am I going to do?"

I let her wail. "Go to The House of the Good Shepherd?" I'm not even sure if the home for orphans, runaways, and unmarried pregnant girls, which Mom used to threaten us with, really exists.

"He says I'd spend the rest of my life thinking about how old it is, what it would be doing if I had it with me."

The prick. I feel like punching Father Anton in the face for bringing up the baby's toes. I feel like slapping myself for giving up Stella. At least I didn't say her name. I just said "a girl."

"Maybe a baby would be nice," I offer, half-heartedly.

"Yeah," she answers, too quickly. "You know, someone fresh, who doesn't know anything about me."

"Yeah, Marie." We're both crying now. "It might be nice. Someone easy to love."

Part 2

Chapter 6

Lorraine and I sit next to each other, decked out in full uniform, like all 383 graduates, cap, gown, every girl with a white chrysanthemum corsage. We're standing in front of our assigned folding chairs in the gym, waiting for someone to tell us to sit down and shut up so we can get on with Chicopee Comprehensive High School's 1970 Commencement Ceremony.

Lorraine is more nervous than usual because the guy she has a crush on, Willie 'Cheese' LaBrie, has been assigned the seat right behind her. Lorraine bites her bottom lip, smearing her teeth with cherry pink lipstick.

Renee and Marie walk over from their seats in the bleachers and stand in the aisle next to us. We have end seats, good for leg room, but bad because I'll have to decide when it's our row's turn to stand to get our diplomas. "Are they ever going to start this thing?" Renee asks, like we would know.

Marie grins at Cheese LaBrie and says, "Look at Lorriane suck that lip, must be thinking of you, Cheese." Marie is wearing jeans. She works at a gas station, under the table, part-time now. Maybe she sells a little pot once in a while, too. She's got a kid, but no diploma. This morning, when I told her she couldn't come to the graduation ceremony in jeans, she rolled her eyes like I was a fool to think the rules applied to her.

Renee, on the other hand, looks like Lois Lane, girl reporter, her stuff carefully packaged, fresh for Superman. She's only a couple inches taller, but she peers down at Marie. "Never mind her foul mouth," she says to Lorraine. I spare a glance at Lorraine. Her face is scarlet. It takes me a second to realize she's mortified. "Marie's comments aren't worth the dignity of response," Renee explains to Cheese. She says shit like that since she started nursing school. She graduated from high school with the class of '69. Dad's so proud of her in her starched blue uniform. She wraps the uniform's white apron tight around her waist and ties it in a big bow in back so her waist looks even smaller than it is. Renee always figures out how to come across as sexy and proper at the same time. She looks like an ad: "Be Somebody. Be a Nurse." She got a scholarship that pays her whole way. Dad almost salutes when Renee walks into the house in that outfit.

She nods to me and Lorraine, says, "See you guys," turns, and walks away. Cheese watches her clutching her purse, swinging her perfect little tush. He explodes in laughter, way after it would have been time to laugh, a nervous yap he can't seem to control. The more he giggles, the redder Lorraine gets. She starts crying.

Halfway through graduation, she's still sniffling. I hand her my last tissue. "Marie should be home, changing diapers." To my surprise, and hers, I give her a sideways hug. She sucks in a series of soft snorts. "Stop sniffling or your great grandchildren are going to see pictures of you getting your diploma with a big red nose." She straightens up, stops crying, but starts hiccoughing.

It seems like ten hours later when I finally get to plop down on a lawn chair in our backyard. The hem of my black gown is dirty from dragging the ground. Marie's kid, Donny, is sitting on a blanket in front of me. He can walk, sort of, but decides to crawl off the blanket for the tenth time and pulls up a clump of grass with his tiny fist. I plunk him and his plastic pail and shovel in the playpen.

Marie doesn't use the playpen much, calls it "The cage." When he gets to be too much for her, she leaves him with Mom and Dad, or Memere, or Renee, or me. It pisses me off that Marie's screwing around somewhere and I'm expected to watch her kid. But Donny's cool. He's cute. You can't help but love him. And he really likes me.

Mom comes out carrying a cake with "Congratulations, Lorraine and Cora Rose" written on it in pink frosting. There's a plastic '70 under the names. I have to share billing on a sheet cake with Lorraine. "Where are your sisters?" she demands.

Donny throws the pail out of the playpen and laughs. I pick up the pail. "How do I know?" A lie. I do know. Marie and Renee went to find Fletcher to get him to buy beer. Donny throws the pail out of the playpen and laughs again. I hide the pail.

"They better show up soon." She goes back in the house.

My sisters' big plans for tonight, after the graduation party at our parents' house, is to ride around in Marie's bombed-out '57 Chevy, a gift from Fletcher, and drink Bud from the bottle. They think I'm going with them. I'm not. Who wants to watch Marie trying to pick up guys and guys trying to pick up Renee?

Dad comes out of the house and grabs Donny. "Hey, little man, give Pepere a smooch." I hate that Dad calls himself that. Andre and Dad were enough names. He barely has any gray hair yet. "Hold him for me a second." He sits Donny on my lap and walks back to the house.

I can't believe this. This is supposed to be a party for me and Lorraine. Where is everybody? Where are Aunt Josette and Uncle Louie? Probably taking pictures of Lorraine in the gym with the gym teacher, Lorraine in the science lab with the science teacher, Lorraine in home ec licking a spoon. It's hot. If Dad wants group pictures with me still in my graduation gown, my sisters and Lorraine better show up in the next thirty seconds.

There's a honk and a screech as Marie pulls onto the grass on the side of the house. "We're home, Dad," Renee yells as the gate swings shut.

"Has she been taking good care of you?" Marie asks Donny. Donny pulls my hair and laughs.

Dad comes back out, jumps off the front steps, and runs to us. Mom is right behind him, wiping her hands on a dish towel. It's 200 feet from the steps to where I'm sitting, but Dad actually runs, stops in front of the lawn chair, and grins. He's handsome in a father kind of way. I wish I was tall and thin like him, instead of a fat, taller, ugly version of Mom. Mom looks really good today with her hair tied up in a French knot and her new polka-dot shorts. It takes more trouble for Mom to look good than it does Dad. He beams at Donny and me. He's hiding something behind his back. I feel it in my gut, he's going to do something corny.

Donny says, "Pip," or something else with a p in it.

Dad, lit up as if Donny recited the Gettysburg Address, lifts him off my lap with one arm, and holds a little jewelry box out to me with his free hand. "Something special, for somebody special."

"Thanks, Dad." I start to hike up my graduation gown. Dad's beaming. They're all beaming, even Marie. I can tell they're going to feel bad if I stash the little box in the pocket of the shorts I'm wearing underneath the gown, so I pull the gown back down, untie the shiny red bow, and open the box. Diamond earrings. "Why?" They're so elegant, so expensive. I'm a little afraid of them. Renee didn't get anything like this when she graduated.

Mom smiles. Renee smiles. Marie smiles. Dad bounces Donny on his hip.

"Graduation," Mom says.

I must look concerned because Dad adds, reassuringly, "Your sisters pitched in. We *all* wanted you to have something nice."

"I love them. Thanks." I wipe my eyes with the collar of my gown.

An hour later, the entire family sits in the yard, eating hot dogs. I finger the earrings every two minutes to make sure they haven't fallen off. Marie puts a dab of mustard on her baby finger and sticks it in Donny's mouth. Donny, looking really cute in his navy blue sailor outfit with the diaper peeking out the shorts, puckers his face like he's sucking on a lemon.

"Don't give him that." Mom frowns. "You'll make him sick."

"Chill out, Mae. He's laughing." Marie puts my graduation cap on Donny's head. It covers his eyes so he can't see. He's wobbly on his feet to begin with. He falls down. The cap falls off his head. He looks around, deciding whether or not to cry.

"Get up." Marie laughs and claps. "That's a good boy."

Donny scrunches up his face, then laughs and claps along with her. The long blonde hair that Mom threatens to cut every time Marie drops him off makes him look even more like Fletcher. He sits on the cap, crushing one side of the stiff band. Marie bites her hotdog and smiles at him.

Mom's working up a head of steam. "He's ruining it." She looks at Dad for support. His eyes are on his second helping of potato salad.

Marie takes a swallow of orange Crush. "So? She'll never use it again."

"It's rented. We'll lose the deposit." Mom catches Dad's eyes. "Andre?"

"Who made this potato salad?" He spoons a bite into his mouth. "Your mother is right, Marie." Mom puts down her hamburger and holds onto the side of the picnic table.

Uncle Louie passes the ketchup, but Aunt Josette's eyes are on Mom and she doesn't take the bottle. Renee and I sit with forks full of potato salad halfway to our mouths.

Memere says, "Eat," and plunks an ear of corn in Josette's plate.

"I'm going to wash the mustard off your face, honey." Mom gets up, swings Donny onto her hip, and carries him into the house.

Marie shrugs. "She's lucky I didn't invite Fletcher," she says as the screen door shuts behind them.

We're all lucky. I feel bad for Mom. She's already raised a family. She loves Donny, so she takes care of him way more than she wants too. But she should find some things to like about Fletcher. She found things to like about Marie and Marie's harder to like than Fletcher. And Fletcher loves Donny too. He could have taken off, but he didn't.

"Well, what are you girls up to tonight?" Aunt Josette asks in her happy homemaker voice.

"Are you going to Lisa Boronski's?" Lorraine chirps.

"Lisa Boronski does not associate with trash," Marie says, taunting Josette.

"What a thing to say. There is no trash in this family." Aunt Josette sits up as straight as possible on an uneven picnic table bench. "There is only room for improvement."

"Lisa *is* a snob," Lorraine says. She must not have been invited either.

"You can come with us. We're just going to ride around," Marie says.

Renee and I look at each other. We look at Lorraine. All of our jaws drop open. Marie has never been seen in public with Lorraine voluntarily. She doesn't seem drunk or stoned. Is she trying to make up for embarrassing Lorraine at graduation? You never know with

Marie. Once in a while, she does something nice for no reason at all.

"With no destination?" Aunt Josette asks, shocked by the concept of four young women riding around in a car on a warm spring night.

"Pizza and a drive-in." Renee dabs her mouth with a napkin and looks Josette in the eye. Doesn't even crack a smile. "Then we'll go to Mr. DeWitt's party."

DeWitt has a party for the graduating students every year. Everybody is invited. They announce it over the intercom during homeroom. He hangs Japanese lanterns and re-used prom decorations in his yard. Renee wouldn't be caught dead there.

"Well, I don't know if that's such a good idea, honey." Aunt Josette squirms, trying to scratch up a good excuse why Lorraine can't go. She smiles across the table at Renee, weighing the question of Lorraine's big night out. On the one hand, there's Renee with her good looks and personality that might rub off on Lorraine. On the other hand, there's the sometimes sweet, sometimes not so sweet, but always diseased Cora Rose. And then there's the big drawback—Marie, the tramp.

"Please, Mom." Lorraine bounces in her seat. The whole table shakes.

"We'll have a good time. It's her graduation, Auntie." Renee displays her sweet young thing smile.

Aunt Josette smiles back and pats Lorraine's hand.

"Let her go," Uncle Louie, seldom heard from, says firmly. "It's graduation night. Honey, we trust you to be a good girl."

"I will," Lorraine answers solemnly.

Aunt Josette smiles like she has gas. "Of course we trust Lorraine."

A couple hours later, Renee teases her hair in the big mirror above the bureau. She's been fixing her hair for twenty minutes, going for the slightly disarrayed, damsel-tossed-at-sea look. She keeps teasing it up, then pulling a few strands loose the way she does when she has to stuff it up under her nursing cap. A few wisps curl around her forehead. It doesn't look much different than when she started out.

I'm sitting on one end of my bed, up against the headboard, drinking Tab. Marie's on the other end of the bed, patting Donny's little bum. Donny's between us, falling asleep, sucking on the receiver of a toy phone. Marie took her bed with her when she moved, so she's sleeping on our couch tonight. Two bureaus fit in the bedroom now. Marie and I are squished on one bed because no one is allowed to disturb the life-size Raggedy Ann and Andy dolls reclining against two big, frilly, mint-green and pink pillows on Renee's bed.

"Get ready," Renee orders.

Marie stretches her neck. "I am ready."

"You're going out like that? Get ready, Cora Rose." She offers me the brush.

"Not everybody primps for three hours to go bar-hopping in Chicopee." Marie's wearing the same faded jeans she always wears. Her t-shirt's a little tight. Her boobs stayed bigger after she had Donny. She looks okay. She looks like a female wrestler, no matter what she wears.

My ears perk up when I hear "bar-hopping." Bad news. I was starting to think I should ride around with them. They pitched in to get me earrings. But I have no interest in trying to sneak into some dive. Renee thinks she's going to get into a bar? She doesn't look twenty-one. She's almost twenty, but she looks more like eighteen than I do. Marie is almost twenty-one. She could pass for thirty if she had to.

"I'm not going." I stretch my leg in back of Donny.

"Yes, you are," Renee says from a haze of hair spray.

"You're coming." Marie pushes my foot away. "Don't spray that crap when Donny's in the room. It's bad for him. Don't they teach you anything in that nurse school?"

Lorraine appears in the doorway wearing checkered green slacks and a matching vest. A home ec project. She's wearing a green blouse under the vest.

Marie raises her eyebrows. "Got a date with Saint Patrick?"

"Ignore any noise that comes from her direction." Renee pulls a paper bag from under her bed and throws it on Raggedy Andy's lap. "Take off your clothes, Lorraine." Lorraine gives Marie a snotty grin before stepping out of her slacks. Renee folds Lorraine's slacks neatly and lays them on the bed. Lorraine disrobes. Marie gawks.

I throw my head back and close my eyes. "Please God, don't let Lorraine get naked. I've made it through three years in the same gym class without seeing her naked." Lorraine ignores me. When I open my eyes, she's slipping into a pointy bra with cups stiff enough to use for Jell-O molds. She peels off her white ankle socks and throws them on top of the slacks. Renee takes a black skirt with a slit up the side, a sleeveless black sweater, black stockings, and a garter belt out of the bag. Everything except the bra and the skirt is Renee's.

"Where'd you get the skirt?" Marie checks out the clothing suspiciously.

"Never mind." Renee holds the skirt in front of her like it's a trophy and smiles with satisfaction. Lorraine sits on the edge of the bed, pulls up the stockings, and wiggles the skirt over her hips.

"The Transformation of Our Lady Lorraine." Marie's head bobs in approval. "Need the shoe horn?"

I mimic Uncle Louie, "Honey, we trust you to be a good girl." I have to admit, under Renee's direction, Lorraine's look has improved.

"I have every intention of being a good girl," Lorraine says from inside the black sweater Renee is tugging over her raised hands.

෬ ෬ ෬

Lorraine and I are sitting at a small round table in a dark room. I'm sipping orange juice. I don't want to get drunk. I've gotten drunk at home twice. It's okay if I'm near a bathroom, but getting drunk at the Limelight would be depressing. It's pretty boring so far, which is okay by me. I'm a chunky brown-haired white girl, wearing black slacks and a loose-fitting blouse, trying not to make eye contact with anyone. If a girl doesn't want to be bothered at a bar, or pretty much anywhere else, I can give tips. A couple of neighborhood guys, almost my father's age, are drinking beer and playing pool. Two middle-aged women, redheads with bad dye jobs, are getting drunk at the bar. Lorraine is getting loaded. Some old guy has plunked himself at our table and is trying to pick her up. His name is Fred. He's sitting next to her, across the table from me. Lorraine giggles every time Fred speaks.

Lorraine says, "I'm a junior at Notre Dame. Law student."

I've never heard her lie before, not a big one like this. Can girls go to Notre Dame? Fred seems real interested in Lorraine's studies. They're leaning on their elbows, looking into each other's eyes. I barely have two inches to put down my orange juice. I try, but it's hard to ignore them. It's gross watching Lorraine flirt with an old guy. Marie is dancing with some guy named Joe, Fletcher's new roommate. He's a hippie.

"Of course I'm twenty-one." Lorraine slaps her ID on the table.

I can't believe even Lorraine is stupid enough to draw attention to her fake ID. At least Lorraine has a real driver's license, some friend of Marie's, a woman with dark brown hair like Lorraine's, and almost the same color skin as Lorraine, only a few years older. My ID is a brown-skinned woman, much older, with hair colored almost platinum. Marie slipped it to me when we pulled into the parking lot of The Limelight Cafe. It's expired.

I complained, "This is Regina DeJesus. I can't be Regina DeJesus."

Marie said, "Why not?" like she was talking to a paranoid she didn't want to upset. "I've been Regina a hundred times. They're just covering their asses. We're not going anywhere where anyone's going to bother you."

Marie, a beer in one hand, Joe in the other hand, comes laughing over to our table. She makes a quick study of Lorraine and her ID on the table. "You're shut off, Lady Lorraine. No more booze for this one, Larry," she yells over her shoulder at the bartender.

The bartender, leaning over the bar talking to Renee, looks up and hollers, "Will do."

Marie pockets the ID and turns to Joe. "This is Cora Rose."

I nod hello and blush.

"He's got money. Machinist. Union," Marie says like he's a pair of drapes she's picked out. She turns to Fred. "Pops, are you trying to pick up Sweet Lorraine?"

Fred sits back in his chair. "Well that depends, Marie, my dear. Claims to be legal tender."

"I like the way you talk," Lorraine slurs, and leans in close to him.

"Well, she's not. Get up, sex kitten," Marie says. "You're going to dance. You might be shit-faced when I take you home, but you're going to walk in the front door all by yourself." She yells, "Larry, play something we can dance to. Something fast."

Larry puts on "Shot Gun." Marie, dancing, spills a little beer.

"Come, my dear." Fred takes Lorraine's hand. Lorraine is a bad dancer. Fred doesn't care. He watches every bad move. He moves worse than she does.

Joe sits down in Lorraine's empty seat. "Buy you a drink?"

"Thanks. I've got one." I lift my orange juice.

Joe starts to get up. "Sorry, I don't mean to bother you."

"Oh, you're not bothering me," I blurt. "Rum and coke, please." That's what Renee's drinking.

We stare at the dance floor. Lorraine's getting really unsteady on her feet. She and Fred are waltzing even though "Mustang Sally" is playing.

"Ask her to dance," Marie yells to Joe. "She's a good dancer."

I am a good dancer. I love to dance. In the basement of my own house. I've danced to the radio or hi-fi in the cellar all my life. In elementary school Renee and I danced to "Shindig!" or "Hullabaloo" when our parents were grocery shopping. Never in public. Never in a bar with a guy I don't know.

"Want to dance?" Joe asks shyly.

"Come on, Cora Rose," Renee laughs. "You'll fall in love with her when you see her dance, Joe."

I could crawl under the table and die. Why can't they mind their own business? Renee's got the bartender out from behind the bar. She's shaking her butt around. She doesn't have to move much to look good on the dance floor. Can't she just be happy with that? Marie's behind the bar, playing bartender, serving herself a free beer. Besides Joe, the bartender is the only guy under forty in the place.

Joe stands. Dance or make an ass of this poor guy. I'm trapped. "How about after this?" I lift my rum and coke. Joe's relieved. We each have two more rum and cokes and use the bathroom twice before we dance. I notice that in bars people use the bathroom a lot.

We dance to "Blue Velvet." I'm glad it's not a fast one. We move slow and stiff, it's better than moving fast and stiff. "Blue Velvet" ends. "You

Belong To Me" comes on immediately. Neither one of us knows how to stop dancing, so we keep our wooden legs moving to Patti Page. Lorraine and Fred are the only other couple on the floor. Fred sways back and forth a little. Lorraine's arms are draped over his back with her head flopped on his shoulder. It looks like he's dragging around Renee's Raggedy Ann doll. Halfway through "Dream Dream Dream," I relax a little. Joe pulls our arms in from the straight-armed waltz thing that I'm used to from dancing with my father and Uncle Louie at weddings. We dance, one arm around each other, our other arms tucked between us holding hands. My neck feels like a board from holding my head six inches away from his. We keep catching each other's eyes, smiling nervously. I put my head on his shoulder. Better. I relax my neck and close my eyes. If we dance any slower, we'll be standing still. My head feels pleasantly heavy with rum now that it's found somewhere to land.

After "Blue Velvet" plays the third time, the only thing still stiff on Joe is his dick. It's all right. He's not pressing it into me. He rubs it against my thigh every once in a while, but not on purpose. It's not so bad. Will he give me a ride home? Kiss me good night? I want to kiss a guy. This one is sort of fat with a belly. I don't care about the belly. I'm fat myself. Joe can't be too old, twenty? It's hard to tell with the beard. When we stop dancing, I'll ask how old he is. He rubs his finger on the front of my throat and brushes his lips against my cheek. I keep my head on his shoulder. I don't want him to kiss me here on the dance floor in front of my sisters.

Smack. Joe and I are pulled apart by the sound of Lorraine's open hand hitting Fred's face.

"What do you think I am?" Lorraine staggers backwards into Renee, who's sitting at the bar, still flirting with the bartender.

Renee stops Lorraine from falling, just barely. "What's the matter?"

"He was grabbing me." Lorraine can hardly stand. Renee hangs onto her.

"My hand was there for the last two songs." Fred holds onto the back of a chair. "I only moved it because it fell asleep."

"I don't even know you," Lorraine slurs indignantly.

"I am the gentleman who has been paying for your drinks all night."
Fred bows and stumbles forward.

"You are no gentleman." Renee maneuvers Lorraine onto a barstool.

"And she is no lady," Fred says, pointing.

"Jesus Christ." Marie swallows the last of her beer. "I take her to the
quietest place in the state and she finds trouble."

"Don't you have a wife somewhere to go home to?" Renee glares at
Fred. Marie holds Lorraine steady while Renee tugs down the sweater,
which has hitched up her back.

"Your little cousin is bad news. A tease," Fred says with his chin in
the air.

Lorraine screams, "He's a, he's a, he's a . . ." She sways backwards and
loses whatever word she's chasing. Renee and Marie each take an arm.

"Shut up, Lorraine." Marie pulls her off the stool. "Concentrate on
walking."

Marie and Renee hold up Lorraine while I unlock the car doors and
Joe rolls down the windows.

"If you're going to puke, do it out here, Lorraine," Renee says, sounding
official. "Breathe. The fresh air is good for you."

Renee and Marie let go of Lorraine's arms. She leans on the hood.
Everyone takes a step away from her. "Oh God." She moans and vomits
by the front wheel of the car. Even though it must be 80° outside, steam
comes up like someone took the cover off a manhole. She doesn't get a
drop on herself or the car. Renee searches her purse until she finds two
moist towelettes. I take a couple more steps back.

"Well, thanks for the dance." Joe steps back, next to me. "Maybe . . ."

"Fletcher has her number." Marie goes around to the driver's side.
"The quicker we're out of here, the better."

"Okay, bye." Joe stashes his hands in his pockets.

"Bye." It hits me that Marie set Joe and me up. I don't change my
expression, don't look at either sister so they won't see I finally get the
picture. I feel like a moron, but I'm glad she set me up and didn't tell
me. I wouldn't have come if I had known.

I help Renee shove Lorraine into the back seat. She's floppy and
hard to move, but doesn't really give us any trouble. She's down for the

count before Marie's out of the parking lot. My sisters and I are crammed in the front. No one wants to take a chance with Lorraine. Besides, she's sprawled out over the entire back seat.

"You like that guy?" Renee raises her eyebrows.

"He's okay."

"You were doing the grit." She wiggles her hips.

"We were not." I look straight ahead. I wish I wasn't sitting in the middle so I could look out the side window and completely ignore Renee.

"Did he have a hard-on?" She pats my thigh.

"God." I don't turn my head to look at her.

"For a tight-ass virgin, you take a lot of interest in the state of other people's crotches," Marie says. "Did the bartender have a hard-on? He's married, you know."

"No shit. We talked about his wife. She wants to go to nursing school. She might call me." Renee flips down the visor to apply fresh lipstick.

"Figures. How come you only flirt with the safe ones?" Marie makes a slow lefthand turn. "We're not going to have to straighten you out, too, are we?"

"I wasn't flirting, I was talking. Cora Rose isn't a lesbian. She just needs more options."

"Flirting with your ass. Options," Marie howls. "You say the stupidest shit."

Renee tosses her lipstick back in her purse. "There's nothing wrong with being a virgin. I'm waiting. When I have sex, I'm going to be in love."

Marie turns right at the last minute. "Saving it." She turns in to the parking lot of The Girls Club. "It's going to go bad before you use it. You're the only one you're ever going to be in love with."

"This is a dyke bar," Renee squeals.

"Maybe Lorraine will stay out of trouble here." Marie kills the engine.

"I'm not going in there." Renee folds her arms over her chest and sits back.

"Me either." I shake my head.

"No shit." Marie holds her long frizzy hair off the back of her head. "Even if we wanted to bump pussies." She gives me a smirk that I ignore. "We couldn't get in. You need real ID here." She motions to Renee. "Gimme a beer. We need a plan."

Renee reaches under the seat, pulls out an empty six-pack. "All gone."

Marie juts her chin out at Renee. "How many beers you have?"

Renee holds up one finger.

"Cora Rose had none. I had one. Lorraine sucked up all the beer. No wonder she's shit-faced. Why didn't you stop that child molester from buying after the first couple, Cora Rose?"

"Me? You're the one who brought us there. I wanted to stay home and watch Lawrence Welk with Mae and Andre."

"Fred is your friend, Marie," Renee says.

"He's not my friend. He's a poor old drunk who hits on anybody who talks to him. You dressed her." Marie leans over me to get a better look at Renee. "If you're going to dress her in a sleazy outfit, you'd better teach her how to handle sleazy men."

"Clothes aren't sleazy, people are sleazy." Renee shakes her head at Marie. "You should learn the difference. You said she looked good."

"Girls who wear tight clothes just to tease are sleazy." Marie's hand is on my leg. She leans closer to Renee. "And if my men are too sleazy for you, how come you and Fletcher spend so much time together?"

"Who said anything about Fletcher? He could use some new clothes, but he's a gentleman. Southern guys have good manners. He's a philosopher." Renee throws her arm around my back.

"You hear that?" Marie nudges my shoulder. "We thought Fletcher was only a pot and sperm dealer who dropped out of school in tenth grade. Renee dug deeper, found a scholar."

"He's self-educated." Renee's practically sitting on my lap. "How many guys do you know who have read *War and Peace* and *The Electric Kool-Aid Acid Test?*"

"It's too hot for this. Shut up and get off of me." I jab them with my elbows and turn around to check on Lorraine, who's on her back with

74

her mouth open, her breasts pointing up like twin cones. "Where did you buy those tits?"

"Mom's old bra," Renee says nonchalantly, then immediately adds, "Shit," remembering she didn't want us to know.

"Let me get this straight." Marie screws up her face. "Lorraine seduced Fred with Mae's tits? Tell me that's not sleazy."

Renee says, "Jesus" solemnly before she bursts out laughing. "Guess what else? That's Mom's skirt, from her cedar chest."

"That's what stinks? I thought it was some funky perfume she borrowed from Josette." Marie and Renee laugh like it's the funniest thing they ever heard. I don't think it's that funny.

"Here's what we do." Marie turns serious and grabs the steering wheel like she's in charge of the first flight to the moon. "We go find Fletcher. He's probably down the street at the gas station. Get him to buy us some more beer. Then we crash at my place until Lorraine comes to."

Renee considers this brilliant plan. "We can't go to the package store with her in a coma." She arches her thumb over the back seat.

"I'm not going and I'm not pitching in for beer," I announce.

"Perfect." Marie jumps out of the car. "Me and the virgin will go. You guard Lorraine from the drunk dykes. And don't fall in love."

Renee jumps out of the car after her. "Cora Rose and Lorraine are virgins too," she giggles. "If anyone tries to pick you up, tell them Lorraine's your girlfriend." Now Renee is going to start with the queer jokes? I give her a filthy look. She stops laughing. "Really, it'll be all right, the keys are in the ignition."

"You assholes aren't going to leave me here alone." I sit back, confident. If it was only Marie, I'd believe it. Renee won't leave me alone in the parking lot of a dyke bar with Lorraine shit-faced in the back seat.

Marie takes off on a slow trot through the parking lot. Renee trots right after her.

"Ten, twenty minutes," Renee yells over her shoulder.

"It doesn't take two," I yell, watching them disappear into the trees that line the parking lot. I look at the lump of Lorraine on the back seat. "Jerks. What am I talking to you for?" I throw a scrunched-up candy bar wrapper at Lorraine. It bounces off her leg. "Jesus, your bootie's hanging out." I lean over and tug Lorraine's skirt. She snores on.

There are about thirty cars in the parking lot of The Girls Club. No one goes in or comes out of the place for at least five minutes. I stretch out in the front seat and fall asleep. I wake up with a start. Some girl is tapping on the car door. "You OK?" she asks, squatting by the car, hands gripping the open window.

"Yeah, fine." I'm confused by the closeness of her face. Between the heat and the alcohol, I'm pretty out of it. I'm not sure where I am or how I got here. I touch the torn upholstery on the Chevy's seat and it all comes back to me. Oh shit, this girl must be a dyke. Why is she bothering me?

"Closing in twenty minutes. Then we turn the lights out in the lot. You sober enough to drive?"

I stare blankly and nod. She starts to walk away, like a boy, with her hands in her pockets. She's big. It's hard to tell how big from my seated position. Maybe six feet? "Do you know . . .?" I want to ask about a bathroom, but I think better of it. The big dyke will just send me into the dyke bar.

She turns, walks back to the car, and offers me her hand through the open window. "Bernice, bartender, bouncer, waitress, parking lot attendant. Friends call me Bernie. Do I know what?"

I shiver. I guess I'm supposed to shake this big dyke's hand. "I'm a little out of it." I stick my hand out the window. I never shook hands with a girl before. Her attitude reminds me of Stella. But not her hands. Her hand is big and hot, not graceful like Stella's. She smiles. She's thin and she has dark hair, otherwise she's nothing like Stella. For all I know, Stella is nothing like Stella any more. "I'm not used to drinking," I say sheepishly.

"You should walk it off." She glances at Lorraine in the back seat.

I glance at Lorraine too, to make sure that all of her parts are covered. I feel sick. I don't want to get out of the car with the big dyke standing there, but I drag myself up and lean on the hood. I hate alcohol. When I stand up straight, I realize that Bernie is only a couple of inches taller than me. How'd she fool me into thinking she was so tall? She leans on the car like it's her personal La-Z-Boy and offers me a Lucky.

"No, thanks."

"Mind if I do?" She strikes a match and looks at me through the flame as she lights her cigarette. She inhales a long, slow drag. The tip of the Lucky glows red. She closes her eyes and throws her head back, enjoying it down to her toes. She puts her whole body into it, relaxing more with every drag, stretching her neck, smiling, satisfied. Every time she inhales, I inhale. When she lets go of her smoky breath and gives me a half smile, I press the backs of my legs against the car to stop my knees from shaking. Fortunately she closes her eyes and throws her head back again. "I'm trying to quit." Her eyes pop open. She looks straight at me. "But I like the rush too much."

The rush I feel is right below my belly. Bernie relaxes her shoulders, leans even further back into the car, sucks in, and exhales. I stretch my neck and roll my shoulders. I should never drink. It screws me up. A cramp distracts me from the itch that's lower. Good. Maybe the cramp is trying to tell me something, a message from God. I look away from Bernie. She's big and mannish and has a terrible haircut. I like real guys. I have a crush on Van Morrison. I liked Joe's hard-on against my thigh.

"You gonna be sick?" Bernie pulls a stick of gum out of her back pocket. "Try this, sometimes it helps."

"Thanks." I take the gum but don't unwrap it. No dyke gum in my mouth. "I need a bathroom." It's an emergency. I'm going to have an accident if I don't get to a bathroom soon.

Bernie nods toward the small brick building. "There's one in there."

"No ID." My gut makes a rude noise. "I'm not twenty-one."

"Don't have to be twenty-one to pee. Jill's at the door." She takes her ID out of her back pocket and hands it to me. "Tell her Bernie said to let you use the ladies' room."

I glance at the back seat. I can't leave Lorraine passed out, alone with a strange lesbian. Does she think Lorraine and I are girlfriends? "She's my cousin. I can't leave her alone."

"Your cousin's not going anywhere. I'll watch her. Give me an excuse to stay out of the noise for a couple extra minutes."

I get a pain that makes me wince. It's me or Lorraine. I'm standing in a parking lot, shooting the breeze with a chain-smoking dyke. May as well be inside the bar. How bad can Bernie be? She must be responsible if they made her the bouncer *and* the parking lot attendant. "Thanks." I take the ID.

Inside The Girls Club, I stare straight ahead and wait in line for the bathroom. I'm shaking with the concentration of holding on and the fear of being alone in a dyke bar. There's a woman ahead of me and one already in the bathroom. I don't get a good look at any of the girls in here. I head straight for the ladies' room, where all I can see are backs. I've made a study of timing girls ahead of me in line for the ladies' room, two-and-a-half minutes apiece, that's the average. I can last if the two girls in front of me are average. Maybe dykes are quicker. My gut's churning, more pressure than pain. I look around quickly, the place is pretty full. A bar in Chicopee full of lesbians on a Saturday night? Maybe some are from other towns or maybe some of them aren't dykes. The women slow-dancing with each other, they've got to be dykes. The place is smoky, smells like beer and sweat, too small for the number of people in it. The music is loud. The bathroom is tiny. I do my business. I'm in and out in two minutes, average.

Bernie is sitting on the hood still smoking when I walk out. I look around. Renee and Marie are nowhere in sight. There's no one besides me and Bernie in the parking lot. And Lorraine. "Thanks." I stick my head through the car window to check on Lorraine. She's stopped snoring, but otherwise unchanged. How do I get rid of Bernie? I want her gone when my sisters show up.

"Welcome." She jumps off the hood and flicks the butt. I try to ignore the way my body vibrates when Bernie moves. Her eyes flicker as she looks toward the building. My hands tremble. She's the real thing. She's wearing men's chino's. I concentrate on how scary it was to be in that bar, how awful it would be to end up like one of those girls.

"Well, thanks again." I grab the door handle to steady myself and to retreat back into the car.

"My driver's license." She sticks out her hand.

"Oh, sorry." I hand back the license. Her hand grazes mine. I'm shaking.

The trace of a smirk on her face lifts up the hair on the back of my neck. It makes me mad. It makes my breasts itch against my blouse. "Thanks for the ID and for babysitting Lorraine." I try to sound confident. I don't think she's falling for it. She shrugs, cool and calm. "My sisters went to get beer. They'll be right back."

"Good for them." She pockets the license and walks away.

I collapse on the front seat, hunch down, and watch The Girls Club customers straggle out, say their good-nights, and drive away. When I think they're all gone, I sit on the hood in the dark parking lot, and look at the night sky. Man, I need a boyfriend.

Fifteen more minutes go by before Fletcher's van pulls up. Marie leans out the window. "What are you, a hood ornament?"

"Where have you jerks been?" It comes out mellower than I mean it to.

"Don't be pissed." Renee sticks her head out next to Marie's. "We had to wait till Fletcher got off work."

"Look who we brought you." Marie points to the back of the van.

A side door slides opens. Joe steps out. "Hi." He smiles shyly.

"Hi." I'm so glad to see him that I have to stop myself from jumping off the hood and running to him.

A half-hour later, me and Joe are in the front seat of Fletcher's van, smoking a joint. Everyone else is inside Marie's apartment. Joe pinches the joint into a roach clip and offers it to me. I've smoked marijuana with Marie and Fletcher and their friends. Joe might have been there, but I don't remember him. Pot makes my gut feel better. We smoke it down to a quarter-inch ember. Joe puts it out in the ashtray, where it joins ten others.

"Wanna go in?" he asks.

"No." I want to go home and climb in bed.

"You have a boyfriend?" He smiles and puts his arm around me. I shake my head.

"I had a girlfriend in high school," he says. "I didn't want to get married right after graduation, so she married someone else."

"You miss her?"

"Sometimes." He kisses me on the cheek. "Your hair smells nice."

His hair smells nice too. It smells like marijuana. His beard tickles my throat when he kisses me on the mouth. It's awkward, sitting side by side. I can see why Marie used to sit on Fletcher's lap when she kissed him in the van.

We start out kissing with our mouths closed. Then we kiss with our mouths open. His tongue feels funny in my mouth, it's too big. I don't know what to do with my tongue, so I move it around a little, that's what he's doing. I liked kissing without tongues better. This sideways stuff is hard. My shoulder is twisted and my neck hurts. He starts breathing heavy. I get scared and sit up. I turn my body completely forward.

"Sorry." He looks sorry. "Should we go in back? It's more comfortable. I won't try anything."

We sit on a mattress that takes up the whole back of the van and smoke another joint, cross-legged, facing each other. It's hot and smoky. Joe cranks open two little windows. It's still hot and smoky. There's a little dome with a tiny bulb that doesn't give much light. "Close to You" is playing on the radio, low.

Joe lays down with his hands folded behind his head. "Wanna dance?"

I lie down next to him. He holds me, doesn't kiss me, but strokes my head for a few minutes. He whispers, "You got beautiful hair." Side by side feels better lying down. I like his bigness better when we're lying down. He kisses me on the mouth, nips on my ear. I worry that he might swallow one of the diamond earrings when he sucks my earlobe. He moves his mouth down my neck and kisses my breast and I stop worrying about the earrings. The whole length of him, chest, belly, hard-on, legs, is on top of me. His big arms are around me. I like his long hair. I stroke his ponytail and take it out of the rubber band. His hair gets in the way so I hold it behind his back. He rubs his hard-on against my thigh. Is that whimpering sound coming from me?

"Oh, baby," Joe says, soft and sweet. "Baby." I like that. No one's ever called me baby. Another little moan that's definitely me. Joe unzips his pants.

"Oh, no." I've never seen a grown man without his pants on.

"It's okay, I'll be careful. I won't put it in."

"Okay." That seems reasonable.

"Damn, you're beautiful. God damn you're beautiful." He's breathing so hard I can barely understand him. I've learned enough from Marie to know it's his dick talking, but I like what it has to say. What should I do? A hand job?

"Take off your pants, baby." He rubs my leg.

"What?" I mean if he's not going to put it in why should I take my pants off?

"I want to make you feel good, honey." He unsnaps my jeans. "I won't hurt you. I won't do anything you don't want me to." We kiss while he unzips my pants. He tugs with one hand and only gets my jeans pulled down a few inches. I don't help him. I don't want to expose myself. He keeps kissing me, touches my belly. My hips move toward his hand. He spreads his hand, reaches further down, and tries to push my legs apart. He whispers, "It's okay." I believe him. He puts his fingers between my legs. He can't get his hand as far down as he wants it. He pulls gently on my bushy hair and presses his fingers right above my clit. No one's ever touched that spot, except me.

"Oh God." I put my hand over my mouth.

"It's okay. No one can hear. Just me. You're so sexy."

"Put out the light."

He switches off the little dome. I wiggle my jeans farther down.

"Take them off." He traces his finger around my belly button. "Help me, baby." I lift my butt. He pulls and I slip one leg completely out of my underwear. He slides his fingers inside me. "You're wet, honey." I want his fingers closer to my clit. I move my hips to try to get his fingers in the right position. He takes his hand away, pulls out his wallet. What's he doing? I'm almost fully dressed from the waist up. I'm glad it's dark so he can't see my naked parts very well. He pulls a little silver packet out of his wallet and tears it open. A rubber. I've never seen one. I can hardly see this one. He slips it on, kisses me, and pushes against me. The rubber sticks to my skin. I liked it better before, with his fingers.

He kisses me and presses harder. "Oh honey. Oh baby." He pants

81

and lies on top of me. Leans on his elbows so his full weight isn't on me. "I won't hurt you. I promise." He enters me part way.

"I never." I don't try to stop him. I don't want him to stop.

"Just a little. I'll go slow. Just a little, baby." He pushes further into me.

"Ouch," I moan, turned on, but afraid.

"Sorry, baby. So sorry." He pulls out, kisses my face, strokes my hair. His breath is hot on my neck. His hard on is outside of me, halfway up my belly. He's still moving like he's inside. I move my hips and feel him, hard, on my clit. I rock against him.

"Oh God." It feels real good this way.

"Go ahead, baby. Go ahead," he groans. His long hair makes a canopy over my face. I moan low, grind against him, and listen to myself breathing hard. He pants, "Come on, cum for me," between his own hard loud breaths. I moan and listen until I can't hear myself or Joe at all.

I lie still, under him.

"Sweet baby," he coos and kisses me all over my face.

My breath calms down. It feels different than when I cum by myself. It feels better. I'm sad and lonely after I masturbate sometimes. I still feel a little sad, but not so lonely.

"Please, baby," he pleads. "You're all wet. Let me try again."

I spread my legs wide for him. It only seems fair. He slips inside me, part way, holds his full weight away from me while he moves inside me. "Does it hurt?"

"A little," I answer.

He puts a pillow under me. It feels better with the pillow.

"Go ahead," I say.

This must be it, normal sex. It hurts, but not real bad. Lots of things hurt worse. I can feel blood on the mattress, pooling under me. I start to cry, not because we had sex; it's good we had sex. I don't want Fletcher or my sisters to see the blood. "Oh God, we messed up Fletcher's van."

He kisses my eyebrows, my forehead, my nose. "It's okay, I love you, honey." He promises to clean it up, promises no one will see but him. I wish he didn't have to see either. He keeps saying, "I love you, baby." I know it's a silly thing to say. I know he doesn't love me. How can he love me when he doesn't even know me? I don't believe it, but he's making an effort, and I don't mind that he's saying it. I stroke his beard. He's a sweet guy. Maybe we'll go on a real date sometime.

He's a sweet guy.

He's a guy.

Chapter 7

"That your young man?" Mrs. Romanski sits in her wheelchair and peers out the window of her tiny room into the parking lot of Riverside Gardens Nursing Home. She's asking about Joe. His green Nova just pulled up. Mrs. Romanski has lived here for eight years. I'm working here for the summer, maybe the rest of my life, the way things are going. I like her because she's feisty and nosy, still interested in the world out there, even though her world has shrunk to the dining hall, rec hall, and the four walls of this room. I like her better when it's not my business she's prying into. I loosen the brace on her right leg. "Anything else I can do for you?"

"Is it a secret?" She grins. There's nothing Mrs. Romanski likes more than a secret. If it's scandalous, all the better. "He a married fellow?"

"No." I roll my eyes at her.

"Second time he picks you up," she muses, raises her eyebrows and leans forward to get a better look out the window. "He your young man?" It's possible she doesn't remember this is the second time she's asked. It's also possible she knows perfectly well and will keep asking until I answer.

"Maybe."

Mrs. Romanski slaps her 'good' leg. "Maybe?" She laughs. "Take my advice. Don't let him try anything until the answer is yes. A girl can't sell herself short these days." She winks. "Never could."

"Next you're going to tell me that he won't buy the cow if the milk is free."

"Sure," she agrees. "Where's he work?"

"At the foundry."

"Welder?" She peers out her window, trying to get a look, but it's too dark. Unless her eyesight is a lot better than mine, all she sees is a black windshield.

"Machinist."

"Working man." She nods. I can't tell if she approves or is just acknowledging that she knows the type. "Seems like a nice enough young man. Right type for you."

I frown. "You can tell by the way he parks his car?" Why is everyone, even an old lady who has never met him, so sure that Joe is right for me?

"Nice fellow." She ignores my comment. The nurses tell us Mrs. Romanski has dementia. I think she decided to weed out reality and toss what doesn't please her. She looks at the clock radio on her nightstand. "Time for you to go, honey." She crooks a finger, signaling me to come closer. I lean in. She takes my hand and drops a piece of chocolate wrapped in gold foil into it, her prized possession, fancy candy that her son brings every Sunday. "Tell him to cut his hair."

"No." I roll my eyes. "When did you see his hair?"

"Ginny says it's down to here." She touches her shoulder. Ginny lives in the next room. "And a beard. I like a beard on a man, myself." The convoluted story of how Ginny knows the length of my 'maybe' boyfriend's hair is going to remain a mystery for now. Someone in this nursing home must know someone who knows someone who knows, or has at least seen, Joe.

"Thanks for the chocolate."

I punch out and walk slowly to Joe's car, believing that Mrs. Romanski is watching from her window, not wanting to lose her gaze.

Joe and I are quiet on the way home, him taking my lead. I've been moody and quiet the last few times I've seen him, half hoping he'll get sick of me and stop calling.

"You okay?" he asks when we pull into my driveway.

"I have to tell you something." I don't want to be in front of my house sitting in his car when I tell him. "Can we go for a walk?"

"Sure."

We walk two blocks without speaking before he's had enough. "Spit it out, Cora Rose."

"I'm pregnant," I say, without breaking stride, looking straight ahead. He stops in his tracks. "Say that again."

"I'm pregnant."

"Holy shit."

I turn and look at him.

"Wow. I thought you were going to break up with me." He looks puzzled. "I used a rubber." This is true. We only did it, the whole deal with him cuming inside, that one time in Fletcher's van, and he did use a rubber.

"It's yours." Ninety-nine percent effective. This is the kind of lottery I win.

"No, I didn't mean it like that." He holds his head between his hands. "Wow. We're going to have a baby." He does a complete turn and repeats, "We're going to have a baby, Cora Rose." The second time he's loud, almost shouting. He holds me at arms length, his whole face lit up. He's happy? He wants this? "I hope it looks like you. When did you find out?"

"A week ago."

"You waited a week to tell me?"

I stare back at him, flabbergasted by his reaction. Not in my wildest dreams did it go like this. I nod. How can I tell him that I told Renee a month ago and she called Planned Parenthood to make an appointment for me talk to someone about terminating the pregnancy, and then proceeded to talk me out of keeping that appointment? "I needed some time to figure out what to do." I called Planned Parenthood back, alone, the next day. I was okay as long as the voice at the end of the line said "Terminate." When she said, "Abortion," I hung up.

"Get married." He shrugs like this is the obvious and only answer. I do a bad job of smiling. His eyes narrow. "Why not? I love you." Now he's wide-eyed and holding his palms out. "You feel anything for me?"

"We barely know each other. I'm eighteen."

"I'm twenty." He shrugs. "We've been seeing each other three times a week." He looks like I kicked him in the belly. "You don't love me. Great." He turns away. I look at the ponytail hanging between his broad shoulders for what seems like a long time. I feel sorry for his big back, which quivers just enough to let me know he's crying or trying not to cry, and sad for both of us, but mostly I feel numb. And mad. I didn't anticipate feeling bad for not loving him, feeling guilty, taking care of him because he loves me. I want this to go away, and if it won't go away, I want the drama of it to be over.

Finally, he wipes his face with his hands and he turns to me. He looks more angry than hurt now. "I grew up without a father. I don't want that for my kid."

"You'd still be the father. We just wouldn't be married." Pregnant and not married; pregnant and married. I've been weighing these words for weeks, imaging them on a balance scale. "If we don't get married."

He shakes his head. "What the hell are you saying? Will you marry me?"

ଓ ଔ ଓ

"Suck it in." Marie attempts to zip me up. "This dress fit last week."

"I don't want to get married." I wipe my sweaty face on the muslin sleeve of my wedding dress. "I barely know this guy." This has been my mantra since I told Joe I was pregnant three weeks ago, then decided, undecided, and re-decided to marry him.

Renee frowns, her hand on her chin. "You can't really suck in pregnancy." Renee's the maid of honor. She's wearing a light blue sheath. Tasteful. For just this one day, I wish she wasn't so competent and pretty. She rifles through the top drawer of the bureau and pulls out safety pins that are linked together in a chain. "Turn around." She pins the sides of my zipper together. I feel the metal of the safety pins straining and the teeth of the zipper pushing into my back. "It'a hard choice." The open safety pins between her teeth distort her words, but her frustration comes through loud and clear. She's spent hours talking to me about whether or not I should marry Joe.

"I'm not sure."

"What do you want from us?" Marie says. "We can't decide for you. If you want more time, take more time."

"She hasn't got more time. I'll be happy to decide for you." Renee spits the remaining pins onto the dresser. "You're pregnant. The father wants you and the baby. Marry him. You can always unmarry him."

Marie strolls to the bedroom door and yells down the stairs, "Mae, crisis. We need your mantilla."

"Brilliant." Renee gives Marie a glance of admiration for her stroke of mantilla genius.

Marie squints at her. "How's she going to feel with a husband she not in love with?" She answers her own question. "Better than she's going to feel without him. I should know."

"A fine time for this conversation." Mom's at the door with the mantilla draped on her arm.

Renee wraps it around my shoulders like a shawl and fastens a knot between my breasts. "The lace matches the muslin perfectly." She nods with satisfaction and looks at Mom. "We need a big pin, a brooch."

"We should be leaving for the church." Mom hurries out of the room, hurries back with a gaudy burst of fake pearls. "Cora Rose." She catches my eye in the mirror as Renee anchors the mantilla to my stiff cotton bodice. "Marriage is a sacred vow, a sacrament. And you *are* pregnant."

"I barely know him," Marie whines, mocking me.

I've been waiting weeks for Mom to have a reaction to my pregnancy. A second daughter knocked up—I thought she'd freak. All she did was look up from the table and ask, "What do you plan to do?" I answered, "Marry Joe?" It was meant as a question. She just nodded and finished setting out the supper plates. Now I look at her and see that she's tired, probably as disappointed in me as I am, probably wondering how she raised such stupid girls.

Mom sighs and clears her throat, like she's about to make an announcement. Marie stops teasing her hair. Renee stops fussing with my dress. Mom looks from daughter to daughter. Her gaze stops on me. She's wearing an A-line dress, the same style as Marie's, a simple dress, the kind of dress you wear to a rushed wedding of a pregnant daughter. "It's a big step," she says.

"Mom, are you telling me to get married or not to get married? I feel like I'm giving my life away."

She stands stiffly, her mouth a tight line. "I'm telling you it's a serious matter." She sighs like she's carrying the weight of the world and turns her back to us to look out the window. She has no more idea than I do about what's the best thing for me to do. I hold onto the bureau and try to stay pinned together. The vital information about life that mothers share with daughters and fathers share with sons at crucial moments is not going to happen—probably doesn't exist. I had no idea how much I was hoping for some last-minute maternal revelation that would make things clear. There's got to be some way out besides abortion or marriage. Something besides binding myself to a stranger for all eternity or raising this kid alone in some dumpy apartment, dragging it to Mom's or Memere's, begging Joe to babysit while I work graveyard at some shitty job and collect food stamps with Marie on Wednesday afternoons. I stare at Mom's back. Renee's hands flutter around the mantilla, adjusting the drape. Marie sprays her hair.

"Here's Memere. If you're going to back out, it's now or never." Mom looks me in the eye. She perks up. "Okay," she says, as if my silence is the answer she's been waiting for, as if Memere making her way slowly up the sidewalk is the deciding factor in whether I should marry Joe.

This marriage is in motion and stopping it will take more energy than letting it happen. How did I get to be this person who just hangs on while things happen to me?

"I'll tell your father to get the car." Mom turns back briskly and gives us her public smile. "You girls look lovely." Then she tilts her head and her smile changes. "It can work out." There's a tear in the corner of her eye. "You can learn to love someone. He'll be good to the baby. He'll take care of you if you get ill."

"Learn to love him?" I want to cry but I won't let tears mess up my mascara and my wedding dress. "*If* I get ill?" I was disgusted with Marie when she got pregnant, the way she blamed everyone except herself. Now I know how it feels to build a trap for yourself and want to rattle the cage at anyone who happens to be near.

Mom winces. "I don't make the rules." Her back is stiff with dignity.

"I'm sorry, Mom." Who does make the rules? "I'm tired. I've got morning sickness."

Mom, Marie, and Dad pile into the front seat of the Chevy. Renee helps Memere and I climb in the back. When we drive up to All Saints, Joe and Fletcher are already standing on the marble steps, talking nervously and gesturing with unlit cigars. They're dressed in glaring white cut-away tuxedos, framed by the big oak doors, wide open behind them.

"Well, don't the men look nice," Mom says overenthusiastically as the car pulls to the curb.

"You told them you were wearing off-white," Marie says, disgusted.

"What do men know?" Renee fusses with the daisies braided through my hair and gives Marie a look that says, It's bad enough; don't make it worse.

Memere, in the stiff black dress she wears to funerals and weddings, pats my hand. "You look beautiful, Cora Rose."

Mom, Dad, and Marie stand on the curb. Renee climbs out, then offers me a hand to help hoist me out. I don't want to get out of the car. I don't want to stand next to Joe in his snow-white tuxedo. I'm afraid if I bend too far forward to lift myself out of the back seat I'll get safety-pinned in the back or brooched in the front. I stare out the window at Joe and Fletcher. Dad opens the back door on Memere's side. "You ladies need a hand?"

"A moment." Memere waves him away and remains seated next to me in her patient black dress. I stare at her pillbox hat, like Jackie Kennedy's except Memere's is black. Joe stares at the car, smiles expectantly. He must have gotten the idea for white tuxedos from the cover of *Abbey Road*, his favorite album. His dream is to become a rock star. I should have had bigger dreams, something besides getting rid of my virginity. Maybe if I had better dreams I wouldn't be sulking in the back seat in my potato-colored dress on my wedding day.

Memere sighs softly, "Scared?"

"This kind of thing ever happen when you were a girl?"

"Since Adam and Eve."

"We don't love each other."

"No?" Memere looks out at Joe's face, lit up, anxiously watching the car. "Maybe he loves you?"

"That's the worst part."

"Love the baby," she advises.

When we don't emerge, Joe walks over to Memere's side of the car, helps her out, then holds the door for me, offering both his hands. "Wow," he says enthusiastically as he pulls me onto the sidewalk. His beard is trimmed to a two-inch bush, his long ponytail looks shinier, darker against the white silk. Big men look good in tuxedos. He takes both my hands and steps back. "You look great."

"Thanks. You look great, yourself." I smile and blush despite myself. He's a good guy, that's what everyone says, and it seems true. Joe.

Dad stands next to me at the back of the church. Both of us fidget nervously. I try to count my blessings; lucky that the church was available on such short notice, that Joe and the priest agreed to a Catholic ceremony, that Joe's not some jerk.

Renee stands alone in front of us in her cool blue sheath with two daisies in her hair to match the ten daisies she braided down the back of mine. Dad winks at me and smiles at the last-minute stragglers escorted up the aisle by Uncle Louie, the lone usher. Mom makes a last-minute adjustment of Dad's tie. Their eyes hold for a second with some hidden meaning. Will Joe and I ever communicate like that, with a private glance? Mom looks at us approvingly before she lets Uncle Louie escort her down the aisle to take her place in the front row.

Dad offers me his arm, solid like the arm of the big sturdy chair he sits on to watch TV in the living room. The look he's giving me, all pride and tenderness, makes him more handsome, makes me want to cry. I wish I could be what he wants me to be. I hang on to his arm and adjust the strap of my off-white pumps. What would Dad want me to be, a teacher, a nurse, President of The Rotary Club? I have no idea. I straighten up and give him a big smile. At least I know that, at this moment, he'd like me to be a sweet young thing who made a mistake.

Marriage, a sacrament, a state of grace. I put my hand on my belly. Move my hand quickly away so I won't draw attention. A baby. Someone else to learn to love.

The organ plays one somber chord. A hush falls over the church and spines straighten against the backs of the pews. The members of the congregation twist their necks, stare down the aisle at us, and wait for the next chord. "The Wedding March," commences, the cue for Renee to take the first step and lead us down the long aisle. Most of the swiveled heads are on the LaBarre side of the church. Joe doesn't have much family. His Mom died when he was born and his Dad didn't stick around. His Aunt Barbara and two of his foster Moms huddle in the first row.

The priest, in his golden flowing robe, stands behind the altar. He raises his hands. The first full measure of "The Wedding March" stomps above us. Renee's silk legs and satin pumps move forward. I hang onto the knot of mantilla at my throat with one hand and my father's arm with the other hand. He steps forward. My feet move with his.

Everyone is staring, smiling. I smile at some people I barely recognize from the factory where my parents work. It's surreal, almost silly, this slow motion march to the altar. I glance at the pews behind and in front of the Kallowitzes. No Stella. Mom sent her invitation to her parents' house. There are rumors about Stella—she joined the Navy, moved to California? In every rumor, she's gone. I kissed Stella and she disappeared. I kissed Joe and we'll be together forever. Maybe first communion and confession and confirmation were the wrong sacraments for me. Maybe marriage will do the trick.

I hang onto Dad. Maybe my best dream is a quiet life, a quiet gut, the chatter in my head a resigned humming like the slow-paced chords of "Here Comes the Bride," soothing and sad as a requiem Mass. I nod and smile at Aunt Josette, who is overdressed in pink taffeta. Lorraine's eyes are wide, excited like she's about to witness John and Yoko exchanging vows. Lorraine, like Joe, loves the Beatles. She's in ecstasy when Joe plays guitar. She sewed a pantset for my trousseau, with an elastic waist so I can wear it as my belly gets bigger. Not that we're going anywhere, except a second-floor apartment with a condemned porch.

I catch the back of Marie's teased-up hair. She's sitting in the second row, her arm entangled in the arm of her date, Eddie. She faces us as we march toward her. Eddie sits rigidly still, straight-backed, facing the altar. Donny, in a little blue suit with short pants, hangs over the back of the pew, teething innocently on the mahogany. Sun streams through the stained glass window and bounces off his blonde hair like a halo. Fletcher's hair. He could be in a pamphlet for Birth Rite if it wasn't for the scab on his chin. I hope my baby is cute.

Eddie whispers in Marie's ear. She picks up Donny and plunks him down in her lap so he's facing forward. He whimpers. Eddie bends his arm so Marie can slip her hand through. She holds on to both of them, like a wife. I smile. I give this guy a month before Marie cuts him loose and tries to patch things up with Fletcher again.

Joe and Fletcher stand at the front of the church on either side of the aisle, hands behind their backs, blinking out at the congregation like albino penguins. The length of aisle between us seems like the Arctic Ocean. We keep moving slowly forward until Renee stops, sidesteps, and takes Fletcher's arm. Dad kisses my cheek, guides me by the elbow, and hands me over to Joe before stepping into the first pew next to Mom. It's embarrassing, being handed off in front of all these people. Joe lifts his arm proudly. I take it. His arm is twice the size of Dad's. I can do this. I can learn to love Joe. He is safe and sturdy. I can learn to love the way it feels to lean on his big arm.

Chapter 8

A love seat with a busted spring smack in the middle of the cushion is the only available seating in Marie's living room. Joe and I sit thigh to thigh on this little couch, but lean away from each other to avoid being stabbed by the uncoiled metal.

"Hey, you guys, this is Dave." Renee walks into Marie's apartment with a new guy dangling on her arm.

Dave is handsome, big smile, gold hair, all man-charm in his creased khakis and boat shoes. Renee's dates are always good-looking, self-assured, save-the-planet types. But there's hesitation in Dave's eyes as he takes a breath and strides into the room. My guess is the walk through the parking lot and up the stairs of the rat project that Marie calls home now has knocked Dave's confidence down a few pegs. He may be wondering if this little corner of the planet is worth saving. If this is true, I can't really fault the guy. It takes time to get used to this housing project. You never know which food smells are going to win out. Pizza and cabbage dominate tonight, and garlic, always garlic. Why do poor people eat so much garlic? And the big brick battleship of a building never seems to sleep. TVs, radios, music, music, music. Spanish music, rock 'n roll, Frank Sinatra. Too much sound and smell. Too many kids laughing, crying, bounding in and out, up and down. As if lack had no place here. If the competition for your ears and nose doesn't throw you off as you walk down the barely lit hallway, the sheer number of doors you pass as you sidestep the occasional beer can or McDonald's wrapper to get to Marie's apartment will.

Handsome Dave smiles bravely, nodding at all of us and the room in general. I feel protective of him. Maybe because I know how it feels to walk into Marie's apartment for the first time. Maybe because I had a baby six months ago and I'm in a protective state of mind.

"This is my sister, Cora Rose." Renee smiles proudly. "And her husband, Joe."

I have to give it to Renee. She's a full-fledged registered nurse with a good job. She thinks she's hot-shit, but that never stops her from thinking well of others. Me for example; she thinks well of me because I'm a good mother and don't complain too much about my colitis. Sometimes, in private, Renee piles on the criticism. But in public, she builds us up if she can. She's gracious. I think that's the word. Where she learned how to be gracious, I have no idea. I can see her doing it, but I can't quite copy it. Maybe it takes a certain amount of self-confidence that I don't have.

Anyway, if Dave's interested in Renee, he's going to have to get used to the rat project because, as much as they fight, my sisters aren't parting company. I wonder if Marie appreciates that Renee introduces us to all her fancy boyfriends or if she just takes it for granted? Marie thinks pretty highly of herself, too. It might not occur to her that anyone would have to get used to her or this place. She might think she's as good as anybody and everybody. Another trait I'd like to develop.

"How you doing?" Joe rises a bit off the love seat and extends his hand to Dave.

Dave shakes Joe's hand and nods, "Hello," to me.

"Look," Renee takes Dave by the hand and pulls him to the window near the loveseat. "See that rooftop?"

Dave squints and says, "I think so."

"That's my house." She beams. She still lives with our parents.

There's an awkward silence. Renee and Dave hold hands and look out the window. I don't understand her enthusiasm for the neighborhood. Maybe because I live a few blocks away and am not likely to move any time soon. Marie once swore she'd never live in these rat projects. I could easily have ended up living down the hall. Because Renee lives with Mom and Dad, she saves most of her paycheck to buy a nice house in a good neighborhood some day. I think it's easier to be proud that you come from a crummy neighborhood if you know you'll be getting out one day.

95

"Oh, yes, I see it, now," Dave says. Bottles rattle and Marie argues with her boyfriend Eddie in the kitchen, which is a few short steps away.

"I'll let Marie know we're here." Renee releases Dave's hand to roust out Marie and Eddie.

Dave looks around the tiny living room with its occupied love-seat and a chair that can be accessed only by moving the playpen blocking it and removing a pile of newspapers occupying the chair's seat. There's yet another silence that Renee would fill in if she wasn't in the kitchen placating Marie and Eddie.

"Have a seat," Joe offers Dave his seat, which is a nice gesture, but weird because that will leave me and Dave on the love-seat, forcing me to decide whether to take a chance on letting Dave get jabbed or warning him and betraying the state of Marie's sofa.

"Thanks. I don't mind standing." Dave rubs his hands together like he's cold. We're on the fourth floor. It's September, but already heat rising from the apartments below make it so hot Marie keeps the windows cracked.

"So, you're a med student?" I smile at Dave who is rocking from heel to heel. "You go to the University?"

"Pre-med hopeful." He corrects me. "I'm taking courses at UMASS." He seems relieved to be in familiar territory.

"That's great."

"I guess. You make it through four years of high school. Then all of a sudden you're first year again. You know how that is." He shrugs and grins his good will.

I nod in sympathy. I'd love to know how that is.

"No," Joe says. "How is that?" He's smiling. I can only hope, smart as he seems, Dave doesn't catch on that this isn't Joe's friendly smile.

"It's, well, it's daunting," Dave says. "What do you do, Joe?"

"I work in a factory," Joe says flatly.

Why Joe is giving this guy a hard time, I don't know. "Joe's a machinist," I say. "He works in a foundry." He's skilled labor, nothing to be ashamed off. Gingerly, I push my knee into Joe's. Joe is usually easy-going. He pushes back, patting my knee, and giving me the fake smile now.

"Oh." Dave nods appreciatively. "Where?"

Joe takes his time answering this question. I don't understand exactly what pushes Joe's buttons. He likes to get along with people and he's good at it, but every once in a while, someone brushes against him the wrong way, and he gets his back up. It can't be just that Dave seems to have had advantages that Joe never had. We run in to plenty of people who have had advantages that Joe never had and he gets along fine with most of them. I'm beginning to wonder if his resentments just kind of pile up and he deposits them on whoever seems worthy and happens to show up when his frustration reaches critical mass. But UMASS doesn't really scream chauffeurs and nannies. For all Joe knows, this guy Dave was bounced from foster home to foster home until he was eighteen, given $200 and told to find his way in the world by himself, too.

I look at the creases in Dave khaki's and smile. For some reason, these pants seem to rule out a history of foster care. Funny, Joe gets along fine with Marie's boyfriend Eddie and Eddie is a pompous ass. But then, Eddie only pretends to have had all the advantages. I try to remember if I've ever seen Eddie in khaki pants.

The guys' conversation, which had been plodding along, stops. They are both staring at me. They must be wondering why I'm smiling. I'm smiling because I've just noticed that Joe is wearing his good jeans.

"Are you going to specialize?" I ask Dave because I don't know where their conversation landed and it's clearly my turn to speak. I'm not trying to piss Joe off. I don't mean to focus on the fact that Dave is in college, but it's all I can come up with.

"Pediatrics," Renee says, at Dave's side again. "Cora Rose just had a baby boy, Sammy, cute as a button." Marie and Eddie make their entrance, too. Renee gestures, "And this is Marie. She has a little boy, Donny, also adorable."

Marie pulls her head back and folds her arms, a gesture meant to let Renee know she better introduce Eddie if she knows what's good for her. Renee is looking at Dave, probably to avoid looking at Marie. So much for gracious Renee.

"That's great," Dave says with way too much enthusiasm. It's becoming obvious that Dave is trying hard not to turn on his heels and run out of Marie's apartment.

"Hey." Marie lifts her chin at Dave, by way of greeting. She glares at Renee as she bends over the playpen and pulls up on its middle. The playpen folds into itself with a sharp snap, becoming half its original size. "This is Eddie. The boyfriend that my rude sister just insulted by not introducing him." Her hands are full so she has to gesture in Eddie's direction with her elbow.

"Oh, Eddie," Renee says unconvincingly. "I'm sorry."

Unfazed, Eddie extends his hand to Dave. "I hear you're in medicine. Good field. I'm in business myself." Eddie is well-groomed and reasonably good-looking. I notice he's wearing corduroy jeans, ironed. He's only twenty-one, but somehow everything he says sounds like it should be coming out of an old man. He works for an insurance company and brings up his degree, managing to make it sound more impressive than the two-year associate it is, every chance he gets. But so what? Renee should just suck it up and be nice to him. He starts to quiz Dave on pediatrics, but runs out of material after he asks, "What's your position on the fluoride question?"

Marie stands with her arms folded, scoping out the situation. She pulls a pillow from either side of me and Joe and tosses them on the floor. "Sit." She takes the newspapers off the chair and carries them into the kitchen.

"I'm going to check on Sammy." I wave at my seat on the couch, offering it up, not waiting to find out who takes my place and who sits in the liberated chair. On the way to Donny's bedroom where the boys are sleeping, I pass through the kitchen and by Marie, who has dropped the newspapers on a kitchen chair and is shoving a six-pack of beer under each arm. "Are you taking beer to the movies?" I ask.

"No. We've got a half hour to kill before we leave. I'm going to need a couple beers before I spend a half hour crammed in a car with Renee and Mr. Kleen. What the hell is her problem?"

I shake my head and step into Donny's bedroom, the smallest room in the apartment. Sammy is asleep on his belly in the crib Donny has outgrown. He's wearing a one-piece baby bunting, a little sack, like a sleeping bag with arms and a neck. Donny is asleep on a mattress on the floor. He grips a little toy truck in his hand, close to his face. I'm afraid he'll roll over and poke out his eye. I loosen his fingers one at a time, and drop his truck in the wooden toy box Dad built. Donny's room is half the size of Sammy's room. There are toys, mostly trucks of varying sizes, covering what little floor space there is. I worry that Fletcher, who is babysitting and should be here by now, will trip over toys in the dark room when he comes in to check on the boys. Or, Donny could wake up and stumble. Or, Fletcher could be carrying Sammy, Sammy awake and crying for me, and wham! Fletcher's foot hits the truck and slides out from under him. I start picking up toys and putting them in the box. The box is soon full, so I'm bent over lining trucks up by the wall when Joe walks in.

"What are you doing?" he whispers.

"Checking on Sammy."

"For the last ten minutes? He's sound asleep."

I kneel on the floor and peer at Sammy, to get a better look at his chest, which rises and falls in perfect rhythm. He's the picture of a safe cozy baby. "Did you talk to Fletcher?" I whisper.

"Come have a beer." Joe shakes his head.

"He's sweating." The hair on Sammy's temple is damp.

"Me, too." Joe wipes his forehead with his sleeve.

"You didn't talk to Fletcher, did you? What if Sammy has an asthma attack?" Sammy's breathing is fine. I keep a bottle of his medicine at Marie's. Fletcher knows where it is. Still, I've never left him alone with anyone besides my mother or sisters. Not even Joe.

"Fletcher's been babysitting for Donny since he was born. They'll be fine. He's sweating because it's hot in here."

"It's not called babysitting when it's your own kid." Why does whispering make everything I say sound more bitchy and everything Joe says sound more reasonable? I stand. "You promised you'd talk to Fletcher."

"What's your problem with Fletcher?" Joe says in a normal volume.

"Shhh. I love Fletcher. I just don't want him taking care of my baby if he's stoned. What's your problem with Dave?"

"Young Doctor Kildare? Did you hear? He's a pediatric specialist," Joe says sarcastically. "Why don't you ask *him* to babysit?"

"Because he's going to the movies with us." I shake my head and smile. See. I have a sense of humor. I'm not just an over-anxious nag. "Give the guy a break. Can you imagine landing in the middle of us?"

"What's the matter with us?"

"You know what I mean. This family can be tough."

Including Joe in the family is a sure way to please him. "Fletcher landed in the middle of *us*, too." He smiles.

"What are you two doing in here?" Marie appears in the door. She's not whispering, but I know better than to shush her.

"Cora Rose is afraid Fletcher is going to get stoned and drop Sammy out the window," Joe says.

"Fletcher doesn't smoke dope in my apartment, because I will kill him if he does." Not counting caffeine, nicotine, the occasional sleeping pill, and alcohol, Marie has given up drugs.

"But does he smoke dope before he comes to your apartment?" I'm the only one whispering, so I stop.

"Joe never comes home stoned?" Marie rolls her eyes.

"Not if he's going to be alone with Sammy." I'm taking a chance that Joe might make a remark about my never leaving him alone with Sammy, but I don't know if he realizes this. Joe says nothing. The front door opens and closes.

"Here's the dope fiend and father of my child now," Marie says.

We can hear Fletcher saying hello to Eddie and Renee introducing him to Dave.

"Where's everybody else?" Fletcher asks.

"Family reunion in Donny's room," Renee says. "I wasn't invited."

It occurs to me, just how rude we're being.

Marie pokes her head into the kitchen and calls, "Fletcher, come here a minute, will you?" The sleeping boys don't even twitch in reaction to her loud voice.

"Pardon, nice to meet you." Fletcher's voice, as always, is soft and polite and southern. We hear his every word as he excuses himself from the living room.

"Hey." He grins, framed by Donny's door. "This is a mighty small room for a party." There's not two feet of space between any of us. It takes one long stride for him to get to Donny. Joe puts his arm around me, motivated by lack of space. Fletcher kneels next to the mattress, puts his hand on his sleeping son's head. He looks up to ask, "The boys okay?" With his thin face and body, long hair, and faded clothes, he looks like a shepherd in a religious painting bending over a lamb.

"The boys are fine. You high?" Marie asks cordially. "Cora Rose is worried."

"No, Ma'am. I'm on probation for possession of marijuana." He stands and raises his right hand. "For the next three months, this boy is straight as an arrow."

"Oh, my God." I unwrap Joe's arm from my shoulder and look for his reaction. Joe's not a bit surprised. "You knew this?"

Joe shrugs. I glare at him.

"I'll take good care of them," Fletcher says, "Sorry, buddy. I thought she knew."

Renee is rummaging in a kitchen cabinet. "Renee," I call. "Did you know that Fletcher is on probation?"

"Well, if I didn't, I found out thirty seconds ago. We're just sitting in there." She points her thumb over her shoulder. "We can hear your conversation." She stands in the doorway with a beer glass in each hand. "Get out of that tiny room. You're sucking up the boys' oxygen. We have company."

Marie, the first to take Renee's advice, steps around her into the kitchen. She looks pointedly at the glasses in Renee's hands. "I forgot. Madame drinks from a glass."

"It's customary to offer guests a glass with their beverage." Renee drops her public voice for a second and smirks.

"Did you know that Fletcher is on probation for possession?" I ask Renee again.

Renee shrugs. "Alcohol is worse than pot." She gives Fletcher and Joe an *I told you so* look. "Don't get bent out of shape, Cora Rose. Fletcher is great with the kids."

"You knew, too?" I turn to Marie.

101

"Yup, and I didn't tell you." Marie folds her arms across her chest. If Memere is right, some day her arms are going to freeze in that position.

"Why am I the only one who wasn't told?"

"Because." Marie leans back, with her elbows on the counter. "You've always been a nervous twit, and since you had a kid you're worse. You've smoked marijuana with Fletcher, so I guess you knew he had it in his possession from time to time?" She delivers this very calmly.

Are they right? Am I some kind of hysteric? "I haven't smoked marijuana since I knew I was pregnant." My effort to control my voice only makes it shrill. "I don't think anybody in charge of kids should be stoned. What's so unreasonable about that?"

"You know Fletcher. If he says he won't get high, he won't." Renee stands next to Fletcher, who has been listening patiently, biding his time until it's his turn to speak. "Will you?" she asks him.

"I am not stoned," he says. "And I will not get stoned this evening."

"I'm the first to admit Fletcher has flaws," Marie says. Fletcher smiles shyly, like this remark is a compliment. "Like his unnatural alliance with this one." She nods at Renee, who smirks in reply. "But he's great with the boys and he's not a liar." Marie's and Fletcher's eyes lock for a second. The rest of us silently watch this oddly intimate exchange between the ex-lovers. "Do you want him to watch the boys or not?" Marie snaps her attention at me. "Or do you think the authorities are going to take Sammy away from you because you let a man on probation babysit?"

"I just want to know what's going on."

"We'll take that as a yes, she wants him to babysit." Marie turns abruptly and marches through the kitchen, proclaiming, "Let's drink beer."

We all follow her into the living room, where Eddie and Dave are sitting shoulder to shoulder on the love seat, sipping Bud from cans. Neither of them looks horribly uncomfortable. They watch us file into the room. I wonder if my sisters' dates have managed to escape the busted spring.

Eddie must know about it. He claps his hands together. "So, everything all cleared up?"

No one answers.

"Anybody besides me need a beer?" Joe looks from Eddie to Dave to Fletcher. All three men hold up the beers they already have. Joe looks down at the beer he, like Fletcher, just accepted from Marie. "Guess I'll drink the one in my hand," he says.

Fletcher chuckles. Then Joe and Fletcher start laughing. Then Eddie shakes his head and starts. Dave joins in and all four men are really bellowing.

"What?" Renee asks. She's sitting on the arm of the love seat next to Dave.

Marie chugs half her beer. "The LaBarre sisters," she says. "We're a barrel of laughs."

Chapter 9

I'm elbow-deep in dirty dishes. The amplified squeals of two guitars, bass, and drums vibrate up the pipes of our second-floor apartment and make tiny ripples in the soapy water. Joe's band, Room for Improvement, is practicing in an empty first-floor apartment. The big old building that we live in is made up of six apartments and there's usually at least one vacant. When Joe's Fender amp finally stops pumping out "Proud Mary," I lean on the sink with relief. "Thank God." Two years ago, on the same weekend I gave birth to Sammy, Joe gave birth to the band. Sammy and I have been listening to feedback every weekend since.

When the music stops, Sammy, on his knees behind me, stops zooming his Match Box Mustang across the cracked linoleum and frowns. Sammy likes the pounding, repetitive beat. He pouts. A second later he says, "Out." His pout turns to a grin that makes craters of the dimples in his fat cheeks.

I stare out the window at a beautiful spring day, barely a breeze to kick up the pollen and Sammy's asthma. I catch my reflection, unexpectedly, in the glass. A dishwatery-looking woman blinks at me. I touch my hair and blink back. My hair shines like patent leather. Dr. Bello says the tissue in my colon isn't looking good, he wants more biopsies. But my hair looks great, how sick can I be? I smile to see if changing my expression makes me look less like a drudge of a housewife. It does. I look beyond my reflection. Bright yellow sunlight blurs my view of the yard.

Sammy says, "Out," again. Maybe it's okay to take him out. He seems fine this morning. The asthma attack he had last night freaked out Joe as much as it did Sammy. Joe's useless when Sammy's sick, worse than useless. Everyone thinks that I'm the anxious parent, but when

Sammy's sick, Joe forgets he's a father and completely withdraws or gets so shook up that I have to take care of them both.

"Okay, little guy, get Mr. Elephant and Pink Puppy." I pull the plug on the sink and wipe my hands on a dishtowel stuffed in the back pocket of my jeans.

"Bottle!" Sammy demands.

The battle of the bottle again. Dr. Bello says it has to go, even at the expense of a mild asthma attack. Mom says it's got to go. Even Renee, with Dr. Spock under her arm and the patience of the childless, says two years old is too old to be sucking on a bottle. Four days, ten fits since Sammy's last bottle. He scrunches up his face, letting me know he's prepared to have a tantrum if necessary. I believe Dr. Bello when he says, "Hold out for a couple weeks, the bottle will be history." But I can't deal with Sammy on his back, kicking his feet and squealing, right after band practice. Not twelve hours after he was fighting for breath and battling the inhaler at the same time. Not the day before I have to go back to Dr. Bello for more tests. I squat to listen to Sammy's breathing. I can barely see his chest rise and fall, barely hear his breath at all. I smile. All traces of the heaving and wheezing are gone. His face is pink, but not too pink. It's amazing how sick he can be at two a.m. and look so well the next morning.

I stand up and say sternly, "You're too old for a bottle," as I reach to the back of the silverware drawer for a nipple. I grab the apple juice out of the fridge.

Sammy watches me seriously until he's sure he's getting his way. "Bottle." He beams and trots off into the living room to fetch his stuffed animals. He sits patiently, leaning against the double-bolted kitchen door, sucking his thumb with his cheek against his pink stuffed poodle, waiting for me to take him and his bottle onto the back porch, down the rickety stairs, into what passes for a yard.

"Good boy, Sammy. You want a ride in the cart?"

He nods yes, his thumb in his mouth, his droopy eyes fixed on me. We study each other and smile in mutual admiration. Sammy's eyes dart to something behind my back. Before I turn to look, Joe's lips are on my neck.

"How you doing, baby?" The sweet smell of pot and beer is on his breath.

I push him away half-heartedly. "You promised you'd keep it down."

He blinks through his crooked smile, humoring me. "It's Saturday." He holds his hands up in a gesture of innocence. "Those black girls downstairs had Marvin Gaye turned up 'til midnight."

"So? Everybody in the house gets to be jerks?"

"*Sammy* likes music."

Sammy, still slumped lazily against the door, says, "Daddy," and puts his arms out for Joe.

"I like music, just not the same song for two hours."

Joe squats next to Sammy. "You falling asleep on the job, little guy?" He twists Sammy's wispy hair gently between his thick fingers. It's hard to stay pissy when Joe's talking baby talk and making goofy faces at Sammy.

"You feeling all right this morning?" Joe's sincerity is his best feature. His concern is real. He's not just sticking in the question to change the subject. Well, partly maybe, but his concern for my health is real. The only sick time he uses is to drive me to the doctor's.

I shake my head. "I'm okay."

He smiles back and opens the refrigerator door, moves the milk and ketchup, looking for beer. He says predictably, "You used to be into music." His voice is even. He doesn't want to fight on a beautiful spring day. He just wants me to know I'm a drag.

"There's not a twenty-minute drum solo in 'Proud Mary.' And there's no reason you can't turn the amp down." I hoist Sammy on my hip. "Come on, Mommy's boy." Jerk. I'm not a drag. I'm tired. "Next time Sammy has an asthma attack in the middle of the night, you take care of him."

Joe, almost in tears himself when Sammy first woke up wheezing and crying, was snoring twenty minutes later, as soon as I was finished giving Sammy his treatment and it was time to walk the floor with him for an hour. What really makes me mad is that Joe gets to sleep and I get to be the bitch.

"What's that got to do with music?" He pulls out a six-pack. "He's getting heavy. Run this down to the guys." He tries to exchange the six-pack for Sammy. "I'll carry him outside for you."

I hug Sammy closer. "Carry your own beer."

"Women." He screws up his face at Sammy.

I tote Sammy past him. The screen door slams behind us.

The yard is mostly rutted dirt with a couple patches of grass that haven't been snuffed out by cars. I put Sammy down and head for the rusty shopping cart left out since last year. It's parked against the chain-link fence. Sammy tugs on the tail of my denim shirt. "Push me." He takes the bottle out of my hand. Except for the back seat of Joe's Mazda, the rusty shopping cart is Sammy's favorite mode of transportation.

"Mus Sang." Sammy points to the shiny new convertible that belongs to the downstairs neighbor. I lay his blanket on the bottom of the cart. He sucks on his juice, double-fisted, the bottom of the bottle tilted toward the sky. I push. The cart and Sammy bounce over the ruts. The sun is bright. I squint and sweat. The shade is on the north side of the house where Room for Improvement practices. Sammy hugs Mr. Elephant's floppy body. We stop in the shade at the side of the house.

Sammy lies on his side and pulls up his feet. The pink stuffed poodle, Gigi, is wedged beside him. He stuffs the bottle between the pink fluff covering her stiff front legs, tilts the bottle toward his mouth, and sucks contentedly. He learned the bottle-propping trick from me. Poor dead Gigi, reduced to this position. Mom says, "Propping a baby's bottle is a lazy, dangerous thing to do." Dr. Spock and Renee agree that it's not a desirable way to feed a baby. Sammy sucks and blinks at me through Gigi's fuzzy pink legs. This is absolutely his last bottle.

I sit on a patch of grass, lean up against the tarpaper shingles, and rock the shopping cart with my foot. Sammy pulls on his earlobe, twitches his foot, and sucks innocently on the nipple. I don't believe a baby can drown in apple juice from bottle propping, but I don't take my eyes off him. I'm never sure when something really is a big deal and when it's just another stupid rule that makes life harder than it has to be. Sammy and I stare at each other. I'm not all that comfortable sitting against the tarpaper. I wish I hadn't thrown the old wooden chair in the trash. I should have left it braced up against the side of the house. It was a functional piece of lawn furniture. Sammy's eyelids flutter and close. The bottle is still in his half-open mouth. He's completely still, except for the gentle rise and fall of his chest. I tug the nipple from between his teeth and tuck the bottle under the blanket. He wakes up, protests with a weak cry, and says, "Ride," but doesn't ask for the bottle.

"Shh." I rock the rusty wheels slowly back and forth over the tufts of grass. Sammy maneuvers his diapered butt until his arms are under his belly and his rear end is sticking up in the air. Within minutes, he's sleeping face down on the bath towel in a little puddle of drool. I love to watch him sleep like this. In the shade, under the open window of the vacated first-floor apartment, I watch his back rise and fall and listen to the soft whoosh of his breath. Inside the apartment, footsteps walk toward the window I'm sitting under, followed by the creak of an old couch. The bottom of the window is even with the top of my head. The smell of marijuana wafts over me and drifts toward Sammy.

"That Eddie guy is a trip," Joe's voice, loud with beer, floats out on sweet-smelling smoke. "Him and Marie make no sense as a couple. Can't believe they're still together."

I scooch to one side, get up slowly, and stand to one side of the window, looking in at a slant, trying to see them without being seen, a peeping Tom. Joe and Fletcher sit with their backs to me on the old couch that was left by the last tenants when they abandoned the apartment. The back of the couch is water-stained because the window was left wide open in the rain. The other two guys in the band must have taken off already. I can tell Fletcher is passing Joe a joint by the way the top of his head turns as the trail of smoke moves.

"Renee's already blown off that guy Dave. She never sticks with them long. Eddie's okay. Marie's a lot more conventional than she lets on. She's attracted to the fact that he's got a decent job, wants to get married, eats all his leafy green vegetables," Fletcher says in his mild-mannered drawl. "Seems to be all right with Donny. Little strict, maybe."

"He doesn't think much of you." Joe's arms are draped over the back of the couch. All I see are his big shoulders and his ponytail dusting the screen as his head moves.

"No, but he pretty much lets me be."

"Doesn't think much of me either. And I got a job. Eat my vegetables." Joe turns to face Fletcher. "Why's he approve of her?" Fletcher says something that I can't make out. "All due respect," Joe says. "That asshole thinks he's Lord of the Manor and Marie . . ." he stops to choose his words or maybe just because he's stoned. "He took her to the Hamptons, but she's still the neighborhood bitch." Joe sounds more philosophical than critical. I can't work up indignation on my sister's behalf. I agree with him.

"They put up with each other. Compromise makes the world go round." Fletcher sucks in a lung-full. "Lot of women would throw him out on his royal ass," he says with his long exhale. It sounds like he's complimenting Marie for her fortitude.

Joe giggles. "Be a trip if they end up married." He blows out a cloud of smoke and exhales a question with it. "You ever getting married?"

"Would have married Marie." Fletcher sits up and stretches. As he inhales and holds in the smoke, I study his profile and try to come up with a reason I'm peering in on them in case I get caught. He shakes his head. He's twenty-five, not handsome, but interesting to look at in a weather-beaten kind of way. If I get caught, I'll just say I strolled over to get Sammy out of the sun and happened to look in. When he's not smiling, Fletcher could pass for forty. His hair is dirty brown, already streaked with gray, pulled back in a ponytail at the nape of his neck. He seems younger when he speaks. He moves his hands, laughs and smiles a lot when he's talking. Mostly he listens—'our philosopher,' Renee calls him. "She was too smart to saddle herself with a draft-dodger."

"Get out of here. You didn't want to marry Marie."

"Didn't say 'wanted to.' Said 'would have.'"

"She's too proud for that," Joe muses. "She ever ask about your family?"

Fletcher takes his time exhaling. "Knows my daddy kicked my ass from the time I could crawl and even my mama doesn't approve of me declining an invitation to Vietnam." He strums the strings of an acoustic guitar.

"You miss Georgia?"

"Sometimes. Beautiful state. Miss my mama and my baby sister. Someday I'll write them, ask them to tell me when Daddy dies so I can go back and see them. For now, the only thing I want to be permanently attached to is Donny." He inhales, and says without exhaling, "And my own dick."

"Motherfucker." Joe laughs and chokes on the dope he just sucked in. "That's a nice thing to say to your best buddy." The back of the couch rocks against the window. He never uses those words in front of me or Sammy. Strange to be married to someone and not know he sometimes says, "Motherfucker."

"Well, I like you, but not as much as my kid." Fletcher strums some more before adding, "Or my dick."

Joe doesn't laugh at the dick comment this time. He says, "What's the deal with Renee?"

Fletcher keeps strumming as he answers, "Renee's my good buddy. You might have to wrestle her for best buddy."

"I mean, what about sex? Her sisters tease her about being a virgin, but hey . . . what the hell, she's got to get lonely." Joe has the decency to sound embarrassed. I was getting ready to leave, but don't move a muscle.

"You confusing lonely with horny?" Fletcher twangs a note and holds it a second.

"Just being a gentleman. She's my sister-in-law."

"She's looking for true love." Fletcher trills his fingers on the back of the guitar.

"True love, whatever that means," Joe says. I agree—whatever that means, but I had thought, until this very moment, that Joe thought he knew.

The marijuana smoke is beginning to worry me. It's starting to drift too close to Sammy. And the guys are getting louder. I push the cart away from the window. I feel kind of sad. I wish I had a friend like that, a confidant, someone I talked to with words I don't use when I talk to Joe. As I'm rounding the side of the house, the women who live downstairs bound down the front steps. Their loud teasing wakes up Sammy.

"Hey. How you doing?" Jackie, in a tie-dyed halter top, tucks a braid into a hive of black coils on top of her head. She stops laughing and smiles.

"Good." I feel my face flush as I pick up Sammy out of the cart. He clings to me, curious, but clearly doesn't want to be put down. I straddle him on my hip. "Hi . . . how you?" I always stumble over my words if I try for more than one at a time when I run into these two.

The other one, Darlene, takes off her baseball cap, runs a hand through her short hair, and rocks on her high top sneakers. "Hi." She smiles at Sammy, picks a rubber ball off the step, and curls and uncurls her fist around it. She makes me nervous. I try not to stare at her hair, which is wiry and close to her head. Or the unshaved legs sticking out of her cut-off jeans. Or any other part of her. "Our music bother you last night?" she asks.

I shake my head.

Now, because I'm too timid to complain, I've given them the idea that it's fine to crank the Motown at one a.m.

"What a day." Jackie pulls her shoulders back and stretches. Her breasts strain at the tie-dyed cotton.

Sammy, wide awake now, and more interested than frightened, stares at them.

"What's your name?" Darlene asks him. She looks up at me. "How old is she?"

"He." I tousle Sammy's brown curls and put him down on the ground. "He's two. His name is Sammy."

"Mine." Sammy eyes the red rubber ball in Darlene's hand and yanks my arm. "Man took my ball."

"Sammy, don't be fresh. The *lady* is just playing with it."

"Ha." Jackie throws her head back, and laughs, a full, throaty laugh. She slaps Darlene playfully. "Turnabout is fair play. Give that smart little boy back his ball." She hooks her arm through Darlene's and bats her eyelashes.

Darlene chuckles and hands Sammy the ball.

Sammy, barely able to hold the ball in his little fist, looks shyly at Jackie. Then he smiles his wide-eyed grin and offers the ball to her.

111

"Kid's got good taste." Darlene slaps the baseball cap back on her head.

"Sweet." Jackie takes the ball and leans into Darlene. "We should take Sammy and his Mom for a ride."

"Ride." Sammy makes airplane noises and runs in a little circle with his arms outstretched. He lands in front of Jackie and takes the ball back from her, grinning, cute as a button. His eyes follow mine to the spit-shined Mustang convertible blinking in the sun behind us. The top is already down.

"We can't. Not today." I look regretfully at the car. "He's got asthma. He was sick last night. It'd be too much wind."

"Some other time, then," Jackie says. "Bye, Sammy." They walk away, arm in arm. "See you."

"Mus Sang. Mus Sang," Sammy sings, accenting the last syllable. He trots after them.

I scoop him up. "Maybe next time, sweetie." Next time could be a long way off. They've lived below us since before Sammy was born and I bet they don't know my name.

Sammy's whole face scrunches up. "Ride?" When he realizes we're not going with them, his face changes from bewilderment to rage. I hold him tight so he won't dart out as Darlene backs the red car down the long dirt drive. Jackie waves. Darlene steers the Mustang around my beat-up old Chevy. "Mus Sang." Sammy wiggles out of my arms. His whimper is the sound of a pressure cooker just starting to heat up.

As the Mustang pulls onto the pavement and speeds out of view, the pang of longing for a strong wind in my hair is so sharp and so sudden that it makes me nauseous.

Sammy wants to take off in a fast car with the two laughing women. So do I. I want the Dreaded Bowel Disease to go away. I want to have friends and listen to "Proud Mary" without going crazy. I sit on the steps and watch Sammy stamp his feet for both of us. It's so hard to know, am I protecting him out of habit? I'm too used to holding back because *I* might get sick. Am I doing that now with Sammy? It's a mother's duty to keep her kid safe, to say no to anything risky. Would a ride in the Mustang really hurt either of us? I thought that by the time I had a two-year-old I would know more than I do. I'm twenty years old and still I don't know shit.

Clouds move slowly through the pale blue sky. "Come here, little guy." I pat the step. "We'll go pick up Donny. We'll get ice-cream cones."

"Hey, baby." Joe calls out the side window. "If you're going out, will you pick up some more beer?"

Part 3

Chapter 10

"I want a divorce, Joe." A bitter word, divorce. It feels like I should have my mouth washed out. "I can't do this anymore. I want a divorce." The word burns as much the second time.

Joe sits on the edge of the double bed. "It's late."

I stand in front of him and sigh. "It's nine o'clock. You don't have to stay with me just because I need an operation."

"Don't make the divorce about your disease. I'm not the one who wants a fucking divorce. You'll be in the goddamned hospital in two weeks, Cora Rose." His voice is measured; anger and frustration are giving way to fatigue.

"That's why we have to talk about it now. If we don't, I'll come home from the hospital and who knows when we'll finish the conversation."

He unbuttons his flannel work shirt. "It can wait."

"That's what you said two years ago when the tests showed the colitis was only getting worse and worse since I had Sammy. That's what you said last year when they put me on the new medicine that didn't work."

"What I said was, we should wait and give it another try."

I can't and don't argue this point. At least he's talking. "We got together because I was pregnant. When they told me I had to have surgery, something snapped. Look how we're living. Don't you want your life back, Joe?"

"What about Sammy's life?" He shakes his head no and says, "Yeah."

"I love Sammy. I love you too, Joe. Just not . . ."

He gives me the look that says he's had enough. He's shutting down just when I thought I got up enough nerve to begin the real conversation or maybe announcement is a better word: I'm leaving this marriage, Joe—I don't need your permission. The circles around his brown eyes are getting deeper. Sometimes he says he loves me. If he loved me, wouldn't he let me go? I can't decide if I feel disgust or sorrow, for him, myself, for our whole situation.

"We're going to be old before we've even grown up." I feel more like Joe's mother than his wife sometimes. Be a big boy, Joe, do the adult thing, get a divorce. "I'm not going to die." Never mind the release forms I had to sign acknowledging death as a possibility. "I'm going to be all right after the surgery. You don't really want to stay married to someone who doesn't want to stay married to you." I'm using the same tone I use on Sammy when I want him to behave.

He answers, slowly and deliberately, like I'm the one who's the child, "You're *not* going to die. So we'll have this conversation after you're home from the hospital." He unlaces one boot. He could cry or he could start yelling. I can't tell by looking at him. He doesn't do either. He crawls under the sheets without taking off his jeans, pulls up the quilt Memere made us for a wedding present, clicks off the light, and turns away.

I stand in the doorway of what used to be *our* bedroom and stare until my eyes get used to what little light is left. Even in the shadows, I can make out Joe's dirty work shirt on the chair and the big double dresser with my jewelry box on top of it. I see the room every day. I come in every morning to get my clothes. It looks the same as it always has, but something is different. It's the smell. The room smells different. It smells of Joe's cologne, his feet, his dirty work shirts. The smell of my feet, my sweat, my dirty underwear and bath powder, is gone.

I close the door and check on Sammy in the next bedroom. He's sound asleep, peaceful; his little boy body so vulnerable, soft, and open, lying on his side, sucking his thumb. Our voices didn't wake him. His chubby body is curled in a ball, just like Joe's. I kneel down and put my cheek next to his face. His breath is a warm steady stream fanning over his knuckles as he makes little sucking movements. His mouth is wet around his thumb. I want him to stay like this, content and undemanding. Sometimes it feels like there's been a big mistake, I caught the wrong bus, I don't know where it's going, and there's no cord to yank to get off. And there's this child with me who is demanding that I be his mother, expecting me to make sure that the ride is smooth and takes us wherever it is we're supposed to be going.

He makes a little snort. His eyelashes flutter but don't open. I close my eyes and feel his breath on my cheek. Running in the backyard this morning on the hard ground, Sammy fell over an exposed tree root and pulled himself up without crying, trying to be a big boy like Donny. He drew his plastic sword, defending the rusty shopping cart that's graduated now from baby carriage to go-cart. Mange, the neighborhood homeless cat, appeared through a big gap in the chain-link fence. Sammy stopped in his tracks, dropped his weapon, said, "Please, Mommy." I knew what he wanted before he asked and I gave it to him, let him feed the cat his soggy leftover Captain Crunch. I was the best, most generous Mommy, a good mother watching to make sure he didn't get too close to the raggedy thing. Sammy hugged me, promised not to feed Mange, not to go anywhere near the cat when I wasn't around. And Sammy was the best, most generous child.

I walk slowly down the stairs to the little room off the kitchen where I sleep. The room is supposed to be a walk-in pantry. I hate the little room. It was all right as a pantry, but it's a lousy bedroom, no heat. The cot I sleep on, borrowed from my parents, takes up most of the space. I have to take my clothes on and off in the kitchen. We should be taking turns sleeping down here. Joe doesn't think either of us should be sleeping down here. He's willing to share a double mattress, sleep back to back in the same bed and pull away abruptly if our butts or big toes happen to touch. I could strangle him for accepting so little from a marriage, for not knowing he's worth more than that, for not knowing I'm worth more than that.

I rock on the edge of the cot, hugging my pillow to my chest. The pillow smells like apple shampoo. I plug in the space heater, the only part of the room that I like. There's something beautiful about the coils if you forget what you're looking at and just watch them circling on themselves, glowing hot and red. The thing that really gets me about exiling myself to this tiny room is that I'm lonely for Joe. Sleeping with him made me miserable, but now that I'm not in his bed, I miss him. He'd have to shackle me to the headboard to get me to sleep up there again, but I wouldn't mind hugging his pillow and taking comfort in the burnt smell of the foundry that never leaves his thick ponytailed hair. I'd steal his pillow, just for the night, if he wasn't lying on it. Too bad I can't *just* be sick and tired of this marriage, or even hate him, plain and simple.

The room is getting stuffy. I unplug the space heater and watch the red light of the coils fade to grayish white. The heater has two temperatures, high and off. I'm sick of turning the little knob to off, climbing in bed before the room gets cold again, and crying myself to sleep. I grab my hooded sweatshirt off the nail on the wall, throw my parka on over it, lace up my boots at the kitchen table, and scribble a note: "Gone for a walk." Halfway out the door, I panic about leaving Sammy, tiptoe back up the stairs, making as little noise as possible in my clunky boots.

I stand by his bed and watch his chest, in and out, a nice effortless movement. He lets out a startled whimper. A dream. He turns in his sleep and fights with his sheets. I pull the cover he's wiggled out of back over his shoulders, trying to protect him from his own imagination. "It's O.K, honey."

"Mommy," he says, in a sleepy stupor. He sticks his thumb safely back in his mouth. It gives me a shiver of tenderness and grief. Joe and I have to break him of this habit if he doesn't give it up on his own soon. We can't ship him off to preschool sucking his thumb. The other kids will make fun of him. Joe and I, how will we take care of him when there is no Joe and I? How do I think I'm going to pull off taking care of a thumb-sucking four-year-old without Joe? I can barely take care of myself. Joe is right, what am I thinking, how could I leave him before the operation?

I kiss Sammy's forehead. I want to take him in my arms, but that would probably wake him. I tiptoe away, whispering to myself, "He'll be okay."

I stand in the middle of the huge kitchen of our five-room apartment. Our place is one side of the second and third floor of a six-family tenement. The good thing about living in this part of town is that most of the apartments are big. I walk around the wooden table that seats six without the extra leaf. I run my hand over the washer and dryer, prematurely mourning, grieving the loss of all this space and all this stuff. "Joe, I'm sorry." I slap the red-checkered curtains Memere and Mom made for the oversized windows. "Stop it." If I want to cry and feel sorry for myself, I should stay in my cot and do it. I'm not even sure if it will be me and Sammy or Joe who will move.

I walk out onto the dilapidated porch and run down the rickety stairs. As I round the corner of the house I see Darlene, one of the black girls who lives downstairs, carrying a big cardboard box full of books. One of the books falls off the top of the heap. I pick up *The Bean Eaters* and hand it to her. Ten p.m. The back of her car is piled high with pots and pans and other kitchen stuff. A rocking chair is strapped to the hood of her car. She and Jackie are skipping out on the rent? Neither of them seems the type to stiff a landlord. But then Darlene doesn't seem the type to have a rocking chair strapped to the hood of her Mustang. She's a five-foot-ten black woman who could pass for a man at first glance. If she's skipping, she better be moving out of state or at least to Boston. Popkos Realty will find her anywhere in western Massachusetts.

"Open the door for me?" She points to the Mustang with her chin. "Where you running off to?" It seems like a funny question coming from a woman who's leaving out the back door with a basket full of unfolded towels and underwear in the passenger seat of her car.

"Can't sleep." I move a toaster oven to make room for her books in the back seat. "Just going for a walk. You moving?"

"Yeah." She dumps the box with a grunt, surveys the yard, and gives the house a long look. "I'm outta here."

"You might miss the big rooms. Where you going?" Probably not too far, her stuff isn't packed for a long haul.

"Edgewood Terrace." She runs her hands over the short hair covering her temples and claps them together at the nape of her neck. "Chicopee's only gated community." She repeats the ad that's been running on the local radio station for the last few weeks.

I can picture her, in her black leather jacket, surrounded by the leather seat of her red car, a cool wave to the security guy as she drives through the gate. "Is Jackie moving too?"

"Already gone. New York City. Gonna be a big star."

I look up the drive and realize her roommate's Citation hasn't been in it for quite some time. She slams the car's back door and gets behind the wheel. "Well, guess I'll see you around. Nice being your neighbor, Kara."

"Cora Rose."

"Sorry. Cora Rose." My eyes move with hers from the sagging chain-link fence to the tarpaper shingles. I appreciate the wistful way she looks around, sees something worth missing in the grubby parking lot of a yard and the big square building in need of repair. She leans on the horn and says, "Bye, house."

I look up at Sammy's bedroom window.

"The kid sleeping? Sorry." She looks at the back door of the apartment and sighs. "Who woulda thought I'd be mourning this place?"

"Maybe it's because you lived here with Jackie. Did she get the job with Neutrogena?" Darlene's roommate once told me she had a shot at a Neutrogena commercial.

Darlene laughs with closed eyes to protect some private thought. I should say goodbye softly and move away. I can feel her thinking of Jackie. She was a good-looking woman with a peppering of freckles sprinkled on light brown skin, who seemed to always be hanging on Darlene's arm. Darlene's hands are folded on the bottom of the steering wheel, her eyes are still closed, like she's praying.

"You okay?"

"Fine." Her eyes pop open like I woke her from a dream. She lays her forehead on the steering wheel for a second before she straightens up. "See ya." She puts the car in reverse. "Sometime, when you pass The Girls Club, stop in. I'll buy you a beer."

I look at her stupidly, not quite sure what she's offering.

"You know The Girls Club? The bar? I'm the bartender." She laughs one of those deep, mocking laughs. "Relax. Lots of straight girls come in for a beer. You might even see a man."

My mouth is open. I close it. "Thanks." I become interested in the knot at the end of the string on my hood. "Good luck in your new apartment."

I walk down the driveway and take a left onto the long empty street. Jesus, they broke up. How will she get along? It always seemed like such a miracle to me that these two women set up housekeeping openly. Everyone knows she's a lesbian and now she's alone.

I walk and walk. It's a beautiful winter night, clear sky, yellow halos around the streetlights. In front of the rectory of All Saints Church, there's a poster of a big thermometer with a line filled in red showing how much money has been donated to the Bishop's Appeal, how much more is needed. The red line is well below the freezing point. I haven't been inside All Saints Church for two or three years. I feel like going in now, talking to Mary in her own house. The heavy doors are locked. I take it personally, kick the doors and rattle the brass handles. I make a lot of noise, but the doors don't budge. No wonder the Bishop's Appeal isn't heating up.

I sit on the marble steps. Just me, the stars, and the lights twinkling in the windows of nearby houses. I tilt my head back and close my eyes. "What am I going to do?" I wait for a flash of divine inspiration. No church bells chime, no vision of Mary appears. I blow my nose, lean on the heavy door, and rub my hand over cold stone.

A light snow starts falling, in April, one of our Massachusetts miracles. I should go home and get some sleep. Funny, advanced ulcerative colitis doesn't make me feel any sicker than when it was just the Dreaded Bowel Disease. I was so sure this last round of tests would show some improvement, that Dr. Bello would send me home, and tell me to come back in six months for another check-up. I roll my neck and breathe in through my nose slowly, out through my mouth slowly, like I saw on Channel 4, "Yoga for Life." It kind of works. I feel suspended, my breath and mind slowed down. It seems like I can feel the world turning, ever so slowly. I sit, let the snowflakes fall on my face, try to capture a quiet moment, so I can keep it like a figure in one of those tiny domes that you shake upside down to make snow. In through my nose, out through my mouth, relax, float.

I get up and walk. Let my thoughts float right out of my head into the night. Forget, just for an hour, that soon some surgeon I've met only once will pump me full of anesthesia, cut out my diseased colon, and hang a plastic bag on my belly. Ostomy. A strange word. I've never said it out loud. No one says it out loud except Renee. Probably most people have never heard the word. In my mind it's "The thing." I'll learn to live with "The thing," take care of "The thing." A plastic pouch that fills with my own waste and makes a bulge under my jeans. I've never even met anyone with an ostomy. Not that I know of. I guess it's not something you'd talk about. Like dying. Like being a lesbian. I wish people would talk to me about dying. So I could tell them I'm not.

I walk a ten-block loop around the old neighborhood where my parents and Renee still live. Snow keeps falling, covering the ground in white gauze. I walk around the old house. Except for a tiny glow coming from the nightlight in the hall, the house is dark. Mom and Dad must be sleeping. Renee's working third shift at the hospital. Smoke is coming out of the chimney of the Kallowitzes' old house. I walk through my parents' backyard, stare at the back of the row of brick buildings. The rat projects. A light is on in the third window, fourth floor, of the last building. Marie's apartment. Should I stop in? No, it's Saturday, Eddie will be there. Saturday and Wednesday are Eddie days. I try to stay away on Eddie days. I don't like all the advice he gives—how to keep house, how to raise kids, how much cream you should put in your coffee. I don't like the way Marie lets him rattle on. She never lets anyone else talk to her that way. I finger my right ear. My diamond earring is secure, soldered in place. My left ear is naked. I lost one diamond the first year Joe and I were married. I still look for it when I vacuum. I stare through the falling snow at the light from Marie's window and look back at my parents' dark window. It's going to kill them if I end up in the projects too.

I detour down the side street where Darlene says she tends bar, shake the snow off the hood of my parka, and lean on a parked car hidden in the dark under a tree. Light is pulsating out the narrow windows of the building across the street. There's a sign over the back entrance, "The Girls Club," in discreet block letters. If the place wasn't broadcasting "Rock Steady," it would be hard to spot it as a bar. The parking lot is full. All these years, a dyke bar going strong, tucked away on a side street, a few blocks from where I grew up, ten blocks from where I live now. Until tonight the bartender was living right under me.

A handful of women spill out a side door, laughing, talking loud, shivering in the parking lot as the night grows colder than expected, and the crazy snow falls. One of them lights a cigarette. It passes from woman to woman. The tip glows bright. The one with the lighter rubs her arms against the cold. A girl behind her in a big cable-knit cardigan wraps it around both of them. The sweater is all stretched out, but they're both covered.

I step back a little farther into the shadows. The two entangled in the sweater kiss on the mouth, a peck, but Jesus—right under the lights. Anyone could drive by, slow down and see their lips touching. They have families? Bosses? Neighbors to see where they are, who they're with, on a Saturday night? Why hang all over each other in plain view?

This is the way they act? I don't know any dykes. Darlene doesn't count, I barely know her, and she's moving. That woman Bernie that I met right there in that parking lot in high school, she just let me use her ID so I could use the ladies' room. Stella. I squirm inside my parka. Even Dear Abby says it's normal for young girls to have homosexual fantasies; it's not unusual for a straight person to be attracted to a close friend in adolescence. Normal people have all kinds of fantasies. It's doing it—not thinking about it—that makes you a dyke.

Maybe none of these girls have families or their families are far away. Or maybe they all have jobs, like driving a truck, where they're their own boss and the people they deliver to are scattered up and down the East Coast, far away, in towns without dyke bars.

I squint and concentrate, pretty sure I've seen a few of these girls around. There's a boyish-looking blonde in a down vest, looks like a girl they used to call Ricki. And an olive-skinned Jewish girl who graduated with Renee's class.

"Darlene," the blonde yells.

There she is; my ex-neighbor in the middle of a gaggle of dykes. I shiver like I stepped out of the shower into the cold night. I want to warn Darlene that no one in this town is going to forget a five-foot-ten black girl dressed in a fringed leather jacket and black Harley boots who's hanging out in front of a dyke bar. The back seat of her Mustang is full of books—she's not smart enough to stay inside? Darlene raises her beer, gestures like the leader of the band. The dykes laugh at whatever it is she says, huddle, let snow collect on their shoulders, talk, pass cigarettes and beer through the cold air.

A carload of teenage boys in a Ford with a loud muffler makes a U-turn. Oh, God, I knew it. The women get quiet. The Ford slows to a crawl, the back window rolls down, a ball-capped head yells, "Dykes."

The dykes huddle closer, there's a murmur, then a hush. Two girls walk back toward the building, disappear in the shadows. If I thought the sudden movement wouldn't attract attention, I'd dive into the bushes.

"Very astute," Darlene says loudly, her hands on her hips, a wicked smile on her face, her eyes focused on the boys in the car. "I am *so* in the mood for this. We have a big pot of boiling oil out back." She draws herself up even taller. "You *boys* cold?" She waves her hand dramatically and leans toward the car, gesturing for them to come nearer. The other dykes laugh nervously.

The guy in the ball cap rolls the window all the way down, leans out so his entire upper body is out of the car, and yells, "Fucking lezzies," at the top of his lungs. He fights his buddies when they pull him back in. The Ford takes off. The kid in the cap yells, "You're all a bunch of pussies." I think he means his buddies.

The women stay huddled and talk quietly for a few minutes, then the group loosens up and they laugh louder than before. My heart won't stop beating like it was me who barely escaped the maniac in the ball cap. Why did Darlene call attention to herself like that? I admit, since I was teenager, maybe before that, I've had fantasies—but I could never be dumb or brave enough to actually be a dyke. They're all crazy—the boys in the car and the dykes in the parking lot. I pull the hood of my parka over my eyes and take off before the punks decide to circle back, or one of the dykes decides to go home and catches me hiding behind her car.

Halfway home, the church bells peal twelve times. I listen in front of the rectory. I've stood in front of the priest's house a thousand times, but tonight, filtered through the streetlights and the falling snow, the house seems unreal, like something out of a dream. In a few inches of snow, in two-foot letters on the sloping lawn, I write O-S-T-O-M-Y. Maybe tonight, before the snow melts, those boys will drive by and think someone wrote a dirty word on the Priest's lawn.

Chapter 11

After the operation, I wake up groggy. Dim light from the hallway stings my eyes. My head weighs a ton, heavy and empty at the same time, like a thick-skinned melon with the middle scooped out. I fight to remember the essentials, who and where I am: Sammy's mother, in the hospital, gutted like a fish. I pick up my head. It falls back on the pillow. There's a bitter, stiff smell in my nose. When I turn my head, the smell turns with me. There's an ache in my gut that doesn't feel like it belongs to me. Morphine? My right hand is tied to a board. I pull down the mask covering my nose and mouth. The pillowcase on my cheek feels nice, smooth and flowery, like clean Saturday night sheets at my parents' house. Oh my God, I have a husband.

"Cora Rose." I wake again to a woman's low dreamy voice, a pressure on the top of my head, a hand placing a mask back on my face. "You have to keep the oxygen on while you're in recovery." I open my eyes. The soft voice comes from a middle-aged woman. She looks like a vision of mercy in the glow of the hallway light that frames her. The buttons on her white uniform strain against her breasts. She lifts the mask up a tiny bit and massages Vaseline on my chin and under my nose. She smoothes her hands over my face, adjusting the elastic bands of the mask. The smell of her working body—sweat, talcum powder, spearmint gum—cuts through the antiseptic smell of the room and the acrid sting of oxygen. I try to keep my eyes open to keep her here.

She pats my left hand as she checks the IV in my right hand. "I'm Norma, your nurse. Doctor wants you to rest. I'm going to give you a shot. When you wake up, you'll probably be upstairs in your room."

My room? "In the hospital?"

"In your hospital room, honey." She calls me honey again before she sticks the needle in. Her thick, white-stockinged calves disappear down the hall. The sound of her padding footsteps is reassuring.

I wake and sleep, in and out of a dream of stockinged legs moving back and forth, up and down the hallway. Curves, soft skin over hard pumping muscle, are framed for fleeting seconds by the slit of my open hospital room door. White nurse's shoes, silky calves at eye level, tensing, smoothing out, tensing back, up and down the corridor, in and out of sight, the top half of my view wiped out by a bag of blood hanging on an IV pole. This must be sleep or something like sleep. Reality mixed with morphine dreams of silky legs. Even in this drug-induced twilight I watch myself and worry that I'll get caught staring.

Daylight streams through the window of a smaller room. The calves in the hallway are gone. The oxygen mask is gone. The pain in my gut is back. I touch my head. "My hair." The yell I attempt comes out as a moan. I grab the bed rail, lift myself, fall back onto my pillow, and press the buzzer at my side. "Nurse."

The nurse, a small woman in white pants and loose fitting smock, asks in a routine work-a-day voice, "You have pain?" She's thin, and pale, and old. Too delicate to take care of someone with no hair.

"My hair," I say accusingly.

"Your *hair* will grow back." She raises her eyebrows in irritation.

"They didn't tell me I'd wake up bald." They showed me a movie, an old man, masked surgeons standing over his open belly, sucking blood into a long hose. After the movie, a social worker asked if I understood that they'd be taking the whole thing, my transverse colon, my ascending colon, my descending colon, even the lining of my anus. They let me watch the gory details, showed me a film to let me know I'd be turned inside-out. They could have mentioned the shaved head. "Why did they shave it?" I didn't have brain surgery.

"It's not shaved. It's cut very short so we can keep it clean. I'll be right back." She marches out of the room and marches back in holding a syringe, needle up. "It will grow back, dear." She taps the side of the syringe to get the air out and smiles, more sympathetic now that she's got the standard cure for crybabies and complainers in her hand.

129

She throws a thick gray braid behind her so it won't smack me as she rolls me on my side, and announces, "Little pinch." She takes aim and jabs the needle into my butt like a dart.

"You just worry about getting some rest." She rubs my back with incredibly strong hands. I try to stay mad at *them*, but the drugs and the backrub work fast and I can't remember who *them* is. In two minutes I'm whispering, "Thank you," and drifting off.

A few days later Renee cranks my bed up so I'm in a sitting position. Mom puts a box in my lap, a present.

"What's this?" I shake the box.

"You're a brave girl." Mom kisses my head. I feel her lips on my scalp. Her hair is getting gray. She's getting that snowman shape that short, busty women grow into as they get older. Her face is softer framed in gray. I wouldn't mind looking like her when I'm fifty.

Renee checks the IV tubes. "Patent."

"Patent is good?" Mom frowns, concerned.

Renee looks at the needle in my hand. "Patent is good. No air bubbles, no red lines, no swelling." She checks out the bulky bandages and the drain tubes. "Everything looks good."

Mom smiles, satisfied by Renee's professional assessment. "Open it." She taps the box.

I pull out a big blue canvas bag with 'La Bag' written in big white letters on the side and study it at arm's length. "What it's for?"

"To hide all your ... things when you get out." Mom waves her hand over the array of ostomy care products on my dresser.

Yes, of course, the paraphernalia connected with my ostomy has to be hidden. People won't want to be reminded that there's something disturbingly different about me. "Hide all my stuff for my ostomy and my ostomy bags themselves in a canvas sack that says 'La Bag' on it?" I keep the thing stretched out in front of me.

Renee says, "It's not to drag all over town. It's for home. Are they letting you take care of the stoma by yourself yet?" "Stoma" rolls off her tongue like she's speaking about a broken leg or a displaced shoulder, not the end of my digestive tract.

"They're not letting me suck through a straw by myself yet." Why rush? I'm going to have this freaky appendage spouting my by-products into a plastic bag below my waist for the rest of my life. "I plan on letting *them* take care of it as long as they want to." The doctors don't tell you, nobody tells you how you're supposed to talk about this *thing*, what you're supposed to think of it. The way you talk about your nose or your elbow is different from the way you talk about your vagina or your butt, or the way you think about your nipples. If your colon has been diverted from your anus to your abdomen does the stoma become your asshole? What if someone asks about the surgery? Can this *thing* be talked about in polite conversation with people who aren't nurses? My own mother can't bring herself to say the word ostomy. "I'm going to close my eyes for a minute." I sink into the three pillows propped behind me.

Mom says, "Rest. We'll go find Dad." Dad's in the gift shop picking up "a little something for the boys." He'll do anything to stay out of the main part of the hospital, away from his mutilated daughter.

"You go. I'll sit here and shut up." Renee leafs through the pamphlets on my nightstand. Mom leaves. Renee reads the title of one of the pamphlets out loud, "Sex and My Ostomy." I've read that pamphlet. Basically it gives you permission to have sex "When your doctor gives you the go-ahead. Usually within six weeks of your operation." The only real information is the suggestion that "at first" it may be more comfortable for a female ostomate to "straddle" her partner and that most ostomates can have intercourse with or without the bag glued on.

"Shut up, Renee," I moan.

She raises her hand, says, "Shutting up," and reads to herself. She places a hand lightly on top of mine.

How come Renee hasn't brought up sex and the ostomy before this? We've always talked about sex. Her entire sex life consists of discussing other people's emotions and the mechanics of sex in the abstract. Her own sister with an ostomy should be right up her alley. Is she letting me get used to the changes one step at a time? Is this ostomy thing so gross that even Renee doesn't really want to talk about how it would be to actually have sex with this little piece of gut hanging there, exposed on my belly? Or is she just, for the first time in her life, respecting my privacy? Why haven't I been thinking about sex with this thing?

Because I don't have a lover? Isn't that when people think about sex? When they're not getting any. I've never talked to Renee about the attractions I've had for other girls. Before Joe, when Marie taunted me, Renee never joined in.

What is Renee's real story about being a virgin? Two knocked-up sisters? Too messy, like she jokes? She stills goes to Mass with Mom and Dad and Memere. Maybe the Catholic stories and all the princess stuff she read as a kid are keeping her chaste? Or maybe she's just not that interested. Says she's waiting for love. Why do I find that so hard to accept? She talks and talks about sex, but I still don't understand how she really feels about sex herself. Does anyone ever tell or even know the truth about sex?

Mom walks back in the room with an apologetic smile but without Dad. She takes La Bag off my lap. "I'm sorry. I thought you'd like it. Marie said you'd think it was funny." She bends the straps neatly inside the bag and folds it in half so it will fit back in the box. We sit and stare at each other. I've never been able to tell whose feelings are hurt when it's between me and my mother.

Renee leaves the room and comes back in carrying a tray. She puts the tray of green Jell-O and apple juice on the bed table. "Your doc says you can give it a try. He'll be here in a minute."

"Green Jell-O?" I sip the juice. My gut makes a gurgling noise. It doesn't hurt. It feels uncomfortable, like I've already eaten Thanksgiving dinner and I'm forcing in dessert. Mom and Renee swallow with me, sip for sip.

The doctor walks in. "How'd it go down?" I've never seen this one. He's handsome in his starched white lab coat.

"Fine," Renee says proudly. "She's got bowel sounds." Mom nods, pleased with my achievement. Who knew I could bring my family honor by having bowel sounds?

"Good." The handsome doctor pats my hand mechanically. "You're doing a great job." He smiles broadly at Renee and leaves.

"He looks married," I say.

"Who cares?" Renee bends close to kiss me smack on the lips. "You're a fucking inspiration. Drink your juice."

"Renee!" Mom says. "Watch your language."

An hour after they leave, Joe comes in with Sammy. I feel uncomfortable around Joe. He feels uncomfortable around me too. A few days before the operation, we were arguing in the living room. Joe got pissed and gave me a shove that made me trip over the coffee table. He shocked us both. I landed on my knees in front of the couch. "Jesus," he said, looking less apologetic than stunned. I said, "Go," and watched him walk out the front door while I was still on my knees. He came home late, tiptoed to the door of my little room off the kitchen, and stared in at me for a long time while I pretended to sleep. I felt sorry for him. I know how it is to want to do what's right, and have the stress of trying to be good freak you out, until you end up doing the opposite of what you wanted to do.

He gave me a bruise on my right knee and that complicates his anger. But he shows up with Sammy every day.

We'd be awkward even if Joe hadn't shoved me. He walks in the hospital room, not sure how to react to me as a patient and an estranged spouse, what his duties are to his soon-to-be ex-wife. He forces a smile and carries on like we're going to walk into the sunset as man and wife. Does he believe that I really am leaving him? Do I believe me?

Sammy runs to my bed, his eyes wide, holding a bouquet of daffodils. I was afraid that the hospital would scare him, but he likes the shiny IV pole, the prepackaged food, the pink plastic basin with the matching cup and toothbrush, and his mother contained in a bed with side rails.

I take the daffodils and kiss him. "Thank you, Sammy. I love them."

Joe sticks the flowers in a plastic water pitcher. Sammy changes channels on the TV with a remote control that's attached to the side rail. We don't have a remote at home. "The flowers are from Donny, too." He watches the changing pictures on the screen above the bed as he speaks. "Daddy was crying last night." I freeze and stare at him.

"Hey." Joe rubs Sammy's head. "I told you, sometimes people cry when they're relieved."

"Boys cry," Sammy says, proud to know this fact but too interested in this new toy to look for our reactions.

Joe picks up the plastic container of half-eaten applesauce. He gestures toward the paper cup of black tea and the unopened cup of chicken broth without making eye contact with me. "You're eating?"

"Kind of." I rip the cardboard top off the broth. It tastes good, salty. I take a bite of the applesauce. My gut makes a noise like dishwater going down the drain.

"You okay?" Joe turns pale. "Should I call a nurse?"

"You're making noises, Mommy." Sammy is examining my room-mate's empty, unmade bed with a stethoscope that her nurse left behind. "Can I listen?"

I let him put the shiny circle of the stethoscope over my johnny to one side of the ostomy. He holds the earpieces against his ears and stares straight ahead, concentrating. My gut gurgles loud enough to hear without any special equipment. Sammy's head jerks back. "Wow." He pulls off the stethoscope. "Can I see it, Mommy?" He means my outside plumbing, the stoma, the incisions, the ostomy bag hanging off of my belly. He's seen pictures in a pamphlet from the Ostomy Association. He wants to see the real thing. "Please." His face is wide open. His sandy brown hair, too long, is falling in his big brown eyes.

"Maybe later," I sigh.

To pacify him, I let Sammy lug the blue canvas La Bag, with some extra ostomy stuff in it, up on my bed. Joe tugs Sammy's sneakers off so Sammy can sit at the foot of the bed without getting it dirty. I'm glad to see that the bottoms of his socks are clean. He surrounds the bag with his bare legs. He can sit with the flats of his feet together, his knees pointing in opposite directions, with no trouble at all. He pulls stuff out of the bag, glue in a tube, glue in a spray bottle, "Stomaease" pads, deodorizer, gauze pads, cotton balls, stoma cleaner, Colly Seal retainer rings, extra ostomy bags. He sits on the bed with all the loot in front of him surrounded by his dimpled knees.

Sammy's got Joe's olive skin and his Auntie Renee's wide round eyes. He loves to wear shorts. He's wearing them today. The dimples on his chubby knees move me to tears. Making it through surgery, getting a shot of morphine every four hours, knowing that our family is about to break up, brings my emotions to the surface. I stick my index finger gently into Sammy's knee. His warm skin surrounding the tip of my finger is too much for me. I turn away.

"Why are you crying, Mommy? Does it hurt?"

"Mommy's glad you're here." I turn back and pat his knees. His legs are cold. Joe shouldn't have let Sammy wear shorts, no matter how much he whined. I keep my mouth shut. Joe would say, "It's spring. He gets a kick out of it."

Sammy picks up a Colly Seal ring. It's flat like a rubber gasket. It's sticky on both sides. Soon the ostomy nurse will teach me how to glue it around the stoma, how to make sure the bag stays stuck on the Colly Seal ring.

"Can I glue it on you?"

"No, honey. There's already one glued on me." Is it taboo for Sammy to touch it? They didn't talk about that in the films we watched, didn't mention it in the *You and Your Ostomy* pamphlet, didn't even go near it in the *Sex and My Ostomy* pamphlet.

"Oh." Sammy's disappointed. "What do you do with the old ones?" Sammy likes to collect things.

"Throw them away," Joe says firmly to Sammy and smiles at me.

"Oh." Sammy's disappointed again. "Memere said *maybe* you'd let me see it."

"Old Memere or Memere Mae?"

"Old Memere."

I touch the bag through the johnny. It's empty. "You want to see?"

"Yeah!"

On the bed between Sammy and Joe, I lift my johnny top and pull the ostomy bag away from the Colly Seal ring. First I pull the waist of my johnny bottoms down, just below the ring. Less of me is exposed than if I was wearing a two-piece bathing suit, but we're not at the beach and it feels like I'm walking through the mall in a bikini. Joe and Sammy watch intently like I'm unveiling a piece of great art. The Colly Seal ring surrounds the wet, red, puckered piece that sticks out three-quarters of an inch from my belly and sits on the right side just below my waist. What a strange little part of me. It doesn't look like me. It looks like something the doctors tacked on while I was knocked out.

The incision that runs down the middle of my belly is still covered with bandaging. I bet Sammy would love to see that, too.

"There's the stoma, Sammy." I wipe it off with a "Stomaease" pad.

Joe pulls away but doesn't take his eyes off the thing.

Sammy stares. "Can I touch it?"

I don't answer.

"Can I touch it, Mommy?" Sammy asks again.

Should I let my little boy touch my stoma? It's clean. I just wiped it off. Even Catholics don't have rules about this one. I look at Joe. He shrugs. It's my call. "Go ahead, honey."

Sammy touches the flabby little piece of flesh with the tip of his finger. He looks at me seriously. "Does it hurt?"

I get a chill, move Sammy's finger, and re-tie my johnny. My son just asked me if my ostomy stoma hurts and I don't really know. The area around it where the surgeon cut still hurts. Inside, my whole gut hurts. The stoma itself doesn't hurt; it feels foreign, strange. Does the stoma have feeling or do I just feel pressure on the tissue below it when the little opening is touched?

"Cora Rose, are you okay?" I feel such a rush of compassion in Joe's question.

"Mommy, you won't have to worry about the bathroom anymore." Sammy jumps off the bed. He knows about my bathroom worries? Why wouldn't he? He lived with them his whole life, over four years.

"Go wash your hands, honey," I say.

Chapter 12

A few weeks later, Sammy collects all the ostomy stuff that's been lying on my bedside table and bites his bottom lip in concentration while he packs La Bag. He seems much older, more capable than he did three weeks ago when I left for the hospital. He snaps the canvas flap shut. His hair falls into his wide-open eyes as he looks at Joe expectantly.

"Go ahead, tell Mommy," Joe says indulgently, giving me a sheepish grin. "He's been saving up a joke for you."

I sit on the side of the bed. Sammy climbs on next to me, puts his face close to mine, and grins a big dimpled smile. "Mommy, you're a bag lady." He waits for me to laugh.

My first instinct is to give Sammy and Joe the look I'd give them if Sammy had repeated a swear word he'd heard from his father. I don't. It's obvious from the expression on Sammy's face that he thought this up himself. One of these days, I'll think being called a bag lady is amusing; this is practice for that day. I should be glad Sammy's comfortable enough and bright enough to make a pun about the ostomy. I smile for Sammy. Then I laugh for real when I realize poor Joe and Marie, who has been taking care of Sammy every day while Joe's at work, must have heard this joke twenty times each. Sammy giggles out of control. Joe lifts him off the bed.

When we get home, Joe says, "You're a strong woman, Cora Rose. Really."

I'm home for over a week before my bravery gets boring. Other people get tired of it before I do. On the third day, Sammy whines for me to get his cereal instead of tiptoeing into my little pantry/bedroom with my orange juice in the morning. By the end of the week, Joe asks,

"What's for dinner?" instead of stopping for pizza or slapping together bologna sandwiches himself.

Renee stops by after her shift at the hospital for a cup of coffee, forgets to check out the skin integrity around my stoma, fusses with her own long frizzy hair in the bathroom mirror instead of trying to style the little bit of hair on my head.

After Renee leaves, I go in the bathroom, close the door, and stare at myself in the mirror. Is my hair a pixie or a DA? Renee thinks I should go for the Twiggy look. I'm no Twiggy and I'm definitely letting my hair grow back. I lift my shirt to look at my midriff and the curve at my waist that has appeared since my operation. I can't decide if my new body is average or still a little chubby. I tuck my shirt in. No matter how much your physical appearance has changed, you can look at yourself only so many times a day before you're bored. Even taking care of the plastic bag that pretends to be part of me is getting routine. I know how much glue it takes to stop it from falling off, how to empty it efficiently, how to take care of the skin around it. I know to take a safety pin and prick a tiny hole in the top of the heavy plastic that the bag is made of so that it won't fill up with gas. I know that charcoal, at one-tenth the price, works just as well as ostomy deodorant. I know that all this equipment costs a small fortune and Joe's insurance pays half. Time to go back to work. I'm ready and I need a job.

Everybody needs a job. I find this out making the rounds at every factory and nursing home in town. My jobs have always been lousy, but except for the last few months, I had one. The nursing home where I worked before I got too sick isn't hiring, but they put me on the list. BuyRite might call me. I hit every nursing home, store, and factory within driving distance. Nobody offers me a job. Maybe it's my medical history, or my short hair. Maybe it's just hard to find a job.

Back home, I pound Swiss steak until it looks like hamburger, fry it in butter, put it on the table, and stand with my hands on my hips watching as Joe spoons peas into a crater that Sammy has made in his mashed potatoes. Joe looks up at me, his face noncommittal the way it's been since I got home from the hospital. "No luck?"

"You going to eat, Mommy?" Sammy asks.

"I need some air." I force myself to smile. "I'm going for a walk. I'll do the dishes when I get back."

"What about Spiderman?" Sammy whines.

I want to give him something to whine about, but I check myself and peck his cheek. "I'll be back in time to give you a bath and read Spiderman."

Joe doesn't question why I'm taking a walk instead of eating supper. He goes for a lot of walks himself lately.

I walk fast, faster than I thought a girl and her ostomy could go. I know exactly where I'm going. I don't let myself slow down enough to think about it. I walk straight to the side street with the dyke bar. I'm on a mission, sort of. Ever since I woke up in the hospital with my head shaved, I've been thinking about Darlene and those girls hanging around under the street lamp. If I had been standing on the same side of the street as those girls, I would have either been turned to stone by humiliation or I'd still be running. Maybe feeling like you're part of a group, belonging to something, even if it's being part of a bunch of lesbians that hangs around at a dyke bar, gives you some kind of courage.

I want to see them under those streetlights again.

I stride up to the parking lot with my hands stuffed in my peacoat. What now? Hang around until some dykes come out so I can stare at them and hope that the wind is blowing in my direction so I can breathe in whatever it is that helps them hang tough?

A trailer truck is parked in back of the lot, a ten-wheeler. A woman who drives a ten-wheeler is tougher than I had in mind. Maybe the big truck doesn't belong to any of the women inside. It could just be parked here, belong to a friend of the owner, somebody's brother, somebody's father. Those big trucks cost a lot of money. A girl who hangs out at The Girls Club or any bar in this part of town wouldn't have that much money. Maybe dykes hang around in the same places just to be with each other regardless of how much money they have, or don't have, because there are so few places for them to go. The lot is crowded with cars, but not a dyke in sight. I want to sit down, away from the entrance, but someplace with a good view where I can see if any women come in or out without having to smile at them or look away. Maybe it's too early for them to be hanging around under the streetlights?

I walk to the back of the lot, sit on the truck's running board, and lean on the wheel cap. It's pretty comfortable. I wish I smoked. It's a good moment to be sucking on a cigarette. It would give me something to do, a reason for being here. I exhale an imaginary drag. I'm warm in my jacket. It's probably 50 degrees outside, nowhere near cold enough for my breath to make a puff. "Satisfying life I've got going here," I say to a mound of dirty slush that's begging to have a cigarette butt tossed into it. Talking to myself in the parking lot of a dyke bar. Smoking a phantom cigarette. Living with a man I'm not in love with. Searching for a job I can't find. How can I raise Sammy if no one will hire me? It's humiliating, not even a minimum wage job offer. I rub my palm on the smooth red paint of the cab's door, nice truck. Steady work. Good money. How hard can it be to drive a truck? You don't have to own it, just drive it. I lean forward, stare at the bar, then pull back. The thought that a female trucker is having a beer in that squatty brick building attracts and repulses me.

"Why not?"

I jerk my head in the direction the voice came from, afraid that it might be addressing me. I'm pretty sure I just said, "Diesel dyke," out loud. I hear another, more subdued voice. I strain my ears, squint, peer around the back of the truck, and locate two bodies that go with the voices, standing near a parked car, forty feet away. Two women lean on the car, speaking in low tones. One of them gestures, the other one listens and nods. One of them says clearly, "Fresh garlic and plum tomatoes, gotta be plum." I've been straining to hear a conversation about spaghetti sauce. I know how to make spaghetti sauce. I reach in my peacoat pocket. I've got five dollars and sixty cents.

The women look up when I stroll by them. I nod nonchalantly, like it's my usual Saturday night thing to walk by two dykes on my way into a dyke bar. They nod back.

"I'm going in." I point with my chin to the sign on the door that says, "Two Dollar Cover. No Exceptions."

"Good for you," the one in the knit cap says indifferently.

There are a lot of women inside the bar and no empty seats on Saturday night at 6:59. Dykes must start early. The place is small, but there must be fifty women and three or four guys in here. It's not like I remember it from the time I used the ladies' room on graduation night. It's smaller, dumpier, and it smells like a place where fifty people have been smoking, drinking, and dancing. So many women want to be in a bar like this so early on a Saturday night in such a small town? There must be a lot of out-of-towners.

Where to stand? Where to look? What to do with my hands? Why do I think dykes are tough? Because they didn't run when a carload of idiot adolescents taunted them? Maybe they feel even more apart from the world then the rest of us do. They're dykes. They must know that normal people think they're disgusting. They must care. But they're here, it takes guts to be here.

I stand behind the row of women seated at the bar and try to catch the bartender's eye. I touch my jeans to be sure the bag is lying flat under the denim. A new habit, a tic. I need a glass in my hand, something to focus on. I wish it was Darlene behind the counter instead of the stocky woman with the crew cut who looks like somebody's mean uncle. Are all the bartenders butchy? I hope I don't look like that with my cropped head. I lift my hand limply when she faces my end of the bar, but she doesn't respond. Should I smile at her? I'm not sure how much smiling goes on here. She turns to work the tap behind her and I stare at the thick neck coming out of her starched collar. She must be used to people staring. She turns around and I stop gawking.

I don't recognize a single face. Not that I really want to recognize or be recognized by some girl from high school or the grocery store. It doesn't matter. I brought myself here. I'm going to make myself stand at the bar for at least ten minutes. I'm here to practice how to hang tough, to prove to myself that I can handle any attraction I have to any of these women. By handle, I mean squash. So far, so good: no attraction. I shove my hand deeper into the pocket of my peacoat. The Michelob clock says 7:05. I came in at 6:59. I'm not leaving until 7:09. I lean on the bar and plant myself like a stubborn child. If I knew how to look cool, I'd give it a shot—but I don't have a clue.

My body starts to twitch involuntarily. Three more minutes, I'll be out of here. Maybe this wasn't such a brilliant idea. I learned how to be uncomfortable a long time ago. Most of them have their coats off, but there's a woman near the pool table wearing a peacoat just like mine. Mine is buttoned up to my neck and, I hope, covering the wet blotch on my jeans from sitting on the ten-wheeler. What would I do with it if I took it off? I try to figure out what these women wear—jeans, t-shirts, some skirts, even some heels, stuff you could buy in any department store. All kinds of hair. A shaved head. My grin, when I realize I don't have the shortest hair in the room, is immediately wiped out when a woman with a Farrah Fawcett cut winks in my general direction. She's probably flirting with someone ten feet behind me. I look through her in case she *is* flirting with me. She's real cute. My heart pounds, my palms get sweaty. Pathetic. I make myself look up at her. I'm grinning at her back. Someone's heavily ringed fingers are draped on her shoulders.

I'm the only jerk in the place standing all by myself?

I study my nails. I pounce on the stool as soon as the big-bodied brunette gets up. I stack and unstack a pile of coasters. I count to fifty. In ten more seconds I'll look up at the Michelob clock. If it's 7:09, I'll be able to leave without wasting money on a drink.

"Buy you a drink?" A tall black woman stands in front of me behind the bar.

I stare blankly before it registers. "Darlene?" I say stupidly. "You weren't here a minute ago."

"No, I was parking my car. What'll you have?" She asks, friendly.

"Orange juice, please." Probably not a very dyke thing to order.

She smiles, a generic smile. Three women sitting at the other end of the bar yell for her services at the same time. She leans in to me. "Two for one hour is seven to eight. Everyone's trying to buy a cheap thrill." She hangs on to the counter and says loudly, theatrically, "Friends, women, lesbians. There are only two of us and so many of you. Have patience."

When she says "lesbians," it feels like she rammed a steel rod up my spine. I twitch with the effort of stopping myself from bolting straight

142

up off my stool. The rowdy women at the end of the bar start singing "Candida" off-key. The bartender who looks like somebody's uncle smiles appreciatively at their effort. The women leaning on the bar drinking, minding their own business, keep doing that. Darlene joins a verse of "Candida" before she heads back with my glass of orange juice. I'm hanging around in a place where they toss off the term "lesbian" and sing Tony Orlando songs without shame.

"O.J." She places a beer mug of orange juice in front of me.

"Thanks." I plunk down two dollars. I don't want her to think she has to buy me a drink. She pushes the two bucks back in my direction. She's wearing a red flannel shirt, the kind that everybody wears, hippies, earth mothers, even Renee when she's cleaning the stove. The collar on Darlene's red flannel shirt is turned up, there's a crease down the sleeves, and it's real wool, Eddie Bauer or Lands End, not the cheap cotton polyester stuff that most of us have. She doesn't look out of place, though. She looks like the place belongs to her. I'm pretty sure she graduated from Chicopee High a year or two before Marie should have. She carries herself like she's proud of every inch. I'd never pick her out as a bartender if I saw her on the street. A dyke yes, but not a bartender. Would anyone pick me out as a customer in a dyke bar if they saw me on the street? I'm really not a customer since I'm not paying for the juice. "How do you like your new place?" I ask, pleased with myself for coming up with something to say.

"Expensive. I'm looking for a roommate that won't drive me crazy." She sticks out her hand. "Welcome to my home away from home." Darlene is the second lesbian I've knowingly had a conversation with, and the second one who wants to shake my hand. She's wearing a thick gold ring. The corner of her mouth turns up, letting me know she's amused that I finally turned up here. I shake her hand. Her expression irritates me.

I drink my juice and nonchalantly check out Darlene's customers, as I watch her slow glide up and down the bar. She flirts mildly with everybody. Friendly, confident, aloof, she looks like she's not looking for trouble, but if you fuck with her, watch out. Her legs slice the air when she moves, her butt steady as a rudder, no swaying from side to side.

143

Must be a jock. Amazing what you can decide about a person by the way her ass moves. Her hair is fixed in some kind of short twists. If it wasn't for the swell of her breasts and butt, it would be hard to tell her muscular body from a guy's under her loose-fitting clothes. I try to watch her without getting caught. I pretend to be interested in the Red Sox on the TV.

I feel a tap on my shoulder. A woman in a short skirt with a ton of makeup stands behind me. "You seen Miranda?"

"Me?" I look at my shoulder like it might belong to someone else. "I don't know Miranda."

"Good." She wiggles her shoulders. "You want to dance?" She smells sweet and musky, amazingly good for someone who must have a belly full of booze.

"I think I want to finish my drink."

"You afraid of Miranda?" She puts her hand on my shoulder. I can smell the beer now. I pull away. "What's your name? My name's Cece. Short for Cecelia. Nice to meet you." I don't say a word. "I forgot your name already." She laughs, puts one elbow on the bar, runs her finger down the sleeve of my coat. I let my arm go limp at my side. She cocks her head. "Shy?" I don't believe that she's as drunk as she pretends. "Lemme wear your coat." She unbuttons my collar. "I'm cold." She must be cold, she's wearing a tank top. "You're new here."

"I have to go to the ladies' room." I take a quick step around her.

"I'll come with you," she coos. Her pretty calf eyes scare me. "No one's going to blab to Miranda."

"I like to go to the girls' room by myself," I say over my shoulder firmly, like I own the place, like I used to practice with Stella in the barn. I try to walk without swaying my butt.

I wait in the bathroom line. The familiar sight of a woman's back waiting in line ahead of me relaxes me a little. I liked hearing myself yell over my shoulder in a strong voice like that, like I belong and Cece was intruding. She did scare me away from my place at the bar. So what? I sounded confident. First you've got to sound like a girl who doesn't give a shit. I wonder how my hair looks.

At the bathroom door, I come face to face with a sign, "DYKE-

144

ROOM," in day-glo purple paint in the place where "Ladies" or a stick figure in a skirt should be. The paint is fresh and it's glowing under a fluorescent light. There's only one toilet and the room is very small. Going into a dyke bar doesn't mean anything, going into a DYKEROOM seems more serious. Men use the men's room, women use the lady's room, dykes use the dykeroom.

I pull down my jeans. I feel claustrophobic, locked in the confessional with my pants down, exposing myself and my ostomy, the Priest about to open the shutter. If I still went to confession I'd have to confess, "Bless me Father, for I used the DYKEROOM."

"Oh my God." I panic and stand without pulling up my jeans. Tears run down my cheeks. Fear is always waiting right under my skin, so familiar that if it wasn't so intense at this moment, I'd be bored with it. But I'm not bored. I'm scared stiff to be alone in the dykeroom. Scared silly. I laugh. "Fear is funny. I'm a funny girl," I say out loud to the back of the door with the DYKEROOM sign glowing on the other side. The sign is funny? I'm funny with my pants down, freaking out in the girls' rooms, spooked by confession memories, blowing my nose, patting my wet cheeks with toilet paper? My bag is funny, hanging innocently, ready to be of service, minding its own business? I can't tell what to laugh at anymore.

There aren't any paper towels left in the dispenser. What kind of a place lets the dispenser run out of paper towels? I'm not a dyke just because I came here. It's not like I had sex with any of these girls. What have I done? Drink orange juice in a bar. Look at some women drinking beer, watching TV, and singing off-key. Now I can leave. I'm not ten years old, this isn't confession. I don't have to wait for penance or the Priest to say "Go in peace." I didn't come in here to repent my fantasies. I came here to dispose of them. I'll find a job in the morning, or next week at the latest. Something will come up. I'll get out of the DYKE-ROOM and that will be the end of The Girls Club.

I pull up my pants. I don't really need the bathroom. It can wait until I get home. There's not even a mirror. My eyes must be red. I splash cold water on my face.

"You O.K?" Someone knocks on the door impatiently. "You all right in there?"

145

"No." I'm sick and tired of lying about being all right. "Be out in a second."

I edge my way sideways through the crowded room, stop at the exit, and glance at the bar before I slide out the door. Darlene, lining up glasses in front of the tap, doesn't catch my nod goodbye. The Michelob clock says 7:27. I've just spent twenty-eight minutes in a lesbian bar. I'm walking out on my own two feet. I can do anything; find a job, bring up a kid on my own.

Chapter 13

After two months of filling out applications and waiting in cubbyholes to be told I didn't get the job, I go for free counseling for women in transition at the community college. I want them to help me get a job as a nurse's aid or as a warehouse worker. I worked a temporary job, second shift in a warehouse moving pallets of paper and drums of rivets. It wasn't so bad. The counselors at the Women in Transition Program aren't open-minded about careers that involve forklifts and minimum wage.

Ms. Blake, in a blue suit with a brown stain on the left lapel that's only partially covered by a button that reads "The Best Man for the Job May Be a Woman," tells me that what today's woman needs is an education and a good self-image. She asks me to write down my most admirable traits and has me describe my fantasy job. She looks up from the neat stack of papers on her desk. "I see that you've had a variety of jobs. Which has been your favorite so far?"

Favorite is not a word I'd use to describe any job I've had so far.

"Nurse's aid." I don't tell Ms. Blake that access to so many bathrooms and working three-thirty in the afternoon until midnight, which gave me quiet days alone with Sammy, were the *aspects* that made it the job I disliked the least.

Ms. Blake has me take all kinds of tests that don't seem to have anything to do with anything. She decides that I should become a nurse. The tests show that I have an aptitude for it. *Of course* it's my decision. Nursing is subsidized.

"It's hard to get into the nursing program, but we give special consideration to women over forty, minority women, low-income women, and men."

147

She can see. I'm white, female, in my early twenties; the operation and the Dreaded Bowel Disease couldn't have aged me that much. I don't look over forty. That leaves low income. Ms. Blake has never asked about my income. I never thought of myself as low-income. I've always thought of myself as middle-income, maybe low-to-middle income, very low-to-middle income.

"I'm visibly low-income?"

"Pardon?" Ms. Blake is a petite, white, woman with shiny dark hair that hangs very straight at her shoulders. Except for the stain on the lapel of her suit, she's neat and clean. Visibly middle-income or doing a good imitation.

"What makes you think I'm low-income?"

Ms. Blake's hair moves in a unit as she leans across the table toward me. "I'm terribly sorry. I don't know why I made such an assumption. My mistake."

I can tell by the way Ms. Blake has asked her questions that she prides herself on objectivity. She just can't stop herself from calling them as she really sees them. I want to push Ms. Blake to explain. What exactly am I doing to give away my station in life? But she's a nice woman, trying to help me find a way to make a living; and she looks really embarrassed, so I let it slide.

I work on my financial assessment. Ms. Blake shows me the graph. There I am, a little dot. Even with Joe working overtime, with my medical bills and Sammy as a dependent, as a family we're a little blip below the low-income line. No mistake. At least we're high low-income. Where would my little dot land if Ms. Blake took Joe's income out of her equation?

I don't mind being a woman in transition on Tuesdays. Tuesdays are for practical counseling, stuff to figure out what I need to do to better myself so I can land a decent job. Thursdays, Ms. Blake wants to get inside my head. Thursday is "Empowerment" day. Ms. Blake seems to think spilling your guts to someone you barely know is empowering. She's especially interested in my ostomy, the history of my "Difficulties." My medical history is part of my file.

"And emotionally, it seems to me, as children who went through childhood," she pauses between phrases, "especially adolescence, with a chronic disease, we get an enormous amount of insight and personal strength from dealing with . . ." she waves her hand, searching for a word, ". . . hardship."

We? I scrunch my eyebrow, knowing better then to ask about Ms. Blake's hardships. "Teaches you to put up with a lot," I say.

The fourth Tuesday afternoon we spend together, Ms. Blake says, "Cora Rose, if you want nursing, it's time to try for pre-placement." We sit at a desk in her office to fill out Chicopee Community College School of Nursing pre-placement and financial aid forms. They want to know my income, my husband's income, my parents' income, my five-year-old's income. Unearned income, stocks, bonds, real estate. Ms. Blake explains the meaning of the word annuity before I check no. They ask if I have any source of income, any savings or other resources I haven't declared.

"Does this mean, am I hiding any money?"

"Yes. Basically."

I'm hiding $2,480.00. I've been saving almost twenty dollars a week for over two years, before the surgery when I was making money to hide. Sealing it in envelopes, one hundred dollars a pop, folding the envelopes in half, stuffing them in a tampon box in the back of my underwear drawer. The tampon box is full.

I can't believe they ask if I'm hiding money. I'd be a jerk to claim it. There must be other people hiding money if the financial aid people ask the question, printed right there on the page. Where do other people hide it? In Swiss banks? How much money can there be out there stuffed in tampon boxes? I check no—no hidden money.

That night, I toss around in my cot, having a bad dream about Ms. Blake. She's disgusted, disappointed with me. It's not clear why or how, but she's on a rampage in my house, grabbing milk out of the refrigerator, spilling it on the floor, pulling Lincoln Logs out of Sammy's toy chest, throwing them around the living room. When she slams my underwear drawer shut, I wake up with a start.

Ms. Blake is not with me. Alone in my pantry/bedroom, I kick at my sheets. Who the hell is Ms. Blake to be disappointed in me? Somebody who's making a living off of the fact that some people can't get work and need help to go to school. How come she gets to call me Cora Rose and I have to call her Ms. Blake? She's not that much older than I am.

I sit up in bed. Oh God, Oh shit, please Mary, Joe hasn't gone in my underwear drawer, has he? Why should he? I swing my bare feet onto the cold floor, walk to the stairs that lead to the second floor, where Sammy and Joe are sleeping. I hold my breath and place my feet gently as I walk up the stairs, but the steps still groan under me. I stop at the top to listen. Joe is snoring. The door to his bedroom, my old bedroom, is open. He's curled on his side, facing the dresser, his knees pulled up, bottom arm cradling his head. Like Sammy—he sleeps like Sammy. I kneel in front of the dresser, pull open the middle drawer, and fish around in the dark. The tampon box is in the back of the drawer right where I left it. I pull the box out and creak the drawer shut.

Click! The light is on. I freeze and clutch the tampon box to my chest.

"What the hell?" Joe says in a sleepy voice.

"Tampons," I answer quickly, out of breath from fear.

"You scared me. Why don't you keep that stuff downstairs?"

I have no answer for that. My underwear drawer stayed in the bedroom I abandoned and so did the tampon box where I hide my secret stash of getaway money.

Back downstairs I shove the tampon box under my cot. I feel like shit. I'll never fall back to sleep now. Didn't I work for this money? Clean, cook, trade babysitting with Marie so Joe and I wouldn't have to pay for someone to watch Sammy when we were both working? I haven't had a job for a few months. So what? Joe spends money, twenty bucks a week easy, on pot and beer. He goes out with Fletcher at least once a week. Thinks it's his right to go out whenever he wants to, and my responsibility to stay home with Sammy when he does. Why should I have to explain my sexuality, something I'm not sure of myself, to him? It's not like he's the perfect husband with his stupid pot and band equipment all over the house. I'm not going to tell Ms. Blake a damn thing about the money. I'm not telling anyone. Not even Renee. Who'd believe a low-income Woman in Transition could save $2,400? I better get a job soon or I'm going to have to start stealing the blood money from my tampon box.

I wait for morning, worrying about whether a job will boost me up over the edge so I can't get financial aid.

The next day I ask Renee, "What's pre-placement testing for?"

"Weeds out sure losers." Renee chomps down on a raw carrot. "So the school doesn't have to waste the full placement test on everyone who wants to apply."

"Thanks. You'll be the first one to know if I'm a sure loser."

She's the only one who knows I'm applying to nursing school. The only one I know who's been through it. Even slouched on my couch, she looks good in her crisp white uniform with the shiny "Renee LaBarre R.N." ID winking on her breast pocket. I want a shiny pin like that, "Cora Rose LaBarre R.N." I want to bring home $287.00 a week.

"You're going to make the perfect nurse." Renee shakes the carrot for emphasis. "Smart. Tough on the outside. Cream puff in the middle."

The pre-placement exam reminds me of the quizzes we used to get in catechism class. The questions are situational and the answers they want are obvious. Renee taught me how to answer these kinds of questions a long time ago: "Pretend you're a very good girl. Answer like she would."

I ask Ms. Blake, "How can they tell by this stuff whether you're likely to pass the placement tests or not?"

"They just want to make sure that the individuals who are offered the placement test have a reasonable chance of passing."

I try again. "What answers would stop a person from having a reasonable chance of passing the placement tests?"

Ms. Blake stops shuffling papers and looks me dead in the eye. "You'll get to take the placement tests."

I'm starting to like Ms. Blake. She's helping my self-esteem.

I make the first cut and wait. Take the placement test and wait. Take the physical and wait. Get letters from my doctor stating I'm physically able to endure nursing school. And wait. By early summer I'm conditionally accepted into the fall semester of the Chicopee Community College School of Nursing.

One of the conditions is an essay to be sent to Sister Mary Margaret Donaldson, Professor of Psychology, entitled *Inspiration, Aspiration, Vocation—Why I Want to Become a Nurse*, no more than 300 words. Sister Mary Margaret's instructions stress, "The essay is not to prove the potential student's writing skills, but is one way of determining motives and intentions of those applying."

I haven't written anything since high school. I start out with the truth. I have no skills, nursing school is cheap—free with financial aid— and I need a job that can support me and my son. The truth makes a bad essay that won't impress Sister Mary Margaret. I don't know Sister Mary Margaret Donaldson. I've never been friendly with any nun, but I have my nun prejudices. On the grounds of the assignment's title, I decide Sister Mary Margaret is a bleeding heart not a knuckle rapper, and write about my roommate in the hospital, Glory.

Cross-legged on top of my cot in the middle of the afternoon, the pad balanced on my thigh, in black ink I write *Inspiration, Aspiration, Vocation—Why I Want to Become a Nurse*, by Cora Rose LaBarre. Renee has impressed on me that nursing school is part science, part psycho-social, part bullshit. I lay on the psycho-social bullshit thick for Sister Mary Margaret. Tell her about the time I spent in the hospital getting the ostomy. Tell her about my roommate, Glory, with the wicked neurological disease that made her twitch and jerk. I write about Glory's ostomy, her chronic neck and shoulder pain. How interested I became in making Glory more comfortable, what drugs she was taking, what her dietitian and physical therapist were doing for her. How my general concern for Glory got me interested in becoming a nurse because it seemed like the nurse was the one with the big picture of what was going on with her care. I don't write about how she coaxed me into talking about Stella by asking about the first person I ever kissed. Not the first boy, the first person. How she made me close the door so we could talk in private. How none of the drugs worked and her twitching just got worse and worse. About how easy it was to talk to her because I knew she was dying.

Ms. Blake makes me revise the essay three times before I send it off to Sister Mary Margaret. She says, "It's best not to overstate the facts." The dramatic part, the lie, where Glory tells me that my compassion and caring has changed her life, is revised right out.

An acceptance letter to Chicopee Community College School of Nursing arrives in the mail. I stash the big white envelope under my cot. Joe doesn't know I've been seeing Ms. Blake, doesn't know about nursing school. I didn't want to tell him unless I got in. I still don't want to tell him. Don't want to give him any information I don't have to. We're being easy with each other most of the time, considerate even, except for once in a while when Joe blows up and takes off for a few hours; but I'm not sure what he wants, who's going to leave the apartment, who's getting the '66 Chevy that probably won't pass inspection, who's getting the '74 Mazda that still has a year of payments. How's he going to be when push comes to shove? I should know him well enough to know how he's going to be, but I don't. I'm not even sure how I'm going to be. I don't care much about the stuff we own. If he wants my parents' old hand-me-down couch, he can have it. If he wants Fletcher's old flowered chair, he can have that, too. All I want is Sammy.

I climb into bed and reopen the big white envelope. It's filled with papers, a bunch to sign, a bunch of instructions about where and when to report. Classes start in September, a couple of months away. I scan the half-inch thick pile of forms, stick them back in the big white envelope, and shove it back under my bed. I got into nursing school; now what? Sometimes Joe seems all right. Sometimes I can tell that he's barely keeping a lid on. One minute, I think my feelings are mine and none of his business. The next minute, I think not coming clean with Joe is the real abomination. This is where I always get hung up. I'm not leaving because I think about girls sometimes. I'm leaving because I'm not in love with Joe. He doesn't have a right to my bad thoughts.

I feel sorry for him. He must be as lonely as I am. It's awful, living in the same house with someone after you've split up. Don't think about it. Think about something else.

I think about Glory and cry. I wonder if Glory is dead. She probably died in the hospital. She had some kind of stroke just before I left. I never said a proper goodbye. Sent her a card once. I could call the hospital, but I haven't. I pull up the shade in the pantry's tiny window and look out at the moon shining over the dark stand of poplar trees in the distance. No one would have called me if she did die. We were people thrown together, like war buddies; never traded phone numbers, never said we'd write.

Glory's not why I'm crying. I'm lonely. I don't want to start sleeping with Joe again, but I'm missing him because I know I'm leaving soon, or he's leaving soon. Somebody better leave soon. Poor Sammy, he's not why I'm crying either. I'm just tired of waiting for my life to start, school to start, my body to heal. Big tears run down my cheeks. I lie on my back with my eyes closed, feeling sorry for myself. I lie like this and cry until I feel like I'm underwater. I blow my nose, and lie here, submerged. I don't hear Joe walk into the room. Don't know that he's kneeling by my bedside until he strokes my forehead and whispers, "It's okay, baby. You made it. It's okay."

I keep my eyes closed and let him stroke my head. He barely fits in the narrow space between my bed and wall. He's a big man, even his hands are heavy. I try to remember the last time we made love. His hands felt too heavy on me then, but now the weight of them feels just right, gentle, soothing. I don't care if he has no idea what I'm crying about. He's stroking my head. I'm glad. It feels good. No one has stroked my head like this in years. Renee stroked my head in the hospital; so did Sammy, so did Joe for that matter. This stroking in the middle of the night is different. His touch is firmer, slower. His fingers squeeze my scalp, gently. He used to touch me like this? Seems so long ago. His hand lingers at the end of each stroke. Sex? After all this time? I could say no thank-you. Send him away. Say I want to sleep now. Say no.

He could leave without any more bad feelings between us. I don't say no. I want him here stroking my head, taking his time, waiting for me to decide.

We haven't made love in many months, maybe a year, maybe more. What does this mean? Does he think we might get back together? No. He knows that's not what I want. I don't even think it's what he wants anymore. What he wants is for me to turn into the woman he thought

I was when we got married. I don't want to be his lover. He doesn't want the real me that way anymore, either. He knows as well as I do that we're not going to find what we want in the same bed. But here he is, kneeling at my bedside, stroking my head, whispering in the night, telling me he's glad I survived, glad I'm in one piece, glad I can eat whole food. Stroking my head so nice. He needs to be gentle. We need something gentle between us. Something final and gentle.

It makes me want a lover. Makes me want to make love, not just make up stories about sex and passion, make love, right now. I could have sex right now. Do something besides cry in my bed. Something hot. With Joe? Passion to help us stay together? No. Passion to fill the waiting and the space between us? Life's not supposed to be a hole you fill up and wait in.

It won't last, not in the long run. We'll go back to the way it's been soon enough. Say hello, maybe even smile when we pass each other in the kitchen, but stay miles apart. My mind races as he touches me, but my body is remembering him, remembering his touch. Joe, the only person I've ever made love with.

He's kissing my neck and I realize that my hand is in his hair kneading the back of his scalp, even as I'm thinking: This will only make it harder. But my body is moving.

I'm thinking how different we are, how much we've withheld, how little we've teased out of each other. Strange; I let go more with Glory in the solarium than I ever did with Joe in the bedroom. I've never trusted him enough to really let go. Never trusted myself enough, either. It's going to be over too soon. His rhythm's not my rhythm. He's going to be breathing heavy in a few seconds, finished a few minutes later, and I'm going to be angry. Angry for not saying no. I can still say no. I'm thinking this and warming to his touch. Allowing his fingers to stop on my face, trace my features slowly. Matching his gaze in the not fully dark room. Who is this man? I thought I would never again be with him this way. Maybe never be with any man, anyone, ever again this way. Seeing the slit of moon in the tiny open window just behind his head, I imagine the moon laughing at us. Laughing at us but still shining on us the way it shines on any other couple. I think the moon is right to shine on us. To hell with it. I'm going to say goodbye as I damned well please.

Joe cries and whispers, "It's going to be all right, baby." It's been a long time since he's called me that. "You made it. You made it, baby. You're alive."

I kiss him on the forehead. He climbs in bed with me. I don't tell him to go. I move with the weight of his sincerity and feel my own longing. There's no desperation in his touch as he strokes me, only relief. He moves his hands over me and sobs, "Thank you for staying with me while you were sick." With no irony, without a shred of sarcasm.

He strokes the inside of my thigh, then pulls back. I like the slow steady climb to passion we're taking. We've never made love this way, building to a sweet fall. This is what I would have chosen when we were in love, if I had known enough to choose, if I had been in love. I pull him close to me.

"Does it hurt? Will I hurt you?" Sweet Joe.

"I don't think so. I'll let you know."

I remember he liked noise when we made love. He liked the noises I made and so did I. I like my own voice, my own heavy breath and high-pitched whimpers. I understand them. I exaggerate my heavy breathing. He kneads my breast slowly. I let out a moan. The noises I make turn me on and tease more noise out of me. He takes my face in his hands, "You're beautiful. You're so beautiful."

I look at his face. "You're beautiful, too."

We're really moving now. I know how to move for him, but I don't play off his desire. I play off my own desire. I feel him moving on me. I think he is even more alone than I am. I pull him into me. Me on top of him, not sure how I got here. I surround him with my arms, my legs, my desire. He's saying something, but I'm not sure what. I feel exhilarated, alive. I lie on him, my body heaving, my mind rejoicing, I'm leaving, I'm leaving. I make love with my eyes wide open, stare at the shelves that used to hold canned peas and corn. I wonder if Joe's eyes are open too.

I haven't thought about the stoma the whole time we've been doing it, haven't worried about the bag breaking or falling off, but now that

I'm lying on top of him, both of us spent, I worry. I squeeze my eyes shut and hold him.

We've been belly to belly most of the time with me on top. He went nowhere near the ostomy, not with his hands, not with his mouth, not with any part of his body, but his belly definitely has been pushing against mine. I wish I'd taken the bag off. Taped a four-by-four gauze bandage over the stoma site like the ostomy nurse in the hospital said I could do. Like I talked about with Glory. "Find a good lover and buy a lot of gauze." That's what Glory said.

"You O.K?" Joe asks.

"I'm fine," I lie. I get off of him like a helicopter, straight up. "Let me see." I feel the ostomy bag. Still stuck tight to the Colly Seal ring around my stoma. I run my palm across his belly, damp with his sweat and mine. Warm and hairy. "You're okay too."

"That doesn't matter to me," he answers.

"I know. Thanks. It matters to me." I wish I could say, "I love you, Joe," and he'd know exactly what I mean.

We lie next to each other for a long time without speaking.

Finally I turn to him. "This is the last time. I'm sorry, Joe. It's not your fault."

"Fault?" He sits up on the edge of the cot. The question in the word, the implication that he had not thought of fault, his or mine, makes me sit up and put my hand on his shoulder.

"We both know how it is." He sits up on the edge of the cot. It sags under his weight. With his back to me, he says, "Goodbye."

Chapter 14

"Never fuck a man you're breaking up with unless he's wearing a rubber." Marie blows this sisterly advice through the phone lines with the exhaled smoke from the cigarette she just lit. "When was your last period?"

It's been three weeks since I slept with Joe. I think it's been two weeks since my period should have started. I stand at the kitchen sink in my terry cloth bathrobe, holding the phone with my shoulder, shaking salt on the counter. Her tone, so rat project, and her logic, so right, pisses me off. "I thought Eddie doesn't allow you to smoke." I make tiny piles of salt with my baby finger. It's seven a.m. on Saturday. I'm lucky Marie's talking to me at all at this hour.

"*Allow?*" She barks out a laugh. "We're talking about Joe. He sleeping with anyone else?" She takes a drag that sounds like she's inhaling through a ten-foot straw.

"Doubtful." I push all the little piles of salt into one big pile.

"Ask him. You're a big girl. Take control."

"Like you've got such a good handle on your own life."

"I took control at fourteen, too young, too stupid," she says philosophically. "Mom should have locked me in the basement. You got the opposite problem. You just let things happen to you. Joe wouldn't be the first man to cheat on his girlfriend with his wife."

I sweep the mound of salt into the sink. "Why did I call you?"

"For a reality check," she answers matter-of-factly, using one of Renee's favorite terms. "You've had it easy. Joe's a good guy. If you don't want him, don't fuck him." The edge is back in her voice. "By the way, if it wasn't for Eddie, Donny wouldn't have a decent pair of sneakers and the rent wouldn't have gotten paid last month. You already got one kid. You end up pregnant and without Joe, your dreams of a starched white uniform and a house in Northampton are shot." She exhales loudly.

"Just because you ended up on welfare, stealing milk from the station where you pump gas illegally, doesn't mean that I'm going to."

The phone slams in my ear.

The plain truth of what she said rings in my head. I don't want another child; don't want to feed it, don't want to grocery shop for it, don't want to clothe it, care for it, or get up at night for it. I don't want to love it; but mostly I don't want to be poor, and mess up nursing school for it. If I end up pregnant a second time, I am out of control. I wish Renee had been home when I called. I bite my thumbnail and stare out the window.

"What'sa matter, Mommy?" Sammy, sleepy-eyed, pads toward me on his footed pajamas. "Who were you talking to?"

"Mommy was on the phone with Auntie Marie. Did I wake you up? Come here, honey." I kneel and hug Sammy. "You want pancakes?"

"Am I going to be late for school?" His face is tight with anxiety.

"Sweetheart, I told you last night; nursery school doesn't start for two more weeks."

"I don't know the bus driver. What if he forgets me?"

"Mommy's going to make sure you get on the bus." I brush the hair out of his eyes. "Then a few minutes later the bus will stop in front of the big building where Donny lives. Auntie Marie will make sure that Donny sits right next to you on the bus. I promise."

I take Sammy shopping for school clothes, buy him Spiderman underwear, and blow a dollar at McDonald's. He picks at the hamburger and looks worried. I eat a couple of his French fries. "You're going to like school. Donny loved nursery school. He'll be in the same building. You might get to play with him on the playground at recess. You'll make lots of friends. The bus monitor and the teachers will take good care of you."

Sammy smashes a French fry on the table with his finger. "How come you didn't get a cheeseburger?"

"I'm trying to save a little money, in case we get a new place to live, maybe closer to Donny." I let him mangle the French fry that he has, but fold the paper down on the little square bag to save the rest of them.

"I don't want to go anywhere without Daddy." He lays his head on his hands and looks up at me from the pink Formica tabletop shaped like an airplane wing. Joe and I haven't talked to him about breaking up, but for the last few weeks we've gotten louder when we talk to each other about it. We've both taken Ann Landers' advice and told Sammy it's not his fault that his Mommy and Daddy argue. That doesn't take away the fact that his world is closing in on him.

"I know you don't, honey. Mommy and Daddy both love you very much. I'm a little scared about going to school, too. But we'll both like it. You'll see." I rub his cheek. "Eat your hamburger. Mommy's going to fill out a job application." I don't explain to him what an application is and he doesn't ask. He's got enough on his mind. He eats half his hamburger while I talk to the guy in the paper hat.

The manager likes me because I'm over eighteen and want to work nights and weekends. But the two-week training period is during weekdays. I'll have to start tomorrow if I want to finish before Sammy and I start school. I slide back onto the seat next to Sammy. "Mommy's going to work at McDonalds." I try to sound enthusiastic.

"Can I come?" His legs swing below his seat. His eyes shine with the prestige of having Mommy work at McDonalds.

"No, but you can play with Donny while Mommy's in training."

"Cool. Can you bring us hamburgers?"

"Maybe."

I snap Sammy into a seatbelt. Will Marie agree to watch Sammy while I learn to flip burgers? Are hamburgers part of the fringe benefits? I flinch at the thought of apologizing to Marie. Memere's too old to watch Sammy every day for two weeks. Mom works during the day. Renee works all hours. I shouldn't have baited Marie with that crack about welfare. She deserves an apology whether or not she babysits for me. If she won't take Sammy, I'm screwed. It's just her big mouth; I can't stand her big mouth.

I stop at the station where Marie works for two bucks an hour, under the table. I'm hoping that apologizing while she's working will soften it if she has a bad reaction. She's nowhere in sight, but Fletcher is. He works here full time now, legally, so he makes almost three bucks an hour. He smiles at Sammy and me and scratches his head while he puts six dollars' worth of gas in my tank even though I asked for three. He looks younger since he went to court a second time for possession of marijuana and his lawyer made him cut off the ponytail.

"That'll be three dollars, Ma'am." He leans over me. "Hey, buddy." He takes five nickels out of his change apron and puts the coins in Sammy's palm. "How much money you got there?"

"Five nickels." Sammy's eyes get big.

"How many gum balls does that buy?"

"Five." Sammy turns his wide eyes on me. "Can I?"

"Yes."

He climbs out of the car and runs inside the station to the gumball machine.

"Only one goes in your mouth," I yell after him and turn back to Fletcher. "How's probation?"

"Sucks. No drugs. No shady characters."

I know from Renee, that Fletcher had only one joint on him. She thinks he was harassed because of his long hair and rusty van. He does seem to get pulled over a lot. His court-appointed lawyer said he'd get him off without probation, but he was wrong. Renee went to court with Fletcher. She thinks the judge was irritated by Fletcher's lack of discretion more than the fact that he had a joint in his glove compartment. The real worry is that the police will pick up on Fletcher's failure to register with the draft board.

He holds his hands up. "That's it for me. Done. I'm too good-looking for jail." He looks at me suspiciously. "You don't take drugs, do you lady?" "Fletcher" is stitched in white on the pocket of his one-piece blue uniform.

I shake my head. "Saving my money, so I can leave my husband." Fletcher takes a half-step back, shuffles his feet, and looks at the ground. "You don't think I'm doing the right thing, do you?" We both watch Sammy through the glass front of the station. He's talking nonstop to the old guy who used to own the place but manages it for BP now, sits all day on a green metal chair, and gets up once in a while to sell a bag of chips or a candy bar.

"Right for who?" Fletcher asks quietly.

"Me, Sammy, Joe."

He rubs the back of his neck. "Joe's my best friend. You really want to know what I think?"

I nod, not sure if I really want to know, and say, "Yes."

"Okay." He folds his tall body and squats by the car. "I think it's killing Joe and it's going to be hard on Sammy."

"We should keep fighting?" I can't keep the frustration out of the question even though I pressed him for his opinion. "Bring Sammy up in a house full of tension?"

"Life is hard. That's all I'm saying."

"We don't belong together."

Fletcher looks at me wearily. "Yeah?" His expression shocks me. In his quiet way, he's angry. I've disappointed him. A guy on probation, estranged from the family who raised him; a father who rarely makes child support on time, he's a hard man to disappoint.

I rub my own neck. "You think we should stay married?"

He folds his hands on the car window. His expression softens. "Joe's a complicated guy. His old man took off." He lowers his eyes. "Doesn't mean you should stay married. Some of us . . . can't." He tilts his head and shrugs.

"I care about Joe," I say defensively. I let my head fall onto the plastic upholstery of the Chevy's seat.

He gives me a look I don't want to understand. "Joe's a family man. It's a strain."

I can't bear to hear about the strain on Joe. "Looks like you're kneeling for confession," I say, way too offhand. "Can I tell you my sins?"

Fletcher grins and, relieved to go along with the change in conversation, squats next to the open car window. "Sure, I'm an ordained grease monkey." He rubs the stubble on his chin.

"I slept with Joe." I check out his reaction. He doesn't have one. Joe already told him.

162

"That's easy." He crosses himself. He doesn't know that he's supposed to start at his forehead, not his shoulder, when he makes the sign of the cross. "You're both forgiven."

"And I was mean to Marie on the phone this morning."

"Because she's marrying Eddie?"

"What?"

"Shit." He hits the window frame with his head. "I thought you knew. She told me last night."

"She's *marrying* him?"

"He just made supervisor. Will never cheat on her." He pulls at a hole in his earlobe where his silver stud used to be. "Never be arrested for drugs."

"Jesus Christ." I lean back again. "She should have married you." Even as I'm saying this, I know it's a shaky statement at best.

"You and me got similar problems." He sighs. "I don't want to be married either."

"Five thousand Hail Marys for both of us." I glance at Sammy, who is still inside the station, using most of his body to animate some story he's telling the old guy in the green chair. "Think that'll straighten us out?"

"Maybe. I know more about sin than penance."

I pull some tissue out of the glove compartment. I want to ask him to take care of Joe, but he's being sympathetic and I don't want to piss him off again. "Sex." I say with disgust. "How many mistakes do I have to make before I smarten up?"

"Sex can get you in a lot of trouble." He taps the window frame lightly with his knuckles. "No doubt about it." He sighs, an old man's sigh.

"Can I ask you something? Why didn't you go to Canada?"

"I was on my way. I got lazy, and stoned, and just feeling too sorry for myself to move on. Then your sister got pregnant." He forces a smile. "My kid's an American." He shakes his head. "Donny and Joe, they're my family. And Renee." He adds shyly, almost apologetically. "You and Marie, too, I hope."

Too sorry for himself to move on; I can't think of how to respond to this. I've never thought of him as family, exactly. We smile at each other awkwardly.

Sammy comes back to the car, rolling ten gumballs in his pocket. "Want one, Uncle Fletcher? Want one, Mom? Mr. Rouseau gave me five more nickels. I'm going to give a gumball to every kid at the bus stop."

Halfway home, Sammy, who has been quiet and seems content enough with his pocketful of gumballs, looks up. "Maybe if Daddy goes to school too everything will be all right."

"No, honey." I take one hand off the wheel and brush the hair out of his eyes. "Daddy doesn't want to go back to school. It wouldn't make everything all right if he did."

He turns his head to the window and doesn't look at me or say one more word for the rest of the drive.

A half hour after we get home, Marie's car pulls in our driveway.

"Donny!" Sammy yells.

"Sammy!" Donny yells as he opens the front door. He flings his arms around Sammy's chest and gives him a bear hug that lifts Sammy off the floor. Sammy squeals in delight.

Donny keeps squeezing until Sammy yells, "Mommy, make him put me down."

Donny's a tough little guy. Dad calls him 'All boy' even though Donny gets more macho from Marie than from Fletcher. How long until he realizes that boys aren't supposed to hug other boys?

"Can I show him the Spider Maker?" Sammy asks. Before I answer, he pulls two old pillowcases filled with snap-on plastic spider legs, spider bodies, spider eyes, and snap-together spider webs from behind the couch.

"Cool." Donny, impressed, takes the biggest bag away from Sammy, and rummages around inside it. He's got Marie's temperament, but he's tall and skinny with his father's bony features. The older he gets, the more he looks like Fletcher and the more he acts like Marie.

Sammy, short and stocky, looks a lot like Joe, with the same wide face and bright eyes, but he's not going to inherit Joe's height or his straight shiny hair. He's going to be a stocky LaBarre with Renee's and

164

Marie's frizzy hair. When Sammy was a baby, he looked just like Joe. Now he looks as much like Marie as he does Joe. Funny, my son looks more like Marie than her own kid does.

"Take that stuff up to Sammy's room," Marie commands the boys, flops down on the couch, and looks at me. "Where'd you find that junk?"

"Tag sale, fifty cents."

Donny drags both treasure bags through the living room, up the stairs. It irritates me that Donny has both bags of loot. Sammy follows him up the stairs happily. I keep my mouth shut and head for the kitchen. I wasn't expecting Marie to drop by before I had a chance to phone her, apologize, and ask her to watch Sammy every day for the next two weeks. I thought she'd be pissed and stay away until I got in contact with her.

"Tag sale." Marie nods in mock approval and follows me into the kitchen. "You're going to have to learn how to stretch a buck."

Shit. She is pissed. She's here to aggravate me. "O.K. Truce. I'm sorry I made the crack about you being on welfare." I fix myself a peanut butter and jelly sandwich at the kitchen counter. The boys giggle in Sammy's room above us. "And I'm sorry I made the crack about your *fiancée*." I say fiancée with a French accent to cover up the sarcasm. "I shouldn't have slept with Joe. I did, now I'm freaking out."

"We're getting married at All Saints." She watches for my reaction to this information. "Who told you we're engaged?"

It's odd to hear the word engaged come out of Marie's mouth. "Fletcher." I answer without looking her in the eye. "I saw him at the station. Donny eat?"

"Fletcher," she says with satisfaction. "If I had my way, he and Joe would be in the wedding party, but Eddie wants you and Renee to stand up with his brothers."

I spread the jelly, wipe the counter, and twist the tie on the bread bag.

"Thanks for the good wishes," she says sarcastically.

Does it always have to be complicated with Marie? Why can't I turn around, smile, and say "Congratulations?" Why can't I just be happy for her? She's not asking *me* to marry Eddie. She's being bitchy, so what? I

165

insulted her. She's pissed. This is what she wants, how she's going to make sense of her life.

I turn around. Before I can force a smile and push out my best wishes, Marie demands, "Make me one of those." She sounds like the leader of the pack in a female prison movie. I hope I don't sound like that.

The boys are still giggling in the room above us. "They play pretty good together." I push the peanut butter toward her.

"For the most part." She builds a triple-decker sandwich: bread, peanut butter, bread, grape jelly, bread. "It's because they're so close in age. Your next one will be, what, five years younger?" That calm before the storm is in her voice.

"Marie, please. I need your help. I'm sorry. I'm *trying* to like Eddie." I drain the last of the coffee into my chipped blue mug.

"And I'm *trying* to help us both out of the shit you're in," she says in her most irritating Mr. Rogers imitation. "Who do you suppose will babysit for this unplanned child while you're at school and everyone except Marie *Belmont* is occupying themselves with an honorable profession?" Belmont is Eddie's last name. Marie has always thought I was a jerk for not taking Joe's last name. This is one thing she and Mom have always agreed on.

I take my coffee and sandwich and walk away from her into the living room.

She tails me and sits a foot away from me on the couch. "Aren't you going to offer me a cup of coffee?"

"Make some."

She takes a sip from my chipped mug.

I slide the cup back to my side of the coffee table.

She slides the cup back and takes another sip. "It's cold." She picks up half of my sandwich and takes a bite. "He knows you and Renee don't like him, but he still wants you in the wedding party because you're family. That's Eddie, solid, like Dad." She takes another bite. "And Joe."

"Put it down." I'm giving her what she wants; she's really pissing me off. "Eat your own sandwich."

She holds my sandwich above her head. I grab for it. She holds it behind her back. "You should be watching your weight. Don't want to put it all on in the first few months. Wait until the Well Baby Social Worker gets a hold of you and makes you keep a journal of everything you put in your mouth."

I cross my arms over my chest. Punching Marie in the face would feel really good.

"Welfare babies can be healthy babies." Her voice is an infuriating sing-song.

"How did you get to be such a bitch? You come from such a fine family." I clench my fists in my armpits.

"You know who Mom's going to blame?" She runs her little finger around the rim of my coffee cup. "Not Cora Rose. Not Cora Rose's hard-working husband. Excuse me, ex-husband. Never Renee, the sweet virgin nurse. Somehow the fact that I'm marrying a nice Catholic boy will be overlooked and Mom's own personal mystery of faith will kick in. My bad example is going to have gotten you pregnant." She holds up two fingers. "Twice." She takes a third bite of my sandwich. I pick the newspaper off the floor and pretend to read it. "If you don't watch out, you're going to end up just like me. Hiding popsicles under the hamburger so the old biddies won't talk about the junk food you buy with their hard-earned taxes. Only you'll have two kids' worth of junk food to hide. And no Joe." She peeks over the top of the paper I'm pretending to read and shows me how to smile pleasantly at a person you'd rather be strangling.

I put down the paper and hum "Alouette." I've forgotten most of the French songs I knew, but I remember they get on her nerves.

"You'll find that men you're not married to don't give a lot of thought to what the children they've fathered are eating. Get used to peanut butter and jelly." She holds out her arm and admires the sandwich. "Cheap protein. WIC gives you powdered milk. Sammy will get used to it. He's young. But you won't. Tastes gross in coffee. Get used to black."

I turn slowly to face her head on, and before the thought forms in my brain, I'm on top of her. I kneel on her thighs, tear half the sandwich out of her hand, and fling it across the room.

167

Marie clenches the other half of the sandwich. "What the fuck?"

I slam her down on the couch. It takes all my might. She lands flat on her back with the wind knocked out of her. I keep kneeling on her, a hand on each of her shoulders, and lean into her body with all my weight. "Don't you think I know how much I've got to lose? You're going to marry Eddie. I'm going to divorce Joe. There's nothing either of us can do about it except help out with the boys."

"You're talking too loud," Marie hisses and looks up at the ceiling. "You'll scare them." She doesn't even try to fight. The back of her head is jammed into the soft upholstery of the couch. Her eyebrows are squished into her forehead. She lays there passive, not giving me the satisfaction of squirming.

I bend her arm back. "Give me my sandwich." Her arm and the sandwich are hanging over the edge of the couch.

"Here." She opens her fist and lets the gooey mess fall on the floor. "What else? You want me to plan a joint wedding and baby shower?" She lies under me, making no move to fight back.

"Mommy?" Donny says, tentative, but not really frightened, from the top of the stairs.

As much as I don't want the boys to see their mothers fighting, I want to keep my sister pinned to the couch more. "Shit. I don't want them to see us like this."

"Then get the hell off me," she snorts. "I hope you plan on setting a better example for the next one." When I don't move, she clears her throat and sings out, "It's okay. Mommy and Auntie are just fooling around." She's not even breathing hard.

As I listen to see if the boys will retreat back into Sammy's room or come down to check us out, Marie shoves me with all her strength. I don't expect it. One of my knees slips off of her thigh and I fall to the floor with a thud. Marie's on top of me. I grunt. Her chest pushes against my back and her lips are an inch from my ear, much closer then I've ever wanted her. "You are no better than I am," she hisses in my ear.

"Mommy?" Sammy's standing at our feet. "You're fighting with Auntie Marie." He sounds more amazed than concerned.

"How come we don't get to play like that?" Donny demands.

Marie gets off me and brushes what's left of the peanut butter and jelly off her hands. She says nonchalantly, "Your Aunt Cora Rose is feeling a little frisky today." Both boys scrunch up their faces, like they don't know what to make of it, but don't quite buy this explanation. Marie sits on the couch, drinking from my chipped mug. "Auntie Cora Rose had the idea that we should wrestle to find out who's stronger."

The boys pick up on her it's-all-over-now attitude and wedge themselves next to each other on the big old chair opposite the couch. "You're stronger. Right, Mommy?" Donny says, bouncing.

"No, sir," Sammy says without conviction.

"It doesn't matter. None of us should play like that." I speak before Marie can get another word in. I pick the goo off the floor. "You guys want popsicles?"

The bribe works when I tell them they can take their treats up to Sammy's room.

I make fresh coffee and place a mug on the coffee table in front of Marie. She says pointedly, "You don't seem to get it. Girls like us, we're not meant to make it unless we walk a real narrow line. Why do you think Renee's such a tight ass? Her looks will only take her so far if she fucks up."

"Marie, what am I going to do?"

"You don't even know if you're pregnant yet. It's 1975. Abortion is legal in Massachusetts now." I make myself look her in the eye. "I would." Her bottom lip quivers, but she checks it.

Then, changing the mood like a light switch, she swings her feet up on the coffee table. "What do you want from me?" Marie's not one to carry a grudge—once she's pinned you to the floor in front of the children.

I sit down next to her. "Take care of Sammy all day for the next two weeks." She'll do it. In some ways, Marie is more generous than most people.

Chapter 15

Joe sits in his favorite chair, the ratty one in the living room. He and Fletcher have already moved the double bed, one of the bureaus, and most of his clothes into the van. Sammy stands in the kitchen doorway. It's four p.m.. The sun is getting low in the sky. I had hoped Joe would finish moving in full daylight while Sammy and I were still in school.

"Come 'ere little guy." Joe holds out his arms. Sammy doesn't budge. "Daddy's not leaving you. I'm just going to live with Uncle Fletcher until Mommy and I decide what to do." He opens his arms wider.

"Why can't you decide what to do here?" Sammy pouts.

"Because it's too hard, Sammy." Joe's walking the tightrope of his own last nerve. "Give Daddy a break," he slumps forward and whines like he's the four-year-old. Sammy, stubbornly refusing to cry, his bottom lip quivering, forces Joe to sit up wearily and be the adult. "You can visit me at Uncle Fletcher's. Donny'll be there too sometimes. It'll just be us guys. We'll have fun." Joe forces a smile.

Sammy narrows his eyes. Joe looks at me like he could kill me with his bare hands. I wish I wasn't still in my student nurse costume. For the last few weeks, ever since we came up with a definite date for Joe to move out, the sight of me in this stiff-collared uniform infuriates him.

I stand behind Sammy and pat him on the butt. "Daddy loves you." My voice cracks. "Give Daddy a hug." Sammy looks up at me. I give him a little push. He runs to Joe. Joe scoops Sammy onto his lap and sways his big shoulders from side to side as he holds him.

"These going?" Fletcher bounds down the stairs with a gooseneck lamp in one hand and a wicker hamper in the other. He sees Joe rocking

Sammy in his lap and stops in front of them. "Don't worry partner, Uncle Fletcher will take good care of your Daddy."

Sammy sucks his thumb, his head on Joe's shoulder. He had given it up, but he's got the thumb stuck all the way in now and rubs his nose with his index finger as he sucks. His head pops off Joe's shoulder and the thumb pops out of his mouth. "We could all just live together," he says, like he's just hit on the perfect solution.

Fletcher kneels next to Joe's chair at eye level with Sammy. "Not going to work, amigo."

"Why?" Sammy whimpers.

Fletcher kisses Sammy's forehead and sweeps him off Joe's lap. "Sometimes grown-ups just can't live with each other."

Joe goes into the kitchen and grips the edge of the sink. I follow and stand behind him, wait and listen as Fletcher opens the front door for Renee, straight from work, still wearing her uniform. She's come to take Sammy to The Big Cheese so that he won't be here when Joe, his bed, and his bureau take off in Fletcher's van. "Come on, Sammy," she coaxes. "We'll pick up Donny on the way."

Miraculously, Sammy goes with her. Joe and I stare out the kitchen window and watch Renee buckle him into the front seat of her Honda. Yellow and red maple leaves blow around in a little whirlwind behind Renee's car as she backs out of the driveway. When Sammy's out of view, Joe says, "This doesn't mean you're getting custody. I'm not giving up my key. I'm not even promising it's me who's going to end up leaving this apartment."

I feel nauseous. I just stare at him and keep my mouth shut, knowing he's ready to blow. I want to tell him how much it helped me that he loved me despite my disease, loved me even more *because* I was pregnant. A miracle really, that he fell in love with me, a miracle that he's finally agreed to be the one to leave. Tell him how sorry I am that I didn't fall in love back. I'm not stupid enough to say any of it. I just want him out so he can cool off somewhere else with Fletcher. I lean against the re-frigerator, tired of hearing him say the same things over and over. Tired of answering him with the same answers meant to get him out, meant to keep as much territory as I can. We said all that there is to say this morning, said it all last night. He wants the fault to be all mine, he wants me to take all the blame. I stand there rigid, refusing. I'll take half the blame. I'll take three-quarters of it. But he's got to take some. I married someone I barely knew. He married someone he barely knew. We had sex, using a condom that promised 99% protection. We had shit for luck. We were young and stupid. Both of us. We're still young and stupid.

"How is this fair? You tell me, how is this fair?" He slams his fist on the sink. I can't go over it again right now. I won't. He is a good man. He's everything he wants to believe he is. But he's also a jerk who refuses to believe that marijuana and tobacco smoke trigger Sammy's asthma attacks. He's the man who got up and changed the sheets, then held me when I had an accident in bed, *and* he's the guy who's outraged if his laundry doesn't appear clean and folded, without him having to give it a thought, the rest of the time. He slams the sink with his fist again, throws his head back, and groans like I shot him from behind. Every hair on my body stands on end. I'm sick of him slamming around the house like a wounded animal, like he's the only one hurting. It's been over for years. For me, it never really existed. I've wanted out of this marriage my entire adult life. He knows it hurt me to stay with him. He wanted me to stay, so he did what he could to get what he wanted. It can't be good for him to be with somebody who wants out. Why can't he see? Why do we have to make each other hateful and miserable before we can let each other go?

"Sammy needs two parents." The despair in his voice reinforces my own desperation to get him out of the kitchen, on the road to Fletcher's apartment.

"Sammy *has* two parents. We can't stay married because your father abandoned you."

"That was a low blow," he says almost inaudibly. Then the full force of his anger booms, "You bitch."

"It's the truth." I try to stand up to his rage by speaking slowly, directly, clutching the edge of the counter. "Sammy's better off with me. I'm a better housekeeper, a better cook. He's used to spending more time with me. You're not good with him when he's sick and it's better for him not to have to move right now." I'm surprised at how even, how reasonable this recording that I carry around in my head comes out. I have to believe Sammy's better off with me. I have to believe we're all injured parties, that Joe and I are both responsible for this mess we're in.

He whips around. "Bullshit, who took care of him when you were sick?"

"My sisters and my mother . . . and—"

"Me," he hollers, "ME."

"You're a good father, Joe, but you got a lot of help when I was sick. Mom and my sisters took turns, cooked and made sure somebody took care of Sammy while you were working."

"So? They offered. What does that prove? You're working and going to school now." The softer I speak, the more incensed he gets, the louder his voice becomes.

"Come on, buddy." Fletcher steps in from the living room. "We better get going."

I sidestep Joe, go into the bathroom, close the door behind me, and vomit in the toilet as quietly as I can.

He bangs on the bathroom door. I pull down the toilet lid, sit, and wait him out. Am I more responsible than Joe is for getting pregnant with Sammy? If I'm pregnant again, is it my fault again? He knocks on the door. Then kicks it. "How do you plan to pay the rent? What about that little detail?" The sob in his voice makes me sit even stiller.

"Come on, Joe," Fletcher says in his soothing twang. "Come on, buddy."

The kitchen door slams.

The sun sets and dark creeps in through the windows. I slouch on the sofa, not bothering to turn on the light. I wait, a half-hour, an hour? Renee's still not home with Sammy. I wiggle out of my student nurse get-up and sit in the dark in my slip. I touch my breasts. They're a little tender, sometimes they're sore like this right before my period, and then again, they were sore for the first and the last three months that I was pregnant with Sammy. I pick up my Anatomy and Physiology book and throw it across the room.

Click, click, click, someone coming up the back steps. Has to be Renee or Mom. They are the only ones who wear pumps. There's only one set of footsteps, so no Sammy. I scrunch up my shoulders; please, Mary, let it be Renee. The last thing I need is Mom lamenting Joe's departure. I kick off my chunky white shoes and put my feet up on the coffee table. Ring. Ring. Ring. Must be Renee. Mom doesn't ring. She bangs.

"Come on in. You got a key." Renee lets herself and a rush of cool air in. I'm surprised how good it feels. "Where's Sammy?"

"We're going to pick him up at Marie's later."

"Later?" I look at my Timex. "It's eight o'clock."

She picks up my feet, slides a Sears catalogue under them, and snaps on the light. "I want to talk. No period yet?"

I shake my head. "I don't want to think about it."

She picks my uniform off the floor, drapes it over the chair, pulls a pen, a checkbook, and a list written in pink on a little spiral pad out of her purse. She puts all the stuff on the coffee table next to my feet. She takes her own uniform off, drapes it over the chair on top of mine, and sits down in her slip next to me.

I pick up the pad and read the pink list, "Bed, lamp, bureau, dishes, hope chest, small marble table, pillows, blanket. What's this?"

She frowns, disregarding my question. "You don't want to think about a decision that's going to affect you for the rest of your life? It's not like you've got forever to figure out what to do. You have to think about it sooner or later."

"Okay. Later." I push the pad toward her, repeating, "What is this?"

"My stuff. I should move in. Think it'll fit?" Renee kicks off her shoes and puts her feet on the coffee table next to mine.

"Joe would go berserk. He still considers half this apartment his. He's making noises about wanting custody of Sammy." I retreat farther back into the cushions. All of a sudden, I'm cold.

Renee sits up straight and faces me. "The apartment belongs to the landlord. Look, Joe doesn't want Sammy to live with him full-time, not really. He knows Sammy's better off with you. He's confused, he's mad. I move in, we'll call it temporary. I pay half the rent. Joe sees Sammy whenever he wants to see Sammy, watches him a couple nights a week while you're working. I look after Sammy when I'm not working." Renee makes it sound so easy, sitting there in her clean white slip.

"He moved out three hours ago."

"I love Joe," she says firmly. "But we may as well piss him off all at once and get it over with."

"You won't like it here. You're used to Mom making meals and Dad offering to drive you to work when there's an inch of snow. Your clothes aren't even on the list. They'd take up half the apartment," I say this nonchalantly even though I know she's offering me a lot.

Renee knows it too, but she's always at her best when she knows she's being generous. "I don't have to take all my stuff. It's time for me to leave the nest. Mae and Andre are driving me nuts. Dad knows my schedule better than I do. Mom's been trying to get me to be a fourth for pinochle ever since Uncle Louie died." She sighs and closes her eyes. "Look, if you're pregnant, I'll do what I can to help out." I take this statement as her vote against abortion. I would have thought Marie would be the one pushing toward having the kid and Renee would be the one advising abortion. I can't separate their opinions from my own. It confuses me that I can't predict their reactions. Renee takes a breath and swings into one of the mood changes she's so good at. "Put on your jeans." She pats my thigh and slips her uniform back over her head. "It's time to pick up Sammy."

She chatters about her personal possessions for the entire drive, what to throw out, what to put in our parents' attic, what to take to my place.

"Come on in," Marie yells. She hasn't asked who it is and barely looks up from her coffee and paper when we walk through her unlocked door.

"Where are the boys?" I drop into a kitchen chair opposite Marie. I let my arms hang straight out, limp as a paper doll.

Marie points at the clock in the shape of a tea kettle on the wall above the stove—9:15. She gives me a look like Mom used to when she didn't want to answer a particularly stupid question. "Snack. Bath. Bed." She spreads the funnies on the table. Is she deliberately taking on Mom's most obnoxious mannerisms?

Renee twists her hair, and sticks a chopstick-like thing through the knot, making a prissy little bun at the nape of her neck. She lets out a surprised, "Lorraine."

Lorraine steps all the way into the kitchen. "Hello, Renee. Hello, Cora Rose." She kneels by the counter and empties a box filled with a bunch of cookbooks and strange-looking utensils.

"What are you doing?" I ask like we're six-year-olds and I caught Lorraine sucking maple syrup from the jug in the corner of Memere's kitchen.

"Nothing." Lorraine stands up, brushes off the skirt of her print dress with extravagant dignity, and smoothes the hair of her French twist. She doesn't exactly have her finger on the pulse of style, but she looks a lot better as an adult than she did as a kid.

"Nothing?" Renee waves her hand over the box.

"Moving pots and pans to make room for my wok."

I give Lorraine a dirty look for no good reason other than I'm tired and I don't know why she's unloading a wok into Marie's cabinet. She steps back like she's afraid of me, bursts into tears, and runs into the bathroom.

"What's that about?" I haven't seen Lorraine in months. Lorraine's always been sensitive, but she can usually stand up to a dirty look better than this.

Marie flaps down the *Union News*, irritated. "She's on my nerves already and she's not even moved in."

"Moved in?" Renee's mouth drops open.

"Temporary. She's got nowhere else to go. Josette kicked her out." Marie shrugs. "I could use half the rent money, if not the company. And it's only until the wedding. You're her favorite cousin, Cora Rose. Talk nice to her. See if you can get the story."

I bang on the bathroom door. "Come on out, Lorraine. I'm sorry," I say half-heartedly. I have more interest in the fact that half the females in my family are moving in with the other half at the exact same time than concern for Lorraine. "Please. I had a real shitty day."

Lorraine comes out and stares at the green speckled linoleum. The linoleum is cracked but shiny. I bet Lorraine polished it. She looks up at me. "I'm sorry about you and Joe. Really." She starts to sniffle again, but stops herself. "How's Sammy?" she asks earnestly.

"Fine." It's kind of touching how concerned she is. I have to be nicer to people. I used to be nice, didn't I? "A little confused, you know, it's hard on everybody."

"You should be telling Cora Rose how he is." Marie rolls her eyes at Lorraine. "You just tucked him in."

Lorraine grabs me by the shoulders and says, "Sammy's such a sweet little boy." She hugs me forcefully. "It'll all work out, don't you think?"

"Lorraine, a little less melodrama." Marie pushes away from the table.

Lorraine exaggerates the good posture Aunt Josette nagged into her. "I'm concerned. I want everyone to end up happy and be friends."

"Well, you better take the first spaceship back to the happy-ending planet you came from." Marie pours four cups of coffee. She pushes one cup in front of me, "You made an appointment at that clinic yet?" I glare at her and sweep a glance at Lorraine. She waves away the consequences of Lorraine's presence with a flap of her own hand, but drops the subject. She places a second cup in front of Renee and another one in front of the chair that Lorraine is standing behind.

Renee shakes her head. "I can't drink coffee after supper."

"Me either," Lorraine says.

"Never bothers me," Marie brags.

"Caffeine causes insomnia. It's a stimulant. You're up until two every morning."

Renee leans back, resting her case.

Marie sends a generic dirty look across the table. It's hard to tell who the look is aimed at. She slides a box of crullers that has been on her kitchen table for the last four days in front of Lorraine. "Eat a donut," she demands.

"Why are you mad at *me*?" Lorraine sits down and cradles her cup of coffee with both hands. She stares Marie down without wincing. Lorraine has learned a few things since we were kids.

"Because you're running into the bathroom, getting all theatrical, and not telling anyone why." Marie dunks a donut in her coffee. "I'm tired of drama. We got enough drama with Cora Rose divorcing Joe and hanging around at that dyke bar."

I'm in the middle of taking my first sip of coffee. "What are you talking about?" I choke. Coffee dribbles down my chin. I grab a napkin and look from Renee to Lorraine. "Where does she come up with this shit?"

Marie raises her eyebrows. "Any takers?"

Renee frowns. "If you have something to say, say it, Marie."

Marie repeats my question, pronouncing each word slowly like the master of ceremonies on Schools Match Wits. "Where does Marie come up with this shit?"

Lorraine wrinkles her brow tentatively. "Because of Stella when we were kids?"

"Go, Lorraine." Marie says, still playing the enthusiastic game show host. "And what bar has she been seen at lately?"

"The Limelight?" Lorraine concentrates like the right answer might really win her a living-room set or scholarship money to attend the Ivy League school of her choice.

"Bzzz." Marie makes a noise like the loser buzzer. "The correct answer is . . ." she pushes the donuts toward me, "The Girls Club."

"You've been hanging around at The Girls Club?" Renee looks at me bug-eyed. "When do you find the time?"

"I haven't been hanging around anywhere." I give Marie a look that only makes her grin wider.

"Who told you such a thing?" Renee crosses her arms and points her chin at Marie.

Marie pours milk in a mug and pushes it in front of me. "You should be getting plenty of calcium. Leave Sammy here tonight. Why wake him up, bring him home, then bring him all the way back in the morning?" She says this like we've been having a discussion about Sammy all along.

I'm so angry I'm shaking. "It's sick. Spying on your sister. I went there once."

Renee's jaw drops. "You *did?* When?"

"Months ago. I had an orange juice." I ball my fists on the table. "Get a life, Marie. Mind your own business."

Marie hisses, unruffled. "Get over yourself. I don't like you in a lezzie bar. Matter of fact, it makes me sick; but you're right, it's none of my business, except when some dyke inquires about you while I'm pumping her gas."

"Big deal." I don't even blink.

"Well?" Renee pulls out the chopstick and lets her hair fall. She massages her own scalp. "What dyke?" She stares at me like I just dropped through the ceiling.

Yeah, what dyke?

"Darlene," Marie answers smugly, "Says, 'hello.'"

"Oh, Darlene," Renee says dismissively. "They used to be neighbors."

"Why don't you both mind your own business?" Renee, thinking she's got the whole thing figured out, irritates me almost as much as Marie does.

Renee says, "Hey, be nice. You start hanging at The Girls Club, you're going to need me and all my bleeding liberal girlfriends on your side."

"That's right, be nice," Marie agrees. "You used to be a very nice girl."

"I am not *hanging* anywhere." I'm on the verge of tears. "Nobody has to take sides."

Lorraine, staring wide-eyed, finally opens her mouth. "Oh. The Girls Club. The dyke bar."

"If you don't want to get shipped back to Mama . . ." Marie points her finger at Lorraine ". . . keep your mouth shut about anything that you see or hear in this apartment. Do not repeat anything to anybody. Especially Eddie."

Lorraine nods her head and bites into a dried-out honey-dipped donut.

Chapter 16

Halfway through Professor Rand's discussion of the human reproductive system, I raise my hand and ask to use the ladies' room. Doctor Rand answers impatiently, "We're all adults here. It's not necessary to ask. Just go." Rand is one of those professors who have been in the same position for so long she thinks that the rules are self-evident and students should be smart enough to know what's expected without being told. I don't fit in with most of the students anyway, so I wouldn't care much about looking stupid if Gabriel, a girl I've been studying with, weren't sitting three seats behind me. Gabriel is the brain of the class. She studies with me because she thinks I'm smart. I want her to keep thinking that.

Walking down the hall to the ladies' room, I'm nervous like I always am when I have to use a public rest room. As I near the door, I hear a couple of students laughing. I don't want the giggling girls inside the ladies' room to hear the noise when I empty my ostomy bag, so I hang around outside the door.

The girls come out of the ladies' room in a pack of three. I slip in before the door swings closed behind them. A harried woman is changing her baby's diaper on the counter by the sink. Piece of cake. Women with little kids are easy. They're too busy worrying about cleaning up their kids' messes to pay attention to anyone else. The girls I hate to run into the most are the ones who finish their business and hang around in front of the sink, checking themselves out in the mirror, looking at themselves in left and right profile to make sure that their blouses are tucked in just right. Sucking up my privacy to adjust their belts. This woman smiles apologetically because her baby's bottom, in its dirty diaper, is an inch from the faucet. The kid's bootied feet dangle in the sink. I smile at her. What's she supposed to do? There's no changing table. I guess there aren't many babies in college.

I watch her in the mirror as I wash my hands. She looks old. Her hair is dyed blonde, coarse and dry, with gray roots at the temples. Her face is dry and gray too, worn-looking, crow's-feet around the eyes. There's something young-looking about the way she's got her hair pulled back in a ponytail. I bet she's not much older than me, too young to look this worn-out. "First baby?" I ask. She raises three fingers. I consider asking her if she wants me to hold her baby while she uses the toilet, but the trapped look on her face when the baby starts to cry stops me.

I slide past her and her bundle of wailing baby, slip into the stall and bend forward over the toilet. Do my business standing up, gently push on my abdomen with one hand, and pull on the ostomy bag with the other hand to detach the thing from me. By now I can tell by the weight of its pull on my abdomen when the appliance needs to be emptied. Appliance, that's what the ostomy nurse called the bag in the hospital. Sounds like I've got a toaster attached to my belly.

My appliance empties into the toilet with a glug. The trick is to empty the pouch when it's only half-full. Nothing spills. Nothing has ever spilled, but it still surprises me when it doesn't. I hitch up my pants and flush. A normal college girl using the ladies' room. I bet the tired woman outside the stall trying to calm her baby doesn't notice my feet are pointing the wrong way. Bet she's not even mildly interested in the toilet habits of the girl in the stall behind her.

I sit on the toilet seat, lean my head against the back wall, and look up at the water-stained white blocks of perforated board that make up the ceiling of the Chicopee Community College ladies' room. I touch the gray metal sides of the bathroom stall. This is college, but the bathroom is public school issue, like the ones in grammar school, like the ones in high school with three feet of exposed space between the sides of the stall and the ceiling.

The woman outside my stall coos at her baby, who is howling to beat the band. Time to get back to class. Time to walk out of here, past her and her screeching kid.

I wash my hands. The woman paces with her fat pink baby on her shoulder. "I don't know what to do for her anymore." Her eyes, blood-shot, meet mine in the mirror. "The other ones weren't like this." She's been crying and it looks like she might start again.

What to say to make her less miserable, to get me out of here? I dry my hands and smile sympathetically. She takes a bottle that's been warming in a sink full of hot water, almost drops it and the baby as she tries to juggle them both and test a squirt of milk on her wrist. I look at the baby's outraged face. No wonder the baby can't settle down, the way she's jerking it around. The woman's eyes are getting more desperate by the second. "My husband's going to kill me if she's screaming like this when he gets out of class."

Why is she telling me this? I haven't said a word to her since I came out of the stall. I say, "I hope she stops." I back away from her and her tear-streaked baby and rush down the hall. My head pounds. My heart beats like I woke from a nightmare. I lean against the wall, and whisper, "Jesus, Mary, and Joseph."

It's not becoming that woman that's got me so spooked, although I am afraid of that. It's the feeling I had when I looked that kid in the eye that's freaking me out. I could have comforted that kid, taken that screaming bundle in my arms and had it snoring those little baby snores in ten minutes. I press my head against the wall. The wall feels like it's pounding behind my skull. I miss Joe. If Joe and I were friends, had only ever been friends, I could talk to him about this—he'd understand why I don't want to take care of anyone else, if he wasn't so mad that I don't want to take care of him anymore. If he didn't love me, if he didn't hate me, if we didn't already have one kid's love to guard, to argue about . . . if the kid I might be carrying wasn't his.

Who's watching Sammy after school?

What day of the week is it? Tuesday, Renee's day off. Did I remind her this morning that I don't get home until four-thirty today? She was asleep when Sammy and I left.

Sammy at the back door locked out, no one answering his calls, no cookies, no milk, no Bugs Bunny. His chubby face streaked with tears.

I run down the hall away from the A and P science lab to find a pay phone. "You're home?" I blurt, out of breath, into the receiver of the pay phone.

"It's Tuesday. I'm waiting for Sammy. That's the plan, right?"

"Right. Thanks. Bye." I reach for my ear. My lone diamond is safe and sound on my earlobe. I dig my thumb into the post until a tingle of pain shoots down my neck, over my shoulder, up my arm. I run back to the ladies' room, but the desperate woman and her wailing baby are gone.

A week later, I'm sitting in Professor Rand's class again. Gabriel takes the seat in front of me. For someone who doesn't speak all that much, she makes a lot of eye contact. I can't get a handle on her. It feels like she wants something from me, but she's too polite to ask. She's too thin and not very good-looking, but there's something solid about her, a confidence that holds you back from thinking of her as homely. Her thick curly hair bounces over her bent shoulders as she writes down what the extremely wordy Professor Rand has to say about the human reproductive system.

My breasts are killing me. They feel like tomatoes, too long on the vine, ready to split their skins. I have the urge to thump Gabriel on top of her dark head with my used volume of *Anatomy: The Study of You and Me.* I have no reason to pick on her except that her calm confidence is getting on my nerves. And she's sitting in front of me.

Maybe I'm not pregnant *or* about to get my period, maybe I'm turning into a vampire. All signs point to it: can't sleep at night, obsessed with blood, run to the ladies' room between classes to see if there's any red on my underwear, sneak hamburgers off the grill at work and eat them half-cooked, pray that the cow's sacrifice will bring on my own blood, and now, fantasizing about blood gushing from innocent Gabriel's skull.

I count backwards as Professor Rand drones on about oogametes and luteininzing hormones, to the approximate date of my last period. I'm not sure when it actually occurred, having had no reason to have kept track until my "Say goodbye with sex" encounter with Joe. Fifty-four days, give or take. Maybe my cycle is still all messed up from the surgery. I fold my arms on the desk and press my breasts. Is this my usual premenstrual swelling? Am I hypersensitive because I'm worried

183

about being knocked up? Or is it the beginning bloat of pregnancy? Too bad I can't ask Rand if there's a way to qualify the heaviness of a woman's breasts to differentiate between menstrual fullness and gestatory fullness, a legitimate, practical, reproductive question. Too practical for Anatomy and Physiology class.

"Ms. LaBarre?" Rand says impatiently, letting me know it's the second time I've been called upon. "Are you with us, Ms. LaBarre?"

"Yes." I can't get used to being called "Ms." "Sorry, could you repeat that?"

"I was asking if anyone could explain why nature designed the human male so as to store sperm outside of the body cavity in a sac before copulation."

"Cold. The sperm needs to be colder than core body temperature to be viable." I retained that information, hoping when I read it that it was too hot in my pantry/bedroom that night for Joe's sperm to be viable.

"Very good." Professor Rand nods, impressed that even pulled from my stupor I know the answer to her question. In fact, I know the answers to most of Dr. Rand's questions. Convinced that the only way to keep up with college students is to read every assignment at least twice and study every new concept until I actually understand it. And, of course, Gabriel and I study before this class every day. My assumption that the average college freshman understands this stuff the first time around or studies it until they do is fading quickly as Professor Rand does her best to knock us down like bowling pins, one question at a time. Gabriel and I are two of the few pins still standing.

Rand walks back to the front of the class, hands folded behind her. She thinks she's superior because she knows something she's paid to teach and has taught twenty times before? Or is it just the way she thinks a college professor is supposed to act? I bet she doesn't know how to change a car battery or an ostomy bag. I shiver, remembering that it was really hot out when Sammy was conceived; must have been 100° in the back of that van. And Joe used a rubber the first time, and every time after, except the last time. Joe's sperm, viable up to 100°. Dr. Rand's chalk screeches and my skin crawls as she scratches the spelling and chemical formula for hyaluronidase on the green blackboard.

After class, I duck back into the ladies' room. Bingo, a dime-sized spot, a red-brown stain on white panties. I throw my head back, raise both arms like the football team is going to rush in and hoist me on their shoulders. Who cares if this Community College doesn't have a football team? I reach for the patient tampon stuffed in the bottom of my bag and kiss the little two-inch plug. I flush twice to hear the double flourish.

Outside of "C" building, I smile, proud, as though it was through my own discipline, hard work, and all-around state of grace that the wonder of menstruation chose me. There should be a football team and it should be carrying me around on the field. Who cares that it was shit luck that I didn't get caught? I don't have to have an abortion. I don't have to have a baby. I feel good for the first time in a long time. I'm going to run with the feeling. In the center of the concrete courtyard, surrounded by white slab buildings, I let the crisp air whip my open coat around, watch the students pour out of the solid, chunky buildings and spill down the stairs around me, to the parking lot below. For the first time, I feel like part of the flow.

I don't have to be anywhere for almost an hour. I boost myself up on one of the white stone walls that surround the cement courtyard and sit down on the hard surface, next to a cement flowerbox full of frozen chrysanthemums which is built into the concrete. Other students hang around on the wall, watching, doing nothing in particular or talking to each other, waiting for it to be time to do the next thing. Two of them sit twenty feet down the wall from me, a young man and a young woman flirting nervously. The way the girl looks down at her hands, looks up only after she's done speaking—her longing for connection so clear even from my casual observation at twenty feet—somehow comforts me and alarms me at the same time. Maybe it's normal to feel like you don't fit, like you've never quite connected. I want to warn her, to tell her she better be careful how she connects, tell her that Newton's Law of Motion doesn't just apply to physics; once something's in motion, it's takes a lot of energy to stop it.

Instead of running to the grocery store before I put in my hours with the frialator, I sit with dead chrysanthemums. The space clears out. No one takes afternoon classes on Friday if they can help it. Within fifteen minutes, I have the courtyard to myself. The light fades. The shadows play on the mass of white/gray buildings, the way it does in autumn. Long streams of light almost perpendicular to the ground are cut off by the elongated shadows of the buildings. I dangle my legs against the cold stone, thinking that the shadows are created by the light itself, thinking that everything exists in relation to something else. I smile at myself for having such a smart, scholarly thought. A strange rush comes over me like a memory. What is this feeling? Seems important to know what it is, to name it, at least as important as learning the name for metabolic acidosis or paranoid schizophrenia. Relief? Happiness? Something else, light and clean, fresh like after a shower, but familiar, like the smell of Memere's powder. Forgiven? Absolved? Innocent, like the slate has been wiped clean? Like when I was a kid, when I was sure Mary, the blessed virgin, was rooting for me. I've been cut a break. Potential, I feel potential.

Driving out of McDonald's parking lot four hours later, I'm determined to celebrate the arrival of my period. In the shower I smile at the red dots, swirling pink as they get sucked down the drain.

"Wanna go to the movies?" I bounce down on the couch next to Renee.

Renee takes a whiff of my neck. "You've got perfume on, Shalimar. My Shalimar." She tilts her head and studies my hair. "You used my curling iron."

"And your mascara and your peach melba body splash."

"What's the occasion? Oh my God. Menses!" She screeches and pulls me up. She tries to twirl me around like we're kids playing statue on the playground, but I plop back down on the couch, laughing. She messes up my curling-ironed hair and plops next to me. We sit side by side, our heads thrown back but facing each other with shit-eating grins. "Jesus, you had me worried." She pushes my face away with her palm and jumps up. "Can't go to the movies. Already made plans. Call that Gabriel person you study with, maybe she'll go." She bolts up the stairs.

"What plans?" I yell after her and get the sound of the shower running for an answer.

After Renee leaves, I do consider calling Gabriel. I fold and unfold a dishtowel twenty times. We're not really friends, just study partners. Today in class I wanted to hit her over the head with my textbook. I've never asked anyone to the movies except my sisters or Joe. I stare at Gabriel's number, pick up the phone, and dial. A man answers. When he says, "Hello," a second time, I hang up. I'm socially inept, can't even make a phone call unless the person I'm calling is a blood relative.

I call Marie. No answer. Probably with Eddie. Where's Lorraine?

I call Sammy at Fletcher's and Joe's place. "Guess what?" he says. "Auntie Lorraine came over with Donny. She's helping us make a tent out of the bunk beds." Sammy races through the words. He doesn't seem to be missing me much.

"I love you, honey. Be a good boy for Daddy. Can I talk to Uncle Fletcher?" Maybe he'll get a beer and go to the movies with me. We're not genetically related, even though he thinks of himself as family, so maybe I'm making a little progress here.

"He's gone to meet Auntie Renee somewhere. I love you, Mommy." Sammy hangs up.

"Well, isn't everyone cozy and paired off for the evening?" I un-crumple Gabriel's phone number and dial quickly before I lose my nerve. A deep voice, says, "Yeah."

"May I speak with Gabriel, please?"

"Gabe," the voice booms. "Phone."

"Oh, Cora Rose. Yeah, hi." She's surprised to hear from me on a Friday night.

I stumble my away through suggesting we catch *Jaws* at the Rivoli Theater.

"Thanks." She sounds almost as flustered as I do. "You mean tonight?" This is worse than I thought. I figured if she didn't want to go she'd just blow me off without all this stammering. "I have a date tonight," she says, finally.

There's a long pause. I'm supposed to say something? "Oh, sorry. I guess Friday night is a date night. I didn't know you had a boyfriend." Nervous comment. None of my business whether or not she has a boyfriend. All we ever talk about is the wonders of cell mitosis.

"Yeah, well." She's flustered again.

There's another painful silence that I fill with, "Well, bye. See you before class to study."

Ten seconds, no reply. She hung up? Just as I'm returning the receiver to the cradle, I hear, "Cora Rose," tentatively. I pull the phone back to my ear. "You're welcome to come with us," she says.

"On a date?"

"I've been seeing this person for a long time. Actually it's a she. We're meeting a bunch of people. I'm sure she won't mind. I've told her a little bit about you." She strings her sentences together without pause. "You're welcome. Really. We're just getting a beer at a . . . women's bar."

A *women's* bar. That's a new one. Does she mean a dyke bar? "The Girls Club?"

After we finish the rest of our short conversation, I hang up and sit down slowly, afraid I might have trouble making contact with the seat of the kitchen chair. She invited me to that bar. Gabriel, a dyke? How many of them are there? She thinks I'm a dyke? That's why she looks at me like I'm some long lost relative she was separated from at birth? She can't possibly know about my (recently nonexistent) fantasy life by the way I study. Minding my business, going to nursing school—bam, the girl I study with, a dyke.

Marie spying on me, Joe and me arguing over who is a better parent, no way I'm going to meet her and her girlfriend. I got into school. I got my period. My life is starting to straighten out a little. I'm not lonely enough to screw it up by going back to that dyke bar. I'll tell her I got sick, tell her Sammy came home and I couldn't find a sitter. Tell the truth, I don't hang out at dyke bars.

Chapter 17

An hour later I'm in The Girls Club shaking hands and saying, "Nice to meet you," to Martha, Gabriel's date. Then I shake hands with Anne, maybe the least dykey-looking redhead I've ever seen.

"So you live in town, Cora Rose?" asks Martha. She's soft-spoken with gray-streaked temples. Older; the vigorous, life-loving type you see in vitamins with iron commercials.

Before I can answer Martha, Darlene is at the table, her hand on the back of my chair. She looks like an advertisement for Champion in her backwards baseball cap and oversized sweatshirt. She nods. "How you doing, Gabe, Martha, Anne? What can I get you, Cora Rose?"

"Orange juice, please." I'm embarrassed to be singled out. I want to tell them I know Darlene because we used to be neighbors and I'm only here because I couldn't find anyone to go to *Jaws* with me. Gabriel and Martha order beers. Anne orders Schweppes Bitter Lemon with two twists of lime.

"Hey, Young Love," Darlene calls over her shoulder to two women entwined in a slow dance. "What'll you have?"

"Two Buds." The taller, dark-skinned woman holds up two fingers behind her partner's back.

The shorter one, wearing a gauze shirt that shows the outline of a black lace bra against pale skin, slides the tip of her finger slowly up the dark-skinned woman's neck. When her finger reaches her partner's ear, she whispers something that makes her girlfriend's hips twitch. Everyone at the table watches the couple dance, hands in each other's back pockets, swaying like laundry in the breeze, pinned at the hips, mouths coming together in gentle pecking kisses, then fluttering apart. The

189

short one stretches, kisses her partner's top lip, then sucks on it and nips at it gently. Even on the barely lit dance floor, I can still see the tug of the upper lip, the swell of both women's breasts in perfect profile. Their heads bob and come back together. They suck each other's top, then bottom lips; let go, come back for more. The tall one takes her hands out of her partner's back pockets, runs them slowly down her girlfriend's ass and back up, reaches her head and holds it firmly in her open hands. A leather armband strains on her biceps as she leans in for an open-mouthed kiss.

"It's not that fun to watch when you're not involved." Anne nods toward the lovers, addressing Darlene.

"I'm surprised to hear *you* say that." Darlene takes a moment to think about it. "Too public for my taste, but it beats a brawl." God, are there brawls in this place? She walks back to the bar with our orders.

"So you've been here before?" Martha, embarrassed, attempts to turn our attention from the two women draped over each other on the dance floor. I attempt to stay calm. Martha and Anne look at me curiously. It's a simple question, not meant to intimidate, but Gabriel snaps a coaster on the table and the sound rips through me like a shot. I'm in a minefield of lesbians.

"Darlene and I used to be neighbors." I take a big gulp of orange juice.

"That begs the question." Anne smiles and leans forward.

"Behave," Gabriel suggests mildly.

Anne folds her arms like a spoiled child. "Like I'm the only one at this table who's curious about what the deal is."

"You find nursing school tough?" Martha rescues me. "Gabe sure does."

"I wouldn't want to be alone in that program," Gabriel says.

Alone. What does she mean by that? There are about fifty of us in the program. "It's tough, nursing school. I was here once . . . a few months ago. I'm separated." Gabriel squirms. "From my husband," I say, wishing I didn't have to drag Joe into this.

"You got a husband. You had some kind of horrible operation. You've got a little kid." Anne grins and pats my hand, satisfied. "Right?" She

190

opens her palm to protest the disapproving stare she gets from Martha. "What? I'm interested. She's cute." She turns to me. I just stare at her and smile limply as the lovers stop dancing, walk over to our table, and stand behind Anne. Anne smiles at them and continues her train of thought. "You see the same faces in here week after week. A new girl comes in, people notice. It's elementary sociology. Or psychology. It's elementary something. People talk."

The short one slides her hand inside her girlfriend's jeans and says, "May as well give them something interesting to talk about."

Anne turns to the couple. Her knee presses into mine. "Since when are you two an item?" The women grin at each other. There's a strong smell of beer. "Well, I'm jealous." She faces the table, fingers my glass, and lets her hand drop next to mine. Our baby fingers touch. "You don't drink?"

"Not really." I sip my juice and avoid her light blue eyes. "A little."

"What are you doing here if you don't drink?" She bats her eyelashes theatrically. I feel myself blush. It's a good question. "You are so easy to tease." She touches my foot with her toe. My heart races. I try to think of something clever to say.

Gabriel says, "Give it a rest, Anne. You're not drinking tonight and you're here."

"But *I* know what I'm doing here." She laughs and throws her head back. Her long dark lashes don't match her red hair.

The lovers, Laura and Billie, pull chairs up to our table. Anne flirts and teases Billie about the leather strap wrapped around her left arm. Then asks Laura to dance. The rest of us watch them shake their shoulders and bump their hips to "Heard it Through the Grapevine" in a pattern that's obviously been danced before. Billie enjoys the show. Gabriel and Martha sip their beer. "Love Will Keep Us Together" comes on. Billie slides into Anne's empty chair next to me. "Dance? This is my song."

She frightens me, and I'm scared of how flattered I am that she asked, but I'm too intimidated to say no. Billie dances conservatively, barely moves her feet, concentrates on a sort of rhythmic bounce of her shoulders, first to the left, then to the right, her hips wide and her feet following casually. I take her lead and hem in my own movements. Laura and Anne get wilder, shimmying up to each other, rubbing shoulders, looking each other up and down, fooling around, pouring on exaggerated lust. I haven't had a sip of alcohol but feel drunk.

Anne waves at Billie and maybe me. Then she makes a pouty-lipped gesture at Laura. Laura throws her head back and looks at Billie, blatantly teasing. Billie smiles like a woman who knows how to bide her time. I start moving to the music in a rhythm more natural to me, push my hips forward with the beat, let years of experience dancing to the radio in the cellar with Renee and Stella take over. Dip and turn when the beat moves me, let my shoulders rotate in their not too subtle movements. It feels crazy and dangerous. It feels good. Billie notices that her new dance partner is loosening up and watches, bounces her head to the music, moves little else. Laura notices her girlfriend's attentions have strayed, squeals, "Hey, that's my girl," and shimmies up to Billie. Anne shimmies up to me, doesn't miss a beat. My composure is rocked, but my body is in the groove, so I keep my balance, and dance.

"You went to Chicopee High School." Anne's lips are close to my ear. "You got a couple of sisters?"

"Yes," I answer, more than a little freaked.

"Don't worry, not everyone's as curious as I am. Small town. I'm easily bored." She switches to my other ear. "Or maybe I'm easily entertained."

"You're So Vain" starts playing. I stiffen and stop dancing. I don't want to keep dancing with Anne. There's an awkward silence that Anne finds amusing. She grins, fondles her rings, and tosses her long hair over her shoulder. I look around to avoid looking at Anne. A woman leaning on the wall in the shadow looks like Stella: tall, thin, dark hair. I used to see Stella everywhere. In the grocery store, when I wasn't thinking of anything really, trying to decide between Cheerios and Raisin Bran, there she was with two kids in tow, rounding the corner in front of me, so I had to put down both boxes of cereal to follow her. But it was never really Stella, not head-on, not headed away. Just like it's not her hugging the wall and slipping out the door tonight.

"Don't be upset. I didn't mean to pry." Anne holds out her arms to dance again. "I'm sorry. Really." She rests her head on my shoulder, puts an arm around my waist, and takes my hand. She flirts with everyone this way? "It's just that I love women. We're so interesting." She burrows farther in to my shoulder. "Don't you think?"

"Yeah," I say, meaning only to acknowledge her comment. Anne is the kind of woman my mother would have warned me about if even her worst nightmare included me slow-dancing with a woman in a dyke bar.

Anne takes my "Yeah" as an invitation to snuggle closer, and squeezes my waist, "*You're* so interesting." She runs her hand under my sweater, causing a jolt up my spine. "And soft." Leaves her hand halfway up my back, just below my bra, and traces dime-sized circles on my skin. The sweet smell of my Shalimar mixes with the spice of her Ambush-scented hair. Her thighs press against mine. "You have a girlfriend?" Even the faint odor of garlic on her breath smells sexy.

"No." I clear my throat. "No, I don't. I'm separated."

"From your husband." She emphasizes husband. "I have a lot of girl-friends. You think that's bad?"

"I'm not actually doing all that much thinking at the moment."

She laughs. "You've never been with a woman, have you?" Her voice lifts at the end of the sentence. I stiffen up again. She squeezes my side. "You're going to love it." She touches my lips with her finger, kisses the back of her own finger and my lips at the same time, pushes the finger into my mouth, demonstrating what she means by "it."

I'm scared, not stiff like usual, scared soft, scared stupid. I look over my shoulder. Gabriel and Martha aren't at the table. I want to make a run for it. My body is not taking orders from the weak messages my brain is sending. Anne stares into my eyes and says, "Relax," in a breathy voice not really meant to calm me. I get a hot chill, on cue, like Pavlov's dog in psych class, salivating on command. I'd probably bark like a German Shepherd if she asked me to right now. I take a deep breath and look away before I turn into a puddle of spittle at her feet.

I see Darlene, one elbow on the bar, talking to Gabriel and Martha, who are perched on bar stools with their backs to the dance floor. Most of the stools are empty. The pool crowd has left. Too early for the drinking and dancing crowd? Darlene waves and keeps talking.

I say what comes naturally to me in a tense situation, "I have to go to the bathroom." I stumble over myself, backing away from Anne. "Excuse me."

"Sure," she says with a toss of her head.

I duck into the DYKEROOM and take a seat. Okay, get it together. Dancing with a girl in a dyke bar—a pretty woman, feminine, but definitely a dyke. A Jamaican woman, or a woman with an accent I'm mistaking for Jamaican, muscles, leather armband. And her sort of mousy, sort of sexy girlfriend. Gabriel a dyke, Martha a dyke, Anne a dyke, means anyone at all *could* be a dyke. Doesn't mean I *am* a dyke.

"How's a person supposed to know?" I'm talking to myself alone in the DYKEROOM again. Just because I was turned on by a beautiful red-headed nymphomaniac? Okay, maybe I am, but I don't have to do it. I don't have to live it. I grab some toilet paper, look down and stop. There's blood between my legs. Did the dancing rip some of the stitches inside me? Kind of late for that. This is what I get for letting myself get all worked up on the dance floor.

"Christ. Get a grip." Menses, the reason I'm here, celebrating in the DYKEROOM, talking to myself like I'm demented. Plain old monthly runoff, like almost every other female of the species.

Dancing with a woman made me forget I have a period, made me forget how happy I was to be out of trouble, back in the safe world of not-pregnant straight girls. I didn't know I was a fucking dyke when I married him. I thought if I acted like a straight girl, I'd be a straight girl. There's no tampon dispenser. I shake my head in disgust. Dykes must get their periods. It's cold in here, but I'm sweating. Sweating, bleeding, and turning into a puddle of lust in the middle of the dance floor. I'm changing physical states? In time I'll be entirely liquid—blood, sweat, tears. A transformation. Maybe that's how I'll change from a good Catholic, a nice girl, a solid citizen—into a dyke.

I walk to the bar and sit on a stool next to Gabriel and Martha, who are nursing tall glasses of something amber-colored on ice. Darlene is changing the roll of receipt paper on the cash register, joking around with a heavily bearded salesman, very male, at the other end of the bar.

"Hi, Gabriel. Hi, Martha."

"Hi, Cora Rose," they answer in unison.

Gabriel stares straight at me with that look of hers, direct, no challenge, just respectful interest. "It's a full moon. Our friends aren't usually this wild." Her plaid shirt is tucked neatly into her black jeans. I've seen the shirt before. It looks more mannish on her straight lean body when the sleeve is covering an elbow propped up against the bar.

"Actually, Anne *is* aggressive." Martha smiles. "Pretty much, all the time."

Darlene, still grinning from some exchange she had with the bearded guy, asks, "You ladies need anything?"

"All set," Gabriel answers for all three of us.

Darlene stacks beer mugs on a shelf under the tap. "You going to be able to make it to my place next week?"

"Looking forward to it." Gabriel raises her glass.

"Like parties?" Darlene addresses me.

"Sure." I've never been to a party as an adult. Not a formal get-together that was planned in advance and wasn't attended exclusively by members of my family.

"I'll be twenty-nine a week from today." She shakes her head like she doesn't believe her own statement. "You should come. Good food. Good music."

"Thanks." I smile, relieved that a woman takes a seat a few stools down and Darlene takes her order without giving me directions or at least a phone number.

CB CB CB

Three hours later, I'm on my bed, staring at the ceiling. One o'clock in the morning. In a few more hours I'll have been awake for a whole day. Renee is working third shift tonight. Sammy is with Joe. The apartment is mine until the morning. My mind races to remember everything that happened tonight. Anne: obsessed with sex, really attractive. Billie: sexy leather armband. Darlene: Harley boots, ball cap, hippest woman I've ever known. Even Gabriel looked good, propped against the bar, shirt neatly tucked, creased jeans. I am fantasizing about every dyke that's ever said hello to me.

So? I can have fantasies, feelings, and not act on them.

Anne kissed me. Doesn't mean she's really interested, that she wants to touch my breasts, run her fingers up the back of my shirt, nip at my neck, my ears, put her fingers back in my mouth and touch my gums again. Who knew gums could be sexy? Enough, Jesus, I already masturbated. I'm still not a bit sleepy. I've got to do something to slow down and get some sleep before Joe shows up with Sammy.

Sammy, Sammy, Sammy. "Sammy's Mommy is a lesbian?" Would a judge take Sammy away from me if he were to find out . . . what? That I've been to The Girls Club, danced with a horny woman, that I want to slide my tongue across her gums, that I'm attracted to a dyke bartender, to my classmate and her gentle gray-haired girlfriend, that I'm lusting after two exhibitionists I barely met? That I kissed a girl the summer before high school and never forgot her?

Anne's hot breath on my throat. The inside cover of Renee's old catechism book featured a young woman in a white robe, surrounded by fire, with her arms up-stretched, reaching; her face lit up by flames, transcending the mundane desires of earth for the glory of His love. My soul is burning a hole in my chest. I take a deep breath, hold it in and try to let the heat out slowly.

I get out of bed, rummage through the medicine cabinet: Percocet, orange baby aspirin, children's Nyquil. A tube of Desitin ointment falls in the sink. I throw it in the trash. Sammy hasn't needed diaper rash ointment for years. Renee's stuff is neatly lined on the top shelf: three lipsticks standing at attention, deodorant, toothbrush in its plastic cup, dental floss, and a bottle of patchouli oil shaped like a little plum. If Darlene, Anne, or Gabriel ever check out the medicine cabinet, I hope they mistake Renee's stuff for mine.

I turn on the shower, pop four baby aspirin in my mouth, and swallow them with a drink of shower water. The warm water calms me some. Eyes closed, I will myself to calm down, relax, get sleepy. Water falls in warm sheets over my bent head, down the curve of my breasts, cascades like twin waterfalls over my nipples, dark against my white skin. Darlene's nipples, darker against already dark skin? Anne's nipples, strawberries? I soap my belly, and run my palm over the stoma. Gabriel's breasts, small, firm, high. My stoma, a little knob, doesn't feel so different from the rest of my wet soapy skin, but out of the shower, lying in bed, the rest of me would be dry, the stoma would still be a moist nipple. What would it feel like to a lover if an ostomy bag or at least tape and gauze weren't covering it? I run my finger around the wet rim. Glory, my roommate in the hospital, once told me that she didn't always cover her stoma during sex. "Depends on my mood," she said. "On Lou's mood. On how recently I had a meal. Sometimes I bury it under a ton of bandages. Sometimes I don't."

"Why would you leave it uncovered?" I had asked.

"Why not? Sometimes sex is more interesting naked. You and me, we got something different." She laughed and her head and shoulders went into their violent dance. "I'm so damned different that my doctors figure there's no way I have sex, period. Fuck them." Good old Glory. She had a hard life, but it was all hers.

Joe accepted me—Dreaded Bowel Disease, stoma, and all. Who else is going to want me now that I've got this "exotic" little thing? I can't go back to Joe. It's too late, even if he'd have me. I'm that scared, but I'm not that stupid or selfish.

I climb back into bed, naked except for my ostomy bag and a dab of Renee's patchouli oil, and drift into sleep: the quilt is a huge soft gauze covering my clean dry skin.

Chapter 18

Awakened from a dream about Joe and Sammy lost in a big dilapidated building, I hear a muffled conversation punctuated by Renee's giggle. Her voice climbs up the living-room stairs and pokes at me in my bed. What day is it? Saturday. Snatches of a woman's gravelly voice, mildly disturbing. I don't want to wake myself up to figure out who the voice belongs to. I peek at Little Ben. Ten a.m. The clink of dishes. Probably Renee having breakfast with one of her work buddies. They're laughing again. Where does Renee get the energy to have these little brunch things after working all night? The thump of soft-soled Nurse Mates padding up the stairs.

There's a knock on my bedroom door. I pull the pillow over my head. Another knock. I open my eyes, close them. I'm not used to waking up in this room again. It's a room built for two, huge compared to the little womb of a pantry I'd been sleeping in, plenty of room for Joe's ghost to float around. I retreat into the blankets, gather them around me like a mummy, and ignore the sound of the door opening.

"Wake up. It's almost ten o'clock." Renee shakes my foot.

"So? It's Saturday." I poke one eye out of the covers. "Sammy back from Joe's?"

"No." She picks my pants off the floor and drapes them over the edge of the bed. I curl up in my cocoon and face the wall. "A friend of yours dropped by."

"I don't have any friends." I frown at the wall. "Who?"

"Darlene." She bounces on the bed. I turn and stare at her at her like she's lost her mind. "The girl that used to live downstairs with the actress girlfriend who was in that Neutrogena commercial. The one who told Marie to say 'hi.'" She smirks.

I try to match the voice I was hearing with Darlene's. "Auditioned. Nobody said the girlfriend was actually in the commercial. Is she still here?"

"Imagine getting paid to just sit there and look beautiful." She ignores my question. "She did have a nice complexion." The mattress springs up. "I'll tell Darlene you're sleeping. We've been having a good time without you."

"Jesus." She *is* still here. I sit up. "How bad do I look?"

She gives my face and hair a once-over, picks a brush off the end table, and drags it across my scalp. "Pretty bad."

I swing my legs out of the covers. "Give her a cup of coffee." I peel Joe's old undershirt off and fling it on the floor. "Please."

With her hands on her hips, she sighs, "We've already had coffee. I'll try to entertain her for a couple more minutes."

I hop around, pulling a clean t-shirt over my head, and try to slip into my sneakers without untying them. My reflection in the dresser mirror shows four inches of hair sticking straight out of my head in wild spikes. My eyes are circled in black. I strip and jump in the shower before I tumble down the stairs, wrapping a towel around my head, zipping my jeans.

"She couldn't stay," Renee yells from her bedroom/pantry. "But she left you something."

Renee's little space, my old room, is all decked out: daybed with sham, pillowcases, matching curtains. The world's smallest desk, red cherry with a little brass hurricane lamp sitting on it. It's the nicest room in the apartment, a miracle of a room with its Lilliputian furniture infused with Renee's patchouli. She hands me an invitation with an African mask stamped in the right-hand corner. "We've been invited to a party." Ten a.m.—she worked all night, but Renee and her mini boudoir are ready for a *House Beautiful* shoot.

"We? It's addressed to 'Cora Rose.'" I give her a dirty look and read the card. "PARTY. Come as you are, 47 Edgemont Terrace, 8 PM, Friday, November 8. NO PRESENTS PLEASE." Six days away. Hand-delivered.

Renee writes "Darlene's Party" on her calendar. "She invited me too. She's sweet."

"I'm not going to this party and neither are you." I wave the invitation at Renee and sit on her freshly fluffed daybed. "I don't care how *sweet* she is."

"Getting bent out of shape because I like your friend?" She says in the restrained, snotty tone she's cultivated for use when the conversation is not going her way. She picks a lacquer tray, two coffee cups, a sugar bowl, and creamer off the seat of her desk chair. "Marie was right. Not only is she a lesbian. She talks about it smooth as silk." She wiggles her shoulders with delight. "I asked her why she moved. She called the Neutrogena woman her ex-girlfriend and she meant ex-*girlfriend*."

"So? You're the bleeding-heart liberal. What do you care?" I roll my eyes to demonstrate how much these irrelevancies bore me. "How long was she here?" I use the nicest tone I can muster even though I'm fuming at the thought of the two of them drinking coffee on the daybed. All of a sudden, it seems like an injustice that my sister got my cozy little womb of a room and I'm stuck upstairs in that uncomfortable expanse. "Wouldn't you have been more comfortable on the full-sized couch or at the adult-sized kitchen table?" Renee's got a ton of people to hang out with. She doesn't need Darlene.

"I'm glad I'm comfortable being straight so I don't have to pretend that I'm not interested in whether a girl is a lesbian or not." Renee is positively gleeful. "She's studying to be a CPA. Practical. I bet she makes good tips at that bar. I always wondered how she could afford that car." She puts the tray back on the chair and sits on the daybed next to me. "She knows that girl you've been studying with."

I stare at her without blinking.

"You know what I think." She pauses for melodramatic effect. "I think that Gabriel person is a lesbian too." She follows me out of the room and sways past me with her tray of dirty dishes. "You'll feel better if you talk about it. You can't really hide these things from a roommate."

"Look, Renee." What made me think I'd be able to sneak anywhere, anytime, without at least one of my sisters butting in? She turns around and looks at me attentively. "There's nothing to talk about. I didn't want to be alone. Gabriel invited me for a drink." My voice is shrill. "It happened to be at that bar."

"That bar?" She concentrates. "You went to The Girls Club again?"

I groan. Why don't I just start writing a diary and hand it over to her every night? "I am not going to that party. Joe would go nuts if he found out."

"Because she's a lesbian? You can go to a lesbian bar, but not a house party for an old neighbor? Calm yourself. You'll be glad I'm with you when you're waiting for Darlene's door to swing open on Friday night."

ෲ ෲ ෲ

She's right.

A few days later as I stare at the oak door and brass light fixtures of 47 Edgemont Terrace, I'm glad she's with me. "Nice, huh?" I say. No matter what she's doing—smoking pot, looking at *Playboy*, waiting for a big dyke to answer the door—Renee makes everything seem so All-American.

"Classy." Renee looks the place over approvingly. Each apartment has a deck in back, and in front a small terrace jutting out from the second floor with scrolled railings. It looks like a train of Swiss chalets stopping for a rest in the middle of Chicopee.

"Charming." I point to the shutters. "Blue mist." Stalling for time, I point to the window casing. "Lemon drop."

"Knock," she commands. We're already late. I couldn't get anyone to fill in at McDonald's. When I don't knock, she pushes in front of me, bangs on the door, and peers in the peephole. "I can't see anything." She bangs louder. "Relax. You look nice. Now if anyone asks you . . ." I'm spared her last-minute advice by the hot air and laughter that rushes at us as Darlene swings open the door.

She hugs Renee like they're old friends. My arms hang at my sides like sledgehammers. Renee exclaims about the linen wallpaper and the assorted masks over the couch. "Where did you get this?" She squeals over the arty photograph of two naked women in an embrace, dark skin bathed in pink light.

Renee has gone to lots of parties. She gushes over Darlene like this whole lesbian thing is just one more reason to put on a miniskirt. Marie's snide remarks and out-and-out hostility don't seem so bad at this moment. Renee bought chapter four in *Human Development and Personality* lock, stock and barrel. Sister Mary Margaret explained that "Chapter Four was revised a few years ago to include homosexuality as a possible cause for emotional problems related to stigmatization as opposed to the old text that regarded this sexual preference as a mental illness in itself." I memorized it. Renee took it for Gospel. Sister Mary Margaret, who usually talks a subject into dust, glossed over it. Sister Mary Margaret and I don't have a firm grasp on the origin and meaning of homosexuality. In one edition I'm flirting with mental illness, in the next edition I'm *exploring* a socially unacceptable sexual preference. Why should Renee understand this?

Darlene pulls me back to the present moment. "Glad you came, Cora Rose." Her smile seems genuine. She doesn't hug me. She's openly admiring Renee in her big blue t-shirt, cinched at the waist, the hem eight inches above her knees. "You look good." She grins at me to back up her statement about Renee. I don't grin back. Renee's body doesn't need me to back it up. Darlene's a knockout herself in a white tailored suit and shiny black wing tips. I stick my hands in my pockets. "May I?" Darlene extends her arm, already draped with Renee's coat.

"Give Darlene your coat," Renee says under her breath.

I'm wearing blue jeans and a plain navy blue sweater over a starched white Ship N Shore blouse. Boring. Renee decided my ass looked best in faded denim. Everyone in the room is more dressed up than I am. The invitation said, Come as You Are. I'm faded jeans, the rest of Darlene's friends are gold ankle bracelets and silk ties.

Darlene introduces us as her "new friends." I wander into the kitchen, stand by the sink, sip orange juice, and study the bowl of Fritos and a half-eaten birthday cake on the counter. There's more food on a table in a breakfast nook in the corner, where four black women are bent over, arguing, laughing, teasing each other, paying no attention to me. It feels weird. I'm not used to being the only white girl in a room. It feels weird wherever I am lately. Lately, since I was twelve.

They're playing charades in the living room. I lean on the counter, position myself in the perfect spot to survey both games. In the living room, fifteen or twenty women and a few guys play with the usual prompting of answers and indignant accusations of cheating from all sides. Renee sits in a prominent spot on the sofa. Darlene directs the action from her seat on the arm of the couch. I strain to hear the conversation. They argue over who belongs on what team. They decide to pantomime countries. I hate charades.

Renee jumps up. "Brussels."

"Brussels is the capital." Darlene laughs. "But close enough."

A guy with a serious Afro asks Darlene, "Whose team are you on?" He's a guy who used to spend the night at Darlene's and Jackie's once in a while. "Her team is correct no matter what answer they give." He points at Renee.

"Bisexuals are not to be trusted," says a woman who is sitting on the floor between his knees and better not be driving herself home, speaking much louder than necessary. "Too many ways to cheat."

"Who are you accusing of being a bisexual?" Darlene fakes outrage. There's a split second of silence before she laughs and the rest of the room follows. "If that is an attack on the sovereignty of *my* homosexuality, I resent and deny it." She raises her arms. "In any case, it's my birthday and I forbid the keeping of scores."

Music floats up the cellar stairs on a cloud of cigarette smoke. The song changes from loud Beatles ("Yellow Submarine") to a low sexy female voice, "I Got It Bad, and That Ain't Good." The softening of the music makes me feel even more out of it hanging around in the kitchen with the white appliances. Bisexual? Darlene's no bisexual. They were just kidding around. Jesus, another fucking option. The women at the kitchen table play a game with round pieces like checkers on a board with black and white triangles. Backgammon? "Hey, you want to keep us honest?" A thin woman with sharp features asks. All four women look my way. "You know how to keep score?"

"No. Sorry. I never played," I answer sheepishly.

They turn back to their game. I venture a few steps down into the smoky cellar, peek through the stair railings, and wait for my eyes to adjust to the dim haze. There are two girls in a shadow at the bottom of the stairs, white women. One has her arms around the other one from behind. Four couples are slow-dancing. Two black, five white, one dark-skinned white or light-skinned black, Puerto Rican maybe, five girls, three guys. Or possibly six girls, two guys; depends if the tall white one in the baseball cap dancing with the white, definitely female one in the tight, green, sequined sweater with the red hair falling down her back, is male or female. Jesus, I'm keeping score by race and gender. Does everyone's mind do this? I squint and run my tongue across my gums. The girl in the green sequins is Anne. I thought she'd be here. I play with the little knob at the nape of my neck. I'd give anything for Lorraine's French twist right now.

The song ends. The person that Anne has been dancing with steps back and bends at the waist. Female. I watch from behind the bars of the stairs as Anne walks over to the tape player and fast-forwards it. Good thing there's already a slit or her movement would rip out the side of her skirt. Anne snuggles up to her partner. They dance in the far corner to "Bewitched, Bothered, and Bewildered." It sounds like something my father would listen to; Ella Fitzgerald, I think. I descend a few steps, wave at Anne who is resting her head on her partner's shoulder. She mouths, "How you doing?"

"Great," I mouth back and make an okay sign with my thumb and first finger. What a lame gesture; what a loser, hanging around on the stairs, gawking at people. Anne's green sequins twinkle in the light of the lava lamp, forty feet away. I covet the entire package she flaunts around the room, her thighs curved under her short tight green skirt, her back swaying under her partner's hand, her long red hair. The way she gives in to herself and lets herself be sexy. Her guts. She's in someone else's arms. It's safe to lust after her without reserve. I'm not sure I like her, but I definitely lust for her.

The song ends, I shove my loose hair behind my ears. Anne's partner walks to the pool table, picks up a cue stick, and waits for her turn while a short black guy sizes up his shot. I'm pretty sure he's a guy.

Anne watches the pool game. I watch Anne. I walk down into the cellar, through the crowd, and lean into her perfume. "Hi, Anne."

She turns. Her hair brushes my cheek. "Cora Rose."

I say, "Hi, Anne," again.

She plays with the three rings on her middle finger, pulls them off, slides them back on one at a time, smiles curiously, but makes no effort to engage me. She has beautiful skin, smooth and clear. Full lips. Her collarbone peeks out under the neck of her green sweater.

My hands are folded in front of me. I wish I could stash them somewhere. Renee keeps telling me to keep them out of my pockets, but I'm afraid they might reach out on their own, glide over the curves of Anne's breasts without her—or my—permission. My hands behave, hang in front of me harmlessly, but they should be covered up, not left dangling below my belt, in full view.

"I like your hair like that," she finally speaks. "When a Man Loves a Woman" starts playing. "I love this song."

"You want to dance?" jumps out of my mouth. I almost look around to see who said it.

"Sure," she answers. Then frowns, considering. "I already asked Jamie, but she doesn't appear interested." Her hand is already on my shoulder. "And you're so cute."

We dance. She leads. All I have to do is follow the sway and smell her sweet-scented hair, but halfway through the song I imagine Renee walking down the stairs. The thought freaks me out. My chest constricts. The air in the cellar seems to be thinning. "Excuse me." I pull away from the embrace. "I think my sister needs me."

"Your sister needs you?" Anne knits her brows.

I nod and bound up the cellar stairs. Thank God there's a backdoor out of Darlene's kitchen. The cold air hits me like a bucket of ice water. I shiver in my shirtsleeves and sweater and stare at the river that runs past the long narrow backyards of Darlene's apartment complex. Before these buildings went up, this spot was a big field. On hot summer nights, high school kids with kegs of beer and transistor radios would watch the river flow. I bet Marie made out on the knoll that Darlene's apartment is sitting on.

That was a close call in there. Anne is real, not some fantasy. She has sex with other girls. I rub my arms. I could freeze to death out here trying to save myself. The knob on Darlene's door doesn't turn. I locked myself out. I knock and peer through the kitchen window. I can't see anyone inside and rap louder. Bob Marley is wailing "No Woman, No Cry." I'm going to have to brave the front door and the crowd in the living room.

As I round the corner of the building, Gabriel and Martha step onto Darlene's stoop, lean against the handrail, and look up at the sky. Martha embraces Gabriel from behind, the side of her face on Gabriel's back. Kind of sweet. Moonlight softens their features. Gabriel gazes up, dreamy, almost pretty. I clamp my hands in my armpits. It's a clear night, plenty of stars. They're wearing jackets, hats, and gloves. They could stand there stargazing for an hour.

I hurry up the walk. "Hi, Gabriel. Hi, Martha."

"Cora Rose." Martha looks concerned about the way I'm shaking. "Better get you inside."

The drunk woman who had been leaning on the guy's knees during charades swings open the door. Waving a drink in her hand, she says "Welcome" flamboyantly, and turns back to a conversation with the guy who was playing pool in the cellar when I left. She lifts her drink to emphasize her point. "No such thing as no-strings-attached. With sex, there are always consequences. I'm not speaking of ethics. I mean practically, it's the way things work in the world."

Gabriel, Martha, and I slip through the crowded living room. Renee stands in the middle of the group that's discussing the consequences of sex. Maybe she'll give a guest lecture on the consequences of abstinence.

We make it to the kitchen, which is now empty, without a ripple of recognition from anyone. "Tea?" Martha puts the heat on under the kettle. We sit in the corner nook sipping orange pekoe. Pool balls crack. As "Joy to the World" vibrates below us, a discussion about monogamy rises above the general din coming from the living room. Gabriel smiles, Martha smiles, I smile. We're not slipping into easy party talk.

"How's your patient profile coming?" Gabriel sounds bored by her question.

"Not so good. I've been having a little trouble concentrating." Drinking tea and discussing gallstones. We're having a Future Nurses of America meeting in the middle of Woodstock.

Darlene enters and says, "I thought I saw you two sneak in." She plunks a glass on the table. "What are you drinking?" She sways a little and catches her balance by hanging on to the table. She holds up her glass. "Gin and tonic?"

"Thanks." Gabriel lifts her teacup. "We're all set."

"Cora Rose? I only drink once a year and this is it. Have a gin and tonic with me?"

By the time Darlene mixes a second batch, I'm almost relaxed. Darlene cocks her ear to the music floating up the cellar stairs. It's Ella Fitzgerald again, "You Can't Take That Away From Me."

"Oh, please." Darlene braces herself with her hands flat on the table. "Who needs to hear this song on my birthday?"

"Memories?" Martha asks with a sympathetic smile.

"Memories will not fuck up the festivities." Darlene takes a big slug of gin. "Anybody want to dance?"

We join the party downstairs. Darlene and I dance to "You Can't Take That Away From Me" twice. It's easy to dance with Darlene. The gin and tonic is sweet on her breath. She doesn't talk too much and she's definitely leading. She's polite, but her mind is far away, not asking much of me except that I relax and follow.

Crack. Crack. Crack. Pool balls. *"The way you wear your hat. The way you sip your tea. The memory of all that. You can't take that away from me."* I'm drunk and happy.

Darlene stops humming. "Did you and your husband have a song?"

"Not really." Joe, my husband, are you drunk and happy somewhere tonight? No. Joe's taking care of Sammy. Don't give Sammy a pop tart for supper, Joe. Put him to bed by nine, don't smoke cigarettes or dope in front of him. Don't smoke dope at all tonight. Don't hate me because I'm slow-dancing with a woman who is thinking of someone else while I'm in her arms.

"I think I got a roommate." Darlene nods across the room at Anne, who is dancing with Jamie again.

I must be high, because I turn around, stare directly at them, and wave at Anne. The music stops, Darlene bows elegantly, and says, "Thank you." I stand alone on the edge of the dance floor for a few minutes, then go back upstairs and visit the gin and tonic and the bathroom before I go outside again, this time with my coat on, to study the train of yuppie dream houses. I'm pleasantly woozy. The party's breaking up. It's nice to watch people float out the door in little clouds that the warm air makes when it hits the cold air.

Renee comes out, says, "There you are," and opens the passenger door to her Civic.

"Don't need a ride."

She gestures impatiently for me to get in. "I am not letting you walk home drunk. It's almost two o'clock."

"Gabriel's giving me a lift." Gabriel and Martha left a half-hour ago, but Renee doesn't know that.

"I knew you'd have a good time." She chitchats about the party. I watch her breath make cool-looking puffs in the air. "You sure they're giving you a ride?" I nod and puff out my own little pillows until she gets in her car and drives away.

I walk in the general direction of home, keep checking my hands and head to make sure my mittens and hat are on. I feel pretty good, false courage being better than none at all. Not so drunk that I don't know it's cold. Drunk enough that I can't feel it. Perfect.

I balance on one foot on top of a little pile of hard-packed snow. Just drunk enough to be proud of this achievement, I slide down, land on my knees, and laugh. "Isn't life wonderful, snow in November?" I say out loud. If I don't think too hard, I'm just exactly drunk enough to believe that I can keep up this balancing act of being aroused by the thought of being with a woman, without actually being a down and dirty dyke.

I'm having a little fantasy about the back seat of Darlene's Mustang when I hear a car pull up, get off my knees, and look up. It's Anne. She's leaning out the open window of her beat-up Camaro. Her chin is in her hands. Her long hair hangs down below her propped elbows. Exhaust pours out her tailpipe. "You're drunk," she says approvingly.

"You look like a movie star. Is it warm in that car?" I've made up a poem.

Her heater is broken, but it's still warmer in her car than on the snow pile. She doesn't seem to think driving requires two hands on the wheel or two eyes on the road. She pulls a bottle of Heineken from under the seat. Her hand, in a soft leather glove, twists off the cap, and brings the bottle to her lips. She passes it to me. Everything about her is sleek. I take a slug and finger my earring. She wipes my lips with the back of her gloved hand and kisses my cheek. Her musk cuts through the yeasty beer smell. She smells powdery, clean, like she just stepped out of a bath, not a bar. I get rigid when she touches me, but lean a little toward her when she draws away.

"Tell me." She smiles. "I like you. You like me?"

"You make me nervous."

"Because I'm forward?"

"You flirt with everyone. It's hard to know if you're serious."

"Serious." She pulls her head back and laughs. "I told you, I love women and I love sex. Seriously. How about you, Cora Rose? It's you that needs to decide whether she's serious or not."

"I'm drunk. Seriously."

She drives without comment for a few minutes.

She takes a right onto a street I've never been on. "Where are we going?"

"My house, unless you say no. I'll drive you home, if you'd rather." She tilts her head coyly.

"I've never said no to anyone."

"You've really never said no to anyone?" This fact seems to excite her. I don't have the heart to tell her that I've only been asked by one person, my husband. "Maybe it's *you* who's obsessed. Tell me, are you attracted to every woman you meet who you happen to know is a lesbian?" She arches her eyebrows. "Darlene? Gabriel? Me?"

"You all make me nervous." I'm liking Anne more every minute. She's direct and so easy to talk to.

"Nervous is serious." She pulls to the curb in front of a big brick apartment building. "We're home." She takes her leather gloves off slowly, biting the tip of each finger, and tugging. When both gloves are off, she lowers her lashes, sticks out her bottom lip, and teases, "Are you going to make me do all the work?" She puts a hand on my cheek. I turn my head and kiss her palm. I kiss her mouth, the kiss I've been hoarding since Stella. I'd hold her and kiss her until we freeze to death in her car, but Anne pulls away, laughing. "Lucky me, you've got a case of coming-out horniness. There's a cure. By the way, you're not that drunk, but if you need to think you are, it's okay with me."

Twenty minutes later, I'm on my back on her satin bedspread, fully clothed, hat, scarf, boots still on, my peacoat a lump by the door. One of my arms is still inside my navy blue sweater. My Ship N Shore blouse is hiked up around my neck.

I adjust my bra and shirt and make a futile stab at the sweater. Anne is also fully clothed. Her green sequined sweater is disheveled, her skirt unzipped. She bends over, rummaging through an old steamer trunk at the end of her bed. The slit of her skirt is ripped almost up to her waist. There's a run in her green tights. I grin, remembering the easy ripping sound of the silk lining, the more resistant popping as the stitches in the slit of the skirt's fabric gave way one stitch at a time in rapid succession as I groped for her, too impatient to wait until my fingers found the zipper. I ripped the skirt of a woman I barely know in a sex-crazed frenzy. Tore her stockings. In the morning I'll feel sordid, stupid, sinful, scared to death. I feel all those things now, but mostly I feel Anne gazing at me like I'm the most desirable woman she's ever laid eyes on. I can't wipe the grin off my face.

I already came twice and my boots aren't even unlaced. I'm not sure if Anne came at all. There was a lot of heavy breathing, a lot of moaning in a short span of time that didn't all come from me. She smiles over the curve of her butt, straightens up, pulls the green sweater over her head, and throws it on a chair. Her hard little nipples, visible through the mesh lace of her pink bra, point downward as she bends toward the contents of the trunk again and pulls out a negligee yellow with age, a man's velvet smoking jacket, and fishnet stockings. She discards them in a pile at her feet and holds up a silk kimono. "Here's what I want." She rubs the silk against her cheek.

She unhooks her bra and lets it fall to the floor. I stare at her breasts. I've never stared at breasts before—seen plenty, but never stared. Hers have strawberry pink nipples just as I imagined. She shakes her long red hair and throws the kimono over her shoulder. It covers one pale breast. She walks to the bay window, naked except for her boots. She faces the street and pulls down the shade on the small cluttered studio apartment.

One foot on the trunk, Anne unlaces her knee-high leather boot slowly, watches me watch her reflection in the oval mirror to her right. Her breasts dip and bob from two different angles as she performs for the glass and me. She walks back over to the bed and kneels on the mattress in front of me. "Here, let me help." She slides her hands inside the sleeve of my sweater, pulls it off my shoulder, and unbuttons my blouse slowly from the top, looking straight into my eyes the whole time. With her hand in the hollow between my breasts, she lifts the bra over them. Kneads my midriff, works her hands up my sides to my shoulders, pushes me back down on the bed, kneads slowly down each of my arms, holds me by my wrists, sucks one nipple, then the other with her insistent moist lips, nipping the hard tip of each puckered nipple. The bra cuts into me above my breasts.

I cum in my pants for the third time in twenty-five minutes.

She pulls back, pleased with herself, and places the kimono in my lap. "You might be more comfortable in this."

A gurgling noise comes from under my still zipped jeans, the last of the gin babbling its way to its logical conclusion. I feel the little bulge of the ostomy. Anne slides onto the bed, straddles me, rests her butt on my thighs. She arches her back so that if I was naked our pussies would be touching. She's surrounded by a halo glow from a candle burning on her night table. I lean back on my elbows, focus on the curve of her belly and the mound of her red bush. She twists one finger in the hair above her clit, otherwise sits very still and lets me look.

There's another gurgle, louder, and a slight cramp. I sit forward, panic like someone switched on a searchlight. Anne balances with the flat of her hands on the bed so she doesn't tumble off my lap. A wave of nausea comes over me. "I'm sorry. Maybe I should go home." I realize how selfish this is. Anne is just warming up, but the booze is wearing off and every fear I've ever had seems to be converging. What if she wants me to get naked from the waist down?

211

She puts one hand around my neck. She says, "Stay," softly, but it feels like a command. I'm afraid of her. She takes her hand from the front of my jeans, slides it to the back, rests her middle finger in the crack of my ass and massages. "Don't be embarrassed. I'm curious." She lies down on the bed, pulls me down next to her.

"I need the bathroom."

"Of course." She rolls over. "I'm sorry, I wasn't thinking," she says sincerely.

When I come back, she's sitting on the bed, her hair draped over her breasts, straddling a pillow, rocking, riding the pillow like she's Lady Godiva on her horse. "Keep your pants on if you want too. But please don't leave. Not yet." The quake in her voice, the raw loneliness, starts a tremor in me. I sit next to her, naked from the waist up.

She sits on my lap and straddles me, one hand on my back, the other hand massaging my ass right where we left before I got up to use the bathroom. She curves her upper body into mine, her breasts an inch from my breasts. She leans closer, braces herself on the bed, and sways so her nipples graze mine. Then she moves her hips like she's pumping on a swing. I close my eyes, grateful she's doing the work, that she's persistent and knows what she wants. She's not going to make me expose anything I don't want to.

Chapter 19

Locked out of the apartment, I fumble in the depths of my book bag, dump the contents on the dirty floor, and rummage through notebooks, empty Frito bags, and tubes of Stomaease. No keys. I bang my head on the door like the autistic kid in the psychology film I just saw. "Autism: a syndrome that exhibits ego-centeredness, the failure to form viable interpersonal relationships, and peculiarities of thought." Sounds like most of the people I know. I bang my head again. Maybe I can knock some sense into myself. Anne will be here in an hour to pick me up. What "peculiarities of thought" make me think I'm capable of being "just friends" with a woman who makes me wet by sitting next to me on a barstool?

From inside the apartment I hear sharp footsteps stopping just short of the door. The handle jiggles and stops without the door opening. Inside, Marie yells, "Tell your boyfriend that me and Donny will be better off without him." I was counting on coming home to an empty apartment. I should be counting my blessings. If my sisters weren't here having their weekly bout, I'd really be locked out.

The door opens with a whoosh. Which sister opened it? They barely give me a glance before squaring off again. Good, let them concentrate on each other. Under no circumstances do I want them to find out about my plans to spend the evening with Anne and Darlene. "Nice to be home." I squeeze between them, drop my junk on the coffee table, and snatch up the keys that are sitting right on top of it.

"I'm trying to leave, but she keeps yapping at me," Marie snaps.

"She's not talking now." I grab a ValuCola off the coffee table and study my sisters, both silent for the moment. I'm pretty sure my failure to form "viable interpersonal relationships" is partly genetic. "Didn't you figure who could hold a stare the longest in grammar school?" Neither of them flinches. "I thought you guys were taking the boys to the mall to see Santa?"

Renee answers without turning her head. "Mom and Dad took them." God bless Mom and Dad. They take the boys overnight almost every Friday.

"Eddie," Marie says in a superior tone, "has a good job. He's faithful *and* reliable. Donny's easier to handle when Eddie's around."

"Donny's afraid of him." Renee snatches the ValuCola out of my hand, takes a swallow, and shoves the can back at me. I flop down on the couch.

Marie says, "Donny respects Eddie. He'll make a good father."

"Donny already has a good father." Abruptly, Renee changes gears. "Donny will be better off if Fletcher gets an education." You can almost hear her voice grind as it shifts into the conciliatory air of a politician working a tough crowd. She stops glaring at Marie, trying to change the rules of the contest from who can keep eye contact longest to who can be least ruffled by the other.

Marie snorts. "Fletcher a college man? That'll last about a week. Where's the money coming from? He owes two months child support."

"He does?" Renee's eyes narrow.

Marie grins. "Your boyfriend didn't mention that?"

"Here's a concept." Renee huffs. "A man and a woman. Friends. No sex involved."

"You're a freak. Here's normal." Marie counters. "A man and a woman. Sex."

I lift up my book bag to demonstrate the weight of my studies. "Why don't you guys fight *somewhere else*?" Anne will be here in forty minutes, and counting. "They're threatening academic probation for anyone who doesn't keep a C+ average."

"Academic probation." Marie pouts sarcastically.

"Fletcher and Renee could never be involved romantically. They're like brother and sister," I say. "Besides, Renee's afraid of sex. And Fletcher's afraid of you."

"I am not afraid of sex," Renee says indignantly. "It just doesn't rule my life."

"The hell you're not." Marie throws her head back and laughs. I sip on my cola. Marie snaps a cigarette from a pack and aims the end of the butt at Renee. "Eddie's not a pothead." She fires off her remarks like she means it to take out an eye.

"Fletcher is clean and sober," Renee shoots back.

"Because he made it to an AA meeting, and plans to enroll in Community College to impress his probation officer? How many times do you think he'll get probation before they throw him in jail?" Marie taps the cigarette on the stair rail. "Too bad he can't switch to alcohol. But he likes his high to be illegal. Taboos are part of the thrill."

"Marie." I attempt a conciliatory Dr. Joyce Brothers voice. "You've been after Fletcher to clean up and get a decent job for years."

"Oh, now you're a relationship expert too?" Marie grabs her parka from the stair post.

I hold the door open for Marie. "Bang your head against something. You'll feel better."

"I meet my problems straight on. I don't have to bang my head." She rams her arms in the sleeves of her parka.

"What's that suppose to mean?" I let go of the door to throw up my hands.

"Renee needs a new rehab project to take her mind off Fletcher. Maybe she can straighten you out before you start buying your clothes in the men's department." Her eyes, slits of light, focus on Renee. "Putting out a stinking thirty-five dollars a week for your own kid is not too much to ask. At least if you were screwing him your *friendship*," the teeth on her zipper grate as she yanks it up, "would make some sense. Fletcher talks pretty, but Eddie walks the walk." She slams the door behind herself.

When I emerge from the shower, Renee is still sitting on the ratty chair, staring into space. "Marie does not love Eddie." She twitches her shoulders to demonstrate her repulsion. "You think she's having some kind of breakdown?"

"No." I give her an annoyed glance from the window where I'm looking out at the driveway. "I think she's living her life."

"You should try to help her. Talk to her." She sounds so earnest that I could smack her.

"Me?"

"You don't get under her skin as much as I do. Are you so self-absorbed that you haven't noticed that Marie is in deep shit here? Did you see her hair? It wasn't even brushed." She stands up to make this last point.

"Maybe we should both mind our own business." I run my hand through my own hair, which is still damp from the shower.

A horn beeps. Renee scurries over to the window. "Who's that? You want to tell me where you're going?"

"Movies," I lie. I grab my coat and run out.

"Hi." I slide in next to Anne and sneak a glance at her suede jacket. The buttons are on the left side. I'm pretty sure that's the female side. It's Darlene's coat I have to remember to check out.

Anne has borrowed Darlene's Mustang. I'm in love with the bucket seats. My estranged husband and my pain-in-the-ass sisters vanish into the leather molded against my neck and shoulders. It's the kind of car that makes you think you're the kind of girl who knows how to kick back and relax. Small talk is not mandatory in a car that has separate temperature controls for the driver and passenger side.

Anne snaps on the tape player and smiles with satisfaction when a saxophone starts to wail. "They never play George Clinton at The Girls Club," she says more to herself than to me. The plan is to stop at a little shop on Chicopee Street to see if she can find something "suitable" for the family get-together she's been pressed into attending. Then head to the apartment she shares with Darlene. When we see the sign for Fashions By Laura, she slows down and says, "Laura," with affection.

"You looking for a dress?" I ask.

"I don't know, something fun but dignified." She gives the finger to some guy who cuts her off. "I want the relatives to see that their lezzy cousin has interesting taste, but I also want the outfit to show how well-adjusted I am."

"You can do all that with fabric?" I ask, half-serious.

Anne walks me past the lemon taffeta gowns in the window. Laura, of Fashions By Laura, turns out to be a grandmotherly type, who greets Anne like she's the Queen Mum. "Don't worry, dear. You have the kind of figure that I just love to outfit." She gives me a wink.

The light in the dressing room is harsh and unflattering. There seems to be no question in anyone's mind but my own that I belong in here with Anne. Laura hovers outside the door with a steady supply of outfits. It's hard to find places to look while Anne steps in and out of skirts and dresses in a five-by-five dressing room with mirrors on two walls. Just for something to do, I pull on a pair of black dress pants and a frilly white blouse that Laura thought were me. Anne doesn't give her own or my state of undress any attention. She's on a mission and it's not flirting with me.

"Any luck?" Laura pokes her head in, squinting thoughtfully at Anne's long half-naked body. I almost take off my thumb trying to zip my pants so Laura won't see the bulge under my panties.

"Too traditional." Anne frowns. "I need a bold statement."

"I have something that just might work."

"Bring it on." Even dressed in cotton bra and underpants, Anne looks confident enough to manage a family reunion. Until Laura leaves. Then she sits down on the little bench attached to the wall and says, "I hate feeling like the hair-brained pervert my relatives think I am." She hugs her slim muscular arms. "Why do I let them get to me?"

I shrug. "Everybody's family gets to them." The frilly white blouse I tried on is too small. I fold it on my lap. Maybe if my bra and panties matched I wouldn't feel so pale and dirty under the fluorescent bulb.

"Knock, knock," Laura chirps. She hands Anne a pantsuit and me a green dress with a built-in bra.

I sit on the little ledge with the dress in my lap. Anne slips into black pants and some kind of short-waist jacket. Laura looks her up and down. The pants are magnificent on Anne. They're silk and they strain a little at her thighs and butt, just enough to show off her curves. Under the jacket are a cummerbund and a white shirt with satin pleats. A row of mother-of-pearl buttons separates and accentuates her breasts.

"Oh," Laura says with her hand to her throat. "Stunning."

"It's a tuxedo." I blurt. And it's more than stunning.

217

"Too tight?" She considers her reflection.

"No, no. You look great. Great. I just wonder . . . will your family think you look *well-adjusted* in a tuxedo?"

Gray-haired, sensibly shoed Laura grins. How does she happen to have a woman's tuxedo in her shop anyway? "Oh, you should see what the girls are wearing." She trills her fingers. "Men's suits. I mean suits *made* for a man, with spike heels and lacy teddies. Evening gowns that you would swear were lingerie. Nipples." She shakes her head. I can't tell if it's mock disapproval or real disapproval. She brightens. "I have some heels that would be perfect. And pearl earrings, I think." The shop bell, ting, ting, tings. "Oh shoot. Excuse me." She bustles out.

"Too extreme?" Anne runs a hand over the man-tailored silk and satin covering her ass.

My palms sweat. "No. It looks really nice. It just needs to be toned down for a family thing."

"Toned down." She twists, looks at herself from every conceivable angle. She bends forward to see if her breasts pop out. Sits on the bench next to me with her legs crossed to see how high the pants ride up. I'd be happy to sit here, until Laura retires, trying to figure out who Anne is, who I am, watching Anne squirm around in that tuxedo.

I make a conscious effort to snap out of it. I insisted that we be "just friends." Anne agreed. She's gone out of her way not to flirt. She hasn't done anything to make my heart race like this. I'm not pressed against the mirror—her mouth's not pinned against mine—my feet are on the floor—she hasn't lifted me up with her surprisingly muscular arms. I'm supposed to be helping her find an outfit that won't freak out her family. A dressing room is not a place where normal people get turned on. Clothes shopping is something I do with Renee, it's not foreplay. Even if I was brave enough to have a girlfriend, Anne is too wild for me. She is cute, though. She is nice. I exhale slowly, preparing for the sight of her stepping out of that tuxedo. Nobody could say she's not sexy.

"What's up?" she asks.

"Anne." I take a second to choose my words. "You look great."

She looks at me skeptically. "But?" She pulls on the lapels. She cocks her head and purses her mouth in parody of some femme fatale that's oddly self-mocking but appreciative at the same time. She slides her eyes in my direction, mocks a kiss, and cracks a trashy smile. She's funny, but her little skit doesn't make me laugh, it makes my thighs ache. It unnerves me. Her mouth, full and wide on her thin face, makes my own mouth itch. Her fingers, not her eyes, not her breasts or her thighs, make me look away. Her hands remind me of Stella. Our eyes meet. Her look is questioning, curious. She likes me flustered.

"Cora Rose?" She stares at me, serious, intent.

"It's too sexy for a family thing. Unless you want them to talk about how hot you are. Then it's perfect."

"Thanks. I needed an honest opinion." She smiles, friendly, living up to her end of bargain. "Try on your dress."

I don't want her to see my hands shaking. I pull the green dress with the built-in bra over my head, slip out of my own bra quickly so my hands are moving and my breasts aren't exposed. Air hits my nipples and makes them hard little pebbles against the smooth lining. The dress, lightweight wool, is lined with something smooth and luxurious. I pull the dress over my pants before I slip out of them. The pants hit the floor and the silky lining of the dress slides over my thighs. Anne bends to move the pants. The smell of her talcum powder fills the room. The curves of her butt strain against the silk pants. I close my eyes, hold onto the wall.

Anne grabs my shoulders, turns me to face the mirror squarely, and zips me up. We stare at my reflection. Even in Reeboks and mussed hair I look reconstructed, well put together. I run my hands over my waist and down my hips, caress the short sleeve on my shoulder, and finger the scoop neck. This is how Renee feels every time she gets dressed?

"Look." Anne runs her hands over my belly. "The darts at the waist are perfect." She cups her hand and lets it rest on the camouflaged bulge.

I step back, confused, angry at the liberty she's taking.

"Sorry," she says.

Who told her she could touch me there? I pretend to be looking for the price tag.

"Hey, I shouldn't have done that. But, Jesus, you look good." She stares, shaking her head with appreciation. It's wonderful and embarrassing. She grabs the tag hanging from the back of the waist, lets it go with a clucking sound. "Ninety-eight bucks."

"For a dress?" I fumble, trying to unzip myself. "I guess money can make anyone look good."

"Keep it on a second." She stands behind me with her chin on my shoulder. "Please." Her eyes are bright. I feel like a kid playing in the barn. It's confusing how the sexiest things sometimes feel so innocent and ordinary. She straightens up, gravely dignified. "Look at us."

We stare at our reflections. Anne—five eight with her boots off, womanly and reserved in black silk. Me—five foot six, as close to stunning as I'll ever get, in green wool.

On the drive to Darlene's we barely speak, but the feeling is different than the stretches of silence that happened on the drive to Fashions By Laura. Instead of calming me, the absence of conversation makes me wonder nervously about what is not being said. Anne pays much more attention to her driving. There's no music this time. I sneak glances at her. Her bucket seat doesn't seem to be fingering her back and fondling her ass in the suggestive way that mine is.

I turn and look at the tuxedo, which is carefully covered in a cellophane garment bag and draped across the Mustang's black leather seat like a reclining dignitary. She'll wear it "someplace where the girls will appreciate it." Just seeing it lying there gives me a cheap thrill. I wish I was the kind of girl who buys ninety-eight dollar dresses I'll never wear so our clothing could be sprawled together across the back seat.

She pulls the Mustang into Edgewood Terrace. It's painfully festive: tiny white lights hang from the peaks of rooftops and twine around the railings of porches. There are electric candles in Darlene's and Anne's windows and a big red bow on the next door. I wish we could get through Thanksgiving before we start on Christmas.

"If it wasn't for Sammy, I'd ignore the holidays altogether. I wish he could see this."

"That can be arranged," she says enthusiastically as she slips her key into the lock. In the living room, there's a real tree, complete with the scent of pine, blinking lights, and presents already wrapped in Santa paper. She throws her jacket on the arm of the couch. "Wow. You guys start early." I throw my coat over her jacket. "Joe used to really get into Christmas." As soon as Joe's name is out of my mouth, I wish I hadn't said it.

She yells, "Hey, Darlene," at the back of the apartment, but gets no reply. "She must still be shopping. Christmas is bullshit. It always makes me sad. Darlene's into it." She frowns. "Maybe if I had kids."

Anne sails around the spotlessly clean kitchen. She's going to cook for the three of us, roasted red pepper pasta. She brings out a little piece of brown pottery that's shaped like a tiny igloo. "Garlic roaster." She grins in reply to my puzzled look. She's happy moving around in the kitchen. "Linguini or fettucine?" She plunks two boxes of exotic-looking pasta in front of me.

"It's all spaghetti to me." The wooden-handled tongs, the swan-necked faucet she rinses them under, Anne wielding a paring knife: it's all exotic.

"Linguini," she answers herself, returning the losing box to the cupboard, and replacing it with a square-shaped bottle of emerald green olive oil and a cork topped bottle of dark purple vinegar. "Balsamic." She plunks the bottle firmly on the counter. "Gotta be the real thing."

Balsamic? "Darlene into gourmet, too?"

"Eating it, sure. Part of the deal is I buy groceries and cook. Secretaries to assistant bank managers can't afford half the rent on a place like this." She talks as she prepares the food, but she seems to have something on her mind. "Darlene makes more tips on a good weekend than I make all week," Anne answers my unasked question.

I rinse off the shiny red peppers. She looks at me fondly, tucks the garlic in its little pottery igloo and sets it to bake in the oven. Her skirt rides up her thigh as she bends to pick up a heavy black pot that looks like it belonged to the Pilgrims. She fills it with salted water and places it on the burner. She crumples cheese into a cobalt blue bowl. "Gorgonzola. Try it."

I pinch a waxy little morsel between my fingers. It has a powerful, surprising, not altogether pleasant, taste.

"Love it." She tosses a bit of cheese in her mouth before she spears the wide end of a pepper with a long-handled fork. "The perfect tool." She demonstrates how well the smoothed-down wooden handle fits her palm. "Control," she says. Something about the way she rotates the fork and the pepper in her long thin fingers embarrasses and thrills me. She removes the grate from one of the stove's burners and turns the naked red pepper slowly over the open flame. This seems dangerous. The fire actually touches the red skin. The skin chars and lifts off in little bubbles of black against red. Her eyes are riveted to the flame.

The smell of the roasting garlic fills the room. "Where the hell is Darlene?" She seems a little nervous all of a sudden, turns the wooden-handled fork faster. "It gets tricky. You have to char the flesh without burning the pepper to the point it's not edible." The pepper is almost completely black. "Done." She steps away from the flame.

First there's a slight burnt odor. Then the smell of the pepper itself. Strong, stronger than I imagined, overpowering the burnt smell, mixing with the garlic. The odor draws and repels me at the same time. "Can you open that sack?" She nods at a brown paper bag, flattened and waiting on the counter.

I spread the paper edges open and hold the bag while Anne wiggles the burnt pepper off the fork. I cup one hand under the sack. The weight and warmth of the pepper is satisfying in my palm.

"Close it up tight," she instructs me. "Or you'll get high off that." She grins, spears another pepper, and offers me the fork. "You game?"

She watches me turn the pepper slowly over the blue fire. A strand of my hair whisks above the flame. I feel the heat on my cheeks. I don't move away from the fire. I want to feel the heat. She pushes the hair behind my ear and leaves her hand there a second longer than necessary. She steps back. I can feel her looking at me. She picks up a cooled pepper and peels the flesh with just the right tension until the skin rips off in long black strips. "Like skinning an animal," she says. I nod, shocked at the comparison. "Cora Rose," she says resolutely. "You told me you didn't want to be lovers, but I'm getting a vibe here. What do we do about it?" Her eyes focus on the pepper.

"The divorce," I say. "My son." I watch the burnt skin give way under her fingers, so agreeably lewd. "It's strange."

"Divorce?"

"Peppers. Why should burnt skin seem sexy? It's kind of horrible."

She cuts the peppers into warm red tongues. "No, wonderful." She places them in a shallow pasta bowl, drenches them with olive oil and balsamic vinegar, crushes rosemary between her fingers and lets it fall over the bowl. She pours a little oil over the gorgonzola.

"That smells so good."

"Twenty minutes until the garlic's ready." She glances at the stove clock and turns the heat on under the pot of water. "Darlene will be home any minute." She leans against the stove. "So, we pretend there's nothing going on?"

I pick a piece of roasted red pepper out of the bowl and suck it into my mouth. "Sorry." I lick the oil on my lips.

She looks at me intently. "You are not sorry." She reaches into the bowl without taking her eyes off mine and holds a wet warm slip of pepper to her own lips. She sucks it down to the sound of the door in the front room opening. She swallows and licks her own greasy lips. "Darlene's home," she says, wiping the grease from my bottom lip with her thumb. "Quit fucking around. I'm willing to give it a try, but I'm sick of the mixed signals." She stands back and looks at me dead serious. "You've got to behave if you expect me to."

"Okay. I will."

Darlene strides into the kitchen and drops three big Toys R Us bags on the floor with a grunt. "I don't get a hello in my own house?"

"Hello," we say in unison.

She scrutinizes first Anne and then me. "What's up with you two?"

Anne shrugs. "It's a 'let's just be friends' situation."

"Dykes." Darlene shakes her head. "At least at The Girls Club they pay me to watch this shit play out."

Chapter 20

A red, white, and blue flag hangs proudly above the roller rink at The United Skates of America the next morning. I sit safely on the edge, outside the action, in a molded plastic chair, watching a mob of screaming kids and a handful of adults attempt to maneuver around the rink in rented skates. Skaters circle, lights flash, "The Hustle" booms over the intercom. My head pounds. Renee lurches off the rink and stops herself from falling on the floor at my feet by falling on top of me.

"That was quick." I brace her shoulders to keep her off my lap. Renee's lack of athletic ability always cheers me up. I grin, despite the pulsing in my head and the promise I made to myself never to grin again.

"This place is a trip." She pushes off my shoulders, deposits herself in the chair next to mine. She dances in her seat, and sings, "Do the hustle," in her squeaky soprano. She kicks the chair in front of her sideways, hoists her feet, wheels and all, onto the chair's arm, and unlaces the skates.

"I feel like shit," I say.

"You deserve to feel like shit." She reaches for her purse and hands me a tiny tin of aspirin.

"Five hundred people had their fungus feet in those smelly things before you did."

I point to her skates, swallow the aspirin dry, and groan.

"That pain is your body's way of reminding you not to stay out all night while your sister worries herself half to death." She stashes the skates under her chair and rubs her feet.

"You were snoring when I got in. Falling asleep is your body's way of forcing you to mind your own business."

"Before I was snoring, I was worrying. If I hadn't fallen asleep on the couch, I would have been driving around looking for you." She pulls her plastic chair up to the safety rail five feet in front of us.

I pull up closer to her. "Thanks for coming." I try to sound contrite, sincere, but all I really feel is cranky. "Thanks. Really. I didn't want to be alone with Joe today."

"Alone with Joe, Fletcher, the boys, and a hundred screaming kids." She gives me a dirty look as she smoothes her hair and captures it in a big shiny barrette.

"You know what I mean." My eyes are burning, my head is banging, the disco lights are flashing. I locate Joe, Fletcher, and the boys on the rink. The four of them are holding hands, barely moving, but I'm still afraid that Sammy or Donny will fall before I can jump up and save them from a pig pile of metal feet. "I'm sorry you worried."

"You're going to have to talk to him alone sometime if you plan to get a divorce. Or get lawyers so they can talk to each other." Renee takes a sip from a star-studded paper cup and makes a face. "This is awful." She balances the cup in a mound of butts piled in the ashtray in front of us.

"Ugh, gross." I look into the syrupy blue stuff. "Like I can afford a lawyer. I feel lousy. Can we talk about something else?"

"School. Divorce. Losing sleep to engage in relationships outside of the social norm. Stress." She pulls her seat, which was only six inches away to begin with, right next to mine, so the plastic seams on the molded arms line up. "Tell me something. Who are you involved with? Darlene?"

"How do you figure that's any of your business?" I roll my eyes. Let her think I'm involved with Darlene. It's better than telling her the truth; I've evolved from a girl too frightened to admit to herself that she's a lesbian into a sex-starved dyke who gets drunk and falls asleep on her hostesses' couch watching *A Christmas Story* on TV instead of fucking. "Thanks for helping me out today, thanks for cooking breakfast this morning, thanks for the new kitchen curtains. Thanks for all the

225

stuff you do for Sammy. If you could just mind your own business and keep it down when I'm trying to sleep, you'd be the perfect housemate."

Renee stares me down. "Can't have it all. Marie thinks you've been sleeping with Darlene right along."

"When we were neighbors?" I ask more amazed than upset, too hung-over to let myself get all worked up. "Fuck Marie."

Her mouth is a determined slit. "Are you ashamed?"

"Why should I be ashamed? It's an accident of birth that we're related to Marie."

"Don't be stupid, I'm talking about you and Darlene. Marie's sure you're having a thing with her. Lorraine thinks so, too." She raises her eyebrows.

"Lorraine," I snort. "Tell your pals that if I ever have sex with anyone again I'll take pictures they can pass around. You got shit on your shoe." I point to a pink glob on her skate. "We live in the same apartment. Do we have to talk about this in an arena?" She dabs at the pink glob with a tissue. I follow the boys' slow progress around the rink. Sammy has an expression on his face that looks more like worry than fun. "Marie's barely even spoken to Darlene. How does Lorraine even know who she is? The three of you sitting around, gossiping. It makes my skin crawl."

"Being secretive makes people speculate." She studies me like I have a disease she might be able to identify by physical inspection.

"Why don't you find a nice Catholic boy and busy yourself procreating his many fair-haired children?" If I thought it would shut her up, I'd tell her that last night I spent the wee hours cradling Anne while she cried like a baby because *A Christmas Story* reminded her of how wonderful and horrible her family is. No sex, just tears.

"I'm not partial to blondes, and, until I meet someone who really interests me, I prefer sex in the abstract." She wiggles her fingers like she's got something sticky on them. "Emotionally and physically: too messy."

I put my attention back on the rink just in time to see Donny fall to his knees. Fletcher dusts him off and has him laughing in thirty seconds. Sammy takes Donny's hand. Their fathers flank the boys on either side, without actually holding on to them. "They shouldn't let go of their hands. Not for a second," I say.

"The boys are fine. You and Joe should quit trying to do things together with Sammy. It just makes everybody nuts." She gives me a sullen look. "Why don't you trust me?"

"Why don't you let me have a private life?"

"You know what?" She drops a lipstick into her purse and snaps it shut. "I don't give a damn who you sleep with. Find somebody else to care. Find somebody else to stick up for you every time the subject of who you're poking, or sucking, or whatever you do, comes up."

I stare out at the ring for several minutes. Renee, mercifully, stares straight ahead too. Finally I say, exasperated, "I know you care, but, Jesus, Renee."

"Sex sucks." She picks at my hair. "Honestly, look at you, not eating right, not sleeping. You look like shit."

"Thanks. I needed to be told I look like shit. I think I'm going to throw up." I'll never eat gorgonzola again.

"Then throw up. It's time for you to get it together." She whacks my shoulder. "I like taking care of Sammy, but he needs more of you. He needs you alert. And Joe better perk up, too. I wouldn't mind a little attention myself. Anything bothering *you*, Renee?"

"What?"

"Fletcher's trial!" She shakes her head in exasperation.

It's true, I'd forgotten. "His lawyer said he could get him off with probation."

"I don't know. He's a three-time loser. For possession, maybe. Draft evasion is another matter."

"They caught up with him? God, that was so long ago. He'll get amnesty or community service or something, won't he? He told you before he told Marie? *Marie's* Fletcher?"

"You know another Fletcher?"

"I was hoping you did." I slump back into the molded plastic chair. "Renee, they won't put him in jail, right?"

"I don't think so, not for the possession charge anyway. I don't know about amnesty, it's conditional. I'm not sure what that means. He's got two weeks to turn himself over to the draft board." She leans into my ear. "In Georgia. Do not tell her."

"When does he plan on telling her? She's going to kill him, and you, if she finds out you knew and didn't tell her."

"She's going to lose it if he ends up having to stay there while he does community service. He figures, tell her at the last minute and maybe she'll cool off by the time he gets back. Really, I think he can't bear to disappoint her again. He's my best friend. He swore me to secrecy."

"Well, your best friend is being an asshole. Do you have any idea how odd it is that your *best* friend is Marie's pot-smoking, draft-dodging ex?" I'm not trying to be insulting, even Memere thinks their friendship is odd. "I don't get it. But then, it's none of my business."

"Fletcher is a conscientious objector. He just didn't fill out the paperwork. Okay, sometimes he is an asshole." She shivers and hugs her arms to her chest. "I've got to tell you something."

"Please don't tell me you're in love with Fletcher. I always wondered if he was why you never. . ."

"Shut up, Cora Rose," she snaps. "Here it is. I have no interest in Fletcher, not sexually. But I'm not a virgin. I've had sex with two different guys. It was fine, just not fine enough to do again until I'm damn good and ready. You and Marie are slaves to sex. That's not going to happen to me."

"How did you pull it off? We had no idea." I'm dumbfounded.

"Oh, it was easy. You and Marie are so sure I'm some frigid prima donna. All I had to do is let you keep believing your preconceived notions about me." She groans. "Why are we talking about sex? I'm trying to tell you something important. If I was you, I'd be worried about Joe."

"Worried about Joe getting busted?"

She nods. "Why not? They live together."

It never occurred to me to be worried about Joe. He buys his pot a joint at a time from some guy at work, or he smokes Fletcher's. Or, that's what he used to do.

"You better talk to him." She bites her lip. "And, what do we do about that Eddie character?"

God, please, no more. "Why is he *that Eddie character*? Marie plans to marry him. Can't we just get out of her way?"

She pulls her head back and looks at me wide-eyed like I've said something astounding. "He's a jerk," she finally says. "He treats Mom and Dad like they're Ma and Pa Clampett." She motions to the edge of the rink. "Here they come."

A serious wave of nausea washes over me. "I'm sorry." I get out of the plastic chair. "I can't face Joe right now."

I stand outside the United Skates of America at the edge of an ocean of parked cars with only Renee's scented tissue to defend me from the smelly exhaust. Disco music bangs out of the big brick building. Before I can decide what part of the lot is least polluted, Joe is at my side. "What's up with you?" he asks in the demanding voice he's been using lately. All the effort I've put out over the last few weeks to make sure I'm not alone with him, and now Joe's got me cornered in a parking lot full of parents buckling in their over-stimulated kids.

"I'm sick." I turn away and take a deep breath of cold air. When did Joe turn into somebody I can't stand being with in the same parking lot?

"Christ, you're not pregnant?" he asks, like that would be one more thing I'd do to aggravate him. He grabs my arm. "Are you?"

"No, Joe." How much longer can I keep myself from vomiting? "Nice of you to ask at this late date."

We glare at each other, letting out the pent-up hostility we try to keep under wraps in front of Sammy. Strange to be face to face and feel so far away from Joe. He's still clenching my arm. My feelings for him have been all over the map. Sometimes I feel a fierce tenderness for him, remorse that I've left him alone in life, abandoned. That emotion shows up mostly if I haven't seen him for a couple days. But lately when I see him he's so cold, and this morning on the phone he was downright nasty. Sometimes I think he really does hate me. Sometimes my body shudders when I think of him.

He fidgets from foot to foot like he does when he's nervous.

"Let go." I tense my arm. He pushes it away. I rub my biceps for effect. My coat is too heavy for him to have caused any damage.

Like an accusation, he asks, "Your checkup at the doctor's went all right?"

I stare through him. Don't get nasty Joe, not about the Dreaded Bowel Disease. Stay my sweet Joe, at least when it comes to that. His eyes are cold little stones. It went great at the doctor's—a clean bill of health that this mutated version of Joe isn't going to hear about.

A second of concern sneaks into his voice. "You're okay?" His mouth and eyes soften.

I want to touch his cheek, to connect with him while that expression is still on his face. That would be one more mistake. For a second it might pull him to me, but then he'd be even angrier. I lean against the building. "Renee and Fletcher with the kids?" I ask even though the answer is obvious. "Dr. Bello says I'm fine. What do you want from me, Joe?"

His arms are crossed on his chest. I close my eyes, try to will him into walking away. I can feel him seething, working himself up, angry that he let his concern for me show. The flat of his hand next to my face when it slaps against the brick makes me flinch. He holds himself against the building, his forearm grazing my cheek. "Are you having an affair with that black woman? One of those dykes that used to live downstairs?"

"Jesus fucking Christ."

"Beautiful." He slams his fist against the wall. I flinch again. "Perfect." He shakes his head and leans in even closer. "Not with my kid living with you," he says nastier than anything I've ever heard come out of him. "You hit the jackpot. Black *and* a dyke, living right under us all those years. Tell me," he spits out, "did it start before or after I left?"

I'm scared out of my mind. "Neither." I look back at him, just as nasty, dead in the eye. My hands form fists. It feels like I'm sitting on my own shoulder, watching. Even my eyes don't feel like my own. It's like I'm looking through binoculars that make everything seem far away and foreign. Joe's eyes are shiny, guarded, like marbles. What he's saying, "My wife couldn't settle for just any lesbian, no she had to find someone that would really make the town sit up and take notice," is strange and detached, not something Joe would say. This can't be Joe. This can't be me.

We stand, making walls against each other with our folded arms.

230

He says, "Don't make me get ugly."

"When did you get to be a crazy racist, Joe?" I'm talking tough, crumbling inside. He couldn't look any uglier to me than he already does.

"Racist? You two are going to get the shit beat out of you and I'm crazy?" His fists open and close. "You got rid of me. How long until Sammy gets in the way of your fun?" He holds his right hand to his chest with his left hand. Both his arms shake. For the first time I'm afraid of his size. "How am I supposed to know he's even my kid?"

Bile comes up in my throat. I spit on the ground, barely missing his sneaker.

"Jesus." He steps back, trembling with rage.

"You're lucky it wasn't your face."

He smirks. "There are a lot of things I never would have believed a few months ago."

I divert my eyes to the cop standing by the main entrance. "There's a cop over there." I hope I'm being melodramatic.

"Call him over." He turns his head, waves at the cop, who is busy directing a swarm of kids, and doesn't acknowledge Joe's gesture. "Tell him about your girlfriend." He gives me an ugly smile.

"Should I tell him about the joint—" I pretend to contemplate where his marijuana might be stashed "—in your glove compartment?" My worst fear: that Joe will take Sammy away from me. What does he know? Obviously, he's getting wrong information. Where's he getting it? Should I stand here and argue with him or just walk away, act like he's insane? I should have practiced what I'd say when he confronted me. "Look, Joe," I say, disgusted, looking him straight in the eye. "You know me. I'm not having an affair with anyone."

He grimaces and makes a face like he has a bad taste in his mouth. "Tell me you're not a lesbian." He gives me that self-righteous look that before the last few months I'd rarely seen but have never been able to stomach.

"I am not a lesbian." I accent every syllable. "But you do use drugs. Your roommate just got busted. You better flush whatever you've got."

He shakes his head. "Don't even try to compare me getting high once in a while to . . ." He releases his fist and takes several more steps back. "We're not through with this. Pick Sammy up at seven-thirty," he commands, turns his back to me, and walks away. "He needs more shirts. Stay in line, Cora Rose." A demand and a threat he lobs over his shoulder without turning around.

"Then buy him some," I yell after him. "Sammy's not going home with you until you clean out your apartment." I step around the corner, and vomit behind the only bush in the lot.

Chapter 21

"I brought you home fries and a cheeseburger. Come down here with your spider bag and your Chinese checkers now," I yell up to Sammy. I'm sitting on the ratty chair, fingering a yellow failure notice. "Or, I won't to be able to play with you at all. Mommy has to study pretty soon."

I don't have to re-read Professor Rand's note, "Your grade average in Anatomy and Physiology has fallen from 92 to 68. To remain a student in the School of Nursing a final grade average of 72 is required. Please see me. 8 a.m., Monday. My office. Bring Extra Credit Project." I have it memorized.

I went from straight A student to flunky in a month. Now I have three days to complete a project good enough to prevent me from getting thrown out of nursing school. It's Friday night. I'll be serving Egg Mc-Muffins to truck drivers and the ski crowd early Saturday and Sunday. That leaves three nights and two afternoons to create charts, graphs, and drawings of The Defense Mechanisms of the Respiratory System which are good enough to convince Professor Rand that I should remain a student in the School of Nursing.

"I want Donny to sleep over." Sammy stomps around in his room above me. He wants a motorized robot and a canopy for his bed that makes it look like a spaceship. He wants his Daddy to live with his Mommy. He wants me to meet him at the kitchen door with a little box of Hawaiian Punch every afternoon.

"I told you, not tonight. Donny can sleep over tomorrow night." Crash! Sounds like his Big Bruiser dump truck hitting the wall. The little shit. I count to ten. First Rand's note in my box at school, then another fight with Joe. "Sammy, behave and get down here. You don't want Mommy to flunk out of nursing school, do you?"

"Yes," Sammy yells in his brattiest voice. "I hate nursing school." He pulls something across the floor.

"Come on, pumpkin," I say with saccharine sweetness. I curl my toes, trying to squeeze out the last bit of patience. "You asked Mommy to bring you home a cheeseburger. Now come and eat it." His food has been cold for twenty minutes.

"I hate cheeseburgers. I hate you." His stomping feet sound like they belong to a two-hundred-pound man. He continues to drag something across the wooden floor, making as much noise as possible.

I hang on the banister. "Sammy, I'm counting to ten. Don't make me come up there."

A bag of plastic spider parts flies down the stairs and crashes at my feet. Spider legs and body parts fly out of the open mouth of the drawstring bag, spewing all over the landing. A piece hits me in the eye. It stings like hell.

"You little shit." My eye tears up. "Get down here and pick up this mess." I'm shaking with anger. "Now."

"You little shit," Sammy mimics me from the top of the stairs. His little Dutch boy bangs almost cover his eyes and are starting to frizz at the ends.

"Get down here, Sammy. Or so help me . . ."

He sits on the top step and sucks his thumb. "I hate you," he says again. His eyes are hard little slits. Just like Joe's eyes the last time I saw him.

I charge up the stairs, grab him by the arm, and yank him down step by step. I drop him on top of the mess at the foot of the stairs. "Pick it up." My hand clamps around his arm.

"Ouch." He tries to pull away.

"Pick it up." I squeeze harder. His lip quivers, his shoulders shake, but he doesn't move to obey me. I've lost enough control in my life, I'll be damned if I'm going to lose any more to a four-year-old.

His spider empire is scattered around him, his mouth contorts like one of those possessed kids in a horror film. "I'm going to live with

Daddy. He's going to let me play with Donny, and Auntie Lorraine's going to make me a tent out of sheets."

"Sammy." My grip loosens. I feel like letting it all go. Joe, Sammy, school. "I know Mommy and Daddy splitting up is hard. But you still have to behave."

"I don't want you. I want Auntie Renee or Auntie Lorraine to be my mommy."

I slap him right across the face. Hard. His head jerks to the side and bounces back like it's on a spring. His tears roll, but his face remains a fierce little mask. He doesn't move a muscle, makes no sound. I stare at him, wait for an inspiration, a way to take it back. "Mother of God." I sit on the bottom step and watch the imprint of my palm and the webbed spaces of my fingers spread across his cheek. "Sammy." I sound hollow even to myself, like I'm speaking from the bottom of a pit. "I did a very bad thing." All I can think of is to say a quick Hail Mary. Let me take it back. Let me start over. I look at my hand, bigger than his cheek. "I'm sorry. Sammy, Mommy's so sorry." You were the easiest thing to hit.

Sammy stares back at me. We sit there and stare at each other. He cocks his head, gives me the lost puppy look he gets when he's hurt or confused.

I touch his face. "It hurts?"

The look he answers me with is not subtle. He pinches his lips together and his whole face shakes. His eyes direct his anger and bewilderment squarely at me. There's no place to divert my own eyes, my responsibility. I put my head in my hands. "Sammy." I have to block the impulse to run away from him, down the rickety steps, out the back door. I kneel to make myself his height. "Grown-ups make big mistakes sometimes, honey." He scrutinizes me, his frown a softened version of his rage thirty seconds ago mixed with a sadness I want to be impossible in him. "I wish I could be home with you more." I lean into him, press my forehead to his. "I will. I will be home with you more." The smell of his hair breaks my heart. "You want Mommy to play with you and not be so tired all the time, like before?" His head and shoulders go limp. I hug him. He pulls back and studies me, cautious. "Sammy, don't be afraid of me. I'll never do that again. I promise."

"You hurt me." He pulls up his sleeve. The red blotch we're staring at reminds me of the time Mom hit Marie with the bristle side of a brush. It happened only once, but after that I knew she could be dangerous. I whimper. The tears catch in my throat, making a loud sucking sound.

"It's okay, Mommy." Sammy, still bewildered, but softened by my tears, climbs in my lap, puts his arm around my neck, and kisses my cheek. We rock. "You shouldn't hit people," he says instructively, repeating what he's learned from me and Joe.

"No. Mommy shouldn't have hit you." His cheek is warm against mine. "Mommy made a mistake. Mommy's sorry."

Sammy and I sit on the couch. He swallows the two tiny orange aspirin I give him and lays his head on my lap. His eyes are heavy. He looks tired—not just tonight, he's been looking tired for weeks. I stroke his hair while we watch Star Trek.

I've got to do better. I will do better.

Sammy falls asleep. Mr. Spock and Captain Kirk make a plan to save some planet or other. I rub Sammy's head and try to make a plan to get through the semester. School. That stupid job. Time and patience for Sammy. All this crazy dyke stuff has got to go. Not just Anne, she's already gone. Poor Anne. I think she really did like having a friend. She needed a friend a lot more than she needed a lover. Renee is right, I can't take the stress. "Oregon Lesbian Loses Custody of Twin Boys." It made the headlines last week. Sammy and I don't want to make the headlines.

Come straight home from school and concentrate on Sammy. No one will be able to tell Joe they saw me somewhere with somebody. No dykes or dyke bars to keep me wired all the time. My nerves will settle down. I'll stop worrying about who knows and who doesn't. No crazy push and pull, no lump of fear, no longing stuck in my throat. So I'm attracted to women? I'll just let it lie there. Plenty of people go through life without sex. Nuns, priests, and, I used to think, Renee. Joe and I didn't have sex for months at a time. It didn't kill me. I never whacked Sammy over it.

"Mommy loves you." I stroke his hair. His head is heavy. I lift the warm lump of his small solid body off my lap and cover him with an afghan.

I put on a pot of coffee and watch it brew while I cap and uncap a felt pen and consider The Defense Mechanisms of the Respiratory System. My attempt to outline a two-foot lung on a flip chart lies on the kitchen table. I try to concentrate, but the thought that if only I could start over, fresh at seventeen, keeps intruding. No Joe. No Sammy. I get the same chill of shame that I get every time I have these thoughts. Wishing my own son out of existence.

My First Communion rosary dangles on a hook with the potholders by the stove. I run my fingers along the beads. I feel so young. Too young to feel so old, to be a wife, a mother. I love Sammy. I do. I wish Memere was younger and lived next door.

I dial her number. She takes forever to answer. "Memere, it's Cora Rose."

"Cora Rose?" She asks, concerned. Memere hates the phone.

"Memere." I can't think of anything else to say.

"Speak up, Cora Rose."

"Memere . . . I just wanted to hear your voice."

"You're all right? You got trouble? Sammy?" Her voice is so old and shaky.

"Don't worry. We're fine. We're going to come see you soon." I shouldn't have called. I know better than to call her unless it's a real emergency, or at least I have something to say. "I just wanted to say I love you. Goodbye, Memere."

Anatomy: The Study of You and Me lies open to the diagram of a lung. My drawing on the flip chart looks more like a diseased liver than a lung. I rip the page and start over. I can do this if I focus. Two months ago, I could focus. Three months ago, I could focus for hours at a time, forget who I was, where I was, while I sucked in the marvels of digestion or the integumentary system. I make a stabbing slash across a fifth attempt at a larger-than-life lung. I can't draw this thing. I'm not an art student. What does my ability to draw an internal organ have to do with being a nurse?

A rap on the back door startles me. Marie walks in, shaking snow off her shoulders. No greeting. She just peers down at my slashed lung and asks, "What is this blob with the black line through it supposed to be?"

"School project." I point to the expanded lung on page 203. "What are you doing here?"

"Pitiful." She picks up the black felt-tip and bites her lip, looking from textbook to drawing paper.

"You can't stay here unless you want to be quiet and watch TV without me. I've got to do this." She studies page 203, paying no attention to me. "Where's Donny?" I demand.

"Sleeping. Eddie's there," she says offhandedly. "Okay, I can do this." In two broad strokes she outlines the two lobes of the left lung, then the three lobes of the right lung. Her drawing is not bad, way better than mine. "You want this thing?" She points to the tracheal cartilage and the left and right bronchus.

I'm subdued by astonishment. "You can draw?" I'm as fascinated by her concentration as I am by the fact that the thing she's sketching looks remarkably lung-like. Not professional, not even good, really; but you can tell what it is. "Since when?"

She shrugs and finishes the whole drawing, bent over the table with her coat still on. I watch her hand hover over the page, then make its marks. She looks up and smirks when she's done.

"That's not bad, Marie. You okay? You look exhausted? You got insomnia again?"

She rolls her eyes. "What else?" Now that she's not so involved with the drawing, anger and irritation creep in her voice. I point to the adjoining page. She outlines a model of a primary respiratory lobule, a complicated system of ducts and sacs that resemble a mutated bunch of grapes. She takes off her coat, pulls up a chair. Then she fills in the intricacies of the alveolar sacs and the capillaries surrounding them. "Fine-line red pen." She puts out her hand like a doctor asking for a scalpel.

I search through my backpack and hand her a pen. "Unbelievable. Marie out of nowhere, drawing The Defense Mechanisms of the Respiratory System." The feeling of possibility runs through me like divine intervention. I thumb through my books excited. Maybe I'll pull this off—add a graph showing the effects of pollution on the respiratory system, a chart with pharmaceuticals showing use, action, side effects. I stop and let the pharmacology book snap shut. This isn't the way my life goes. This is too good to be true. I don't deserve it. I hit my kid. "What made you come over here, Marie?"

"Memere called." She turns the pad and leans into the drawing. "She's never called me before." Calmly, way too calmly, she continues to fill in the veiny red lines. "What's the matter with you?" She pauses to give me a deadpan face full of attitude. "I mean besides the usual. You scared her. Leave her out of your mess. She's eighty-seven years old."

"Do you know you're giving me that look that Mom used to give you?" I touch the drawing. "I know how old Memere is." Why can't Marie just be nice or just be an asshole, why does she have to be both at the same time? "I had no idea you could draw. I didn't think a phone call would scare her."

"You may as well cry. Your face is all blotchy already," she says. "What happened to your eye?"

I cry, no noise, just tears, a steady stream.

"I'll need coffee if it's going to be a tear-jerker."

I give her Renee's best pottery mug. She holds the coffee in one hand and flips through my anatomy book with the other hand while she waits for my tears to stop.

"I hit Sammy."

"Hard?" She closes the book. "Not just a slap to get his attention?"

"I dragged him down the stairs. There's a bruise on his arm. Maybe on his cheek."

She scrunches her eyebrows and sips from the mug. "You're really queer?" It's half question, half statement.

"Queer?" The word hits me like a brick. "What does that have to do with Sammy?"

"Kids get hit over things that have nothing to do with them all the time. If you plan to be a dyke, you better toughen up."

"Plan?" My plan is to bury my sexuality in a dark corner and hope it dies for lack of light. "I'm not like you, Marie."

239

"You're damned right." She laughs sarcastically, then turns deadly sober. "But you're my sister. I haven't slept in three nights, but I never hit my kid." She shakes her head. "Why didn't you just call somebody? You want to lose Sammy? You're really pissing Joe off. He's had it with you. You better talk to him and you better make nice."

"Talk to him about what?"

"About not taking your kid away from you. Tell him you're sorry. Tell him you need help. Appeal to his manhood. His fatherly instincts. They love that shit." She puts down the pen she's been twirling. "Sooner or later he's going to find out, and he better be good and buttered up when he does. He loves Sammy. He working tonight?"

I nod. "He already knows. He accused me of having a thing with Darlene."

She sits up. "Who told him about Darlene?"

I shake my head. "Did you tell Fletcher?"

"You think I'm a moron? Someone must have seen the two of you together someplace. Deny everything."

"I'm not having a thing with Darlene," I say wearily. "I already denied everything. We had a fight at the rink."

Her brows knot in concentration. "Whatever you do, don't tell him you hit Sammy. We'll have to keep Sammy away from him for a few days. Whatever he says, don't admit you're a dyke. Get your ass moving, cry, whatever it takes." She waves her hand. "I'm telling you, he's pissed and he's talking about court. Judges don't think divorced lesbians make good mommies."

She doesn't bring up marijuana to be used as a threat or bargaining point, doesn't bring up Fletcher at all, barely speaks about him since he left for Georgia.

A fine tremble starts somewhere in my trunk and spreads over my whole body. "I can't. I'm too afraid."

"So? You think Joe's not fucking terrified of you? You think he wants the world to know that his wife's a lesbian?" She laughs, a tired laugh. "Afraid?" She leans back and closes her eyes. "Some days, since Fletcher's been gone, I can barely get out of bed. Do it anyway."

I have no idea if Marie is giving me good advice or not, but I walk to the parking lot outside of the foundry where Joe works, stand across the lot, and look through a huge open door that a ten-ton truck has just passed through. The shadows of the workers crawl across the inside wall of the huge brick building. It's cold. My breath comes out of my nostrils in short blasts. The shadows of the men grow taller. Their heads hit the twenty-foot ceiling as the light, made by heat strong enough to melt metal, flashes. Goggles, protective headgear, belted jumpsuits: they look like giant upright ants moving slowly, cautiously around the pit of smoldering metal.

It's 8:30, dark and brisk outside. Snow is falling, lightly. I feel like a speck, cold, small, and anonymous, as I watch them. I'm glad to have a few minutes to see the slow dance these guys are doing around their cauldron before I have to face Joe. Outside, my world is falling apart. Inside the foundry, these guys have created a strange harmony despite the heat and the danger. Maybe because of it.

The foundry. The guys call it The Pit. Joe likes his job in The Pit even though it makes him tired and dirty. He's in a good union, working overtime tonight, same as most Friday nights since we met. He gets time-and-a-half for the first four hours, double-time after that. He always feels good about himself when he works overtime.

I've got to figure out a way to make it easier for Joe, for myself, for Sammy, so we don't break. I've got to make myself love him more than I hate him, so we don't break Sammy. Joe can work with ten other men, for twelve or fourteen hours, to forge a ton of boiling metal into something useful. He likes most of the guys he works with, but some of them he can barely stomach. He should be able talk to me without exploding.

Feel good about yourself tonight, Joe; generous, industrious, virtuous. He'll be walking through the big iron gate with thirty other guys in orange asbestos suits any minute now. Sammy and I used to wait by the gate with a meatball grinder and a thermos of black coffee for him on overtime nights. Wish I had a meatball grinder for him now. I finger the crumpled failure notice in my pocket and practice what I want to say to him. The shriek of the 9:00 whistle cracks my nerve. I hang onto the iron fence post.

Men pile out the side door. A lanky guy, Garry, a friend of Joe's, is walking fast, fifty feet ahead of the crowd. He takes change from the pocket of his orange jumpsuit, runs toward the gate and the canteen across the parking lot. Garry slows down when he sees me. "Cora Rose?" He looks over his shoulder. "Joe's coming," he says nervously. He adds, flustered, "Good to see you."

"Thanks, Garry. Nice to see you, too." I've become a woman who can make Joe's buddy blush just by standing outside the gate. Men gossip too, I forgot. Joe's pals know his story—errant wife left her hard-working husband. I can't get all worked up. I did leave my hard-working husband. I am the errant wife, here to make peace and reconcile our differences.

They squeeze through the gate, two or three guys at a time. Seems like every one of them is talking. When the furnace is blasting, they can barely hear themselves think, never mind hear someone else speak. Lots of conversation gets backed up in the four hours between breaks. Joe is in the middle of the pack. He strolls casually, laughs with a guy walking next to him. He sees me and stops dead in his tracks. The guy with him stops, too. They create a bottleneck by standing right in the middle of the gate. The whole pack stops.

One of the guys behind them says good-naturedly, "Come on, move it. There's working men here need fuel." I stare at the guy until our eyes meet. He says, "Oh." Recognizing the delicacy of the situation, he pushes the man standing next to Joe through the gate.

Joe steps to one side and calls after his buddies, "See you in a minute." When the last of them are out of hearing range, Joe says gruffly, "Sammy all right?"

"Yes, but we need to talk."

"You got brass balls coming here." He clenches the iron bars of the fence.

"We have to figure out a better way to take care of Sammy." I pull the yellow failure notice out of my pocket. Even as I'm doing it, I know it's a stupid place to start. "I'm flunking school."

"You think I give a damn if you flunk school?" He starts to walk away.

"Joe, you have to listen to me. This is about Sammy."

He stops, turns back. "I thought you and your sister had the arrangement all sewn up. What do you need me for? It's a little late for you to start worrying about Sammy."

"Joe, he's still *our* child." Should I beg?

'That's why you came here, because I made a crack about Sammy not being my kid? I know he's mine." He's shaking his head, walking away with his hands clenched at his sides.

I follow him. "Joe, I'm not going away until we figure out how to make this break-up work. For Sammy." Come back, Joe, my old dependable Joe who loved me, who put Sammy's best interests above his own. I don't want this Joe. Why is he pretending he doesn't care about me? Why do I have to pretend I don't care about him? "Joe." His big arms, his wide rigid shoulders are moving away. "I'm sorry, Joe. I've done some things wrong. We both . . ." I'm talking loud, desperate to stop him. I'm panicked. I'm sorry. I want to slap him, knock him down, make him stop walking away.

"I slapped Sammy," I say loud, accusatory, like it's his fault. I didn't plan to say it. I planned not to say it, but there it is, almost solid, hanging in the cold night air.

He stops, suspended, doesn't turn around.

"I flunked a big exam and he kept whining." I hug myself through the bulk of my coat. I try to be angry, so I won't fling myself at his feet.

He turns on his heels. "Did you hurt him?"

"He's okay. I didn't mean to. School, and work, and us fighting." I'd rather be hit by his clenched fist, than by the look on his face. He hates me. He cared for his wife, not this Cora Rose.

"Where is he?" he demands, cold and self-righteous in the knowledge that he's been screwed by life in general and me in particular.

I concentrate on the part of me that's angry with him and his pig-headed refusal to ever take any blame at all, let it piss me off, let bitterness rise in my throat, let the sharp taste of his shortcomings keep me from choking on my own guilt, and keep my words from drying up in my mouth. "Marie's with him." I recite what I've memorized in the cold yard of the factory. "Sammy is a piece of us both. We can't hate each other. You have to forgive me or a part of you will always be mad at Sammy. We have to stop thinking about ourselves and start thinking about our responsibilities to Sammy."

"We? *I* am not responsible for you hitting Sammy." He's enraged. "And I'm not responsible for you being a dyke."

"No, you're not responsible for me hitting Sammy." I keep my body rigid. I will not fold. Now I have to pull out all the stops if I want to get through to him. "You can't just be his father when you're in the mood. You have to be consistent. We need some kind of schedule," I say, firm and business-like, hoping my voice will hold me up, hoping my tone won't piss him off even more. I step toward him. "You can't decide at five-thirty that you're going to take him for the evening. You can't decide a half-hour before you're supposed to pick him up on Saturday night that you're not taking him until Sunday morning. It's not fair."

"Fair to who?" He's shaking with rage because he knows what I'm saying is true. He's getting less dependable every day. I'm never sure if he's going to show when he's supposed to. Sammy is never sure.

"Sammy. All you see is his relief when you show up. You don't see how nervous he gets waiting. How depressed he is when you cancel. Four-year-olds aren't supposed to be depressed." I'm shaking, too. "We're not taking good care of Sammy." I could just as easily be sobbing, but I'm talking loud, in his face. "If doing right by our son helps me out, you'll just have to live with that."

"God damn you." A hot angry tear slides down his cheek.

"God damn you, Joe. You didn't slap him, but you drink too much beer. You smoke pot. Even if it was legal, he's got asthma, he shouldn't be around that stuff. Tobacco too, not if he's in the room. When Fletcher gets back, if he doesn't watch out, he might end up in jail."

He snarls. "He's your friend, too."

"You give Sammy ice cream for dinner; let him stay up until ten o'clock even if it's a school night. He's got rings under his eyes. Part of it's my fault. I've got to do better. But part of it's your fault. Have you taken a good look at him lately?" I lower my voice. "You know how to be a good father. Be one." He winces and turns away. His big shoulders

244

shake. Men talk about caving under a woman's tears, but this is how he always gets me. A tenderness hits me so physically that I touch his arm to steady myself. He lets me keep my hand on his arm. I know how to get him, too. I whisper, "He's a little boy who needs a good father. You used to be a real good father. I used to be a real good mother. Sammy is hurting. We're hurting him, Joe. We've got to help each other."

He stands there expressionless. If only he'd let me in. If only it was safe to say how we really feel. He stares straight ahead. I start to whimper. My little speech isn't working? He's going further inside himself?

The barely audible broken sound I'm making turns into full blown shaking and sobbing. It's an act in a way, meant to wake him up, meant to soften him up, but it's not really fake. All I had to do was let go. I've been close to tears since he walked through the gate. This sobbing and shaking has been in me the whole time. I just had to stop blocking it. It's no more an act than facing him shameless and yelling with folded arms. I rest the top of my head against his chest and whisper, "Please, we got to work this out."

Softly, almost delicately, he says, "Damn you," and lets his hand rest on my back.

A second later, he steps back, recovering his anger. "Okay. We work out a goddamned schedule. For Sammy. I show up on time. No beer, no dope for me." He grabs my shoulders hard. "No slapping, no dykes for you."

Part 4

Chapter 22

I'm bent over a little blonde kid. "We're going to play pin the tail on the donkey," I chirp, trying to convince him that his mother has not forsaken him forever to the chaos of Sammy's fifth birthday party. "Then we'll have birthday cake. Won't that be fun?"

"No," he wails, showing me he still has all his baby teeth.

"Your Mommy left you here because she knew you would be a big boy."

Marie, tacking a dog-eared poster of a donkey without a tail to the fake wood paneling on the wall behind us, draws her hand across her neck trying to get me to shut up, but I keep on talking. I made it through Christmas, New Years, and into my second semester of nursing school by unrelenting plodding and I'll make it through this party the same way. I haven't even come close to slapping Sammy again. Deep breathing, calm talking, warm baths, prayer; I'm doing whatever it takes.

"Mommy will be back to pick you up in a little while. Crying is just going to make it seem longer." I know this won't work on a four-year-old, but I already tried to bribe him with candy and pointy hats.

"Grammy," the kid wails louder.

An eight-year-old girl sits on a balloon right next to the little blonde kid. Marie trips over her, trying to get close enough to me to have a private talk. The balloon pops under the girl. The little boy and I gasp. The girl giggles and Marie puts her in charge of blowing up balloons. When Marie finally reaches my ear she whispers, "His mother's in a halfway house. He lives with Grammy."

"Oh shit." I shake my head trying to erase the swear. "Sorry. Your Grammy's coming back. I promise."

Marie slaps her forehead. "Your *Daddy* will be here in an hour." She smiles at the poor kid, pats his blonde curls, and motions at me to zip my lip. "Mae," she yells over to Mom, who is orchestrating some kind of a clapping game from the couch. The game inspires the already over-stimulated kids to bounce on the sofa, roll around, and giggle uncontrollably on the carpet in front of her. Mom stops her hands in mid-clap to look up at Marie. "We need a Memere type over here," Marie bellows above the din as she moves toward the door to answer a knock. "Cora Rose is traumatizing this poor kid."

Mom responds to this plea for her grandmotherly attention and trots over. "There, there," she says solemnly but kindly to the blonde kid. "Can you keep a secret?" She takes the little boy's hand and puts her finger to his lips. "I need one little boy who can keep a secret. Is that boy you?" He stops crying and looks at her wide-eyed. Mom's eyes scan the room suspiciously to be sure no one else is listening. "We have a big cake that needs candles," she mouths, her words barely audible. We both watch her lips intently. She looks around again to be sure no other little eavesdropper is listening in to try to steal this child's glory. "Think you can do that?" The little blonde kid nods seriously.

I follow them uninvited, into the kitchen, amazed at what an exceptional Memere Mom has turned out to be. I don't remember her being an exceptional mother. I'm right behind them as they head toward the refrigerator. What will Sammy's memories of her as a Memere be? He sees her once or twice a week, not every day like I used to see my Memere. Memere, I promised to take Sammy to visit her. She'd hate all this commotion at Sammy's party.

"Auntie Lorraine," Sammy squeals from the living room.

I go back to the pack of kids in the next room. Sammy is bouncing on his heels in front of Lorraine. What will his memories of me as a mother be? Maybe I'll get the hang of it by the time I'm Mom's age. Lorraine takes her coat off, revealing a full-skirted Donna Reed dress complete with a stiff wide belt of matching material. She's holding a huge present. She looks pretty miserable considering she's only just stepped into the party and hasn't had time to get a headache yet.

Donny spots the big box wrapped in clown paper and squeals, "Auntie Lorraine."

"Wow." Sammy springs up and down. "I bet it's a sleeping bag."

Marie hooks her fingers around my forearm. "Come with me." She drags me out of the living room full of children who have temporarily stopped bopping each other with Nerf balls so they can ogle Lorraine's oversized gift.

"Wait here." Marie deposits me on top of my chenille bedspread.

"What am I waiting for?" I don't mind taking a break from the squealing kids.

"A favor-in-kind for letting me know what an asshole Renee is."

"This is too long to hold a grudge, even for you, Marie." My sisters are still feuding over Fletcher and he's been gone for months. I warned Renee I wouldn't lie if Marie asked me a direct question and Marie is queen of the direct question. "Fletcher would have told you himself if you'd given him one more day."

"He would have told me the day before he was leaving. I have a right to know that the father of my child is taking off for Georgia to turn himself in to the draft board. Donny has a right to know what state his father is in."

Yup, that's why I tried to talk Renee into telling you. "Renee tried to get him to tell you sooner. She thought she was doing the right thing."

She turns on her heels and leaves the room. I have a bad feeling about Marie's favor. You don't remove the adult host of a kid's birthday party from an apartment full of hyped-up kids, unless there's a serious problem. I don't have time to invent trouble. The door opens and Marie shoves Lorraine through it. Lorraine snivels in front of me.

"Tell her," Marie orders. "Or I'll call an ambulance so they can cart you away after I break your neck."

"You're horrible," Lorraine is using her fifth-grade voice; this is not good.

"You left Mom and Renee alone with twenty screaming kids?" I sit cross-legged on my lumpy bed, trying to prepare myself for whatever hideous statement is about to erupt from Lorraine.

"It's not like she's innocent, either." Lorraine swallows a sob.

Marie leans against her closed bedroom door. "Spit it out, Lorraine. I got cake and ice cream to dish up."

"Joe and I," Lorraine starts, stops. Her lip quivers but she looks Marie in the eye. "You're not going to make me ashamed. You're not going to turn this into something dirty."

Marie rolls her eyes impatiently. Somewhere in my gut I know what's coming, but if I needed a concrete thought to save my life at this moment, I couldn't form one.

"Joe and I." Lorraine straightens up, her chin in the air. Then she's kneeling on the bed in front of me with her hands wrapped around mine. "We're in love."

"In love." I pull my head back and smile. Then the meaning rushes over me. "Love." I stare at her like she's some exotic bird. This love didn't even take him out of my family—and yet, I didn't know about it? Joe's life so separate from mine, I never got wind of his new girlfriend, not a whiff in the air? "Jesus."

"Cora Rose," Lorraine pleads. "Please don't look at me like that."

But, I can't take my eyes off her. Joe has been fucking Lorraine, actually fucking her. Of course. It makes sense if you look at it from a certain angle. Sammy and his "Auntie Lorraine tent houses," his "Daddy and Auntie Lorraine said I could." What did I think she was doing in Joe and Fletcher's apartment all the time? Cooking, cleaning, baby-sitting the boys. And fucking Joe. I don't want him. I gave him up, and yet it feels like she stole him.

All the while he's been making me feel dirty and guilty, keeping me in line with threats to take Sammy, he's been getting naked with Lorraine. I tilt my head, but Lorraine still looks like my loser cousin. My loser cousin is fucking my salt-of-the-earth husband. Won't Mom and Dad be surprised? Fletcher must know. Renee will kill him for not telling her. Unless Renee knows. Then I'll kill her. On some level Sammy must understand Auntie Lorraine is the new woman in Daddy's life. I'm dumber than my five-year-old. I try to look at Lorraine through Joe's eyes, through the eyes of someone that didn't grow up with her as their loser cousin. She has Aunt Josette's tweaky nose, but

252

she's almost pretty in a severely wholesome kind of way. Some guys might be attracted to her schoolmarm look. But Joe? Or is he just that lonely? Lorraine and Joe, confusing; who are these two if they're together? I shake my head and immediately an image of Joe shaking his head at the thought of me getting naked with someone who is not him pops up.

I look down at Lorraine's hands, still entwined around mine. The drama of the situation makes me laugh, a short burst of a laugh that comes and is gone in a split second.

She pulls away and stands up. "You think it's funny?" she asks in an almost hysterical hiss. "I've been beside myself. My doctor says I have an ulcer. I can barely keep down Cream of Wheat." She wrings her hands, tears stream down her face. "My own mother is not speaking to me."

Sweet Jesus, even Aunt Josette knows. "That's why she threw you out." I tsk, tsk half-heartedly. "Lorraine, you've been telling lies. You're a fallen woman."

I marvel at her ability to produce so many tears. It must be a relief to let it rip like that. It's a bad habit, making someone feel bad because they are the cousin that's always been the scapegoat, because you can, because she's fucking your husband and anger is more satisfying than confusion. She doesn't need me to berate her. She's upset enough with herself. I feel a kind of generic awe at the way things can turn out. These last months, I've been confining myself to a safe tight space, but I see the world isn't secure or predictable no matter how small you make yourself. The world is off tilt, or maybe I'm off tilt, seeing things from a skewed angle. Maybe I should thank Lorraine for righting me, helping me get my equilibrium back. It's liberating, knowing the last person you'd suspect of it, is capable of taking this kind of fall. Lorraine's head hangs down in front of her. She just confessed a grievous sin, a mortal sin. But not an abominable sin. A tear drips off the tip of her nose. I register that she's distressed, but I don't feel it. This thought—Joe's fucking her and it's not even an abominable sin—makes me furious. My sex is loathsome. Their sex is run of the mill, just another normal mortal failing. They can go to confession and communion. I can be annulled. They can get married, all will be forgiven.

I have to admit I'm not confused about one thing; I'm jealous of her being with Joe. How absurd, but there it is. Jealous over a man I don't want.

I adjust my weight on my lumpy mattress. If Joe's a hypocrite, what in the world is solid? I glance at the spot where Marie was standing, but she's gone. Another piece of reality hits me.

I glare at Lorraine. "You miserable bitch."

"Cora Rose?" Lorraine takes a few steps back like she's ready to make a run for it if necessary.

"You're the one who told Joe I was sleeping with Darlene." It's been weeks since I've seen Darlene, Anne, or the inside of The Girls Club. I get an image of Joe and Lorraine, post-coital. Joe's hands behind his head with that satisfied look he gets on his face, Lorraine snuggled up on his shoulder, discussing Sammy, what's for supper, his job, her career punching holes in notebook paper, congratulating each other for curtailing my perversions. "You sit in Marie's kitchen with your hands folded on your lap and you spy." I squirm with disgust. "Lorraine on dyke patrol."

"I never used that word." She sniffles, makes a tiny sign of the cross on her forehead with her thumb. "I'm sorry. I am so sorry."

What penance will Lorraine give herself for sleeping with a married man, especially this married man? How many novenas? How many sleepless nights? I have to get her out of here before we end up crying in each other's arms. "Stop sniveling. Say ten rosaries and go in peace."

"I will. I will say ten rosaries." She sits on the edge of the bed with her back to me and collapses her shoulders. "Don't be mad at me and Joe," she sobs into her hands.

"Would you tell Marie I'll be right out?" I ask, the way a boss would ask a private secretary. "And here's a message for your lover: I'm not having sex with anyone at the moment, but it's none of his business. And close the door, please."

A few minutes later, I'm back in the sea of kids seated on my living-room floor. The paper plates in front of them are soggy with melting ice cream. Sammy spots me as I wade through the tired little bodies. "Will you buy me Star Trek sheets, Mommy?" he asks excitedly. He and

Donny and another chosen little boy are sitting with Lorraine's huge present in the middle of them. I sit down on the floor next to him and feel a sweet pang of pride that he's asking me, not Lorraine. "Will you?" Sammy rocks with excitement.

"Yes, honey." I hug him. "Mommy will get you Star Trek sheets." I smile dishonestly at Lorraine, who is on the couch across from us, looking desolate. Why doesn't she just leave? Is this penance? I better watch myself. She's in Sammy's life whether I like it or not. At least she is Lorraine; one of the few people in the world who I've grown up to believe is below me in pecking order. Such a sad state of affairs, that this should give me comfort.

Mom, hearing my statement about buying Sammy the sheets, knits her brow in an almost indiscernible gesture of disapproval. If she wasn't my mother, I wouldn't have caught the expression. If I wasn't her daughter, I wouldn't know that it was my remark that displeased her. I watch her face. An hour ago I would have carried her frown on my shoulders, in my belly, or maybe right behind my eyes, and felt annoyed with her judging, her interfering. Now I watch her check her own reaction as her face smooths over into a smile and wonder why my telling Sammy that I'll buy him sheets annoys her. Is it because I can't afford it? Because I'm spoiling him? Does she feel guilty because she's raised an imperfect daughter who's raising an imperfect son? As Mom stoops to pick up an empty soda can, her face turns from a smile to a frown again. This smile and this frown have nothing to do with me. They're directed at Renee, who is sitting on the couch, daintily eating cake, ignoring a spilled plate of goo two feet away. Renee has not involved herself with the birthday clean-up the way she usually does. She didn't help decorate. She didn't even bake. She's moping until Marie forgives her for not telling her about Fletcher leaving for Georgia. She's moping until she forgives me for telling Marie. She's moping because she can't spend an hour on the phone with Fletcher every day. She's moping because her best friend and her sisters are ignoring her counsel; Fletcher and I have not gotten lawyers and Marie won't even discuss going for the free therapy Renee set up to prevent the breakdown Renee predicts if Marie goes through with her marriage to Eddie. Renee continues to pick at the rocket ship cupcake that Marie made sure to point out was bought and delivered by Eddie.

"Let me do that." I take a corner of the plastic bag hanging from Mom's hand. Does Mom think Eddie's a jerk? Does she suspect I'm a dyke? "You must be tired."

"Tired?" She pulls her head back, insulted, refusing to give up her sack of garbage. "I raised three girls." She stoops and sweeps the goopy plate next to Renee into the green bag. "The bags are under the sink. There's enough trash to fill two."

After the party, Sammy and I take the short walk to Joe's. The front door opens. "Hey, pal." Joe greets Sammy with a big grin, ignoring my presence at his door. "What you got in that sack?"

Sammy opens the wrinkled grocery bag and sticks his head in. "Devil Dogs and balloons." Sammy talks fast, wired from the party.

"Where's your Auntie Lorraine?"

"Cleaning up," I answer.

"Auntie Lorraine got me a sleeping bag. Mommy says I can bring it here sometimes."

"Can you put that stuff away for Daddy, pal?" Joe runs his hand through Sammy's hair.

I kneel and give Sammy a hug. "Bye, honey. I love you."

"I love you too, Mommy." Sammy squeezes me. We rub noses. "She's going to buy me Star Trek sheets, Daddy."

"She is?" Joe nods. "Go on." He pats Sammy on the butt. "Put that stuff away and change into your jammies." Sammy trots through the kitchen. When he's safely out of hearing range, Joe says abruptly, "What are you doing here?"

"I know about you and Lorraine," I report confidently, my arms crossed over my chest, my eyebrows arched. I stop to savor his reaction, but he's poker-faced.

He takes a pack of Marlboros out of his shirt pocket. "Me and Lorraine?" His face is a blank.

"I know you're fucking Lorraine."

"Nice language." He taps the pack on his thigh, nods toward the bedroom and Sammy who is too far away to possibly have heard, tears

256

off the cellophane, and taps out a cigarette, eyeing me critically the whole time. This is not the way I expected things to go. He's supposed to be tongue-tied. Ashamed. He puts the cigarette in his mouth backwards. "What makes you think I'm sleeping with Lorraine?" He stares me down. The filtered end of the butt wags at me as he speaks.

I pick a silver lighter from a wicker chair, snap it open, and offer him a light. He bends toward me, eyes intent, and takes a drag. The filter goes up in a blue flame. He fumbles with the burning cigarette. It falls to the floor.

"You did that on purpose." He dances around, stomping on the butt.

"Cigarettes are bad for you, Joe." He glares at me. "And you're not very good at it." I sit down in the chair.

Joe grabs the arms of the chair on either side of me, leans in within six inches of my face. "What exactly do you want?" This maneuver, meant to cower, infuriates me.

"You're a big bully and you smell like an ashtray." The bitchiness in my voice gives me a strange thrill. I meant to be philosophical, detached but generous, thinking only of Sammy's well-being as Joe groveled in shame, even willing to admit I may have given him a little push toward Lorraine, if things went well and he was contrite; but he's not cooperating.

"What do you want?" he repeats, turning, listening for Sammy.

"I want you to concentrate on your sex life with Lorraine." I push back against the chair to distance myself from him. The wicker doesn't have much give. This is what he does when he's really angry—puts his face right in mine like he's going to take a bite. "Coward. Get off me." I'm trembling. Joe's trembling. "You're a liar and you're a hypocrite."

"You're still my wife." He steps back.

"That's right, Joe. That's why society would find it disturbing that you've been sleeping with my cousin behind my back." He sets his jaw, hoists up his jeans, and glares at me. "But that's not what I'm most concerned about." I speak quickly because I have the idea he might do an about-face and leave me sitting alone in his living room. "I want to make sure that we have an understanding about Sammy. That we don't use Sammy as a weapon, especially after you and Lorraine get married."

"Married?" he repeats, incredulous. "It's not me and Lorraine we have to worry about. Do you think that the kids at school are going to have an *understanding* when they find out Sammy's mommy is a dyke?"

"Kids can be mean. It's our job to protect him. I am worried about you, Joe. You used to have a mind of your own. You don't really care if I'm a lesbian. Your pride's hurt and you're worried what other people will think." Once the word lesbian is out of my mouth, I feel almost giddy. "What are people going to think about you having an affair with my first cousin?" It sounds less lurid than I hoped.

"I don't give a damn if you screw the whole softball team at that fucking college as long as you're not raising my son." His baritone gets squeaky. He's not bothering to control himself for his pride or my benefit.

"It's a community college," I say flatly. Amazing, how removed you can be from another person's misery when you're really angry. I give him credit for not bringing up the fact that I hit Sammy, for knowing me well enough not to be worried about that. "There are no sports teams."

"You ended our marriage." He wipes his nose on his sleeve and stares me down, like a great big copy of Sammy when he's being a brat. Too bad their mannerisms are so much alike. It makes it harder to hate him. For the rest of my life, whatever happens between us, every time I see Joe, I'll see Sammy. Suddenly, I feel really tired, like I could close my eyes and fall asleep with Joe standing there in front me. Joe looks like he could use a good long rest too.

"Daddy," Sammy yells from three rooms away. His voice jolts us both. I have to stop myself from jumping out of the chair and running to him.

"Daddy!" Sammy likes this yelling from room to room.

"I'll be right there, Sammy. Pick out a book," Joe calls back. He lowers his voice. "He's not growing up in a house full of lezzies. I'll take you to court. I'll bring everyone in on it, your sisters, everyone."

The phrase "take you to court" scares me. "No, you won't." My face is so close to his I can feel his cigarette breath on my cheek. "Don't be stupid, Joe. My sisters will side with me."

There's a moment of silence. He is still leaning over me as I sit on the chair and the intimacy of it is awkward. We both feel foolish and exposed, but neither of us are willing to give up our positions. His breath on my face has that same animal 'kill or be killed' odor that I smelled as I shoved toilet paper down Bobbie Lee Paterson's throat so many years ago. How am I going to protect Sammy from the cruelty of other children?

"And Lorraine won't lie in court. Not even for you." I say this confident, cocky, like I know Lorraine better than he does, like I'm not scared to death of what I've done, what's been done to me, what could be done to Sammy. "I won't do anything to hurt Sammy. You better not either."

He takes a step back, glowering at me. I stand, turn on my heels, and walk out the door.

As soon as the door shuts behind me, I want to sneak back in, snatch Sammy out of the bathroom, and run like hell. I should have yelled one more goodbye to him. I sit in my car, stare at the depressing brick and green wood of the buildings. I bet Joe misses Fletcher. We all miss Fletcher. Marie can barely stand to mention him except when Donny asks when Daddy will be home, which happens every day. It's no wonder Marie hooked up with Eddie. He's going to pull her and Donny out of the rat projects, plodding like a packhorse in his arrogant, steady way.

I don't want to be alone. I don't want to go back to Marie's. I don't want to go home to my empty apartment. I drive to The Girls Club and sit in my car, thinking about Sammy, Joe and Lorraine, Marie and Eddie. Sex, I think with a shudder. What do I want? I look around the lot. I want to tell someone about Sammy, how I just left him at his Dad's; that Joe was furious, and I won't see Sammy now for twenty-four hours. I want to talk about how it is to love a kid and be so ill-equipped to take care of him. I want to tell someone about Joe—how it was to be close to him, how it feels to lose him. I want to talk to someone who is not a member of my family.

I sit in my car, listing all the things I'd like to tell someone. Finally I see Anne, out of the corner of my eye, crossing the parking lot. She walks straight to my car and raps on my window. "I thought it was you. You're not sitting out here in the cold to avoid me?"

I don't say anything. My eyes tear up.

She purses her lips. "Look, I'm really a very nice girl. Being dumped is the only thing I hate more than being tied down." She smiles. "Can I buy a friend a beer?"

"I'm not up for noise and smoke. How about a cup of coffee?" Over coffee, I'll tell her why I'm terrified to go inside The Girls Club.

Chapter 23

Darlene and I sit at opposite ends of her couch, sipping cocoa. I've reached a milestone: called a friend, and gone to a movie with her. And, I've spent several hours with a dyke without getting turned on, just scared that someone will report back to Joe. "How did you get so comfortable with being a lesbian?" Ironic; I'm finally convinced I'm a lesbian and my desire is at an all-time low.

"Who says I'm comfortable?" Darlene unlaces her green high-top sneakers and kicks them off.

"The way you carry yourself. Nobody intimidates you."

"Have you noticed I'm a black girl? I lived in Atlanta, where they smile whether they like you or not. I lived in New York City, where they don't smile whether they like you or not. Now I live in a small town in Massachusetts where you have to be introduced five times before they acknowledge you one way or the other."

"Really?" I ask, wanting to know if this is real information or she's messing with me because I'm such a small-town hick.

"You see me bartending. I don't wave any flags at school. My policy is *Don't deny the obvious, but don't put a target on your back as you're walking away.* It is a big, messed-up world." She takes a sip of hot chocolate. "Jackie loved Christmas. New Year's. Fourth of July. Valentine's Day," she says mournfully. Valentine's Day was a month ago. She's told me, more than once; she's bored with lesbians obsessing about being lesbians. Darlene prefers to obsess about one particular lesbian.

"Think you'll ever stop missing her?"

"Doesn't look that way tonight." She tosses a pillow from the couch to the chair.

261

What are the rules here? It seems like she wants to talk about Jackie, but it's always the same. She brings up her name. Then she skitters away from the subject. If she was Renee or Marie, I'd just butt heads with her, but I'm pretty sure that would be a bad move with Darlene. She frowns.

"Tonight?" I'm trying for Sister Mary Margaret's recommendation; the open-ended empathetic return of a word or phrase, to put the person you're conversing with at ease. Doesn't work, she just frowns.

"Darlene," I lean in awkwardly. "You'll get over her." She gives me a mildly disgusted look. Bad move, downplaying emotional struggles with dismissive platitudes.

I walk across the foam green carpet to the phone. "I'm going to call Sammy to say good-night, okay? He's got a cold."

"Be my guest." She waves at the phone.

I dial home. Then I dial Joe's.

"What's up?" she asks in response to the scowl on my face.

"There's no answer at my place or Joe's. Sammy should be getting ready for bed by now." I bite the nail on my thumb, hoping my intuition is off.

"They would have called if something was wrong with Sammy," she says reassuringly.

"I didn't leave the number."

"Why?" She eyes me critically, slowly placing my refilled mug on the coffee table in front of me. "Don't want your sister to know you're here?"

"It's not what you think," I answer.

"What do I think?" She pulls her head back in an attitude that lets me know I better be ready to elaborate, showing me an alternative approach to Sister Mary Margaret's method of getting a person to open up.

"I just want a little privacy. I want a friend of my own." I offer part of the truth.

"And what did I think?"

"I don't know. That I'm afraid that people will find out about me, by association."

"What people?" She folds her hands on her lap.

"The court, my parents, Memere, Sammy's teacher, everybody."

"You're afraid the good people will accuse you of hanging around with a black lesbian."

"If I told you all the things I'm afraid of, you'd be surprised I ever left the house."

She frowns and nods in irritated agreement. She taps her mug, rearranges her body on the sofa, stretching her long legs under the coffee table, and stares at the ceiling. "My father never met Jackie. For him, she never existed. So when I went home for Christmas, I had to pretend nothing was wrong. I can see how having a kid would make things harder." She offers me a complicated, maybe consoling shrug. "Look, I don't really know about kids and divorce."

"You know about losing someone," I say.

We agree, silently, to talk about something easy. We both seem to need the company tonight, so we're watching a boring rerun about grizzly bears when she gets up to answer a knock at the door.

"I'm looking for my sister." Marie, out of breath, spots me over Darlene's shoulder. "Cora Rose," she says like she's talking to a naughty child. Her face is flushed with cold and agitation.

"Sammy?" I tug on my boots, my heart in my throat. Marie is already headed away. "What happened?"

Darlene hands me my coat and holds the door. "I'll be right here. Let me know if there's anything I can do."

"Thanks," I yell over my shoulder as I trot behind Marie. We're at a full run before we reach her car, which is parked across the street. "Is he all right?" I struggle with the busted handle on the passenger side.

"Just get in." Marie plugs her key in the ignition.

"Where is he?" I compete with the engine's loud complaint.

Marie, in deep conversation with the '63 Chevy, ignores me. "Come on, baby," she begs, then demands. "Don't stall on me now." She lets the clutch out too quick. "Jesus. Fuck." Her urgency raises the level of my own panic. Did Sammy choke on an apple core? Crack his head on the icy steps? My car is parked at home.

"Take a breath, Marie." *Concentrate Prioritize Initiate*, pops into my head, a new prayer from nursing school. "Concentrate on the car. Only the car." She shoots me a look but takes a deep breath before she starts the engine up again. The wheels spin on packed snow. She slams into reverse. The car jerks back five feet. She slams back into first.

Darlene knocks on my window with the keys to the Mustang.

"Come on. We'll take Darlene's car," I bark. I don't even know where we're going.

"No!" Marie sucks in a determined breath.

I fight with the door handle. It jams. Darlene steps away from the car. Marie lets out the clutch, steps on the accelerator and leans forward, gripping the wheel so tight in her gloveless hands that her knuckles turn white against her chapped red fingers. "Move, bitch." She slams one fist on the wheel. We lurch forward.

When it's obvious the car is going to stay in a forward motion, I grab her knee and squeeze. "Asthma?"

"He's in the hospital but he's okay." She glares at me. "I looked everywhere for you, the cinemas, the mall. Renee finally told me to try here."

I shake her knee. "Sammy?" I say. "Tell me about Sammy."

"You have to sign a paper so they can give him a shot. His spray thing didn't work." She gives me a dirty look that is several degrees less intense than the looks she's been giving me and relaxes her hands on the wheel slightly.

"He was fine when I left," I whisper.

"He had a reaction to incense. They need the parents."

"Incense?" I cut in.

"A kid needs two parents. Where the hell is Joe?" she asks through gritted teeth. It's unnerving how much she sounds like Mom, the same raw pride, the same indignation when the world doesn't behave the way she wants it to. She speeds through a red light blowing her horn. "It's not bad enough we don't know when Fletcher's going to be back—now Joe disappears. If Donny ever ends up in the hospital, I'll kill Fletcher if he doesn't leave word . . ."

"Sammy's all right, though," I insist. "Right, Marie? You said he's okay."

"Renee didn't know where you *or* Joe were. I tore your kitchen apart looking for phone numbers. Even the pediatrician's phone number is on scrap paper," she says passionately. "You've got to put them in a book. In alphabetical order." She's hysterical, or close to it, Marie.

"You're giving me hell about housekeeping?" I lean close, trying to draw information out of her with the gravity of my body. "Sammy had an asthma attack, but he's okay?"

"They'll take care of him without your signature if things get bad enough." She's talking fast and driving faster. Her eyes are riveted on the road. "You can't just say fuck 'em all. Everybody'll know about you if you don't watch out." Her words come so fast and high-pitched that I can barely follow. "You don't know how hard people can be. You're off in some fairy tale. People are mean. Life is harder then you are." She stares straight ahead. We're barreling down the main drag now. I try to calculate how many minutes we are from the hospital. "That Darlene." Her voice becomes distant. "She's so obvious. Why doesn't she just wear a fucking suit and tie. We got kids." She looks at me strangely, almost tenderly. She's scared. "Sammy is going to be okay. Donny is going to be okay. Fuck 'em all. Like being straight is so easy."

"Her name is Darlene."

"What?" Marie screeches into the parking lot of the emergency room.

"Her name is Darlene. Not *That Darlene.*"

"Darlene?" She says, confused, like I brought her name up out of nowhere. "It's about Sammy and Donny. Don't you see it? Joe has to hate you, so he can let you go. Fletcher wouldn't let me love him. What could I do?" She grabs my wrist tight, trying to talk some sense into me. "Somebody's going to beat the shit out you." Exactly what Joe said.

"Yeah, well it doesn't have to be my sister." I stare down at her hand locked around mine. "You're hurting me. We're here. Let go."

Marie stares at me for a suspended second, not comprehending my point, not letting go of my wrist. In the split second I take to actually look at her, I see that she's gloveless, hatless, her coat's not buttoned, and her blouse looks like she slept in it. She releases my wrist. My hand is shaking as I brush her frizzy hair out of her face. "Thanks, Marie. It's over. Come in with me. You shouldn't be driving."

"Fletcher could have gone to jail. He's down there with his horrible father. Donny . . ." She looks, forlornly, straight ahead and revs up the car. "Oh God, what if me and Eddie end up like you and Joe." Poor Marie, she's ready to open up, but her timing is monumentally bad.

"You'll figure that out, we'll all help you. As long as Sammy's all right," I say in one quick breath, glad the door handle doesn't jam again. "Park the car."

"And Donny," she says.

"And Donny." I jump out of the car and run toward the hysterical lights that announce the Emergency Room. Over my shoulder, Marie is headed toward the road not the parking lot.

Inside the glass front of Emergency Services, a young nurse stands impatiently behind me while a quick-handed receptionist slides three sheets of paper through a slot on the bottom of a caged window.

"Can I see him?" I look around, trying to figure out which corridor has swallowed up Sammy.

"That's up to Doctor. Read and sign these please," the receptionist says, with a wave of her hand.

The nurse hovers at my shoulder waiting to scoop up the paperwork. "I need these permissions pronto," she says brusquely.

The lines on the paper blur. I look desperately from the fine print, to the nurse, back to the fine print. "Here." The nurse slides her finger dismissively over the bold letters that read; THIS IS A RELEASE FORM PLEASE READ CAREFULLY BEFORE SIGNING. I sign, "Cora Rose LaBarre." Relationship: "Mother."

The nurse whisks the paper away from me. She has a stethoscope around her neck and a watch pinned to the breast pocket of her pink scrubs. "It's amazing how many mothers leave small children without letting anyone know where they'll be in case of emergency." Why is she wasting time to take a dim view of me? She doesn't look old enough to be out of high school, never mind lecturing on motherhood.

"He's all right?" I grab her shoulder. I don't care what she thinks as long as she gets the shot of adrenaline she's holding into Sammy. She frowns. "Sorry." I pull my hand away. "Please. My son?"

"He's okay." She gives me a grudging half-smile that implies "No thanks to you." "He's in the holding room. Wait here." She looks me in the eye. "Allergic reaction. Pine incense, of all things." I cringe when she holds up the hypodermic needle. "This will cure him. Doctor will probably order Benadryl. You'll be taking him home in an hour or two. He'll be asleep before you get there."

She takes off through a set of swinging doors. It takes me ten seconds to come to my senses, look around to make sure no one is watching, and follow her through the "Do Not Enter" sign. She's nowhere in sight. I stand, eerily alone, in a starkly lit hallway with a scrubbed white floor, a white ceiling, and rows of white curtains on either side. Sammy is in one of these white-draped holding rooms. I listen. A baby's weak cry is partitioned off at the far end of the corridor. The sound of an old lady whispering, maybe praying, comes from behind an ominously stained curtain on my right. I have to stop myself from humming the "Hail Mary" that I feel pushing up my throat. I need to be quiet, even inside my head, to listen for Sammy.

A nurse with an emesis basin and an arm full of towels breaks through the swinging doors hip first. She pulls an IV bag on a pole behind her. I expect her to throw me out, but she asks excitedly, "Which one is Doctor Stillman's burn patient in?"

A testy male voice answers, "Right here, Peggy."

Curtains part and swallow her up.

I stand still and close my eyes until I pick up what I'm straining to hear. Sammy is whimpering, "Mommy," weaker than the baby crying, higher pitched, but not as loud as the old lady praying. I move cautiously toward the sound of him.

"Mommy's here. She's waiting for you," Renee's voice comes low from the last cubical on the right. Reassuring and tender, but firm with authority, she says, "This nice nurse is going to give you a shot, a little pinch in the arm. Then you can see Mommy. The doctor will give you a little green pill, and listen to your lungs again with the stethoscope, and you'll feel better, and Mommy can take you home." Her voice is an even chant.

I know what Renee's doing. I've seen it. I've done it myself. She's distracting him, playing good nurse, comforting nurse, while the other nurse, the young scolding one, draws up the adrenaline, getting ready

267

to stab him. Student nurses are used to comfort people long before we get to stick needles into them. I walk quickly, lightly to Sammy's end of the hall and stand as still as I can, holding myself back from entering his little space, breathing as deeply and quietly as possible, in sympathy with his own labored breathing, which I can hear over Renee's persistent hum. "We'll make a tent under the kitchen table with the Star Trek sheets Mommy got you and we'll play Monopoly Junior and have a snack there." He can't be ten feet away from me now, but I don't separate the curtain. I force my feet to stay planted on this side of his draped cubicle. He's safe in Renee's arms. If I part the curtain, it might startle him or distract the nurse with the needle in mid-jab. The nurse with the needle is right. I should have let Renee know where I was in case of an emergency. I should have told her I was going to the movies with Darlene, left the number on the fridge, hung a little book with tiny flowers on its cover on a nail by the phone with names and addresses and numbers in it. The Girls Club should be scribbled in right before Gleason's Garage. In case I go back there. In case Joe decides to forgive me for not wanting him. In case the world changes and the courts stop punishing dykes by taking away their children.

"You're being so brave, sweetie. Here, look at Auntie Renee." She doesn't want him to watch the stab. It's supposed to hurt less if you don't know exactly when it's coming. A needle hitting Sammy's relaxed muscle should slide in easier than a needle hitting his hard muscle, tense with anticipation. The nurse must be pulling up his sleeve, swiping his arm with an alcohol pad, aiming the syringe. "What do you think Donny's going to say when he finds out what a brave boy you are?" Renee asks earnestly, not quite blocking the apprehension in her voice. She's given a thousand shots and the stick Sammy's about to get still scares her.

"Little pinch," the nurse's voice rises cheerfully now.

I flinch. Rub my arm like it was me who took the needle.

"Mommy," Sammy cries loudly. "I want my Mommy."

And then he's in my arms and we're both crying and rocking. His hair is wet from tears. His heart races from the struggle for air. Soon it will be racing from the shot of adrenaline. His small chest heaves against me. I can feel his flesh sucking in and out between his ribs with each breath, a small, crashing motion. He clings to me. I wrap myself around him and breathe in each of his inhalations, breathe out each exhalation. "My brave boy."

By the time the doctor pokes his head in, reassures me that Sammy will be fine, and kicks me out of the holding room, Sammy has swallowed the Benadryl and is twitching in a fitful sleep under stiff hospital linen. The doctor doesn't kick Renee out. Professional courtesy.

I sit in a row of hard plastic chairs and wait for someone to come out and tell me that Sammy's breathing and pulse have calmed down enough for us to go home. Joe is with Lorraine somewhere. Why else wouldn't he leave a number for Renee? Until the last couple of months, both of us have always left word where we could be reached. Do we think we're protecting our privacy? Everybody in this family finds out every damn thing about everyone else eventually anyway.

In a way, Joe and Lorraine did me a favor by getting together. I'd be even more paranoid of people finding out I'm a lesbian if Joe wasn't carrying on with Lorraine. As if my sexuality is any less of an offense depending on who my husband is sleeping with, but somehow it feels that way. Marie said it, Darlene said it, the world is a mess.

Looking at the situation from here in this depressing waiting room, with the rest of these tired, anxious people, it doesn't matter who knows I'm queer, who knows I have a friend who isn't a straight white girl. Half the disgust, the racism, the fear is in me. What else is in me? Darlene would have come to the hospital with me. If I'd let her drive us here, maybe she would have met Joe and my worlds would have collided. With barely a thump, I bet. Sammy's in the emergency room. That changes everything, for the moment at least. We all would have studied the floor, anxious and tired like everyone else. I'd like to throw back my head and wail. I look around instead.

Two seats to my left there's an old woman in a shabby gray coat, rocking a colicky infant on her shoulder. Across from me there's a young guy holding his head between his knees. His fingers worry the heavy links of chain hanging from a silver key ring that's attached to his belt loop. The keys jangle as he hangs his head and works his fingers from link to link. There are other people sitting in the row of plastic chairs behind me, but I don't look at them. The baby lets out a yelp and the young guy looks up for a second. He's got tired eyes. He catches me staring at him and gives me a look that's meant to intimidate me. But he doesn't fool me, he's dying inside. His expression makes me want to laugh, or hold him and tell him it can't possibly be *all* his fault. Whatever it is, it's at least as complicated as the knot of pain on his face. We both look away. I want to borrow his key chain so I can work the links.

Renee comes out and sits in the chair next to me with a heavy sigh. "God. I'm so sorry. It never even occurred to me that he might be allergic. Great nurse. Pine incense, what was I thinking?" She shakes her head and starts crying.

I put my arm around her, pick a piece of fuzz off her sweater, and let it fall on the linoleum, which is incredibly dirty compared to the spit-shined tile and freshly painted walls of the holding room. "Thanks for taking care of him."

"We're going to have to air out the house before we bring him home." She blows her nose and straightens up.

I nod. I don't want to comfort or be comforted by Renee, not physically anyway. I just want to be quiet and watch the young guy finger his chain. The baby is asleep on the old lady's lap now, and the shabby waiting room with the too bright lights seems like a holy place, a place to think clearly. Marie is an idiot for being so freaked out that I'm a dyke. It's easy for me to understand how she feels because I'm so close to letting my own fears turn into repulsion. I turn to Renee. "I was with Darlene at her place."

She scowls. "I wish I had known that." She leans back in her chair and closes her eyes. I bet she has to work in a few hours. The old lady gives me a sympathetic smile. I close my eyes and wonder if Sammy is going to be better or worse off in the long run without all the religious stuff I was fed when I was a kid. I'm humming "Hail Mary," wondering what She would think of homosexuals, wondering if She'd offer amnesty to draft-dodgers, when a cold blast of air barges through the emergency room doors, accompanied by Joe and Marie. Everyone except the young man with his head between his legs turns to watch them.

"Sammy's okay. We're waiting to take him home." I stand to greet them. Joe looks confused and scared. "He's okay, Joe." I smile. I know he's assessing Sammy's condition by the degree of my anxiety. Marie, right behind him, looks less agitated than she did an hour ago.

He collapses in the seat next to mine. "Thank God." He puts his hands over his face. He's shaking.

I touch his shoulder. "It's just an allergic reaction to incense."

"I'm so sorry, Joe. Worst idea I ever had. We have pills in case it ever happens again." Renee pulls the bottle of Benadryl out of her purse.

Marie sits down next to the guy who had been handling his key chain like a rosary. He sits up and stares at her. "Got a cigarette?" she asks him.

"Can't smoke in here." He reaches into his shirt pocket and hands her a half-full pack.

She says, "Thanks," slips two in her coat pocket, and holds the pack out for Joe. Joe is too busy looking at me like he's seen a ghost to accept Marie's offer. "Jesus, it was like you were sick all over again," he says. "What did the poor kid do to deserve this?"

"None of us deserves it. At least with Sammy, it's simpler. You just want to hold him. You don't want to wring his neck, too." I bite my bottom lip.

He half-smiles and looks at his feet.

"Here he is." Renee stands. We all stand and stare at the nurse as she walks toward us carrying Sammy cradled in her arms. He's asleep, wrapped like a newborn in a thin hospital blanket. Joe takes him from her.

"Daddy." Sammy clings to Joe's neck and falls back to sleep while I sign more papers.

I hold the revolving glass door of the emergency room open for Joe and Sammy and follow them to Joe's car. I sit in the back seat with Sammy's head on my lap and stroke it all the way to Joe's place. Joe sits alone in the front, driving slowly, cautiously; spooked by the hospital, nervous about taking Sammy home to his place and being in charge of keeping him comfortable and safe so soon after a crisis. I barely glance at Joe and we don't speak to each other, but I can feel his changing moods. I can sense his state of mind by the tilt of his head, the slope of his shoulders, and his fleeting glances in the rearview mirror as he shifts from anxiety, to relief, to anger, back to anxiety. I feel the subtle charge of his brooding physically on my own skin, at the back of my neck, on my scalp, and especially in the base of my belly where my gut used to be. I'd forgotten how nervous he gets when Sammy is sick. How panicked he was to be left alone with him when I went off to the drugstore the first time Sammy needed medication. How he sat by the crib and wept with relief when I got home and Sammy's wheezing finally calmed down. The last thing Joe wants tonight is to be left alone with his son.

We tuck him in together, our upper bodies bow into each other as we bend so our heads will clear the top bunk of the bed. Silently, I thank Lorraine for having the grace to stay the hell away. Sammy is sleeping in the bottom bunk. If Donny were here, he'd be sleeping above Sammy in the top bunk. I try to remember: Is this like the old days, Joe and I hovering, attentive? It was usually me who put Sammy to bed, occasionally Joe, rarely both of us. If it was both of us, we'd be having a conversation that might involve Sammy or might not. Joe's face is wet with sweat. He straightens up and actually wrings his hands.

"I want to sleep at home in my own bed," Sammy says in his slushy Benadryl and fatigue voice. "Can Daddy come home with us just for tonight?" Poor Sammy; barely able to pick up his head, limp from the drugs and his struggle for breath, but still fighting to put his world right. He's so young to find out that being sick isn't necessarily enough to get him what he wants. I feel a hollow victory. See Joe, Sammy thinks of "home" as his life with me. His real bed is his bed where I am, in my apartment. See Joe. You need me. You don't really want to stay here alone with Sammy when he's sick, you don't really want to have sole responsibility for a child whose chest might start heaving again, whose voice might desperately call "Mommy" in the middle of the night.

"You have two homes now, Sammy, one with me and one here with Daddy." I hug him. "You're a brave little boy."

"Don't cry, Daddy," Sammy says. "It scares me."

272

With a look of surprise, Joe puts a hand to his face and wipes his cheeks on his sleeve.

"Daddy's crying because he's happy that you're feeling better, honey," I say.

Joe looks at us with an expression I can't read, some combination of gratitude and resentment. Or maybe I'm putting my own feelings on him. Then he breaks into a forced smile. "I sure am happy you're better. You gave us a scare. We have to get rid of the incense smell before you can go back to Mommy's." Joe's voice is tender. He kneels next to the bed and strokes Sammy's head with his hairy knuckled hand. "Maybe Mommy will stay here just for tonight, little guy." Crouched low and kneeling, Joe's bulk is exaggerated. "You could sleep on the top bunk." He addresses me without looking away from Sammy.

Sammy stares at me with his glossy eyes.

I look up at the top bunk, remembering how relieved I was to find out that Donny, not Sammy, would be sleeping four feet off the ground. "I'll be right on the floor next to your bed in the sleeping bag."

We stay like that, me standing on one side of Sammy and Joe kneeling on the opposite side, each of us speaking in turn, gently, re-assuringly, until Sammy's eyelids flutter and close without opening again. Then I move to the windowsill and Joe moves to the foot of the bed, both of us looking down at Sammy's chest, rising and falling at an almost normal rate and depth now. I tiptoe out of the room. Joe follows me.

When we reach the kitchen, he sighs heavily several times, working up steam, getting ready to talk. I want to speak before he does, before I get distracted by his version of the truth. Before I believe the sweet, tender version I just saw kneeling at Sammy's bedside is all of Joe that there is. I want to tell him what I have to say before my skin hardens into a shell that protects me from any version of Joe and any chance of real communication. But I need something to do while I collect my thoughts.

"Cup of coffee?" I ask even though it's Joe's kitchen not mine.

"Cora Rose . . ."

"Joe. I want to say some things." I drop into a kitchen chair. "Please."

273

I motion to the chair opposite me, the place at the table with its back to the door, where he always sat when we lived together. "Before I lose my nerve."

"Your nerve?" He smiles bitterly and pulls out the chair, looking me up and down. "I don't know you anymore. You're a hard woman. The only time you're soft now is with Sammy." He gets quiet and runs his hand over the pockmarked wood of the old kitchen table.

Thrown off balance by the regret in his voice, I lift myself out of my seat and move toward the counter. I'm still soft. In the hospital when I'm playing student nurse, I'm soft with the patients, especially the old people. Joe just doesn't get to see the soft parts of me anymore. I fumble through his cabinets, searching for coffee. He doesn't stop me. I realize on my own that I have no right to be rummaging through his cracked measuring cup and Flintstone jelly glasses without permission. I turn back to him empty-handed. "I want to say this because we've been through a lot together, but mostly because of Sammy. We have to straighten things out for Sammy."

"This is getting to be a broken record. It's *you* who has to straighten out," he says wearily, but confident of the point he's laying out once again. "What you're doing with your life is not good for Sammy."

"Tonight—" I grip the back of the wobbly wooden chair. My voice is low. I want to keep my emotions level so I can think, so my frustration won't carry through the rooms and wake Sammy. "—was supposed to be *your* night with Sammy."

"Renee offered. I should have told her where I was, but *you* live with her." He looks sheepish until he hits the word *you*, then his fisted hand falls to the table with a thud.

"What's that got to do with it? Get over it, Joe. How I live, who I live with, doesn't make you any less responsible as his father." Joe sets his jaw and narrows his eyes. But his expression doesn't shut me up. "And it doesn't make me any less responsible as his mother. Being a lesbian isn't a sin or a disease." I force myself to keep eye contact with him, very careful not to say *my* being a lesbian. "It isn't good or bad. It just is."

His face gets tight with anger. "I don't give a damn about sin. It's..."

He opens his big hands and slowly stretches his fingers wide across the tabletop. ". . . disgusting. Maybe it *is* a disease, but not like when you were really sick. You can walk away from this. You said it yourself, you're still his *mother*, for Christ's sake." His voice collapses. He sits back, incredulous that we're in his kitchen having this conversation. "Cora Rose," he says like he's talking to a ghost. "Where are you?"

"Here's the thing, Joe." I look away, trying to make my voice indifferent. The chair I drag out from under the table makes a horrible squeal before I slide into it. "You don't have to understand me. You can think I'm disgusting." My heart is breaking. Disgusting. To Joe. He found the one feeling to really humiliate me. "Disgusting." I spit the word back at him. He'll never get the satisfaction of seeing how much it hurts. I brace my back against the slats of the chair. I start out in the most serious, formal tone I can manage. "You can hate me for being a lesbian, but you better not let Sammy see how much I disgust you." But I can't sustain it. I feel naked and disgraced, just plain dirty. My words dissolve into a lament. "Don't. Don't do that, Joe. Please don't."

Tears run down his cheeks and splash on the table. The little tremor around his mouth makes me afraid of what he's about to say. "You expect this not to disgust me? It's not about hate," he says in a strange, out-of-body voice. "Don't you get it? I'm trying not to love you."

"You've been talking to Marie," I say to myself as much as Joe. "You used the same words, almost exactly."

Joe doesn't look at me. He's too busy crying.

I push myself away from his table and walk out of the kitchen, through the dim living room, to Fletcher's room. I sit, inert, on top of a pile of clothes on Fletcher's bed, and let fatigue numb my emotions before I take a deep breath, and pick up the phone on the orange crate that serves as a nightstand. I call to tell Darlene that Sammy's okay.

She answers the phone on the first ring. "Thank God," she says.

After I hang up, I have the odd unreasonable urge to go back to the kitchen to talk to Joe about Darlene. I want to talk to him about Stella too, from all those years ago, tell him I understand how it is to be in love with someone and be forced to let them go. I want to talk to Marie too, tell her I'm sorry that she still loves Fletcher.

I walk into the tiny room where Sammy is sleeping and stare down at him. It seems like he was an infant yesterday. How he loved to sleep on his hands and knees with his rear end sticking up in the air and his face in a puddle of drool, while I pushed him around the yard in that rusty shopping cart. The nightlight throws a fluorescent green shadow on his pale face. I still love to watch him sleep. The bunk bed, the small bookcase cluttered with toys, and the tiny bureau that was Donny's when he was a baby crowd the space and remind me of the three beds pushed together when I was a kid. I'm glad that Sammy's not always alone when he sleeps in this roomful of shadows, that sometimes he has a cousin, asleep on the top bunk.

I fall into a deep sleep, cocooned on the floor in a sleeping bag. I wake up with a start and stare at Sammy. He's sound asleep. I hear murmuring, wisps of conversation making their way through the train of rooms. I strain to be sure it's live human voices, not the TV. It's Lorraine talking to Joe. Except for a lone light in the parking lot below the apartment, the naked window is framing a pitch-black night.

I crawl out of the sleeping bag and tiptoe through the empty bedrooms to the dark living room where Joe and Lorraine sit, facing each other on the couch, huddled in conversation. Lorraine whispers plaintively, consoling, but trying to convince him of something, too. I'm riveted to the sight. Joe and Lorraine look like an old married couple, licking each other's wounds after some family tragedy. Joe, his back bowed, shoulders rounded, lifts his head to speak to her. I can see how they would be drawn to each other. They make perfect sense together in the dim light of the four a.m. living room. Lorraine has been ready to be someone's lover, someone's wife, since she hit puberty. Joe will let her take care of him. He'll be loyal. He'll love her. If he doesn't love her already, he'll learn how to love her. He'll take care of her, too. I bet they have three kids. She's living with her mother again. I wonder how she explains slipping out of the house in the middle of the night to Aunt Josette.

They touch foreheads. "You have to be able to bend," she says, placing a hand on his already bowed shoulder. Grown up, not the flitty sixteen-year-old I have trapped in my brain. Lorraine, I suddenly understand, will take my side if she can, if she doesn't have to betray Joe to do it.

They straighten up, simultaneously sensing my presence; look at me like I'm an apparition, look at each other for confirmation on how to react.

"Hi." I stand motionless in the doorway.

Chapter 24

"Daddy says we might get a slidy chute as soon as it's warm enough to dig holes for the feet. Slidy chutes have feet that get buried." Sammy delivers this bit of knowledge as he pushes peas around his plate and takes a bite of a drumstick. It's been a long, hard winter. We're all hoping for a warm, easy spring. "Big as the one at school."

"Big as the one at school?" I doubt Joe's considering a fifteen-foot slide. "Don't talk with your mouth full." I stick an apple and a box of raisins in his backpack, last-minute insurance that he won't starve in the shadow of the swing set Joe put up in the grassy, fenced-in yard behind his new apartment.

"Daddy!" Sammy responds to the distinct sound of the engine knock coming from Joe's Mazda. It's 6:45 sharp. Joe has cut back his Friday overtime so he doesn't have to wait until Saturday morning to pick up Sammy. Lorraine drops him off at school on Monday morning.

"Are you going to that phone place with Auntie Marie again?" Sammy stands still while I comb his hair. It's a new unspoken thing between us, he lets me fuss over him at the last minute before he leaves for Joe's, and I let him go with a warm but time-limited hug and a smile. Friday night is the worst. Before he leaves, I feel like I'm abandoning him. After he's gone, I feel abandoned.

"We'll see. Maybe I'll stay home and study. A few more months and Mommy will be a real nurse." I pat the backpack and remind myself that a lot of mothers would be thrilled to have long weekends without their kid. "You've got your heavy jacket if it gets chilly." It's April. The jacket will come back crumpled but unworn no matter what the weekend brings, but I feel better packing it.

When Sammy's gone, I set the timer on the stove for twenty minutes, preparing to sink into a time-limited period of acute anxiety and depression. It's a trick I learned from behavior modification class. "If you can't stop yourself from certain nonproductive behaviors, put a time limit on them. Then systematically shorten the time."

Months ago, Joe and I agreed that he would take Sammy every Wednesday and every other weekend. This was the arrangement I wanted, a definite routine, with Joe showing up when he's supposed to. Then, about three months ago, Joe started pushing for every weekend. The paralegal assigned to my case by Legal Aid convinced me to agree to weekends in exchange for taking Wednesday night back. That's when the wallowing and withdrawing into self-pity started. The first week of the new arrangement, I spent all of Friday night curled up on the ratty chair, immobilized by the fear that Joe's demands would expand to the whole week, one night at a time, until Sammy moved lock, stock, and Star Trek action figures into Joe's half of the new duplex two streets away.

The stove timer ticks off the seconds and I sit on the ratty chair rehashing the paralegal's pointed remark. "The mother-gets-custody bias applies to heterosexuals. Relax. Let your husband co-parent. He's not asking for anything outrageous yet."

Yet. I'm asleep in the chair when the timer goes off. A few minutes later, Marie calls. "We're meeting Renee in twenty minutes."

"The Exchange again?" I moan. The Exchange is a new "Café" with a red phone at each table. You sit in a booth with a big red number above it and hope someone thinks you're cute and gives you a call. We went three weeks ago. Within an hour, Marie was paired off with Larry Shimpsky and his glass eye, and Renee had taken the phone off the hook so she wouldn't be disturbed while she lectured me on letting myself be happy. "Come pick me up. All you have to do is sit there and look like a straight girl. Put some lipstick on." Marie thinks I should be seen in public, surrounded by as many horny straight men as possible, as often as possible.

Almost before we're seated in our "phone" booth at The Exchange, the waitress brings us three pink drinks we didn't order. "Lady Slippers from table 13," she announces. Marie does a 180 and raises her glass of pink stuff to the same three adolescent-looking guys at table 13 who tried to pick us up last time. She swivels back, takes a sip.

"How is it?" Renee asks.

"Free." Marie shrugs.

"This is the most depressing place I've ever been." I cross my arms over my chest and settle in for a long sulk. "Maybe Lorraine will get pregnant soon and Joe will have to split all this time he's found to devote to Sammy between two kids."

"We brought you here to rescue you from morbid self-indulgence," Renee scolds.

"Lorraine pregnant wouldn't be in your best interest." There's nothing but pink froth left in Marie's glass. "You gonna drink yours?" I slide my Lady Slipper over and she continues her evaluation. "Sammy'd get attached to little Joey or Josette. Ugh, that would make Josette, Memere Josette. Screwing your wife's cousin hasn't turned out to be the bombshell we'd hoped," she says regretfully, sucking down half the Lady Slipper. "It *would* speed up the divorce." She swivels around again. "See anybody you like?"

"No." Renee scowls. "This isn't a fish tank. Don't drink so fast and stop bobbing around."

"Of course it's a fish tank. You're the only two people in the place who didn't come to catch something. Now that President Carter has granted amnesty and Fletcher's back, clean and sober, with his bona fide belle, living once again, in northern splendor, you're going to have to snag some other sucker to celebrate your virginity with on Saturday nights."

"He didn't go to jail. He was on work-release." Renee fiddles with her feather earring. "And I'm not a virgin."

"He lived with a father that he can't stand for months. That's jail. You'll always be my little virgin sister." Marie swats Renee's earring. "And this is a fish tank. You're wearing lures." The booze is starting to hit. Renee is worried about the recent spike in Marie's alcohol consumption, but I like Marie's personality better after she's had a couple. "Joe spending time with Sammy isn't the tragedy she's making it." She speaks directly to Renee. "To hell with what any court says. She'll always see plenty of Sammy. Look at the family he's got. We'll never let go. Him and Donny spend at least a day a week at Mom and Dad's." She jerks her chin at me. "We switch off once a week." Then she jerks her chin at Renee. "You're always taking them somewhere. You even snatch him from Joe and Lorraine sometimes. Neither of us have had custody of our kid for more than a few days at a time since the day they were born. And neither will Joe."

I say, "Sometimes I think Mom and Dad believe he'd be better off with Joe."

Renee looks surprised that I'm putting in my two cents. Marie raises her eyebrows, like maybe she agrees with the sentiment I'm accusing my parents of harboring.

"What?" Renee slaps Marie's arm with the back of her hand. "You've had too much to drink if you think Joe should get custody because she's gay."

"Give that a rest." I'm not sure if Marie means the gay or the too much to drink comment. She leans back in her chair without acknowledging the slap. "If Eddie and I had gotten married and he had adopted Donny before we split, I could see an argument for him getting custody." Apparently the trauma of giving up Eddie and his promise of respectability has receded far enough into Marie's past that his name can be spoken without her flying into a fit of angry remorse, at least after two Lady Slippers. "Joe's a good father. I'm just saying. Why should the mother always get the kid?"

"You don't think that." Renee rolls her eyes.

"Oh," Marie says sarcastically. "I thought I did." She tips her empty glass at me. "You know what else I think?"

"There's more?" I say.

"Plenty. I think it's your turn to be the bad sister."

I watch Larry Shimpsky hand over two bucks and get his hand stamped with a little red phone. "Here's your boyfriend." I nod toward the door.

Marie must really like him, because she says, "Larry?" without trying to hide the interest in her voice. "Is he coming over?" She doesn't even

281

swivel her head. Larry breaks etiquette and walks straight to our table without dialing us up first.

Renee and I watch them slow dance. Renee purses her lips at me. "She's right; it's time for you to move on."

"I should stop fighting for Sammy?"

"Stop obsessing. Joe will come around. He listens to Fletcher and Fletcher listens to me."

"Fletcher's got a new girlfriend to listen to." I grab my sweatshirt and stand.

"So? We talk all the time."

"You're the one who convinced me that Joe would never really want Sammy to live with him when Joe first moved in with Fletcher."

"I still say he won't go for full custody when push comes to shove." She grabs her purse. "What are you doing?"

"Moving on." I slide out of the "phone" booth. "Give Marie a lift, will ya?"

She raises her voice above the din. "Larry, can you give Marie a lift?" She rushes after me without waiting for an answer.

"Sorry." I unlock the Chevy. "You're not invited." Renee opens the passenger door and scoots in next to me. "I don't want you to come with me."

"Too bad." She bounces in the seat. "Where we going?"

I switch on the radio loud enough to discourage conversation and drive. Renee bobs her head and hums along with "Yellow Submarine." She's still humming when she jumps out of the car into the parking lot of The Girls Club. "I haven't been here in years."

"You've never been here." I walk in front of her, pull the three-dollar cover from my back pocket. I hand her my keys. "Bye. Take the car. I'll walk home."

"Aren't you afraid Joe will find out?" She takes the keys, but doesn't leave.

"You're a boring little fake virgin. Go back and bother Marie." I'm walking away.

She's right behind me. "Well, he did live with a druggie. The draft-dodger thing isn't going to do you any good now." We've been musing over the relative weight the court is likely to give Joe's and my infractions. "Marijuana should be legal. Lesbian love should be legal." I make a gagging gesture, which she ignores. "Is it actually illegal for gay people to have sex or is it just legal to discriminate against them if they do? I always wanted to see the inside of this place." She walks faster, right into the bar ahead of me.

I walk back to the car and smack the hood when I realize I gave her the keys. I walk to the edge of the parking lot, just needing a minute, not even fooling myself that I'm going to walk home. She's got my apartment keys too. I retrace my steps through the parking lot and hand over my three dollars at the door.

It's after ten and the place is filling up. Women are joking around, checking each other out, making noise. Renee sits at a table, studiously not looking at me when I walk over to her. There are no unoccupied tables. "One drink, then you are out of here." I sit down opposite her. She cranes her neck to get a good look around the room. She pays no attention to me. I'm happy to be left alone.

Finally, she gets her fill and asks me what I'm drinking. "Bud," I answer, deadpan, trying to bore her so she'll go away. She doesn't look bored.

"Yeast," she frowns.

"What's it called when you kill your own sister?"

"Murder," she answers cheerfully. "Definitely deny custody for that."

"Sororicide," I whisper and watch her walk up to the bar. She's wearing tight faded jeans and a French cut t-shirt. I've spent a considerable amount of time helping her decide which jeans make her ass look good and which color blouse shows off her blue eyes best. Usually, it's like looking in the mirror. You get so used to yourself that you never really know what you look like. Now, looking at her sidling up to the bar, I realize it's not just her physical beauty that makes her good to look at.

I must be seeing what other people see when they first look at her. She's a pretty, shapely, white girl. All curve in tight clothes, but that isn't what gets my attention. What amazes me is you can see her gutsy personality in the way she moves, the way she carries herself. I always knew she had a certain kind of courage, but I never knew you could actually tell by looking at her.

Darlene greets her with a big smile and Renee leans into the bar to talk. Her butt sticks out far enough to stop traffic. Who she is—it's all over her, even in the way she angles her hips. She's hot and she knows it. Darlene sees it. Darlene, too—she's got a whole different personality and way of moving, but you can see she knows who she is just by the way she stands and moves around the bar. I keep watching Renee. She's smaller, prettier, she's got on tighter clothes, but she looks a lot like me. She looks the way I used to feel. When did I feel as good as she looks right now snuggled up to that bar? Maybe she looks the way I've always wanted to feel.

Something about the easy laugh that spreads across Darlene's face makes me sit straight up; reminds me of a feeling, like when I was a kid, before I got really sick, lingering in the barn to whisper to the cow, even though Mom said I should spread the hay and come right out. When I rubbed Molly's cow neck, I wasn't as afraid of being found out because I didn't believe in the sin of it. It just felt right.

It's not that I never feel good anymore. It comes and then it's gone. Maybe Renee's right, I should figure out what's right about me and concentrate on that. I'm a dyke with an ostomy.

I watch Renee walk back to the table. "Quit staring. Pick out a nice woman who is not your sister and stare at her. See anybody you like?" She mimics Marie and turns around in her chair to take in every woman in the place.

"Shut up."

"What's the point of going through all the trouble you're going through if you're too depressed to even look at women in a bar?" She pulls her head back and says mildly, "For the record, times are changing. Sooner or later people are going to wake up and being a lesbian won't be a big deal. In the meantime, don't overreact."

"I'm capable of reacting without your instruction." Am I over-reacting? The possibility makes me smile at her despite myself. "What would you know about how much trouble it is to be a lesbian? Or depressed. You're too busy poking your nose in other people's lives to get depressed." She keeps looking around, watching women on the dance floor. "And you don't know how it feels to have an ostomy."

"Who said anything about the ostomy? You know I'm working on being supportive without being intrusive." She folds her hands into their social worker position on her lap.

"Well, then." I wiggle my fingers at her. "Goodbye."

We sit in silence, nice and quiet, sipping our drinks. Suddenly, I've got all her attention. "Let's dance," she says.

"Dance?"

"Dance. See all those women shaking around? They're dancing. Afraid to dance in a room full of lesbians?"

"You don't know a damn thing about it. I've danced here. I don't want to dance with you."

"When was the last time you danced? Even alone in the apartment with the boys? We used to dance with the boys all the time." She gets up and starts dancing with me still seated.

"*This* is intrusive. Now you're confusing support with participation."

"Up."

She should be struck dead by the look I'm giving her. Dancing with your straight sister in a dyke bar, now that's depressing. She knows I'm pissed, but she ignores it. She dances around me even though I'm planted in my chair. She won't let go of my hand. It's getting embarrassing. She's making a scene. I get up and move around a little on the dance floor. They're playing some whiny disco music with no beat. I'm making plans to kill her as soon as this dance is over.

Then one of those little miracles happens. Without so much as a fraction of a second between songs, Aretha Franklin comes booming over the speakers. Aretha "R.E.S.P.E.C.T." Franklin. No two white girls have ever danced to Aretha Franklin as well, as often, or as devoutly as me and Renee. She brought Aretha and headphones to the hospital after my operation. I can move to R.E.S.P.E.C.T.

"We used to dance to this in the cellar." I say flatly, trying to tone down my enthusiasm.

"You and Stella used to dance to this. I always got stuck with Lorraine."

"I'll dance this *one* dance with you if you promise to leave and *never* come back here."

She squeals, "R.E.S.P.E.C.T. find out what it means to me," and pulls me to the middle of the floor. She dances and shakes her sisterly ass at me. My ass shakes back. It takes no effort at all. I can do it without a girlfriend. I can do it without a colon. I can do it while I'm still legally married. Our asses shake back at us from three mirrored walls. We admire ourselves. I gain new respect for the lighting and mirror arrangement at The Girls Club. We display ourselves generously. We know when to shake our shoulders. We know when to grind our hips. She knows how many steps I'll take to the left. I know how many steps she'll take to the right. We meet in the middle, shake our asses some more, then step back, the same way we've been doing since 1967.

When Aretha's done belting it out, I bow to Renee. "Now, please. I mean it, *please* go away. I want a whole chunk of life that does not involve my sister."

"I'll leave when I'm damned good and ready." She teases. "It just so happens I'm ready now." She kisses my cheek. "My baby sister is all grown up and throwing me out of her bar." She's genuinely pleased that I've passed this developmental hurdle. "You know I'm *trying* to back off. It's hard."

I step away and walk to the bar in case she wants a hug. I watch her exit. Darlene stops wiping a glass and watches with me. "When you're done staring at my sister, can I have an orange juice?"

"You sure you don't want to play ball?" Darlene tilts her head. "Your sister would make a great cheerleader." We grin at each other. Darlene, bartender in the only dyke bar in the county, knows my story well enough to tease me about my sister, knows my son, has his school picture in her wallet—surely this qualifies as a miracle.

I stand alone, leaning on the bar, nursing my orange juice with my butt sticking out. I touch my diamond earring, secure as always on my ear. I touch my other ear, naked as always. Somehow the fact that one ear is studded in diamond, one ear is naked, makes me grin. The bar cuts into my ostomy bag, so I sit on the stool and listen to the faint glugging noise. My hand slips over the slight bulge in my jeans even though I know I'm all right. One day soon, I'm going to stop doing that. I fold my hands on the counter. I look around. Marie would fit right in here if she could just get over it. She'd be a ringer for a patron, a serious butch with an attitude. The girls in heels with ankle straps would go nuts for her. I shake my head. What a thought. Marie is the last person in the universe that I would ever want to show up here.

A woman on the stool next to me says, "You okay?" She's not a regular. Or at least, I've never seen her before. Maybe she's been coming here for months. "Adjusting my ostomy bag." It's the wrong thing to say to a woman you've just met in a bar. It's kind of fun to say the wrong thing and not really give a damn. By the look on her face, she has no idea what an ostomy is and she isn't asking. I can't take my eyes off her hands. Something about the way she pours her beer and plays with the big silver ring on her baby finger intrigues me. "I'm fine, thanks. I came to dance. Do you wanna dance?"

The following acknowledgments represent excerpts or short stories that evolved into the novel *The Girls Club*.

"The Girls Club," *The Sun*, edited by Sy Safransky, The Sun Publishing Company, September 1993.

"Dancing Sisters," *Sinister Wisdom*, edited by Caryatis Cardea and Sauda Burch, Sinister Wisdom Inc., Fall 1993.

Excerpt from *The Girls Club*, *The Best of Writers at Work*, edited by W. Scott Olsen, Pecan Grove Press, 1995.

"*The Girls Club* - Chapter One," Quarterly West, edited by Margot Schilpp, University of Utah Press, 1999. First Place. Best of Writers at Work.

"The Girls Club," *Love Shook My Heart*, edited by Jess Wells, Alyson Books, 2001.

"A Very Nice Woman," *Bedroom Eyes*, edited by Lesléa Newman, Alyson Books 2002.

"Breaking Vows," *Cutthroat*, edited by Pamela Uschuk, William Pitt Root, and Donley Watt, volume 2, number 1, Spring 2007. First Place. Rick DeMarinis Fiction Prize.